RON GAMBRELL

The Fisher Man

Rough River Publishing LLC
7819 Bramble Ln.
Louisville, KY 40258

www.roughriverpublishing.com

The Fisher Man
Copyright © 2022 Ron Gambrell
All rights reserved.

Release date: May, 2022

ISBN: 978-0-9908562-7-6

To all who pre-read my manuscript during the creation of this book, I humbly thank you for your time and suggestions—all well taken. Further thanks to the editors whose keen eyes, sharp minds and ruthless critique makes me a better writer.

Editors: Larry Myers, Christopher Smrt, Suzie Nicklos, Jiniece Goodman, Rachel Rice and Christy Mudd

Cover art created by Rough River Publishing LLC

Dedicated to all those who work covertly with little or no recognition.

The Fisher Man

Part I
Why me?

Elijah Haycraft
Wilson County, Kentucky

Six years old.

As a child, there were times when sitting in the kitchen corner came as a relief. Better there than bent over receiving my father's leather belt, or the toe of his boot, or the back of his hand. One particular time, however, it felt as if I might die. My mother stood nearby, hands over her eyes. She, too, held back tears.

"Stop crying!" Dad screamed as his hand struck across my face.

"Honey, please don't!" Momma shouted. When he showed her his doubled fist, she backed off.

Even at a young age, I had begun to endure pain on the outside. It only went on a few minutes until Dad's rage subsided and my mother would patch me up. But this time, things were different. The pain came from inside my body and wouldn't stop. For several nights I'd laid awake trying to understand the pinching, biting sensations inside my ass. With no clue, I had scratched myself raw. Blood on the sheets and my underwear had enraged the monster inside of my old man. He slung me into the corner and dared me to move. Each time I cried, he hit me again.

Snot ran freely from my nose. Weak and struggling to hold back tears, I pleaded, "Daddy, please. I hurt inside. I don't wanna cry. I'm trying, but it feels like there's bugs in me, biting me."

1

I could smell his hate. He stared as if I'd lied. His nostrils flared. When his hand drew back, I could hold it no longer. Vomit exploded out of me onto his pants leg and shoe. More heaves filled my lap. I couldn't breathe.

"Dammit," he screamed. "You little shit! Look at this mess!"

White worms filled the bile like small spaghetti. He struck me again, and I got the sleep I so wanted.

* * *

Eight years old.

We lived in a small house on ten acres that used to be part of Grandpa Haycraft's farm. My father worked at a packinghouse twenty-five miles away. My only sibling was a border collie named Nellie. We grew up together. She and I used to take naps in the grass on sunny, cold days. In the summer, Nellie would roll over and let me search her belly for ticks. She even allowed me to swat flies right off her back. I loved that dog.

Now and then, Dad and Grandpa would go fishing on Todds Creek at the back of the farm. They brought back fish, cleaned and ready to be cooked. I recall the first time I went along. After Grandpa Haycraft rigged a seven foot cane pole with a hook, line and a lead sinker, Dad guided me through the process of running a fishhook in one end of a worm and out the other. The worm wiggled. "Is it in pain?" I asked.

He said, "Who knows? Don't think about it. Just lower it in the water and let the fish feed on it."

I did, and one did. When I jerked the line, the fish became hooked. It struggled, swimming back and forth, bending the pole. Concerned, I asked, "Don't it hurt the fish when we hook it like that?"

Granddaddy Haycraft got all excited and hollered, "We'll ask it, boy. Just bring it in before it gets away."

When I pulled it out of the water, Dad held it up by the line. "Good job, son. That's a nice size bluegill." He took it off the hook and I could see it gasping for air. Did it suffer? Moments later, as he held it down on a hardwood board, Grandpa used his special spoon to remove scales from the fish. The spoon is one of a kind. Someone in our Scottish ancestry had crafted it from pure silver. The metal is all one piece, but it looks like someone took a fancy crucifix, cut the top portion off and welded on the end of a soup spoon. Even more unique is the way the wooden handle slides off and the stem is sharpened into a knife. Grandpa used the blade to cut the fish open and remove its guts. The little creature continued to gasp for air and its tail flopped back and forth. I couldn't understand why the fish didn't make noise. I asked, "What does it make us when we do this to a fish?"

Grandpa spit tobacco juice and said, "Boy, this here's what man's been doin' for a million years. We catch or hunt somethin' down, and then we butcher it and eat it."

My father added, "When you do this to a fish, Son, it makes you a fisherman."

After a moment of thought, I asked, "If we did this to a man, would it make us a man-er-man?"

Grandpa Haycraft looked at my father and said, "Your boy ain't right."

* * *

Eleven years old.

During my middle school years, kids picked on me. They'd seen me flinch and cower when someone raised a hand towards me. We were at a tractor pull at the county fair when my parents overheard some boys calling me a sissy. Next day, Dad took me to the garden and made me beat the heck out of a scarecrow. It seemed kind of stupid until I began to imagine I was hitting one of the boys from my school. I got to hollering and it scared my dog Nellie so bad that she ran off back to the house. When we were done, it became my chore to rebuild the scarecrow. After that day, whenever I felt like beating on something, I wrapped a blanket over a bale of straw in the barn and went off. Nellie got used to my rage and laid watching. It somehow made sense to release my emotions while Dad was off working at the packinghouse. Mom walked in on me one day and seemed to approve. To my surprise, she taught me her own version of what she called the one-two-three.

Fronting up to me, she said, "One, bring your fist up slowly as if you're gonna hit me up under my chin." I did. When my fist touched her, she leaned her head backwards and said, "Now two, before I can recover, hit me low in my belly."

"You want me to hit you?"

"No, dammit. Just act like you are. I'm tryin' to show you something."

When I brought my fist to her belly, she doubled over and said, "Now three, grasp both your hands together in one big fist and come down on the back of my head."

As if in slow motion, I came down and she went to the floor. Looking up, she said, "At this point, I'm done and you can kick the tar out of me if you want."

We practiced several more times. I asked, "Who taught you to do this?"

She grinned and said, "My mother. Believe it or not, Elijah, girls do fight."

"Oh yeah, then why don't you beat Dad up for me?"

"Elijah, knowing how to fight is one thing. Knowin' when and who to fight is another. I seen a boy hit a girl out back of her daddy's barn once. When I went at him, he hurt me real bad. Pulling back her hair, Mamma showed me a scar on the side of her face, close to her ear. "He hit me so hard right here that I couldn't see. While I was down on the ground, he kicked me until he broke two of my ribs. My brother beat hell out of him the next day, but it sure took me a while to get over that whoopin'... and honey, your daddy's bigger and a whole lot meaner than that guy was."

"So you just let him be mean?"

"That's not fair, Elijah. Only way for me to stop your daddy would be to kill him. And I sure don't wanna do that. I don't want you and me to be alone. Believe it or not, mean as he is, your daddy loves me and you both. He'd protect us no matter what. It's just that when he drinks, his own upbringin' comes out and he becomes an angry man."

"What's that mean, Momma?"

"Honey, it's too complicated for a boy your age to be worryin' about. You'll figure it out some day."

I stood there thinking, *Shame Momma's brother had to get killed overseas. Maybe he could beat hell out of my dad.* When I said, "Sure wish I had me a brother," Mamma cried.

From that day forward, I stacked my straw bales so that the top one hung out several inches. It became my imaginary chin. Boy did I wear me out some blanket covered straw heads.

* * *

Thirteen years old

For over a year, I helped my father restore his father's old Cessna airplane. Grandpa Haycraft had been a pilot in the Vietnam War. After the war, he bought the used Cessna from someone. He taught my father to fly well enough to get his pilot's license. I never knew the full story, but apparently Grandpa had nearly crashed the plane while trying to do barrel rolls with my father and his two sisters on board. After that, the plane sat in the barn, slowly rotting. When Grandpa died, my father and his sisters sold the farm, paid off debts, and divided up what little the old man had. My aunts had no interest in the Cessna, so Dad decided to restore it. I remember how we drug it up on a farm wagon, high enough for the wings to clear fences, and then pulled it from Grandpa's barn to ours. The engine had locked up over time. Dad and I tore it down and completely rebuilt it. He also insisted on reinforcing brackets and supports so he could "play around in the sky." He apparently wanted to do some of what his father had tried to do. When I asked about the day they almost crashed, Dad said Grandpa stayed inverted too long and should have known that the gravity fed fuel system wasn't designed for that. I dreamed of the day I would go up with Dad and learn to fly.

One night, my friend Billy Henderson had walked the half mile from his house to mine. That's a long walk for him considering he walks with a limp. His right leg is twisted. Some sort of birth defect. My parents had gone somewhere and I was alone. Billy knew we were working on the plane and wanted to see it, so I took him out to the barn. Nellie followed along. Billy and I climbed into the cockpit and it surprised me that Dad had left the key in the ignition. I figured he'd been drinking whiskey the night before and simply forgot. "Can you start it up?" Billy asked.

"Dad would kill me."

"Would he even know?"

I considered and said, "Only for a few seconds." The engine turned over slowly and then ignited, filling the barn with noise and smoke. Billy shouted, "Hot damn. We're goin' to war!"

I shut off the engine. "Oh no! Now I'm gonna have to air out the barn or he'll smell it."

As I spoke, my father stepped in through the doorway. "Get the hell out of my plane!" Nellie sensed his anger and snuck out the door. My friend and I came off the plane as Dad stood shaking his head. "Billy, you best take your ass on home."

Billy gave me a look and then left without saying a word. Dad opened a cabinet on the wall above his workbench and removed a bottle of whiskey. I remained frozen as he stood in the doorway guzzling and monitoring Billy. Often, waiting for an ass whooping from my father was as bad as the actual beating.

"I'm sorry, Dad. I was just—"

"Don't you even talk to me, boy!" he shouted as he put down the bottle and picked up a rope from the workbench. While he made a slipknot, he said, "Take off that shirt."

"But Dad—"

"Every time you open your mouth, I'm gonna add another lick."

He put the noose around my wrists, tying me to one of the vertical six-by-six barn supports. With my back to him, I stood there needing to pee. I turned to see him taking another swig of the whiskey. Then he removed his belt.

I closed my eyes and waited. Suddenly, he lashed me across the back. It shocked me like no licking I'd ever taken before. Trying to grip the post, I held my breath. Another lashing came before I could fully recover from the first. I wanted to hold my piss, but another lash came and hot urine filled my drawers and ran down my legs. I needed to cry out but knew if I did it would only add to my agony. In my mind, I began to chant what my mother had once said. *It's only a sensation. It's only a sensation. It's only….*

By the time he finished, my head leaned against the post. My arms were stretched and my knees were on the dirt floor. Throughout the abuse, my father never said a word that I recall. I hung there numb, waiting for more, when his whiskey bottle clanged against the metal wall. Things got quiet. Seconds passed and I didn't know if he had left or not. My mind allowed the return of senses and I began to feel the pains of my injuries. The light in the barn went out, and I could hear his feet in the gravel outside. The smell of cigarette smoke drifted in.

While I wanted him to release me, it came as a relief that he went away. After what seemed like forever, I heard the slam of the screen door to the back of the house. Relaxing my head against the post, I wondered, *Is this what it felt like for Jesus?*

A whisper inside my head said, *Yes.*

The floodlight on the front of the barn bled in enough for me to see. As the sound of a distant freight train subsided, the night became deadly silent, and I began to hear the high pitch buzzing sounds of mosquitos. One by one, they found the blood on my back. I cried until Nellie came in and started licking my wounds.

* * *

Fourteen years old.

The Burton twins, Allen and Barry, lived just up the road from us. First week of the summer break between middle and high school, they invited me to camp out on a flat spot next to Todds Creek on the back of their place. Their father had given us permission to explore all we wanted as long as we didn't leave the farm. We hiked in, set up camp and fished for a while. During the two weeks prior, I had been sneaking a small amount of whiskey from different bottles that my father had hidden in several different places. It amounted to a full pint bottle. That night, after pigging out on fried bluegills, we began sipping. Half the bottle had us dancing around the campfire and howling at the moon. At some point, our tired butts crashed for the night.

Next morning, we slept in until the rising sun heated up our tent. After a brunch of canned bean soup, the twins took me out on a hike to teach me how to identify ginseng. They said their daddy digs it in the fall and sells it for a whole lot of money. They also told me that if someone got caught digging their daddy's ginseng, he might shoot them. During our search, they began talking about how they'd love to search the woods near the thoroughbred horse farms, since rich folks don't need to hunt ginseng.

Allen said, "You do know that if you cross Todds Creek, it's not that far to the Proctor Estate."

"I seen the entrance," I replied, "but that's about it. Sometimes I hear a helicopter back that way. Dad says that place belongs to a politician that he don't like."

Barry said, "Our daddy says it's odd how people say they don't like the man, but he keeps on gettin' re-elected."

Allen asked, "Hey, you wanna go see it?"

"See what?" I replied.

"The Proctor place. Me and Barry know just how to get there. We snuck up to the fence one day while we were out huntin' mushrooms."

"Really? But we're not supposed to leave the farm. What if your daddy comes back here to check up on us?"

"Hell, he ain't gonna cover the whole farm. We'll just say we were out looking for arrowheads."

We returned to the camp, ate some snacks and then started our adventure. I imagine we looked like three commandos hiking off with our .22 caliber rifles, canteens and backpacks. Recent rains had widened the creek at our camp, so we headed upstream to a spot where we could cross on a fallen tree. The water ran swift and clear over large rocks. We took turns balancing our way across and then headed up into the woods.

Barry led the way up that hill of old, tall timber. Heavenly streaks of sunlight penetrated through the high canopy of leaves. Blue jays screamed at our intrusion of their woods. Occasionally, I glanced back at how things would look on our return to the camp. In a matter of fifteen minutes, we were sneaking along near the backside of the Proctor Estate. "This is where we were before," Allen whispered.

Barry said, "Sure is a lot more leaves now."

Uphill and to the right of an old wooden horse barn, I could see the big white mansion. A four-rail wooden fence ran along the back of the property. About twelve foot of clearing lie between the fence and the woods we were in. The edge of the woods grew thick with underbrush. "You sure they don't have dogs?" I asked quietly.

Allen replied, "Never saw one last time."

As he spoke, the sound of voices caught our attention. Barry used his rifle scope to look up toward the house. "Hot damn!" he whispered loudly. "It's a woman. Y'all stay here. I'm gonna find a better view."

Allen and I watched as Barry crouched, rifle in hand maneuvering along the slope to an opening. Seconds later, Barry lowered his gun, looked our way and motioned for us to join him. When we got there, he got close and said, "You ain't gonna believe what I just saw. She ain't wearin' no top."

Side by side, we all three had our guns up, using our scopes to check out the backside of a tall woman with long dark hair. I could barely see her bikini bottom. As we waited in anticipation, a whitetail deer that had been bed down close by jumped up and started snorting as it bolted through the woods. The woman, now joined by a man, wet from the pool, turned toward the noise. Her boobs were awesome.

"Oowee!" Allen spoke louder than he should have.

"Who's out there?" the man shouted.

We all three turned and took off running downhill making more noise than the deer. No one spoke or stopped until we reached the creek. Bent over, catching his breath, Allen said, "Sorry guys. Just ain't never seen anything like that."

I stood staring back in the direction we'd just come from. "One thing for sure. They know we were there."

We crossed Todds Creek and walked the rest of the way back to camp. That night it rained like cats and dogs. We hunkered in the tent finishing off the rest of Dad's whiskey. I fell asleep thinking about those boobs I'd seen.

By daylight, the rising water had started up over the creek bank. We packed up and hiked home.

Two days later, the Sheriff and a man in a black suit came to our house. Dad wasn't home. None of us had a cell phone back then, so mom left a note and went with me to the Sheriff's Station down at the Wilson County Court House. Allen and Barry's mother, Flora May, sat in the lobby with their ten-year-old sister in the seat next to her. She looked up at my mother and asked, "Do you know what's going on?"

"No, I don't," Mom replied. "But I sure do hope to find out before William gets here."

I asked, "Are Barry and Allen here?"

"Yes," Mrs. Burton answered with a smirk. "They got them and their daddy in a room back there. What the hell did you boys get into?"

Before I could answer, Mom and I were led to a room. The man in the black suit was from the government. Turns out, there were cameras at the Proctor Estate. They had a picture of me, Allen and Barry, standing side by side in the woods. They wanted to know why we had our guns pointing at Senator Proctor's house. I clammed up, not wanting to say what we were looking at with my mother sitting there. Suddenly, the door opened and in stepped my father. "I wanna know what the hell's goin' on here?"

The man introduced himself and then handed Dad the photograph. "Sir, these boys were caught on video at the Proctor Estate. Their guns are pointed at the house. We need an explanation."

Dad stepped closer. I could smell whiskey. "Boy, you got five seconds."

"Dad, I can explain, but not in front of Mom."

Allen and Barry told me later that they got an ass whooping for leaving the farm and for pointing their guns at that house to stare at the woman's tits. My old man took me to the barn because he'd figured out that I had been stealing his whiskey.

* * *

Fifteen years old.

One afternoon, Billy, his sister Sissy and I were walking down the road. Two guys from my school, Brad Stone and David Weeper, were up on Brad's porch, about 150 feet from the road. Brad's big, mean dog sat watching us. As we passed, Brad hollered out, "Look at that freak! Boy, can't you walk like a normal human being?"

"Ignore 'em," I spoke softly as we kept walking.

"Why?" Sissy asked. "Why should we let 'em talk about Billy like that?"

"Because," I replied, "They're just punks. And besides, I don't wanna mess with Brad's dog."

"He's right," Billy spoke. "Same dog that chewed up little Jimmy Higdon."

Sissy stood there rubbing the back of her right hand, and then her face when David spoke loudly. "Hey Billy! I'd sure like to suck your sister's tits and do her up the ass!"

Billy couldn't help himself. When he gave 'em the finger, Brad stood up and hollered, "Go get 'em, Bruno!"

Damn dog came running out across that yard, barking and growling. It didn't worry me as much as it did Sissy. She got all scared and took off. The dog caught up and knocked her down. It was damn near dragging her by her hair when I started kickin' it with my pointed-toed boots. It let loose, and we all ran home. At suppertime, I told my father what had happened.

"Are you shittin' me? Is that the same dog what attacked the Higdon boy?"

"Yes, sir."

Mom said, "Dog shoulda been put down."

"Only reason they didn't," Dad growled, "is because them people are somehow related to the Sheriff."

Later that night, after Mom went to bed, Dad came to my room. "Get up boy. We got work to do."

I had no idea what he meant, but pulled on my jeans and boots and followed his orders. When I climbed into the cab of his old pickup, Dad handed me a plastic garbage bag and said, "Put it in the floorboard."

The heavy bag stunk terribly. Afraid to ask questions, I did as told. Before we reached the blacktop, he finished off a half-pint of whiskey and threw the bottle out the window near our mailbox. "Tomorrow morning, I want you to pick that up and put it in the garbage, ya hear?"

"Yes sir," I replied.

He lit a cigarette and began to explain. "Boy, there comes a time when a man has to take things into his own hands. Those pricks, Stone and Weeper, they crossed the line today. I've seen that girl Sissy and she's got all the makin's of a woman. I can understand them boys thinkin' about doin' stuff to her. That's normal at their age. But shoutin' it out in front of her like that ain't right. Damned disrespectful. If'n her daddy had heard 'em talkin' that way, they might get buried in a ravine on the back of his farm. And what really pisses me off is them a sicin' that dog on ya'll. Me and you are gonna teach 'em a little lesson on that."

It only took about five minutes for us to reach the road that Brad Stone lived on. Dad drove by slowly and we could barely see Brad's dog lying up on the porch. "That the dog that came after ya'll?"

"I'd say it is," I replied. "Didn't see any others."

A quarter mile down, Dad parked the truck behind the Little Rock Baptist Church. When he opened his door, he said, "Bring that bag with you boy. That there's our bait."

11

We walked at a pretty good pace until nearing Brad Stones house. There were no other houses within sight. I followed my old man into the wet ditch on the side of the road. "This ought to be close enough," he whispered. "Take that hambone out. Stick the bag in your pocket. We'll need it later. I'm a guessing that dog's gonna catch wind. When he does, he'll come off the porch and head our way."

"Then what?" I asked.

"Don't you worry about that right now. Just do as I say."

The hambone was nasty. Maggots were all over it. I'd say daddy had dug it out of the trashcan. I didn't want maggots in my pocket. When I started shaking the bag, Dad punched me in the chest and held his finger to his lips.

The sound of a vehicle drew our attention. We squatted low in the ditch. Moisture absorbed through the knees of my jeans. When the car had passed, Dad took the hambone and held it up with one hand. After about a minute the dog hadn't moved. Dad licked the index finger on his other hand and held it up in the air to judge the wind direction. He motioned with his head for me to follow. We quietly moved further down the ditch. When we were almost to the Stone's mailbox, he stopped and held the meat up again. Hungry mosquitoes buzzed their satisfaction at our arrival. Seconds later, the dog raised its head. Dad grinned and whispered, "You know its name?"

"Bruno," I whispered back.

"Good."

The dog climbed to its feet, stretched, and then slowly came off the porch. In a way, I admired my father's composure. While he squatted like a statue, my heart pounded and I literally shook. It reminded me of my first deer hunt. Instead of using the gravel driveway, the dog came straight out across the yard. Same path it took earlier in the day. As it drew near, it slowed down like a cat in stalk. At about thirty feet, it stopped and began a low growl, its white teeth glowing in the dark. Dad held up the hambone with one hand while using his other to pull out his folding hunter's knife.

Oh no! He's gonna kill it.

When he held the knife out, I knew he needed me to open it. I flipped out the five inch blade and handed it back. Dad spoke quietly, "Bruno. Bruno. Come on boy. Come and get this meat."

The dog's head tilted. After a few seconds, its ears rose up straight and it stepped closer, tongue flicking in and out. He wanted that meat. My father laid the hambone down in front of him, on the edge of the ditch, but held on to it with his left hand. "Good boy. Come and get it."

The dog never even paid attention to me. When it reached the meat, it first licked and then began tugging. Dad dropped the knife and grabbed Bruno's collar with his right hand. The dog went off, growling and tugging, its hind paws throwing moist dirt. Letting go of the meat, Dad used both hands. "Get the knife, Eli," he whispered loudly. Stab it behind the ribs."

"I don't wanna kill it, Dad."

"Do it, boy. Now!" Apparently the dog couldn't bark as it struggled against Dad's tight hold. "Do it, dammit or I'm gonna kick your ass."

I mumbled, "Sorry, Bruno," while pushing the whole blade in and downward, ripping it open. The warm smell of flowing blood filled my nostrils as the dog let out a muffled whimper, jerked several times, slowly stopped tugging, and then stretched out. My father released his grip. "Good job, son. Damn good job."

Sitting on my heels, I stared at the dead dog and then the house, thinking, *how would I feel if someone did this to Nellie?* I wiped the bloody blade off in the grass, and said, "Let's go."

"We ain't done yet, boy. I want you to take that knife and start skinnin' this thing out. Just like we do a deer. Only I want you to leave the head on it. I'll keep watch."

Are you kidding me? Confused, I proceeded to do as told. The job seemed morbid, but at least the dog was dead and felt no pain. Mosquitoes tormented me the entire twenty minutes it took to turn Bruno into what looked like a canine version of a bearskin rug. I finished with blood stains on my neck and face from swatting.

"That'll work, son. Now we're gonna sneak up there and lay it out on the hood of that shiny new pickup. Tomorrow morning, they'll find it."

The next day, all hell broke loose. The sheriff and a deputy came to school and took me out in handcuffs.

Killing the dog bothered me. Mother seemed to notice and asked me what was wrong. When I explained, she said, "Honey, you know your daddy kills animals for a living."

A couple days later, she kept me home from school and took me to where my father worked. The people there gave us both a yellow hard hat and then led us on a tour of the slaughter process. As we approached what they called 'the kill floor', I could hear the non-stop squealing and mooing of pigs and cattle as they waited their turns to be slaughtered.

From an overhead catwalk, Mom and I stared down at my father's work area. "Dad!" I called to him. He turned for only a second to look up and acknowledge our presence. He wore a yellow apron and tall rubber boots and literally stood in six inches of blood. His jaw bulged with chewing tobacco as he steeled his knife and then continued to cut the juggler veins of hogs at the rate of 400 per hour. The reality of what he did didn't seem to concern him at all. The overall butchering process consisted of an assembly line—dead hogs hanging on a rail, moving around the room as workers cut this or that from the carcasses. Men and women chitchatted among themselves while mindlessly butchering animals. Hog guts and fetuses were removed and discarded as nonchalantly as a barber cutting hair. It truly was a kill floor. At a distance, I could see cattle hanging and meandering around the room while being butchered in much the same process. I stood there thinking, *No one considers this when they buy meat.*

Mom put her hand on my shoulder and said, "Eli, this is an ugly process that your daddy participates in every day, just so people who claim to be animal lovers can with clear conscious, eat meat. And honey, these animals never did anything bad to anyone.... Can you understand now why your father had no problem killing a dog that had already chewed up one kid and was about to do the same to your friend Sissy?"

That night I lay in bed wondering if God favors the life of one animal over another.

* * *

Fifteen-sixteen years old.

Now and then, I spent the night with my grandparents on my mother's side. One night in September, Grandpa Smith and I stood outside in the dark, next to the barn. He had just snuck me what he thought was my first taste of whiskey. We split a half pint. Me feeling all brave and stuff, I started talking bad about my father, and how mean he could be, and how mad it made me when he talked down on my mother. Guess I got a little loud when I said, "He ain't nothing but a no good son-of-a-bitch, and I'd like to go home right this minute and—"

"Whoa, now," Grandpa interrupted. "You need to calm down. Your daddy hears you talkin' like that, he'll take to wearin' you out."

I turned, started taking a piss, and said, "Oh well. One of these days, I might just take to wearin' *him* out."

Grandpa waited until I zipped up and then took ahold of me with both of his big hands on my shoulders. "Now you listen to me, Elijah. If your daddy gets outta line with you or your momma, you let me take care of him. And if you got somethin' to say about him, believe you'd be better off sayin' it to me."

"Sure," I replied, "and what if you ain't around when I got somethin' to say?"

For a few seconds, Grandpa seemed lost for words. He took out a pouch of chewing tobacco, made a wad and stuck it in his mouth. After about a minute, he spit and said, "Look up yonder, boy. You see that star out a piece from the big dipper?"

I nodded.

"That there's the North Star. She's always up there, right in that exact same spot, day or night. Even when you can't see it, she's there. When I've had me drink or two and your grandma goes to gittin' on my nerves, I find it's a whole lot better if I just come out here and talk to that star."

Not long after that, I sat on the back steps, frustrated, watching yellow maple leaves float to the ground. Nellie came trotting in from the field in a hurry. She had gotten old and couldn't run like she used to. For the past year, she had been unable to hear me calling her name. Instead of heading straight to the house, she ran the edges of the barn and then followed the well-used path on up to where I sat. As I greeted her with a head rub, more movement at the barn caught my attention. Two scraggly coyotes stood staring our way. "Were they chasing you?"

The next evening, Dad and I watched as Nellie limped along the edge of the garden spot looking for a place to poop. I said, "Last night, the coyotes were chasin' 'er."

Dad adjusted his cap and said, "Reckon we oughta put 'er down before that happens."

"Couldn't we just build a kennel with a top on it to keep 'em out?"

When Dad hesitated to answer, I could tell he wasn't enjoying the conversation. He loved that old dog as much as I did. Finally, he said, "Nellie's goin' on seventeen. That's way over a hundred in dog years. She ain't never been caged up. Wouldn't seem right to do it now."

Tears ran down my cheeks. "I'm gonna miss her."

Dad put his hand on my shoulder. "We're all gonna miss 'er, Son." After a few seconds, he said, "Tomorrow, when you get home from school, I want you to go ahead and dig a grave. We'll take care of it when I get home."

I remained, watching Nellie, as my father walked to the house. Later that night, I couldn't sleep, and so I went outside, found Nellie and fed her a half bag of Animal Crackers. It killed me that she couldn't hear my voice, telling her how much I loved her.

There was no way I could go to school the next day. Mom and I talked at length about Nellie. Like Dad, she convinced me that putting her down would be the right thing to do. We both were tore up just talking about it. She said, "Elijah, if you want, I'll dig the hole."

"No. Hell no. I'll do it."

Nellie napped in the sun nearby as I cried while using a long handled spade to dig the hole. When Dad got home, he wasted no time. Seeing his .22 caliber pistol put a knot in my stomach. He put a leash on Nellie and led her to the gravesite I'd created in the grassy spot where she and I used to nap in the sun. Nellie had no clue as she sat next to the grave. I looked back and saw Mom staring out the kitchen window. Dad rubbed Nellie's head between both his hands and said, "You've been a good one, girl. Gonna miss you." He turned to me. "Okay, boy. Say your goodbyes."

He didn't know that I'd been crying, hugging and saying my goodbyes for hours. "Go ahead, Dad. Just get it over with."

He seemed surprised that I would be ready. "Oh no. She's been more your dog than anyone else's." He cocked the hammer on the gun and offered it to me.

"No, Dad. I don't wanna do it."

"I didn't ask if you wanted to. Just take the damn gun. Lay the muzzle right behind her ear and pull the trigger. She won't feel a thing."

I took the gun and held it right where Dad said to. I had killed a lot of animals in my life, but this felt different. "Goodbye. Nellie. I love you."

When I pulled the trigger, she fell immediately to her side and began jerking. Without thinking, I cocked the hammer, stuck the gun to her head and pulled the trigger again. As I started to cock it again, Dad grabbed the gun. "That's enough, son. She's done." Nellie's body stretched out straight and then relaxed.

Losing Nellie sucked. I often found myself, outside, alone in the dark and missing my best friend. One night, while coyotes howled in the distance, I looked up to Grandpa's star and complained. "Why did Nellie have to take a bullet while the coyotes get to live on?" That same whisper that answered *yes* to me in the barn, when I asked about Jesus, came again.

Elijah, think about how a Coyote's life ends.

On a Sunday morning, as I sat next to Mom at Church, Preacher Herman talked about how suffering the loss of a loved one is often self-inflicted pain. He said, "We tend to want to live in the past and our soul suffers because we desire something that cannot happen." His eyes fell on me when he said, "Each day, God gives us hope. If we just pay attention to the present and not the past, something beautiful comes along and it heals the heart." I prayed for something beautiful in my life.

That night, I dowsed Nellies doghouse with gasoline and burned it. As I stood watching the flames, my parents rushed out of the house. When the door slammed, I turned expecting a scolding. Instead, Dad said, "Thank you, son. I've been wantin' to do that myself." Mom just nodded.

Days passed and my unanswered prayers for something beautiful diminished. Memories of Nellie were again haunting my quiet moments. Living each day in wait for a new beginning was not easy.

My parents talked me into a long-weekend camping trip to a place called Natural Bridge State Park. About an hour from home, my mother loved the place because it got her out of the house and she got to talk to people. Dad liked it because he enjoyed sitting around a fire with men who drank as much as he did.

A girl named, Kelly, from Lexington, had come there with her parents. She wasn't the prettiest girl I'd ever seen, but her smile and her laughter lit me up. She had beautiful long, wavy red hair. We took hikes together. On the third day, as we climbed up the mountain, Kelly reached for my hand. Her touch felt electric. No one other than my parents and grandparents had ever held my hand. I wondered if it meant as much to her as it did to me. High up on a ridge in that forest, I got my first kiss. Kelly healed my heart. After that weekend, I called her up on the phone at least three nights a week. At our house, we had no internet connection. Therefore, Kelly and I did it the old fashioned way. We mailed each other our wallet sized school pictures with a note written on the back. Weeks and months went by in anticipation of seeing her again.

Just when I thought I'd found a girl who actually cared about me, Kelly told me she'd gotten sick and might not live. At first, I thought it could be a lie, some cheap way of breaking off our relationship. I was wrong. We continued to talk, but I only got to see her one more time.

In the end, my father would not drive me to Lexington to see Kelly in the hospital. With only a learner's permit for driving, I considered stealing the truck and going anyway. Mom sensed my intentions and talked me out of it. When Kelly died, I wanted to go to the funeral. Dad said, "You barely knew the girl." More than all the beatings he'd given me, I hated him for that. He had no idea what Kelly meant to me.

That night, after Dad had fallen asleep, Mom came to me with an envelope. "This came in the mail today. Didn't want to give it to you in front of your father."

I hugged her neck and went to the back steps. My fingers shook, opening the letter from Kelly.

> Dear Elijah,
> I told my mother not to send this letter until I was gone. When I told her how you said that you were mad

at God for letting me get sick, she said we're like all other animals. We're stuck with what the world puts forth, be it good, bad, or ugly. She says how we react to what nature puts us through may be what we get judged on in the end. I don't know if she's right, but at this point it no longer matters.

I'm glad your father wouldn't bring you here. Don't want you to see me like this. Please remember me the way you remember your sweet dog, Nellie. Remember the good things!!! When I think of you, I think about hikes in the mountains, and the beautiful moments we had on top of that ridge. I will take your smile and our kiss to Heaven.

While I never got to experience love like most, I do believe that you love me. And for that I LOVE YOU ELIJAH.

Kelly Armstrong

After reading the letter, I could hardly breathe. The back door opened and my mother stepped out. She sat down and wrapped me in her arms. I handed her the letter, she read it, and we cried together. "It's a beautiful letter, Eli. May I show it to your father?"

"No. He wouldn't understand."

"Honey, I believe you underestimate your father. Despite all his flaws, there's a sweet guy in there somewhere. Perhaps if he reads this, he will understand how much Kelly meant to you."

"I don't think he cares."

"Please, Elijah?"

"Okay," I agreed for my mother. "But I want it back tonight."

Mom stood and said, "You go for a walk. After he reads the letter, I'll leave it on the kitchen table."

The next morning, during breakfast, it pissed me off that Dad didn't mention the letter. He went about his bacon, eggs and biscuits without a word. My appetite disappeared. When I stood to walk away, he looked up, wiped tears from his face and said, "Believe today's a good day for me to start teaching you how to fly the Cessna."

I looked at my mother. She winked.

* * *

Seventeen years old.

It's not easy standing in front of the class, senior English, dry-mouthed and dreading the task of presenting a personal narrative. Old Mrs. Effinger had said, "Pick something unique about your life that people might find interesting." For over a week I had planned to talk about flying my father's renovated Cessna. That idea got ruined when Brad Stone did his speech on flying a Learjet that belonged to his uncle who trained thoroughbreds. I considered not speaking and taking a zero, but knew if I did, my father would go off.

"Elijah Haycraft," Miss Effinger spoke from the back of the room. "You've delayed long enough. We're running out of time."

On my way to the podium, I grabbed a flyswatter from the teacher's desk. "The title of my speech is, Pain." Holding the flyswatter up vertical, I said, "We all know how to use one of these. When a fly bugs us, we go after it. We do the same to mosquitoes, and don't we all step on ants and roaches? Darn near anything that bugs us, we kill, and we do it so often that killing becomes natural." Smacking the swatter on the podium, I said, "Question is, does the fly feel pain? And does anyone even care?"

Sherry Brown, in the front row, said, "Nooo, it's a fly."

"Ah, but what if it's not a fly? What if it's something bigger?" Reaching back to the teacher's desk, I grabbed a rubber mouse and her wooden gavel. Someone had placed the mouse in her desk drawer the day before to scare her. Holding the mouse up by its tail, I said, "My mother goes after one of these with a broom. I'd rather use a hammer." Laying the mouse on the podium, I smacked it, thump, thump, thump, three quick times with the gavel. Several in the room jumped, including Mrs. Effinger. I asked, "Does a mouse feel pain? How about a pig or a cow or a chicken? We kill 'em every day for food. We do it quickly, but the question remains, do they feel pain or think of it the same way we do? Do we even care?" Lifting the gavel again, I said, "And what if I miss the mouse and hit my hand?"

I came down twice on my left hand with the gavel. It sounded about like hitting the rubber mouse. When I took a deep breath, Mrs.

Effinger threw up her hands. "Elijah Haycraft! There will be no more of that!"

While she lowered herself into a desk in the back of a row, blood ran onto the podium from skin hanging off the knuckle of my thumb. I exhaled slowly, grinned and continued. "As children, our mothers tell us that it hurts when we fall. So, we cry and our mammas give us attention. But then, daddy says, 'Don't cry boy. You ain't hurt. I can give you somethin' to cry about,' and he does, often. Not sure about you guys, but eventually, I learned not to cry. Over time, pain became just a different kind of sensation." Looking down at Sherry Brown, I said, "Shocking, but somehow interesting."

As she frowned, someone in the class said, "You're sick."

My friend, Billy Johnson, shook his head. Brad Stone and David Weeper sat in the back of the room rotating their index fingers around the side of their heads like they thought I was crazy. Mrs. Effinger tilted her head and asked, "Elijah, are you sure you want to talk about this?"

"I'll stop now, ma'am, if you'll give me an A."

"You know I can't do that."

By then my adrenaline had begun to flow and I was having a good time speaking. "Then I guess I'll have to continue." I thought for a few seconds. "We all go fishing. Everybody I know uses live bait even though it has to hurt like hell when we put a hook through the worm or cricket or minnow or whatever. And no one ever seems to have a problem with butchering a fish alive. My father says it makes us a fisherman. But where do we draw the line? What is it that makes a psychopath advance from a fish to a man?"

Sherry turned and said, "Mrs. Effinger, do we have to listen to this?"

Mrs. Effinger said, "Elijah, your subject is a little frightening."

I replied, "Do you know how boring it was when she talked about her first experience riding a bicycle? I'm trying to talk about how we all learn to kill things without even considering the pain we inflict. She might find it uncomfortable. I find it ... interesting." I held my injured hand up. Blood dripped.

"Oh my God!" echoed across the room.

Mrs. Effinger nearly fell trying to get out of the desk while shouting, "That's it, Elijah! You're done!"

David Weeper said, "I told you all, this guy ain't right. Now you can see why Sheriff Johnson told us to stay away from him."

The class continued their snickers, snarls, and innuendos as Mrs. Effinger dabbed my hand with tissues from her desk and then applied a Band-Aid. It reminded me of the way my mother fixed me up after I'd done something wrong, and my father had beaten the heck out of me. When Mrs. Effinger finished, I whispered, "Thank you."

Quietly, she said, "Elijah, I believe we ought to speak with a counselor about your issues."

"Issues?"

"Yes, dear. Everyone knows you've had a troubling childhood and about your dealings with the law. I understand your need to talk, but I'm afraid you might upset some of your classmates."

The bell rang, and I stood up to leave. Several students gathered near the door. "What about *their* issues?" I asked while stepping away.

On my approach, Sherry Brown moved over to block the door. "How's your *pain*, Elijah?"

Purposely flaring my nostrils, I said, "Are you trying to *bug* me?"

Her forehead wrinkled and she stepped aside. "Hey!" one of the guys shouted as I left the room.

Billy worked to catch up with me in the hallway. "Slow down. What the hell's wrong with you?"

Without stopping I said, "It's lunchtime. I'm hungry."

The two of us sat alone at a table on the outside terrace. I had become accustomed to a few people staring, but suddenly it seemed they all were. Billy read my discomfort. "What the hell do you expect? You took a gavel and busted your own damn hand."

"Oh well. It's my hand."

"Come on Elijah. The Sheriff's done told the whole county to watch out for you. Now they're gonna believe you're some kind of psycho. And no wonder. You said pain can be interesting."

"And?"

"And it makes you sound creepy. Like you're one of those freaks that gets off on pain."

I bit through a carrot stick, and said, "What's wrong with that?"

"You're trying to be funny, right?"

"No. Not really. I'm just saying—"

Before I could finish, Brad Stone and David Weeper stepped to the table. They had another guy with them, an underclassman that had only been at our school for a few weeks. I didn't know his name. "Stand up," David demanded.

I remained seated and said, "What's your problem?"

Brad said, "You threatened Sherry. We all heard you."

David spoke loud. "Should we call the Sheriff before this moron goes off on Sherry?"

Nearly everyone eating outside stood to see what was going on. Someone hollered, "Kick his ass!" My gut churned as I began evaluating. I didn't care if they called the Sheriff. I'd dealt with him before. His deputies roughed me up more than once. Brad and David didn't really worry me. They were all mouth. But this new guy looked stout. His neck barely protruded his collared shirt. Father had once warned me that it's hard to knock out a man with no neck. The guy stared at my eyes and asked, "What are you looking at, Freako?"

"Guess that's what I'm trying to figure out."

His lip curled as he spoke again. "What's with the long hair? You two's a couple of them gay boys, ain't cha?"

Billy said, "How about y'all go on so we can eat our lunch."

David shoved him in the shoulder and said, "How about you shut your mouth before we kick *your* ass."

The hairs on my arms began to stiffen. I rose slowly and spoke softly, "Believe you should think twice about puttin' your hands on my friend."

"Oh yeah? What if I do?"

With the crowd closing in, I said, "Come over here and I'll tell you."

Asshole grinned and said, "Really?"

As David came around the table, Brad said, "Watch him, he might have a knife."

I held my hands up to show him I didn't. No Neck remained quiet but seemed to be sizing me up. I leaned toward David's ear and whispered. His face turned red, his eyes bulged. Terrified, he backed off. Moving towards me, the new guy barked, "What the hell? You afraid of this creep?"

He hit me hard, right in the nose. My world exploded into darkness and sparkling stars as I fell backwards over a chair and then to the ground. Blinded, I sat on my heels expecting to get kicked or pounded. It didn't happen. Vision began to return as I caught warm blood from my nose, dripping off my chin. Laughter and ugly comments continued from the crowd that surrounded me like planks in a fortress. Though my insides were shaking, I climbed to my feet. The crowd got quiet. I stared at my attacker while licking the blood from my hand. Then I said, "My name is Elijah. What's yours?"

The guy squinted and said, "You really are weird."

At that moment, I felt more frightened than weird. Many of my classmates had made fun of me, yet they all seemed afraid to beat on me. This idiot was different. He didn't know me. My mind flashed back to the scarecrow in Dad's garden. Glancing towards Brad Stone and David Weeper, I asked, "Did they put you up to this?" The guy shook his head as if to say no. While pointing at my nose, I began slowly rotating and speaking loudly to the crowd. "See what he did to me! It's broken! Does that make you people happy? Y'all think it's okay to pick on someone because they're not just, like, you! Wanna know how this feels? It's like a thousand nerve endings playing heavy metal in my head! And it's awesome!"

In my peripheral vision, I could see that No Neck had relaxed his hands. Continuing to turn, I shouted again. "Do you know what happens when you hit someone who ignores the pain?" Still in motion, I brought my fist up under the guy's chin so hard that he nearly came off the ground. Blood shot from his mouth as he bit his tongue. Before he could recover, I began pounding the sides of his head left, right, left, right, left, right fast like a machine until he collapsed to the ground. It felt good to finally be the aggressor. I kicked his side once, twice, three times. When he curled up into a fetal position, I pushed him to his stomach, put my knee into his back and pulled his head up by his hair, like a trophy. Blood ran from his mouth. His eyes were barely open. My heart pounded as I looked up at the shocked crowd. "There will be no happy ending for anyone who bullies me or my friend!"

Rising to my feet, I felt stronger and meaner than at any time in my life. I stepped to Billy and put my arm around his shoulder. David and Brad stood next to one another, ten feet away. Facing them, I said,

"Now, which one of you wants to try and kick Billy's ass?" They both held up their open hands up as if to say, not me. I wiped blood from my face. "If you even put your hands on him, we're gonna find out if you enjoy this as much as I do."

* * *

Eighteen years old.

When I graduated from high school, I thought about applying for work at the packinghouse. My father said he didn't want me working my ass off there like he'd been doing for years. Said I should join the military and get me some free college. During my senior year, recruiters had come to the school to pitch the benefits of signing up. Free college. Travel the world. All that stuff. The recruiter seemed to think my arrest record could be overlooked due to no convictions. One hot summer morning, I decided, what the hell, and went on down to sign up. I left there thinking I'd soon be a soldier. However, by the time I returned for my physical, the recruiter said I had been turned down due to psychological restrictions.

"What the hell does that mean?" I asked.

He said, "Without going into details, I'd say it has to do with your local Sheriff's department expressing a fear of mental instability."

"Sheriff Johnson told you I'm unstable. Did he tell you how many times he and his deputies roughed me up?"

Being of age, I decided to go ahead and get away from my father. My mother's parents let me move in with them. A few months later, Mom started working part time at the Wilson County Library. Suddenly, she began wearing makeup and dressing nicely. Dad wasn't stupid. He knew someone at that library was paying her the attention she deserved. I stopped by on a Saturday night and found my mother alone, sitting on the back steps smoking a cigarette. I'd never known her to smoke. She had a black eye.

I became enraged. "I'll kill that sonofabitch!"

Mom shook her head. "No, Elijah. I deserved this. I met me a man who treats me like a lady. Talks to me. Smiles at me. I don't know what I'm gonna do."

Holy smoke. "Where is Dad?"

She said nothing, but nodded towards the barn. I walked out there with intentions of doing something I'd always wanted to do. I was going to try and kick my father's ass. That didn't happen. I found him, sitting on the floor, leaning against a bale of straw, crying like a baby. The smell of liquor hit me. His bottle sat on the ground next to him. The old single barreled shotgun I'd used to kill my first rabbit leaned against the six-by-six post he had tied me to. I'd never seen him that way before. Suddenly, I wondered what it felt like to find out that your spouse had been cheating on you. I didn't know whether to knock his sorry ass out, or give him a hug.

He looked up. "What am I gonna do?"

I reached for the bottle, took a swig and said, "That's that same thing Mom said."

"Ain't never been one to say pretty things, or dress my woman up and take her out on the town. Reckon I brought this on myself."

When I picked up the shotgun, he said, "Go ahead. Shoot me. I'd just a soon die."

I breached the gun, removed the shell and pitched it across the barn. That night, I got drunk with my father. He opened up and told me things I couldn't imagine. He let me ask questions, and he gave me answers. He described his childhood and how Grandpa Haycraft had mistreated his mother and him and his two sisters. It turned my stomach, and I cried.

A couple days later, I sought out the man who had been talking to my mother. He seemed nice enough, clean cut, good looking guy, perhaps a few years younger than her. When I asked about his intentions, he said, "Look, kid. Don't know what she told you, but it's not like I'm trying to bust up her marriage."

"So what exactly are you trying to do?"

"Don't act stupid, boy. If your old man was doing his homework, she wouldn't be giving it up to a guy like—"

The words weren't out of his mouth before I busted him up aside of his head. When he reached for his pocket, I pointed my finger and said, "Don't go there. That punch was for my mother. I tell my old man what you just said, he'll do his homework when he cuts your throat and watches you bleed out."

The next day, that man left town. She didn't say so, but I could tell my mother was crushed and blamed me for the guy leaving. My parents stayed together despite their differences. I could tell they were not happy. Dad fell deeper into the bottle. Every time he got drunk and upset with me or Mom, he threatened to kill himself. One day, I said, "Go ahead. Quit talking about it. Mom and I would be better off without you anyway." That was on a Saturday.

Next morning, when she didn't show up for Church, Mom's parents and I got worried. I borrowed a cell phone and called the house. No one answered. Grandpa and I left service and went to check on her. Dad's truck was in the drive. Entering through the back door, we found two kitchen chairs overturned and an empty whiskey bottle in the sink. "Mom! Dad! Y'all in here?"

With no answer, I ran up the stairs to my parents' bedroom. Their bed had been made. I bounced back down the stairs as Grandpa came out of my old room. He shook his head.

As we stepped out the backdoor, the sound of Dad's Cessna drew our attention. The plane left the barn and headed down the field. Grandpa shouted, "Check the barn!" I ran.

By the time Grandpa reached the barn, I knew Mom wasn't there. On the floor, scratched in the dirt, were the words: SORRY SON.

Grandpa said, "This ain't good, boy."

We stepped out the back of the barn and watched as the Cessna approached. I said, "Know damn well she's not with him. She would never get in that plane!"

As the Cessna roared by, some sixty feet away, Dad glanced our way and nearly lost the plane. "He's drunk!" I hollered.

"She's not with him!"

"Good!" I shouted back. "Bet she finally left his ass."

We watched as Dad regained control and lifted off nearing the end of the field. He flew out a half mile and then turned back.

Grandpa said, "Hope he can land that damned thing."

"He ain't gonna land. He knows we're watching." Nearing the field, Dad pulled up. "He's goin' into a loop!"

Grandpa said, "He'll kill himself."

"That might be his intentions." Flashbacks of our fight the night before made my stomach ache. The plane inverted perfectly. "Come on, Dad. You can do it." He stayed inverted too long. "Pull it down, Dad!" The engine began to sputter. "No, Dad! Please, please don't do it!" The engine quit and the plane went into a free-fall.

Before the plane hit the ground, Grandpa grabbed me and held on. The impact threw debris in every direction. I beat Grandpa to the plane, but couldn't get close enough as the flames were too hot. I'm not sure how long we stood there watching the plane burn before a neighbor's pickup came flying down the drive. It never even slowed down as it busted through the fence. The sound of sirens followed in the distance.

Mr. Burton and the twins jumped out of the pickup and ran to us. By then, the flames were beginning to subside. Allen and Barry followed as I tried to get closer. Mr. Burton hollered, "You boys need to wait for the fire truck! That thing could blow up!"

The volunteer firemen arrived and had just enough water on board to extinguish the flames. Smoke continued. They made us stay back while they inspected the wreckage. By then, the Sheriff had arrived. As Grandpa described what we had seen, Wilson County's Fire Chief left the plane and came our way. He nodded at Grandpa and me and then spoke to the Sheriff. "The coroner's gonna be here soon. We can't do much more until he takes a look and starts working on identification."

"It was Dad. We saw him."

"Yes," replied the Chief, "but it appears he wasn't alone."

"No," I screamed and took off running to the plane.

The two firemen there grabbed me. One said, "We can't disturb anything until the coroner gets here."

The other man had tears in his eyes when he said, "Elijah, you don't wanna look."

I looked anyway and immediately threw up. As I went into dry heaves, Grandpa put his hand on my shoulder. He looked in at what I saw, and said, "Come here, boy." When we had stepped away from the firemen, he hugged me and whispered. "I'm gonna rub out what he wrote in the dirt. When you get back to the house, straighten up the kitchen." I pulled away and looked into his eyes. He said, "Ain't neither one of us sure about what happened here, but for your grandma, and for insurance, best this was an accident."

* * *

Twenty four years old.

For nearly five years, I lived in my parent's house while working at the same meat-packing facility where my father had spent most of his life. Didn't make a lot of money, but as a country boy with no college, I did okay. Didn't mind working hard, five days a week. On Friday nights, I partied. On Saturdays, I slept. Did Church some Sunday mornings, then back home is where I'd be. Figured I'd stay in those hills till the Lord comes after me.

None of the girls that I had gone to high school with would even consider a date. Now and then, at Church, I'd get a nod or a smile, mostly from those already married. No one went out of their way to speak. Sheriff Johnson had done a good job of convincing the whole county that I was some sort of a lunatic. Even the preacher man kept his distance.

One of the guys I worked with at the packinghouse lived in nearby Madison County. On Friday nights, he spent half his wages at the bars in Richmond, home of the Eastern Kentucky University. On one particular night, Gary asked me to meet him at a new place that featured live music and a ton of college girls. Turns out, the bartender was Billy's sister, Sissy. When I bellied up at the bar, next to Gary, Sissy approached.

"Elijah Haycraft! Ain't seen you in a while."

"Good to see you, Sissy."

As Gary and I began drinking beer, I started checking out a lady at the end of the bar. She sat with a black couple and seemed a little older than the crowd. While pulling her long blonde hair back out of her eyes, she gave me a glance. They were drinking shots. When Sissy came our way, I asked, "You know them?"

"I know Tamara, the black girl. She's in one of my classes at Eastern. Believe the guy's her cousin. The white girl came in with him. Heard her say she's a med-student at UofL."

"Med-student!" Gary huffed. "There you go, Elijah. You need you one of those prissy doctor types."

"Not sure I'd call her prissy," Sissy replied. "Girl's got a mouth on her, and that's her third shot of Jack Daniels in thirty minutes."

"Damn," I mumbled. "A whiskey-drinkin' woman. My kind of girl."

Sissy smiled. "Elijah Haycraft. I've known you most of my life. Ain't never seen you with a woman. Even Billy thinks you're gay."

"Bull! Trust me, darling, your brother knows better."

"Really?" she replied. "Well, if she's your kind of girl, go on down there and introduce yourself."

"Hell yes," Gary agreed. "Show us whatcha got."

"Y'all can both kiss my ass." As I spoke, the woman looked my way again and sort of smiled. I downed my beer and said, "Give me a shot of Jack Daniels."

As I started that way, some guy approached the lady. "Damn!" I thought out loud. He started talking to her and put his hand on her shoulder. She pushed his hand away and said something that I couldn't hear. When I stopped and set the whiskey on the bar, she sort of tilted her head. I pointed at the shot, and then at her. Believe she and the guy knew my intentions.

He said, "Bug off, man. She's talking to me."

I picked up the shot glass and said, "No offense, pal. Not trying to start trouble, but I just bought this for the lady."

"I'm not your pal," he spoke with a slur. "And you need to walk away."

When I reached to give her the drink, the guy smacked it out of my hand. Whiskey flew and the shot glass rolled across the floor. Several people noticed and began to watch. When my nostrils flared, the man drew back. Before I could react, the lady grabbed his wrist and said, "Mister, you just cost me a shot of whiskey. Now you need to move on before *I* kick your ass."

The black guy said, "She's not kidding. You best back off."

The woman released her grip as Sissy stepped up. Apparently, she knew the guy. "Jason. You need to leave this alone. If you don't, I promise you're gonna get hurt."

By then, the band had quit playing and everyone in the room watched. "Like hell," the guy sputtered. "Ain't no woman gonna kick my ass."

Sissy said, "Don't know about her, but I know this guy, and you don't want no part of what he's gonna do to you."

By then another guy came and took ahold of the jerk. "Come on, Jason. You're too drunk to be fighting."

While his friend pulled him away, the guy shouted, "Ain't afraid of his ass!"

As I watched them disappear into a dark corner of the room, the band started playing again. Sissy leaned on the bar in front of the woman. "You okay?"

She looked up. "I'm good. Sucks about the whiskey."

Sissy poured another shot, sat it down and said, "I'm Sissy. What's your name, Honey?"

"Jane."

"Well, Jane, this here shot's from my friend, Elijah." Turning to me, she said, "Elijah, this is Jane. Now you two talk while I go do my job."

I took a seat on the bar stool cattycornered to Jane and her friends. Sissy brought me another beer. When I took a sip, the other girl stood and said, "I gotta go pee."

Jane said, "Elijah, this is my friend, John Evans."

"How you doin'?" I asked, trying not to stare at the long thin scar that ran across his cheek.

"Pretty good." He raised his shot. "And boy do I feel safe around you two bad asses."

"I wasn't tryin' to start trouble."

Jane spoke, "Thanks for the shot. You from around here?"

"Wilson County," I replied. "Ain't nothin' goes on there. Come here to party after work on Fridays. First time in this place."

"Then," she replied while holding up the shot, "I'd say we have something in common."

John asked, "What kind of work do you do?"

With my elbows on the bar and my hand on the back of my neck, I said, "I work at a packinghouse."

"What do you pack?"

"Meat."

"Meat? You kill animals?"

"You wanna eat a taco, sir, somebody gotta kill somethin'."

Jane downed her whiskey, exhaled and said, "Sounds manly." The band began a slow song. She stood and said, "Come on. Dance with me."

Part II

Chapter 1

Louisville, Kentucky
2018

For better or for worse, marrying Jane changed my whole life. My mother's parents thought I had been kidding when I told them I might be marrying a future doctor. Then, to my surprise, they liked Jane. Grandpa said, "At least she ain't highfalutin' like the doctors I know."

Grandma had a different take. "She's pretty as can be. You two ought to give us some beautiful great-grandbabies."

I sold my parents' place and came to the city, a move regretted almost immediately. John Evans says opposites attract, and that's why Jane and I hooked up. I'm thinking it's why he and I became such good friends. I let him talk me into taking a job where he works. It's an internet service provider called Indirect Cable. John's a computer engineer. I answer phones. There have been days when I felt I'd rather be back at the packinghouse, killing animals and talking with my old friends. Jane assured me that after she became a doctor, I could find a more interesting job. Maybe even go to college. That was about a year and a half into our marriage when she spent day and night on med-school. I had become so bored that I met someone interesting and it nearly broke up our marriage.

When Jane graduated, she asked me if I'd be willing to move to Indianapolis. I said, "Hell no! If you have to go, fine. I'll move back to the hills."

Somehow, she managed to stay in Louisville, starting her internship in the Emergency Room at University Hospital. Three years later, she continued her trauma surgeon residency. I still had the same job and no college. With Jane working nights, I struggled with my sanity.

The workout room at our condo complex kept me in shape, yet teased my hormones. Several shapely ladies worked out there on a regular basis. My instincts warned me against striking a relationship with a neighbor. Therefore, I tried to keep conversations to a minimum.

Some days, I drove to a park for a run or a walk in the woods to clear my mind. Mostly, I spent evenings bored in our downtown, high rent condo, watching my savings disappear. Too many nights ended in bourbon and memories of my sweet mother and the man whose worst addiction was becoming my own. Despite his abuse, my father loved me. He taught me how to be tough. He taught me how to withstand pain. He taught me how to flip the switch. I knew things were bad the first time Jane said, "The whiskey's making you mean."

Just when it seemed I might go off the deep end, strange things began to happen.

After work on Wednesdays, John and I typically stop off at a nearby place called Del Junco's Bar and Grill. John likes a cold beer. I prefer a shot of bourbon with a beer chaser. Weather permitting, we sit outside. On a hot day in late July, I adjusted the umbrella over our table as a waitress delivered our drinks. When she walked away, John took a sip and asked, "You sure you want to sit out here? Heat index has got to be over a hundred."

I said, "I'm fine. Told you before, I believe that heat index was invented to make us think it's hotter than it really is."

John wiped his forehead with a napkin. "That's what the heat index is for. Lets us know when it's hotter than it really is."

"Do you know how stupid that sounds?" Checking the weather app on my phone, I said, "It's ninety degrees. Don't be such a wuss. I thought they brought you people over here because you could withstand the heat?"

John squinted, "Don't go there, bro."

"I'm just saying you wouldn't last a day on a farm. Look around. See all these people out here enjoying themselves. What good's a cold beer without a hot day?"

John leaned back and said, "Sounds like a beer commercial." While holding up his mug, he added, "But I still say no one should be working in a field when it's a hundred degrees."

I popped my mug on the mesh metal table, spilling a small amount, and said, "There you go again, talking that one hundred degree stuff. I looked it up already. When do you think it last reached a hundred in Louisville?"

"Probably last week."

"No."

"Last year?"

I shook my head and said, "It hasn't been a hundred degrees in Louisville since 2012."

John picked up his phone. "Don't believe that for a second."

While John searched I noticed a man who seemed to be watching. That would be strange considering he wore dark glasses and had with him what appeared to be a service dog. I'd seen him there at another table the week before. Both times, he sat by himself, positioned to face our way. This time, his Cincinnati Reds baseball cap had been replaced by a light colored fedora. He was white, had dark hair that hung past his broad shoulders, and a full beard like an Amish man. Occasionally, he appeared to be talking to himself. I figured he had Bluetooth earbuds. Then something odd happened. Two attractive ladies walking down the sidewalk seemed to draw his attention. His head turned slowly as if following them, yet the dog, sitting on its haunches, never looked that way. *This guy's a fake.*

John laid his phone down without speaking, which meant he'd found out that I was right about the temperature. Instead of boasting, I brought his attention to the man who still appeared to be checking us out. My friend laughed. "Elijah, I saw the guy walk up a while ago. That's a guide dog he has with him. He can't see, dumbass."

"Or he wants us to think he can't see." As John rolled his eyes, I asked, "Do you know who Sherman is, the blind guy that works with us in the call center?"

"I've seen him."

"His hair's always a mess. Now look at this guy. Beard's all scraggly, yet his hair looks more like a woman's. Layered and neat. I'm thinking it's a wig."

"Damn Eli. You sound infatuated."

"Bet he's a cop."

John leaned back, checking out the man and said, "You think I'm paranoid about the weather. Now look at you, all worried that some blind guy is spying on us."

A few days after that, on one of Jane's rare days off, we went to the park for a walk. After a mile or so, Jane wanted a break. We stopped and sat on a bench. Jane lit a cigarette. As she paid attention to her phone, I noticed a man and a dark, long legged woman standing a short distance away in the direction we'd just come from. They were dressed to run. The woman stood with her back to us. I began to focus on the man, his dark sunglasses, broad shoulders and his Cincinnati Reds baseball cap. *No visible hair. No beard, But* "Damn," I mumbled.

"What?" Jane asked.

"That guy standing down there. He looks familiar."

Jane looked up from her phone to check them out. "Yeah, right. I see what you're looking at."

"No. I've never seen her before. But that guy. He reminds me of someone I've been seeing at Del Junco's. It's almost like I know him, and it feels like he's stalking me." As I spoke, the couple began jogging away.

Jane put out her cigarette and said, "Guess they're through watching. Let's go."

As we continued our walk, I said, "That couple didn't run by where we were sitting. They had to come from the same direction we did."

"You think they were following us?"

"Not sure, but it didn't make sense that they jogged off in the direction they came from." In my mind, I kept thinking, *I know that guy.*

On the first Wednesday of August, after eight hours on the phone with snarling, whining, bitching, unsatisfied customers, I met John for our usual stop. A storm system had left behind a few scattered clouds and an unseasonably cool breeze. I said, "Wonder what the heat index is today?"

John picked up his mug. "Hot one day, cool the next. All part of the climate change." When I shook my head, he grinned and said, "I'd gladly pay the carbon tax if every day could be like this."

I sipped my shot and chased it with beer. "So tell me John, how's the carbon tax gonna make it cool in the summer?"

"It's a lot about pollution. Theory is, if we quit pumping greenhouse gasses into the atmosphere, average daily temperatures will drop, sea level will no longer be rising, and..."

As John spoke, I noticed a young woman taking a seat, alone at the furthest table from us. She put her purse on the table and then held her phone up while sipping from a cup with a straw. I couldn't tell if she might be reading from the phone or using it to video us. Her long dark legs were crossed under a short, khaki skirt. She wore black heels. *Hmmmm. That's not a Del Junco's cup.*

John pulled up a graph on his phone that supported his concerns for increasing greenhouse gases in the atmosphere. "Look here, Elijah. CO_2 levels are way higher today than they've been in the last 450 thousand years."

"How can you say that? Wasn't anybody checking CO_2 levels back then."

John shook his head. "Don't they make you hayseeds take science in high school? We have ways of identifying levels of many different compounds throughout history."

I downed my shot and asked, "Are you calling me stupid?"

"No, I'm not. I'm calling you uneducated."

I sat glaring back through my mirrored sunglasses. John turned away as he always does when anyone looks at his face for more than a few seconds. Figured it has something to do with that scar across his left cheek. Not bad, but noticeable. He had never offered an explanation, so I never asked. Rising from his chair, he adjusted his belt and said, "Be right back."

As John headed inside to use the restroom, my phone dinged. A text from Jane read: **Must be a full moon. ER is swamped.**

I replied: **Got it. See you tonight**, and then added a red heart emoji. Before I could lay the phone down, it began to quack. The caller ID displayed my own name and number. *What the hell?* I answered the call. After a moment of silence, I hung up. "Stupid calls."

As I sipped beer, my attention went back to the woman across the way. Her hair reminded me of the lady I'd seen in the park. I didn't get a good look at her face that day, but....

John returned, plopped down and motioned toward the building. "Believe I saw your blind spy guy inside."

Glancing that way, I said, "Show me where he's at. I wanna go introduce myself."

"Too late. He left out the back door."

"Did he have the dog with him?"

"Yes."

At six feet one inch and strong as an ox, John is an extreme techie whose size made him a natural for football. Not long after Jane introduced us, she told me how his all-state senior year as a running back had fallen short when he got diagnosed with a pre-existing heart condition. Regardless, he never lost his love for the sport. That day at Del Junco's, while I nursed my beer and monitored the woman, John switched from spies and weather to his fantasy football picks for the upcoming NFL season. Occasionally I'd say, "Yes or no, or okay." When the waitress came to ask if we wanted another round, I didn't even notice.

"Wake up!" John complained. "You want another beer or not?"

"Oh ... a...." Picking up my half full mug, I said, "No thanks, I'm good."

When the waitress walked off, John asked, "What the hell's wrong with you?"

"I'm fine. Why?"

"Never seen a beer last you that long."

Raising my mug to John, I said, "Reckon I'm thinkin' more than I'm drinkin'."

"Jane up your ass?"

"Not really. She can't give me a hard time when she's not around. Woman spends way too much time at that hospital."

"Yeah, and you knew that would happen when you married her."

"Yes I did, but it's a lot more than I expected. Hell John, I'm thirty. What's wrong with wantin' a kid, maybe two, and a place of our own with a yard and a garage?"

"So buy a house. You guys make enough."

"Not right now we don't. Jane's a resident, and she's got way over two hundred grand in college debt!"

"Ouch. I thought she got free college."

"Hell no," I replied. "Her bachelors got paid for by the government, but not her masters and not med school."

"But Elijah, in two or three years your girl's gonna be making bank."

"She's already thirty-four. By then she'll say she's too old to have a baby."

"Didn't I warn you about that? Don't believe Jane's interested in kids."

"And that pisses me off. What woman doesn't wanna have a baby?"

John's face distorted. "The one you're married to, country boy. I love you man, but if you keep talking down on my girl, I might have to come around this table and whoop up on your lily-white ass."

"Your girl?"

"You know what I mean."

"Lily-white ass? Sure you wanna go there?"

John winked and offered me a fist bump. If only all people could get along like we do. We appreciate the honesty, respect our differences, and enjoy being friends. "Just give Jane a break, Elijah. She's come a long way. Most people who go through what she has wind up on drugs or homeless or both. You're Jane's rock, and I love you for that."

I sat mulling on John's remark, my eyes still watching the woman.

John asked, "You know her?"

"Who?"

"You know who. You think because you're wearing those glasses I can't see you checking out the sista."

"She's black?"

John studied a few seconds. "Mixed, I'd say."

"She keeps staring at me."

"How you know she's not looking at me?"

"Last week, Jane and I were walking. I saw a man who reminded me of the blind guy. He was with a woman. They appeared to be following us. Can't be certain, but I'm thinking that's the same lady."

"Did the guy have his dog?"

"No."

"Was he holding on to her?"

"No, he wasn't, and guess what? No beard. And if he had any hair at all, it was under his cap. I told you it was a wig."

John laughed. "You see a guy with no hair and no beard and somehow associate him with a blind guy who has long hair and a beard? You are one paranoid mo-fo."

Taking my sunglasses off, I looked toward the woman who then lowered her phone and stared back. "You can call me paranoid all you want, but there's something going on. Man keeps showing up. Watching. Now he leaves and she's here?"

John took a longer look and said, "Elijah, we come here every week. Other people have the same right. Why in the hell would they be spying on you?"

"Okay then, let's say you're right, and I'm not being stalked. In that case, she's still staring ... and she's hot."

"And you're married, boy! That's another thing I warned you about. Ain't no man supposed to be with the same person forever. But you just had to go and get married. Now she's at work most the time and you're all lonely, feeling sorry for yourself and about to mess around, again."

"Bull. I'm not gonna mess around."

"Then what are you doing?"

"Come on, man. You know what I'm doing. Just because I'm on a diet, doesn't mean I can't look at the menu."

"Bro, that line's older than me."

My eyes were glued to the woman. Hers were on me. Something floated between us. I said, "It's ... like a car. You love your old one. No intentions of getting rid of it. But then you see a new one, and you start thinking about how it would be to, maybe, you know, sit behind the wheel."

"Not sure which is bigger," John said while rising from his chair, "your libido or your imagination."

"You leaving?"

"If you ain't drinking, I got other things to do." He put three ones under his mug for a tip and stood there looking towards Miss Suspicious. "You know, just because you can't take a ride, that doesn't mean I can't."

Damn. "Well, good luck big boy." As John took his first step, I said, "While you're over there, ask her what her problem is."

He looked back. "Tell Jane I said hi and that her husband needs to get laid."

I sat there, jealous and contemplating what John might be saying. Miss Suspicious glanced my way several times as they talked. After three or four minutes, John looked at me, shook his head and then walked off. The lady watched until he was out of site. Just as I picked up my phone to call John, she stood and began walking in my direction. She had the small purse hanging on her shoulder and carried the drink. Her short black hair and delicate features reminded me of actress Halle Berry. By the time she'd reached my table, I could feel a hammer pounding in my chest. Trying not to be obvious, I asked, "Is there something I can do for you?"

She grinned. "I hear you need to get laid."

Damn John. I took off my sunglasses, scanned the lady up and down, and said, "You don't look like a hooker."

"Thank you. I'm not. May I be seated?"

Leaning back in my seat, I said, "Sure, but I ought to warn you that my wife's a closet sociopath."

"Doubt that," she replied while taking a seat and setting her cup on the table.

The waitress walked by glancing my way. I said, "Another shot, please."

"How about you, ma'am?" the waitress asked.

The lady shook her head to say no. As the waitress walked off, I asked, "You know my wife?"

"Not as well as I know you."

Now she had my attention. "Am I in trouble?"

"No, but I have my own issues that need fixing, and I think you might be the man I'm looking for."

"Really? Why me?"

She stared before speaking. "You've been described as a man who can come across as, shall we say, plain and simple—"

"Lady, where I come from people don't appreciate being called simple."

She ignored my comment and kept talking. "—but I'm also told you might have a mindset similar to the way you describe your wife."

She thinks I'm a psycho? "I'm afraid someone has misled you."

"Comes from a pretty reliable source."

"Really?" I crossed my arms with my elbows on the table. Leaning forward I took in the details of her eyes, her nose, and her thick lips. My stare dropped to her chest.

She said, "Excuse me?" as if offended.

I looked back at her eyes and asked, "What person would tell you such things about me?"

She rocked her head back and forth and said, "One of your high school classmates."

"I'll be damned! David Weeper! Boy he's put on some weight!"

"I wouldn't know."

"He's the one you were with in the park? The one who's been hanging out here every week?"

"We've both been here every week. Apparently you pay more attention to men."

"Fuck you, lady."

She took a sip from her McDonald's cup before speaking. "You have a bad mouth."

"Yeah, well, I didn't invite you over here. What are you, some kind of Jehovah's Witness?"

"My, my. And he's politically incorrect."

"What did you and my friend just talk about?"

"John?"

"Yessss," I replied.

While scanning the area, she said, "I told him I wasn't interested."

"You busted his chops?"

Still looking away, she said, "Then he told me you think I'm stalking you, and that you're married, and that I should leave you alone."

"But you came over here anyway." I stood, looked around for my waitress and said, "The fact that you hang out with David Weeper tells me I don't wanna know you."

"He told me what you whispered into his ear. Could you really do that? Could you butcher a man alive?"

"You think you know me lady, but you don't."

"If I tell you something that only you and I know, will you give me a few more minutes?"

"Ain't got time for you lady."

"I know your mother was dead before the plane crashed."

Whoa! My heart raced. It felt like someone had struck me. No one had ever said that to me. No one other than my grandfather even knew of the possibility. I lowered back into my chair. "Why would you say that?"

"I read the NTSB report. You and your grandfather both told them that you saw your mother in the cockpit with your father."

"And?"

"And when I talked to the old Sheriff, he said you thought your father was alone. That tells me she wasn't sitting in the cockpit."

"You talked to Sheriff Johnson?"

"Yes, I did. Mr. Haycraft, your father knew that plane had a gravity fed fuel system. You and I both know he tried to make it look like an accident."

"So I *am* in trouble."

"No. That's not what I'm here for."

There I sat, with a stranger who had her hands around my balls. My instincts said, *leave*, but I wanted to know what she was up to. Why she and a man who hates me had been spying on me. It couldn't be good. I asked, "What exactly do you want from me?"

Instead of answering, she stood, leaned over the table and slapped me across the face. *What the?* Muscles in my groin tightened as I contemplated screaming the F-word, tipping the table, stepping around and beating the heck out of her. Instead, I remained frozen the way I often did as a child when my father struck me for no apparent reason. Always in the end, he had a reason. *This woman has a reason.* Moving my eyes only, I observed people gawking. Two tables away, my waitress stood frozen, holding a dripping mug of beer in each hand. My attacker stared, waiting. I rubbed my face and said, "I'll ask again. What do you want from me?"

She glanced around as if to tell people to mind their own business, and then turned back to me. "I'd like to know if you found that to be a painful experience or an interesting sensation."

Weeper told her that. "Your issues, lady, do they have to do with pain?"

She took a seat. Chatter began again at other tables. The waitress moved on. "Weeper believes you're the kind of guy who can take it or inflict it, and not fall apart afterwards."

"No comment."

Relaxing back in her chair, she steepled her fingers and asked, "Do you like taking chances?"

I looked around to see if anyone might still be paying attention before replying, "Do you?"

"Yes, I like taking chances, and I do quite often. How about you? When was the last time Elijah Haycraft took a chance?"

"About five minutes ago."

"When you let me join you?"

"Exactly."

As I spoke, the waitress came back with my shot. She seemed nervous as she set it down and asked, "You ... need another beer?"

"No thanks," I replied. "Believe we're about done here." Picking up John's tip, I added a ten and said, "Keep the change." She thanked me, gave the lady a look and then stepped away.

While I slipped my wallet back into my pocket, Miss Suspicious said, "I need someone I can trust. Someone who can trust me."

I downed the shot, let out a deep breath and said, "Only woman I trust is the one I sleep with."

She raised an eyebrow and then asked, "Is Elijah interested in a bit of excitement? A little danger maybe?"

I stood, put my sunglasses on and said, "I really do have to go."

"You seem like a smart guy, yet you have no college degree."

"Not sure how you know that, but it's my business. Not yours."

"You need a house. You want a baby."

"I'm gonna kick John's ass. He had no right to—"

"Your friend didn't tell me that."

"Then how the fu— did you know?"

As I spoke, the phone in her purse alerted a text. She pulled it out, glanced at it and then back at me. "The same way I knew you need to get laid."

"John didn't tell you that?"

She finished a quick reply to the text and then slipped the phone back into her purse. While picking up her cup, she said, "You and your buddy sit down out here every week. First thing you do is lay your phone on the table."

Each table on the deck had one or more phones visible, either flat on the table or in the hands of its owner. *Damn.* "So you've been listening through my phone?"

She stood, stepped closer and asked, "When can you have a free day?"

"Lady, I don't do free days."

Quietly, she said, "I'll give you a thousand dollars in cash for the first day, regardless. If you like my proposal, you'll be extremely well compensated. Maybe enough to pay off your wife's student loans or to buy that house you want."

I looked away, thinking, *This feels like a trap.* Turning back, I said, "Tell me something. This proposal you have. If I should happen to be interested, would I have to worry about going to jail?"

"Let's just say, if this were a movie you'd be one of the good guys."

"Really? So, if this were a movie, would David Weeper be a good guy?"

"Yes," she replied.

Leaning forward and to the right, I took in the curvature of her butt. She said, "Is it your nature to gawk?"

"A few minutes ago, you smacked my face. How about I smack your sweet ass and see if you consider it an interesting sensation?"

"Sweet ass? You meet a professional woman and that's your first impression?"

"Professional women don't start a conversation with, 'I hear you need to get laid.' Besides, I drew my first impression when I saw you in the park."

"You were with your wife and you stared at me?"

"Dark blue running shorts. Yellow hems on the legs."

"Nice recall. Can you describe my running shoes?"

"I wasn't looking at your shoes."

"Oh, I see." She made an ugly sound by sucking the straw in her empty cup, sat the cup down on the table and said, "For the record, only three people have smacked my ass. My mother is still alive."

Maybe I do like this chick.

You need to get away from her.

"Shut up," I accidentally spoke.

"Excuse me?"

"Sorry, I was talking to myself." The sun popped out, and she removed sunglasses from her purse. I said, "You know my name, but I don't know yours."

"Sarah. Sarah Smith."

"Sounds fake."

She slipped on her glasses and tilted her head. "Does it matter?"

"Sarah Smith, I'm not sure I wanna spend a day with you."

"Liar. I believe you do." Leaning close, she said, "Elijah Haycraft, if you'll give me one day and promise not to discuss it with anyone else, I'll let you sit behind the wheel."

Chapter 2

Meeting Sarah Smith lit a fire in my mind. For the rest of that day, I worried over what I might be getting into. As the sun went down, I sat alone as usual at the condo on the balcony with a four dollar cigar and a bottle of bourbon. The more I drank the more promiscuous my thoughts became. Grandpa Haycraft had once told me, "A man doesn't become wise until his dick quits gettin' hard." Guess I've got a ways to go.

While Sarah Smith's beauty took my breath, her mind gave me chills. She seemed really smart, like Jane. I've always been impressed by brilliant women, and especially those who aren't afraid to speak their mind. What worried me the most about this particular smart lady would be her association with David Weeper. I couldn't imagine him doing me any favors. The fact that he described me as some kind of a psycho pissed me off. I should have kicked his ass years ago.

Jane got home late after working in the emergency room. When she came to bed, I held her tight while thinking of the other woman. *Either she's a liar and a bad person, or she's a cop.* Neither option seemed trustworthy. With my eyes closed, I recalled Sarah Smith's face, her hair, her small breasts, long legs, and the way she walked to my table.

Jane startled me, rolling over and asking, "Honey, are you okay?"

"Yes. Why?"

"Your heart's beating fast. I can feel it."

"Guess I was having a bad dream."

"You weren't asleep, were you?"

I turned my back to her and said, "Go to sleep."

Jane snuggled against me, kissed my shoulder and wrapped her arm over me with her hand against my chest.

The next day, Thursday, I didn't see John until right before the end of lunch. In passing, he asked, "How long did you stay at Del Junco's?"

"Long enough to see you get shot down."

"What do you mean, man? Me and her's gonna hook up."

I grinned and said, "Not what she told me."

"Oh, so she did come over there. I told her you were married and she'd best leave you alone." Before I could say anything else, John's boss called him into his office.

That night, my conscience—yes I have one—would not allow me to totally lie to Jane. It was late and she had already fluffed her pillow and positioned herself in the bed to watch cable news. I sat on the side pulling off my socks. "I won't be going in to work tomorrow," got her attention.

"And why not?" she asked.

"Something weird goin' on. I've been approached with an offer."

She hit the mute button on the TV remote. "A job offer?"

"I'd say."

"Good for you. You need a better job."

I shook my head and said, "Thanks for the ego boost."

Turning the sound back on, she said, "Eli, we've already agreed that you won't spend the rest of your life answering phones."

Lying down, I said, "Sounds like it's temporary."

"Most jobs start out that way these days. What kind of work is it?"

"Some kind of project. Supposed to be exciting."

"Exciting?" This time Jane turned the TV off and asked, "Details please?"

"That's just it, I don't have any, but it sounds like there might be a lot of money involved."

"Really. Then I guess you need to check it out. How were you picked for this job?"

Sometimes I feel Jane should have been an attorney. Her ability to cross examine comes naturally. I have to pick my words carefully. "Remember when we were at the park? The man I thought might be stalking me?"

"Yes, dear. He was with a woman."

He's the one who recommended me. His name is David Weeper. We went to school together."

"So you'll be spending the day with this Weeper person?"

"Well, not exactly."

Jane sat up in bed. "You're sounding vague, Eli. What is it you're not telling me?"

"It was the woman who approached me."

"The woman? The one he was with?"

Leaning on my elbow, I said, "Look, I'm trying to be honest. This lady has some sort of an offer that apparently takes more than a few minutes at Del Junco's to explain. She says if I like the offer, I'll be extremely well compensated. Enough to pay off your student loans or buy the house we want."

"That much money?"

"That's what she said."

"How does she know about my student loans or that we want a house?"

"Apparently she overheard John and me talking." Jane tilted her head forward with her hand over her eyes, as if she had a headache. After several seconds, I asked, "You okay?"

She looked up. "Come on, Eli? You said these people have been stalking you. She's eavesdropping on your conversations. Don't you find it at all suspicious?"

"Well, hell yes I do. Honey, I'm not stupid."

My dear sweet wife took a deep breath, squinted and said, "So then, Mr. Haycraft, what do *you* think she wants you to do for all that money?"

"I've got no idea."

"Bet it's illegal."

"Hope not." While reaching over to turn off the light, I said, "She says if it were a movie, I'd be one of the good guys."

"Do what?" Jane replied in the dark as she crawled across me to turn the light back on. "Eli, that means she's some kind of a cop?"

"Yes dear. That was my first thought. But why me?"

"The guy you went to school with, Weeper. He's told her something."

Pulling the sheet up, I said, "You know, you could have broken my rib just now with your knee."

"But I didn't, and don't try to change the subject."

She's not going to let this go. "I told the lady that if David Weeper had referred me, I probably wouldn't be interested. He and I were not exactly friends."

Jane glared, jerked the sheet back off and said, "But you're going with her tomorrow anyway?"

Walked into that. "Yes. I'm interested in the money."

"Eli, I'm a doctor. I've busted my butt to get where I am. We make enough money for now. Soon it'll be a lot more."

At that point, I just wanted to go to sleep. "Honey, you know living in this condo is killing me. I need space. And I wanna do my part. You just said I need a better job. Doesn't that mean I need to make more money?"

"No dear. It means I want you to feel good about what you do. I want you to have a job that challenges you."

"Oh, really? How do you know that this job, whatever it is, isn't gonna satisfy all that?" Jane growled a couple seconds, and then sat shaking her head. "Dammit, Jane. Do you know how bored I am sitting around here at night while you're at work? You come home with all these exciting stories of how you helped save someone's life. I sit here night after night doing nothing. So dammit, I need a little excitement in my life." My dear wife stared at me, stumped with no logical comeback. I said, "I know you, Jane. If you were me, you would at least be curious? You'd wanna check it out? See what's required. How long it'll take?"

I could see Jane's eyes moving behind closed eyelids as she made her creepy, barely audible purring sound. Sort of like a cat. She tilted her head back, opened her eyes and said, "How old is this woman? What does she look like?"

"You saw her."

"I saw her ass. I didn't see her face. I want to know how old she is."

"Are you kidding me? I didn't ask her how old she is. My age, I guess. Maybe younger."

Jane growled again, louder and asked, "Is she pretty?" When I tilted my head and shrugged my shoulders, she knew. "Hell no! So, you're telling me that while I'm here washing your clothes and getting ready for work, you'll be spending the day with some young, beautiful woman who offers you excitement? What the—"

"Jane—"

"Don't Jane me, boy! How can I trust you after what happened before?"

"I'm interested in the money, not the woman. It's about a job and that's it."

Jane's eyes squinted. "When did you meet her at Del Junco's?"

"Yesterday."

"Is that what you were thinking about last night?"

"What's that supposed to mean?"

"Relaxed, in bed, your pulse was eighty-five."

Rising up, I said, "Are you kidding me? You counted my pulse?"

She reached over and started twisting my right nipple. "Asshole. You were excited just thinking about her!"

I took a deep breath and let it out slowly. Leaning forward, I stared down at my chest. "Now, you know you have to do the other one."

She did with vengeance. So hard I nearly pissed myself. When she finally let go, I fell back onto the bed. Jane glared and said, "Bet your pulse is over eighty-five right now!"

I said, "You did the second one harder. Can you give the first one just a little more?"

"No," she snarled, but then did it anyway.

In my head, fireworks exploded. "Thank you," I whispered, relaxing into my pillow.

Jane glared and said, "If you want more, I need more ... information."

"I already told you, the woman didn't go into details. Considering the amount of money, I can only assume it involves a certain amount of danger."

"Well, duh." Jane leaned back against the headboard of the bed, rubbing her spread fingers up and down over her nightshirt. "See what you've done to me with all this talk about danger and excitement." One thing for sure, she wasn't lying. Her fingers were sliding over the hard proof. "Where exactly are you going with this woman tomorrow?"

"She didn't say."

"Then I think you should take me with you. Can we be back before my shift?"

"Honey, this ain't about you, and I have no idea what time we'll be back." Jane's lips puckered out. I said, "It's just one day. You know I'm not afraid of a little danger. It can't hurt to check it out."

"Damn you, Eli. I don't trust you."

"I'm not gonna sleep with the woman. Why would I? I've got you."

"Didn't stop you before," she replied while pulling off her night-shirt. "Guess I'll just have to wear your sorry ass out tonight."

Chapter 3

First week of August, 2018

On Friday morning I pulled into the Starbucks parking lot around 6:25, five minutes early for my rendezvous with Sarah Smith. The sun rose above steamy, still wet buildings across the street. I lowered the visor while trying to recall details of the woman's appearance. I had no idea what she would be driving. After staring toward the front entrance for a moment, I turned back and there she stood at my door. "Damn," I mumbled. When I lowered the window, her familiar clean scent drifted in.

"Good morning." Reaching in, she dropped an envelope into my lap. "That's half your money for today. You'll get the rest later."

Leaning to the window, I checked out her sexy black blouse. It had buttons all the way down, short sleeves and hung loosely over her broad shoulders. The V-neck revealed enough to suggest she wore no bra. After giving me a behave-yourself look, she said, "Stay here. I'm going in to get us both a double shot of espresso."

"Do I look that tired?"

"No, but you're gonna need lots of energy where we're going."

"And where exactly are we…?" She didn't answer. As she walked away, I stared while ripping open the envelope. Her skirt and heels had been replaced with jeans and hiking boots. My mind flashed back to Del Junco's when she had called me a liar. She was right. Despite all the uncertainties, I did want to spend the day with this lady who calls herself Sarah Smith.

I stuffed five well-used one hundred dollar bills into my wallet. Not knowing how long we would be driving, I decided to go in and use the restroom. Inside Starbucks, Ms. Smith waited near the counter. Ahead of her, one of Jane's college friends, Lisa, and another lady that I did not recognize, waited for their order. Avoiding Lisa, I went straight into the restroom. On my way back out, she and her friend were seating themselves at the far end of the room, both staring my way. Sarah Smith stood at the counter as if waiting on me. When she turned with my small to-go cup of espresso, I accepted it, waved a lazy salute to Lisa and started toward the exit. Sarah caught up as I held the door. In passing, she said, "I gather you know those ladies."

A few steps into the parking lot, I asked, "Are you driving?"

"Yes." Sarah used a remote to unlock the doors of a solid black Camry SE. It had a Kentucky license plate that read 100-ASS.

"Nice ass you got there."

"Excuse me?"

"Your plates," I said with a grin.

"Just get in," she said, motioning toward the passenger side.

"Hold on. I need to grab my stuff."

Lisa and her friend stared out the Starbucks window as I transferred my backpack from the pickup to the floorboard behind the passenger seat of Sarah's car. When I slid down into the front seat, trying not to spill my drink, Sarah had the engine running and sat sipping her espresso. "What's in the backpack?" she asked as I closed the door.

"Survival stuff. Knife, rope, boots. First aid kit. Change of clothes. You did offer excitement."

"No guns?"

"No guns. Would that have been a problem?" I didn't see the need to tell her about the small .380 auto in a leather pouch resembling a wallet in my right front pocket.

She hesitated and said, "Probably not. You won't need one where we're going."

I took a sip of my drink and thought out loud. "Dark windows, black paint, and a black interior. Is this a government car, or is it just a black thing?"

"Look asshole, I'm half black. Is this a conversation we need to have?"

"Not really. I mean, I didn't even pay attention to you being mixed until John pointed it out."

"Mixed! My, my. You're just full of micro aggressions. Hope you're not a racist?"

"Whoa! Hell no, lady. We need to get something straight right now. If you're gonna expect me to be all politically correct, I might as well get out and go home. What if I call you black, or woman, or lady, or pretty?"

She tilted her head and said, "I like pretty."

Instead of replying, I just stared thinking, *This ain't gonna work.*

"Elijah, you can call me anything you want, but if you really do offend me, you'll know it when I knock you out."

Whoa! My girl is a badass. Relaxing back into the seat, I winked and said, "I'll keep that in mind."

She held up her espresso like a toast and said, "You're a real cowboy, aren't you?"

I touched her paper cup with mine and said, "Giddy up."

She finished her espresso, put the car in gear, and said, "Buckle up baby, I drive fast."

I downed my first ever cup of espresso as though it were a double shot of bourbon. It didn't seem as strong as I expected. Fastening my seat belt, I settled in for the ride. Leaning forward, Sarah glanced past me and asked, "Did you tell your wife about me?"

"Why would you ask?"

"One of those ladies in Starbucks is on her phone. Does she know your wife?"

Glancing over, I could see it was Lisa. "Yes, but what makes you think she's talking to my wife?"

"Call it a woman's intuition. Would you like to listen in to see?"

"You can do that?"

When she nodded, I said, "No thanks. I don't spy on my wife."

On our way out of the parking lot, I could see Lisa through the Starbucks window, phone still against her ear. Seconds later we were accelerating up a ramp to the interstate. Sarah drove like a NASCAR driver, using the merging lane to pass a big truck hauling building supplies, and then launching across three lanes of traffic into the fast lane. "You're gonna ... get us ... killed."

*   *   *

"Wake up Eli."

At first I thought it was Jane's fingernails running through my hair. I'd been dreaming something sexual it seemed, and I felt aroused.

"Wake up Eli. We're here."

Her words were fuzzy. Groggy, I opened my eyes but couldn't see. My senses again recognized Sarah's clean fragrance. It covered me. I could taste it. "Where am I?"

"We're at our destination."

"What ... what happened? The espresso? You drugged me?"

"Yes," she replied while continuing with the fingers.

"And you're not afraid I'm gonna go off?"

"I haven't harmed you, and besides, if me knocking you out for a few minutes frightens you, you're probably not the man I need." Then she spoke in a sweet enticing voice. "Please don't hurt me."

I might as soon as I can see. I could hear crows cawing somewhere nearby. "Am I blinded?"

She chuckled. "No, it's just dark."

"Are we alone?"

"Yes."

A horse blew somewhere at a distance. "Was that a—?"

"A horse? Yes."

Reaching, I noticed my zipper was partially down, and my gun was gone.

She asked, "How do you feel?"

"I'm thirsty and a little hungry." *And mad and hard and I wanna hurt someone.*

"We'll eat in a few minutes."

"You drugged my drink. Not sure I trust your food."

"Speaking of trust, give me your right hand."

"Excuse me?"

"Just give me your hand please."

When I reached across, she took my right hand and slid it inside her unbuttoned blouse over one of her bare breasts. It was firm and her skin felt warm and moist as if she had been sweating. Her stiff nipple rested between my first two fingers. When I started to pull back, she held my hand in place. "Eli, do you know what we're doing?"

"Ahhh, no."

"At this moment, you're sitting behind the wheel. You said you only trust the woman you sleep with. I need to earn your trust. If this is what it takes I'll let you take a spin, right here, right now, in the dark. No one has to know, and then we can go about our business as if nothing had ever happened. What do you say?"

Hell yes. The man in me wanted more, but it seemed wrong. In my mind, she had some sort of night-vision camera and was setting me up for blackmail. "No." I pulled my hand out and said, "I'd love to touch you all over, but I'm pretty sure this is not why you brought me here."

"Okay, Eli. But remember this moment. I'm trying to earn your trust."

"Why you calling me Eli? Only Jane calls me that."

"While you were asleep, I listened in on her call."

"That pisses me off."

"Get used to it."

Wonder how long she's been listening in on my calls? I asked, "What were they talking about?"

"Let's just say, I could tell she was talking to her best friend. And it sounds like maybe you and Miss Jane have a little history with trust issues."

"Lady, you ain't ever gonna gain my trust by drugging me and listening in on my wife's phone calls, and stealing my gun." Reaching for my back pocket, I said, "And where's my phone?"

"Sorry, but you lied about the gun, so I searched you and your backpack."

"Why's my zipper open?"

She chuckled again. "I do a thorough search. Looked through your wallet, but I didn't keep it. Your phone and your gun and that odd spoon slash knife or yours are in the trunk of my car. Are you in some kind of a cult?"

"No. It's an heirloom. I carry it for luck."

"Or to cut a man's throat," she mumbled. "Your bag's in the back seat. By the way, why do you have cigarettes? We've never seen you smoke."

We? "The cigarettes are my wife's. Brought 'em along in case I want one. Why do you care?"

"Your wife is a doctor and she smokes? That makes no sense."

"My wife's an adult. She can smoke if she wants. It's none of your business." I could feel anger building. "I want my stuff back, now."

"I'll give your phone back for emergency use only, but you have to keep it turned off while we're together. The gun and knife stay in the trunk. Agreed?"

As soon as I can see, I'm gonna kick your ass.

Don't underestimate her.

"Agreed?" she asked again.

"For now."

"Be careful getting out. Don't bang my door."

She opened her door and got out. The light still didn't come on.

Why am I going along with this?

Because you can't see, dumbass.

I reached for my backpack and unzipped it. As Sarah stood behind the car opening the trunk, I found the glove box and opened it, hoping for light. Inside, a small bulb shined on a set of handcuffs. *Nice.* After a quick visual of my backpack, I slid the handcuffs inside, under my extra clothes.

As Sarah closed the trunk, I closed the glove box and climbed out of the car. She turned on overhead lighting and it about blinded me. We were inside a wood framed garage. An older model Chevy pickup sat next to the Camry. Looking around, I saw nothing special—work bench with a vise, rows of hand tools hanging on the wall, an air compressor, and an old fridge in the corner. *This is a man's garage.* As I had suspected, the windows were covered with plywood. Sarah stood by the side entry door with a small backpack on her shoulder. She held out my phone and said, "Come on, Cowboy. Let's go." Her blouse had been re-buttoned. She grinned and said, "You had your chance."

We walked out of the garage and into a rural setting. I used my hand to block the bright sun rising well above the eastern tree line. Remnants of rain dripped from the metal roofing on a white-framed story-and-a-half farmhouse. Two large sugar maples and a barbed wire fence divided the forty yards of grass and weeds separating the house and a small barn. Chickens cackled as they mingled in and out of the barn. Well beyond the old wooden structure, beef cattle grazed on an open pasture.

Motioning around the place, Sarah asked, "What do you think?"

Still scanning the area, I said, "I like it."

"Let's go inside. I'll make sandwiches."

We stepped up onto the porch. While Sarah unlocked the deadbolt, I stared first at her butt, and then down the lane that disappeared into a thick stand of hardwoods. We were indeed isolated, and yet for some strange reason I felt safe. If the lady wanted to hurt me, she would have already. Even the mystery of not knowing our whereabouts felt exciting. I asked, "We still in Kentucky?"

"Yes," she replied while stepping through the doorway.

Inside, it looked a lot like the old house my grandparents lived in. The air smelled similar to my mother's fragrance. Four feet from the door, carpeted stairs with wooden balusters and a handrail led to the second floor. I stood there for a moment, taking in details. "This your house?"

"No," she replied from the kitchen. "Bologna and cheese okay?"

Joining her, I asked, "You got pickles and mayo?"

"Yes, and how about a slice of home grown tomato?"

"Sure, if you have it."

"For you, sir, we have it all."

We? Watching her work, I decided she must at least live there. Her backpack and keys lay on the table. Windows behind the kitchen sink provided a scenic view of the farm. "So," I asked, "when do we discuss your dilemma?"

"Over lunch."

A slight creak in the ceiling worried me. *Are we alone? Is it just the old house expanding and contracting, or do we have company?* "How long was I out?"

"Longer than I expected. About ninety minutes. It took a while to search you and...."

"And what?"

"Nothing really." She cut our sandwiches in half, added chips to the paper plates and then opened the fridge. "We have sweet tea and water. That's it."

"Tea's fine."

While pouring us each a glass, Sarah said, "Let's eat on the back porch. I'll explain my situation." Sounded like a plan to me. So far it seemed as if we were playing house. Sarah shouldered her backpack before handing me my plate.

On the back porch there were two wood slat rocking chairs facing the barn. Sarah placed her backpack on the floor. I did the same. Then we sat side by side with a small table between us. I switched plates. She grinned and said, "We *are* going to have to fix the trust issue."

After Sarah swallowed part of her sandwich, I picked up mine. Even then, I gave it the smell test. Having swallowed my first bite, I said, "It's good, but I'm not a very patient man."

"Okay, okay, Eli. If you don't mind, I'm going to continue to call you Eli, because I like it better than Elijah." She hesitated as if waiting for my reaction.

Jesus.

"If that's okay?" she added.

"Eli's fine, but if you haven't revealed your purpose by the time I eat this sandwich, I'll be ready to go."

"Very well. I should start by saying that I work for the government."

Figured that. "Am I supposed to believe that the government lets you go around drugging and kidnapping people?"

"For starters, I didn't kidnap you. You voluntarily got into my car. I simply relaxed you for the ride."

"I didn't feel relaxed when I woke up."

"Actually, I didn't trust you, and I didn't want you to know where I was bringing you. As for the government, you need to keep in mind that most of what I'm about to reveal to you is not known to those I work for. I'm recruiting *you* because I want to keep it on the down low."

"Yet, David Weeper knows."

"He does, but only because he's helping me. It's complicated."

"I'd say it is. Sounds like you're trying to involve me in something that you're hiding from the government."

Tilting her head, she said, "Basically."

I took a bite of my sandwich and spoke with a mouthful. "And why the hell would I wanna do that?"

"Money, excitement, and because it's the right thing to do."

"Believe I'll decide that for myself."

She stared at me for a moment as I enjoyed my sandwich and the scenery of the barn and beyond. "Okay," she started, "I already told you I'm half-black. My father's Emirati."

"An Arab?" I asked, turning back to her.

"Yes. He lives and does business in Dubai."

"So he's rich?"

"Very much so. When my mother was in college, she did a semester overseas. A woman approached her with a proposition that involved her receiving a considerable amount of money in return for having a man's baby."

"A surrogate mother."

"You could say that."

"So your mother changed her mind? Didn't wanna let you go?"

"No. It wasn't quite that simple. She was never expected to give me up. Part of the deal was that she should raise me as an American. The man needed his child to be an American citizen."

"Your mother involved herself in some sort of a conspiracy?"

"If it wasn't complicated, we wouldn't be here."

"Is she still alive?"

"Yes."

"Hope to hell this ain't about terrorism. I don't—"

"Please, Eli, hear me out."

"Why? The more I hear, the more I could be accused of being involved."

"But you're already here. Just hear me out."

"Not sure I want to."

"Mister, you asked my daughter to tell you what's going on, but you won't shut up long enough for her to explain."

Sarah and I both rose and turned quickly to the voice. In the doorway between the kitchen and the porch stood an African American woman, dressed in a house robe and wearing a scarf over her head.

Chapter 4

Whether or not Sarah and I were truly alone at the farm was abruptly verified. The woman who crashed our back porch picnic looked old enough to be her mother.

"Momma, I would have called you down when I was ready."

"Well, I'm not gonna stand by and listen to this white man interrupting you like he—"

"Ma'am, I wasn't trying to be disrespectful to your—"

"There you go again! Do not interrupt me or my daughter in my house."

"Momma! I'm interrupting you. You're being careless, and you're about to run him off before we even get started!"

I must be out of my mind.

Sarah focused my way and said, "I did bring you here to meet my mother. My intentions were to fill you in a little beforehand. She hasn't given me that opportunity."

Both women turned to look at me as though it was my turn to speak. "Ah, okay. Let me guess. Your mother's gotten herself into some trouble, and you're trying to clean it up."

The woman stepped down onto the porch and glared at me. "I'm not a bad person."

"Didn't say that, ma'am, but your daughter's going to a lot of trouble to fix something."

"Mister, I'm a proud American and I'm equally proud of my daughter. I might have made a mistake in my youth, but without that mistake this beautiful girl would not exist today."

"Well I'm sorry lady, but your beautiful girl just drugged my ass, stole my gun and my phone, and while I was passed out, she even ... never mind."

Glancing at Sarah, the woman asked, "You did all that?"

Sarah gave her a look.

Backing up a step, I said, "Please, take my seat." When the woman had lowered into my chair, I crossed my arms and said, "Providing I make it through this day, I might try and pretend I never met you people. But since I am already here, how about you explain the mistake you made, best you can, and then I'll decide if your daughter made a mistake bringing me here."

The woman looked up at her daughter. Sarah said. "Go ahead. Tell him what *you* think he needs to know."

The mother stared past me toward the field for a moment and then spoke. "Thirty years ago, nobody even talked about terrorism. When I reached eighteen, my daddy said I wasn't the woman my age would indicate because I didn't have me a child and a first-of-the-month check. He didn't want me to go to college. That drunken-ass son-of-a-bitch wanted me to stay home and have babies so *he* wouldn't have to work. With grants and scholarships, I managed to go to college. When I left those housing projects behind, Papa swore I would never make it in the white man's world. Now, can you understand how it affected me when a woman came to me with an offer that included more money than anyone in my poor-ass family had ever seen?"

As she spoke, I reached down for my sandwich and drink and took a bite.

"Are you paying attention to what I'm saying?" she asked.

"Yes, ma'am," I answered while taking a swallow of tea. "You go right ahead. I'm listening."

"While I was in high school, my oldest sister turned tricks on the streets of Louisville's west end for twenty dollars a pop. My whole goal in education was to make sure I never felt the necessity to do such a thing. When Sarah's father counted me out ten thousand dollars in cash, I felt like the richest person in the world."

Your sister charged twenty dollars a pop. You got ten grand. Not bad.

"And that wasn't all of it," she continued. "He said he would give me an additional five thousand dollars a month in support while I raised our child in America. The man also paid for her education, and he showed her the world."

"Sounds like a pretty good deal to me."

Sarah sat back down. "Momma, please, let me finish this."

Once again, mother and daughter stared at one another. Finally, the elder faced me, offering her hand. After cramming the rest of the sandwich into my mouth, I reached down to shake her hand. She took mine between both of hers and said, "My name is Ella. I'm glad you came. Listen to what we have to say, and if you decide not to help us, please, don't you go spreading our dirty laundry."

When I nodded, she released my hand. Though early in the day, the lady looked exhausted. It reminded me of my Grandma Haycraft in her final days. "Ma'am," I asked, "are you not well?"

"Excuse me?"

"You look like, well, like you might be suffering."

She looked at her daughter. "Did you—"

"No Momma, you know I wouldn't."

Looking back at me, Ella asked, "What exactly do you mean?"

"I'm sensing that you have a sickness. I see it in your eyes."

Ella leaned on the chair's armrest. She reached up and pulled off her scarf. Her head was practically hairless. "Yes, I am a sick woman, on a mission, determined to rid my daughter of a situation that I put her in. My days on this earth are numbered, and that's why I'm begging you to consider helping us."

I backed up against the porch post, turned to Sarah and said, "I'm gonna be honest. All things considered, I'm wishing I hadn't gotten into that car with you. But I'm here, so tell me what you want."

While she removed a folder and an iPad from her backpack, I finished off the rest of my tea. From the folder she offered an 8x10 photo of a man. "This is Amor Saline Al-Riase. He's my father."

The man looked to be about sixty years old, well dressed, and very much Middle Eastern. Sarah opened the iPad and initiated a video. "This," she said, "is from a national newscast."

In the video, three shirtless men knelt, facing away, heads hanging, hands bound behind their backs. The newswoman spoke:

The three men in this video were arrested late last evening in Al-Karaieed, a small isolated district on the southern border of the African nation, Vitora. Their arrest is part of a multi-national effort to apprehend those responsible for a recent series of street bombings throughout the region.

"I seem to recall this like, what, six months ago?"

"Yes," Sarah replied. She paused the video and then zoomed in on the back of one man's head. He had very little hair. "Notice the shape of the mark on his neck."

Just under his hairline, I could see what looked like a small birthmark, maybe one inch wide. "Okay."

She then zoomed out and back in enough to see that the guy next to him also had an identical marking in the same spot on his neck. Had he not been hanging his head, his hair would have covered it. "Are they twins?" I asked.

"Don't think so," she answered while zooming in on the third, a larger man. "Look closely."

Through the man's hair a marking of the same size and similar shape could be seen. "Interesting. And obviously not triplets."

"Exactly," Ella stated.

"Okay. So these terrorists are all carrying the same mark?"

Ella said, "When I saw this on the news, I recognized it." Turning to her daughter, she said, "Show him."

Sarah leaned forward, hanging her head and pulled her hair up. In the pit of her neck, she had the same marking as did the three men in the news clip. "What the hell? You're associated with these men?"

"Not by choice," Sarah replied while straightening up. "Best I can recall, this happened to me when I was maybe seven years old. At the time, I thought they were removing an embedded tick. Mamma told me it left a mark."

"After that," Ella continued, "we never paid any attention to it. But now—"

"But now you're thinking you were somehow marked on purpose? By who? Who did this to you?"

"The old man who lived here had a visitor that day. Mother had gone off to grocery shop. They told me I had a tick, and I believed them."

"So you're saying the man you lived with and his friend, were somehow associated with the men in that news clip?"

"Apparently, yes," Sarah answered.

"A terrorist group?"

"Yes."

I knew this was going to be about terrorism. Jane would say, get the hell out of here. Holding up the photo of Sarah's father, I asked, "So how's this guy involved?"

"It's a long story, but I'll try to make it short. Every year when I was a child, we traveled to the Middle East to be with my father. As I grew older, Momma got sick and stayed here while I went alone. Early on, my father let me know that under no circumstances was I to behave in any way that would be disrespectful to his religion. He would pay for my Catholic education but reassured me that Christianity was not the right way. Before my first grade year, we moved here."

"Mr. Haycraft," Ella interrupted, "I wanted to stay away from the city and all the drugs and shootings that I grew up with. When Amor offered me the opportunity to live here, free, in return for helping to care for the old folks that owned the farm, I saw no reason to turn it down. I no longer had to work nine to five in the city, and since I had studied finance in college, living here free provided an opportunity to invest a large portion of my monthly support from Amor."

Sarah said, "At that time, all I knew was that my mother had gotten pregnant while overseas in college. I knew my father had been sending money, but I had no idea how much. And at least he seemed to care about me. Every year, I got to spend one of my summer months overseas. In the end, I got to attend Dartmouth and Oxford."

"Oxford. Were you like, a Rhodes Scholar?" I asked.

"No, and I only went to Oxford for my Masters. You might say I got in because of my grades and my travels, and my fluent Arabic. It didn't hurt that my father paid the tuition."

I stood there a moment, contemplating. "Your travels?"

"By the time I turned thirteen, I'd already seen much of the world," Sarah replied. "My father had taken me to the Pyramids, the Alps, Iran, North and South Korea—"

"North Korea? Is that legal?"

"Now it's not. It was before last year. Besides, if you're from the Middle East, traveling with your father, no one asks."

"It sounds like a good life to me."

"Exactly," Sarah's mother replied. "So you can see why I went along with those opportunities for my daughter."

Opportunities and money, I thought.

Sarah said, "It was all good, except for one thing. My father continued to insist that I live my life according to his religion."

"He's Muslim, right?" I asked.

"Yes."

"There's lots of American Muslims."

"My father's not an American Muslim. He believes in Sharia law and warned that if I dishonored him, there would be grave consequences."

I began to read something in Sarah's voice. She certainly had bad feelings for the man who had financially supported her and her mother.

"Mr. Haycraft, there came a time when Sarah began to reject her daddy and his religion—to me, not to him. I encouraged her to go along with his ideologies at least until she completed her studies."

"When was that?" I asked.

"I received my Masters two years ago," Sarah replied.

"So what am I missing?"

"My father attended my graduation. Prior to the ceremony, I saw him watching as I spoke with one of my classmates, a guy. Before walking away, my friend gave me a hug and a kiss on my cheek. Right after the ceremony, my father came to me and said that I had dishonored him by my actions and that by tradition I should be punished. As I stood there, analyzing his arrogance, he further informed me that he would be arranging my marriage. He said that he would soon be traveling to America to introduce me to my future husband."

"So he like, betrothed you?"

"No. Betrothal would involve a proposal and acceptance. In this case it's an arranged marriage."

I said, "Damn, that sucks. Has he already picked your husband?"

"Yes. We were introduced about a year ago."

"And that was like six months before your mother saw the video of the terrorists."

"Correct."

Sarah's explanation sounded like a drama on TV. On one hand it all made sense, but on the other it seemed too outrageous to be true. I asked, "The man he picked for you, is he American?"

"Yes," Sarah replied. "His name is James Davis Proctor."

"Proctor? I know that name."

"He lives near Morganville, Kentucky. When I visited his house with my father, that's when I realized he is the son, or I should say, the adopted son of—"

"Kentucky U.S. Senator, George Proctor," I interrupted.

"You know him?" Ella asked.

I stared at the woman. "Lady, something tells me you already know I grew up close to the Proctor Estate."

"No, I didn't know that." She looked across to Sarah. "Did you?"

Sarah nodded and I began to understand why me. Jane had been right when she said David Weeper probably told this woman a few things about my past.

You need to get the hell out of here.

I asked, "Isn't the Senator's son running for office?"

"Yes" Sarah replied. "He's running for a seat on the Kentucky State Senate. Have you ever met James?"

"No. Can't say that I have. But like every other kid in the county, I knew of the Proctors. That's about it." Looking out the window, I asked, "Are we close to the Proctor Estate?"

"No," Sarah answered quickly.

"Would you tell me if we were?"

"No. Not at this point."

Turning back to her I said, "Go ahead. Tell me about James Proctor."

"Well, believe it or not, I found him to be charming. He's handsome and his daddy is rich and powerful."

"So marry the guy and live happily ever after."

"There's more," Ella admitted. "Tell him, Sarah."

"When mamma told me about the marking on my neck being like those on the terrorists, she also told me about her arrangement with my father all those years ago. Along with the initial shock, some things just didn't make sense."

"Yeah, like how a strict Muslim would want you to marry an American?"

"Correct again," Sarah answered. "That alone would dishonor his religion, unless—"

"Unless that American turned out to be a Muslim."

Ella said, "You're a quick study Mr. Haycraft."

66

"Mom asked me to check and see if any of her classmates that were overseas with her might be raising a child of similar circumstances. I found one who had raised a daughter and two who had given up a child for adoption. Both adopted were boys, and each had an adoptive parent with ties to the US Government."

"That's interesting."

Ella said, "The girl she speaks of died two years ago in an attack while vacationing overseas."

Sarah handed me a photo of a woman who looked to be her age, and then said, "I researched statements taken at the time. It's no surprise that the news media never reported on how she had allegedly been executed after being accused of an act of promiscuity."

"Damn," I said. "Guess you best not dishonor your father. What about the other two?"

"They're both still alive. One has been raised as the son of the late Marshal Wellington, US Ambassador to the East African nation of Vitora."

"The same country where they caught those three terrorists?" I asked.

Sarah nodded.

"Ambassador Wellington," I continued, "wasn't he the one that got assassinated?"

"Yes, that's him."

"And isn't his kid running for Congress?"

Ella said, "You certainly stay up on politics."

"My wife watches cable news constantly. She likes to talk about it. So the other adopted guy, let me guess, James Davis Proctor?"

Ella let out a sigh and said, "There you have it."

I studied for a moment and then asked, "What else am I missing? There's got to be more."

Ella began rocking in her chair. "Don't you find it strange that both of these men are running for political office?"

"No stranger than your daughter working for the government. But I am interested. Does the Wellington guy know the Proctor guy?"

Ella stopped rocking and grinned again while nodding her head.

Sarah took a drink of her tea and then rose from her chair. "I first drew the connection while watching news footage of Ambassador Wellington's funeral. It showed James hugging Timothy Wellington's neck. Not a likely act, unless the two were already acquainted. Then further study revealed that they had once worked together."

"Okay," I said, "but when it comes right down to it, there's nothing illegal about them knowing one another. I'm sure political families associate."

"Yes," Ella agreed, "but it concerns me that the Wellington boy never expressed public interest in running for office until after someone killed his father."

"You're not just a little paranoid, are you?"

Ella looked back at Sarah and said, "Show him."

Sarah removed yet another photo from the envelope. "About two months ago, I took this from a distance, a high spot near the Wellington Estate. It's located in the mountains near Covington, Virginia. This is Timothy Wellington."

The picture showed a man standing next to a pool, bent over and drying his hair. "And?" I asked.

Removing another photo, she said, "This is a zoomed version. Look closely."

"So," I mumbled, "he has the same mark on his neck."

"Exactly," replied Ella.

"What about the guy you're supposed to marry?"

"To this point, I've not been able to verify that, but I'd bet money he has one too."

"Jesus. This stuff's crazy. No telling how many times it's happened."

"I've been running checks on the children of members of Congress and as yet have not found another one who matches the MO of these two."

"You mean these two and you."

"Yes, and me."

"Earlier you said you didn't want your superiors to know what you were planning to do. What exactly is your plan?"

Ella said, "I didn't make an arrangement with the father of my child because I had feelings for him. We made a business proposition. He kept his end of the deal as I received monies for all those years. Initially they told me he wanted an American child so that if the world went to hell, he could easily and legally move to America. Now, I think I've learned differently. I believe Amor participates in an effort to infiltrate our government."

I need a drink. I pulled Jane's half full pack of cigarettes from my backpack. "May I?"

Ella nodded her approval and then continued. "I'm sure Amor preferred a boy child. A son that could grow up some day to be in Congress."

"Ma'am, don't we already have Muslim women in congress?"

"This is true," Sarah spoke. "But I doubt my father anticipated that happening twenty-eight years ago. Plus, I'd say he has his eyes on something bigger than Congress."

"The White House," I replied.

"Exactly. He wants Muslim blood in the White House."

I took a draw and turned my head to exhale before speaking. "Some would say that's already happened."

"I hear you," Sarah replied. "I checked Obama's pics to make sure he doesn't have the tattoo. If he is part of a conspiracy, it doesn't appear to be connected to ours."

Would she even tell you?

Maybe not. "So your father's plan is to have you marry someone who came about just like you."

"Seems that way."

"Your babies will have two natural born American parents. No one's even gonna ask questions."

Ella pulled herself up from the chair and said, "I want no part of it, and I certainly don't want my daughter involved."

"From what I'm hearing, she already is. And I still don't know what your plan is or how it includes me."

Sarah said, "It's pretty simple. I have no intentions of marrying James. Who I marry will be my choice."

"But what about your father?"

"He can't make me marry a dead man."

"Oh. So you want to...?"

"Mr. Haycraft, in my mind, Proctor and Wellington are terrorists. They have bad intentions for America and they want to involve my daughter. As such, I want them dead."

"Is that right? And you want me to kill 'em?"

"I want you to help my daughter in any way you can to get this over with. Whatever it takes. Sarah says she needs you to help her get information. I'll pay you to make sure neither of them survives."

"Well, therein lies the excitement. You ladies think I'm some kind of an assassin?"

Sarah stepped close and stuck the point of her index finger into my chest. "Already told you, I heard you described as the type of person I need."

"David Weeper told you that?"

"Yes, he did."

"David Weeper doesn't know me that well. I find it very suspicious that he would refer you to me."

"David works for Homeland Security."

"Really? Is that who you work for?"

Sarah hesitated. "Yes, covertly, and I hope you won't blow my cover."

Might blow your brains out if you're lying to me. "So why doesn't Weeper take care of these guys himself?"

Sarah shook her head. "David's more of a tech guy. I don't think he would have the stomach to, to—"

"To kill a man. He's a pussy. Always was."

"But he's a nice guy, and he is a patriot. What I need from you is way beyond David. I need information. I need to find out who the fathers are of Timothy and James. We need to know how widespread this thing is. I need someone to make them talk. And I need someone who is not going to fall apart afterwards."

"Are you saying you want me to torture someone?"

"Whatever is necessary to get them to talk."

Weeper told her I can do that? "Damn. That's a tall order." I took a hard draw off of my cigarette. "Doesn't sound like a personal vendetta to me. Sounds like something for the CIA. Don't they have people that can take care of this stuff?"

"I can't involve the CIA. They already know who my father is. They follow his financial dealings as they would anyone who has international dealings and investments. They also follow him because he's my father, and I work for the government. I have a Top Secret Clearance. They check out everything."

David Weeper knows what's going on.

She added, "My biggest problem is that I have an ISOPREP on file."

"What the hell is that?"

"It's an Isolated Personnel Report. Basically just a file that an at-risk-operator fills out as a way to be identified either in a rescue situation or in case of death."

"So," I asked, "what's wrong with that?"

"Up until recently, I thought the mark on my neck was unique to me. Therefore, I listed it on my ISOPREP. If my father gets identified as a terrorist and he happens to have one on his neck, I could be in big trouble. Mom saw the marks on those men's necks in a short news clip. Chances are someone in an agency has already made note of it. It might even be something they've known about for some time."

"Update your file," I thought out loud.

"I need to, but if I do it right now, it might set off an alarm, so to speak. One would typically only update right before going out of the country."

Why would a Homeland Security Agent be working out of the country? "Interesting," I mumbled.

Sarah continued, "Can you see now why it's vital that I do not involve the agencies?"

This is about me and my mother and my father who plans to use me in some sort of a terroristic plot. Are you willing to help us or not?"

Why would you want to get involved?

Sounds like David Weeper has already gotten me involved. I need to find out why.

"Can I look at that thing on your neck again?" Sarah leaned over and pulled her hair up. "So it's a tattoo?"

"Yes."

"How come they choose this shape?"

She raised her head and said, "It took me a while to figure it out. It's the shape of the country we spoke of. Vitora, in Africa. My father has business ties there. I suspect he's somehow a part of the terrorist cells operating out of Vitora."

There were too many unanswered questions. I pinched my cigarette out, dropped it on my plate, and said, "Perhaps you should take me home now?"

Ella looked disappointed. "Mr. Haycraft, we have opened up our lives to you. We've revealed information that you could use against us. Are you saying you're not interested?"

"Ma'am, I work in a room with three Islamic women. I'm not afraid of 'em. Actually, I've become quite comfortable being around them. I realize that like every religion, Islam has its share of weirdoes. People like those you describe seem to wanna destroy the country I love. The bad things they do make it hard for Americans to accept the good Muslims who live here now. I'll try to buy that your concerns are for the country, to some extent. And maybe I am interested, for my own reasons. But let's be very clear about one thing. The guy that referred me to your daughter hates me. David Weeper was an ass to me in school and he knows I don't like him. I can't imagine any scenario where he would want to do me a favor. So, I need to think about it. I need to somehow make sense of why I might put myself into such a position."

The woman took a deep breath, exhaled and said, "Are you saying there's a chance you will work with my daughter?"

"I'm interested."

"Good. I'll pray about it, and I hope you will too."

I turned my back to Sarah and her mother and stared out across the view. Everything about the farm, the cattle, the chickens, horses, it all took me back to my youthful days. "It's been a while since I rode a horse."

After a moment of silence, Ella suggested, "Sarah, honey, why don't you saddle up the horses so you two can take a ride before you take him home?"

Chapter 5

Sarah opened the ten-foot wide fence gate that separated her mother's back yard from the slight downhill walk to the barn. She stepped through and waited for me before closing. "You could have left your backpack in the house. Mom wouldn't go through it."

Yeah right. "I'll leave it in the barn."

A warm breeze, the smell of livestock, and the sound of flies, bees, and other bugs buzzing reminded me of how much I missed the country. "Watch your step," Sarah warned while pointing out fresh piles of cow manure. During our walk on a wet but worn grassy path, she asked, "Are you a proficient rider?"

"I'm no expert," I replied while still considering whether she might be carrying a gun. "You?"

"I rode show horses up until college."

"Saddlebred?"

"And standard."

"Do any good?"

"Got a room full of ribbons and plaques."

Watching her walk, I said, "So that's why you carry yourself so well."

"Excuse me?"

"All the ladies I know who ride show horses have really good posture."

As we stepped into the barn she asked, "How many ladies do you know who ride?"

I stopped, glancing back to verify that Ella couldn't see into the barn from the house. "Thought you said you knew me?"

She answered, "Apparently I don't know everything about you."

"I can pretty much guarantee that."

The barn turned out to be much nicer inside than I had expected. Not new, but well kept. The first room on the left had no door. Feed bags were stacked along its walls. A big cat, lying on the highest feed bag, raised its head as we passed by. I assumed the next room to be for tack since it had a steel door with a lock. After that, an open space looked to be for grooming and farrier services. Apparently, the last room on that side was for the chickens. One cackled in. Another cackled out. I said, "I'm surprised you have chickens in a horse barn."

"Those are mom's babies."

On the opposite side of the runway, there were four stalls. Each had a wide window with steel bars, and a sliding, wooden door. A harness, bridle, and lead hung next to each stall door. In the loft area above the stalls, bales of hay were stacked two high. The familiar aromas of aged oak, sawdust, hay, and the distinct sharp smell of horse waste, brought back more memories. I asked, "How many horses do you have?"

"Three. That first stall is Callaway, my show-horse. He's twenty-one. The other two are trail horses. Both are like, fifteen years old."

"They stay in the stalls all day?"

"Mom lets Callaway out some every day. The others get to graze a lot. They're in here now because it stormed last night."

Near the end of the barn, a wheelbarrow and pitchfork reminded me of sweaty middle aged women mucking stalls on hot and humid summer days. The second stall had no horse. When I stepped to the third window the bay inside came close, pushing its nose through the bars. Sarah said, "Best watch that one. We named him Lucifer for a reason."

I blew long and softly into the gelding's nostrils to introduce myself, likewise savoring his hay tainted exhale. When Lucifer's ears rose upright, I felt safe rubbing his head. Sarah said, "You do have a way with horses."

"This guy likes me. Mind if I ride him?"

"Not at all. Mom won't, so I usually do. But I'm okay with riding the mare. If you change your mind, we can switch." She pitched me her keys and said, "Saddles are in the room with the door. Use the shiny key. Both saddles are the same. Grab one while I get Ruth. You can hang your backpack in there."

"Ruth?"

"The mare." As I walked away, she added, "Bring a blanket too!"

Stepping toward the tack room, I verified the handcuffs key on Sarah's key ring. At the door, I glanced back to admire her model like stride. She had changed into riding pants. Though she didn't have her blouse tucked in, it still didn't seem bulky enough to conceal a gun.

While sliding the last stall door open, she threw me a look as if to let me know she knew I was watching.

Inside the tack room, I quickly removed my backpack and pulled out the handcuffs. *She's right handed. I'll want to be on her right side.* Emptiness fluttered in my chest. I stuck the cuffs in my right back pocket and then hung the backpack on a tack hanger.

As Sarah led Ruth out of the stall, I returned with a blanket over my shoulder, carrying one of the heavy western saddles. She took the blanket and laid it over the mare's back. I slung the saddle on. Positioning myself, I waited for the right moment. With my hand already on the cuffs, I said, "You finish this. I'll go get the other one."

"Okay," she replied.

When she bent over to get the cinch, I reached under and popped handcuffs onto her right wrist. Instinctively, she tried to rise and swing. The mare jumped, snorted and stepped several feet away as I nearly jerked Sarah off the ground, snapping the other end of the cuffs onto one of Lucifer's stall window bars. The gelding threw a fit as I rebounded out of Sarah's reach. "What the hell?" she barked while awkwardly cross grabbing for the gun or keys that weren't there.

"Calm down," I said, walking to the mare.

"What are you doing?" she asked as I tied the mare's reins to a metal loop on the wall.

"I'm making sure Ruth doesn't run away."

"No dammit! What are you doing to me?"

"Please, don't ask questions." Stepping back toward Sarah, I removed Lucifer's leather lead from the wall and said, "I need to secure your other hand."

"You're out of your mind!"

"No dear. I'm quite sane." While creating a slipknot loop in the lead, I looked into Sarah's eyes for fear but saw none. I said, "You need to do as I say."

Looking at the cuffs, she asked, "Are those mine?"

"Yes."

"Why? Why are you doing this?"

"I wanna spend some time with you. Call it entertainment. And I want you to be as helpless as I was on our drive this morning."

"I didn't restrain you."

"No. You did worse. You drugged me. Put me at your mercy, and then did who knows what while I slept. Now, it's my turn."

"What if I don't play along?"

For a moment, I stood there contemplating. "You want me to trust you? You want me to put my life on the line to save yours and your mother's asses from whatever? Can't you trust me enough to do this?"

"No. Hell no. What you're asking goes way against protocol."

"Oh really? You think what you're asking me to do doesn't go against my protocol?"

"Just let me go. I'll take you home and we can forget this day ever happened."

"Yeah, right. And you'll keep spying on me and listening to my wife's phone calls, and I'll still have to deal with David Weeper." She stood there, dark eyes dilated. I said, "If you can't do as I say, maybe I'll just have to go back to the house and party with Ella."

"I'll unlock these cuffs, and I'll kill you."

"Don't think so. I've got your keys. For some reason it looks like you trusted me enough to leave your gun behind. You might figure a way to pick the lock on those cuffs, but in the time it takes, Ella and I will be finished."

"Finished what?"

"I don't know? She's already dying a slow death. Cancer, right?"

"Yes."

"She's gonna suffer. Maybe I could do her a favor."

Sarah's nostrils flared. "You're a sick bastard."

"You said you knew everything about me. You said David Weeper told you I'm some kind of a psycho, and yet you act surprised at what I'm doing. You're asking me to torture two men and then kill 'em, and now I'm supposed to flinch when you call me a sick bastard?"

She hesitated. "Surely you wouldn't harm the woman who plans to pay you?"

"What makes you think I'm in this for the money?"

She again stared as if trying to read me. After a silent moment, she said, "I'm not sure you've ever done anything like this."

Hmmm. Now she wants to try and mess with my head. I remained quiet.

"I'm not sure you have what it takes. You're a mommy's boy, aren't you?"

Same thing my father said.

She continued, "I don't think you have the guts to—"

Whop. I struck her across the face. Her head flew sideways against the bar and then recovered without any expression of pain.

"Entertainment?" she asked softly.

Chickens clucked nearby. Cows mooed in the distance. Flies danced about on Sarah's chained arm with no reflex. I admired her coolness. "Look," I said, "if I put this loop on your wrist, as long as you don't struggle, it'll remain loose enough to wiggle out of. If you struggle, it'll tighten and you won't." I removed the handcuffs key from the key ring. "I'll put this in your pocket." Sarah concentrated on the leather loop as if considering. Holding the key up in front of my face, I began inching backwards. "What's it gonna be, you or Ella?"

Sarah said, "I'll call your bluff. Know damn well you want that money. If I play along, you have to promise that no matter what happens here in this barn, you will not harm my mother."

"I don't have to promise anything. No one knows I'm here. I can pretty much do what I want. But if you do as I say, you'll have my word. I will not harm your mother."

With her free hand Sarah rubbed her face, one side and then the other, scratched both ears. "Key please?" she asked.

After I slid the small key into her pants pocket, Sarah held her arm out. I put the leather loop over her hand and tied it off on another bar. She stood with her back to the stall, arms stretched. Checking out my handy work, she asked, "Now what?"

"Do I need to secure your legs? If you kick me, it'll be a mistake."

"What are you going to do to me?"

Without answering, I began slowly sliding my hand around her waist to guarantee she wasn't armed. A delicious heat radiated from her body. My hand moved up to the back of her neck, under her thick, dark hair. Spreading my fingers, I massaged the base of her skull. She squinted and it excited me. "Tell me, how does one learn fluent Arabic while on summer vacation?"

"Interrogation?" she asked. "Is that your game?"

"Call it anything you want. But when I ask questions, you best have answers." Moving my hands to her blouse, I released the top button.

"I didn't learn it overseas. The old man and woman who lived here spoke Arabic. They were of Middle Eastern descent."

Like two large spiders, my fingertips crawled up the sides of her neck. I began lightly reading her face the way a blind man would, taking in every soft detail. "You said you have National Security Clearance?"

"Yes."

I had not been so close to another woman since Margaret, a little over a year after Jane and I got married. Touching Sarah felt like an addiction luring me into relapse.

You promised you would never do this again.

"Shut up," I whispered.

"Who are you talking to?" Sarah asked.

"Not you."

"You have issues."

"I have questions. Earlier, you said *we* need to know how widespread bla, bla, bla. If you're keeping this from your superiors, who is we?"

"It's a figure of speech."

"I don't believe that. David Weeper knows what you're up to or he wouldn't have referred you to me."

"David came to me with suspicions. He said I needed to look into my father's financial dealings to make sure there wasn't anything there that could come back on me. I had already started researching when Mom noticed the markings in the video."

"You already knew your father was a terrorist?"

"No. I hadn't gotten that far. I knew he had dealings in Vitora. After watching the video, things started adding up. I told David that my father's dealings might not be on the up and up, and that I'd like to gather information on my own."

"None of that explains why he referred you to me."

"A week later, David called me. We met. He said I would need to gather as much information as possible. Names, dates, etc., and that I should keep the project from the agency, otherwise my mother and I could be suspects by association. When I said I might need help, he told me about you."

Why? He hates me.

"Doesn't the government know about the support money your mother received?"

"They do."

Her eyes remained on mine as I unbuttoned a second button. "Then why can't you just come clean? Tell them you think your father is involved with terrorism. They'll surely appreciate the heads up."

"Eli," she spoke with shortened breath, "for years, my mother lied to me about her involvement with my father. She told me she had sex with him overseas, at a party. In actuality, she was artificially inseminated."

"Okay, so you're a test tube baby. Is that a big deal?"

"It is, considering she lied under oath to the FBI."

"Perjury?"

"And treason, if you add what my father's involved in."

"Why would they ever doubt what she told them?"

Sarah tilted her head as if carefully deciding what to say. "If we go to the Agency now, they'll question my father. What if he tells them he never had sex with my mother?"

"He can't deny paying support for all those years."

"True, but they would know my mother lied. It would raise suspicions of her involvement, especially when they consider how we lived for free on the farm with my father's Islamic associates."

What she said made sense.

Sarah added, "And what if they do a DNA test? What if by some chance it doesn't match. We'd be cooked. They'll think we're both part of this stupid terrorist group. They'll indict my mother and accuse me of being a double agent."

My left thumb ran smoothly up and down the shallow pit behind Sarah's ear. With no reaction, I began working on the third button.

"I don't get it," she pleaded. "You had a chance to do this in the car."

"In the dark," I replied, continuing with the button. "Does Sarah Smith lie a lot?"

"No. Please, we can talk without all this. I promise I will not lie to you."

That's a lie.

"Why are you doing this to me? Do you have to tie a woman up before you can enjoy her?"

I refused to answer.

"Do you tie Jane up? Or is it the other way around? Does she tie you up?"

"This is not about Jane. This is about you and me." Running my fingers through her hair, I said, "It felt awesome when you did this to me in the car." Her eyes closed. Leaning closer, I inhaled her fragrance. It stimulated me. I lightly nibbled an earlobe. There was a shuddering and Sarah's head tilted backwards. I cupped her right breast.

"Please?" she whispered.

"Please don't? Or please do?"

"Please, don't."

"Earlier, in the garage, you asked me to do this. Now you say no. Do you only get freaky in the dark?"

"I was trying to gain your trust."

"Yes you were. And you were willing to go all the way."

"Not really. I was testing you."

"Testing me? Are you saying you had no intentions of letting me go for a spin? Wasn't that a lie?"

"Not exactly. I was gambling that you wouldn't want to."

"You lied. I wanted to touch you, but I didn't trust you. I wanted to see you. I'd like to see you now."

"You said it wouldn't be right by your wife."

I released the last button. She closed her eyes and took a deep breath. "May I look?" She said nothing as I pulled open the blouse to see what had been on my mind for nearly two hours. They were small. They were beautiful. And they moved up and down with each heavy breath. Wanting her to say something, I asked, "Are you ignoring me?" With no answer, I moved to her side and slid my hand down to her navel, lightly reading its moist perimeter. Her stomach sucked in. "Was I dreaming earlier, or did you get carried away during your thorough search, in the dark, in the car?"

When I slipped three fingers inside the top of her pants, she jerked, her eyes opened wide and she pleaded, "Please, don't. Don't do this. Don't take my clothes off. Hurt me if you wish. Kill me if you must, but my mother doesn't deserve to see me that way."

Thank you, I thought. "Just answer my questions."

She stared and said nothing. Using the back of my fingers, I rubbed across her limp nipples. They began to harden almost immediately. Sarah took a deep breath and her head leaned back. For a moment, I thought she might be enjoying my touch. When I continued, she squirmed and asked, "Is this your idea of torture?"

"It's a start. When you quit ignoring my questions, I'll stop."

"Are you kidding me?"

I stepped back. "You drugged me, and then you abused me in my sleep. You got freaky didn't you? Didn't you?" When she refused to answer right away, I took her beautiful hard teats between my fingers and began squeezing and pulling.

"Stop that! What the hell is your problem?"

"I want you to answer my questions. She began turning her head back and forth slowly and said, "You're a mess, Elijah Haycraft."

"You have no idea."

"What do you want from me?"

"I want the truth. Did you get freaky with me?"

Her eyes became glassy. "Yes, I touched you. Now, are you happy?"

"That's it?"

"I rubbed you through your clothes, and…."

"And what?"

"I kissed you."

"No shit?" I said, releasing my grip. "Why?"

"I don't know why," she mumbled like a kid caught misbehaving. "I just did it."

The horse behind her kicked its stall, yet Sarah did not flinch. "You molested me in my sleep?"

"I did not molest you."

"Then what the hell do you call it?"

"I did you no harm."

"Jesus! You got any more of that drug? Can I put you to sleep and have my way with you as long as I promise not to harm you?" With no reply, I stood staring, running my hand through my hair and thinking.

Sarah said, "If you feel the need to rub me through my clothes the way I did you, I deserve that."

I laughed a little. "Now you want me to rub on you?"

She glanced back and forth at her hands. "I'm sort of tied up here. If that's what you want to do, I don't see where I have much choice. I do still need to earn your trust."

This woman's playing me like a fiddle.

A part of me said, yes. A part of me said, no. Moving closer, I placed my hands on her hips. When she turned her head and leaned back, the horse came close and started lipping her face through the bars. "Get away!" I huffed.

Sarah said, "It's okay. He won't hurt me."

That's weird. When I began moving my hands, she breathed heavily. I felt myself doing the same. "So you trust me to do this, to like, massage you through this awesome feeling material?"

Her weight shifted as she moved one of her feet further away from the other.

You need to stop this.

She closed her eyes again. "Touch me, gently."

Oh, my. She's all in.

Backing off a couple steps I said, "Sarah, open your eyes." When she did, I said, "I think we're done here." She stared past me into the loft, taking deep breaths and slowly exhaling like a runner after a race. It reminded me of a few disappointing moments between Margaret and me. A tear ran down her cheek. I felt guilty and wished I could hold her.

She shook her head and said, "If you're done with your little game, and I'm done getting teased, you need to release me before my mother comes out here."

"Can we still go for a ride?" I asked. She stared. Her eyes reminded me of Jane when she wants to hit me. I stepped to the door to make sure Ella wasn't heading our way. On my way back, I said, "She's not coming."

Sarah looked into my eyes and said, "You are one strange man."

"Thank you," I replied.

"It wasn't a compliment, asshole."

"Oh well. Do you trust me now?"

"I trust you know how to torture a woman."

"Ouch. By the way, you do know I was never gonna hurt your mother."

"Yes, I figured that. I couldn't imagine a guy who hates bullies wanting to abuse an innocent woman."

I stood there thinking how much I was beginning to like Sarah Smith.

"What's wrong?" she asked.

"You know, I did this to clear up a few details, and for you to see what it's like to be abused while powerless. The way you did me in the car."

"All this for that?"

"Call it a dry run. Isn't this what you want me to do to your guys? Restrain them, and then get them to say what you want them to say? I could have gone further, but I didn't have to. I learned what I needed to know."

"You learned what you needed to know?"

"Yes."

"And what exactly did you learn?"

"I learned that you would be willing to suffer, or even to put your life on the line to protect your mother. That means a lot to me."

"So then," she asked, "did I earn your trust?"

"I'd say we should now have a certain amount of mutual trust."

Glancing at one and then the other of her bound wrists, she said, "But I don't feel trusted."

As I moved to untie her wrist, she said, "Wait. Before you do that, could we maybe, seal our mutual trust with a kiss?"

Chapter 6

Sarah had not lied about the horses. Both proved strong and spirited. She seemed to be testing my riding skills as we galloped a path that crossed rolling hills and grassy meadows. Not knowing the terrain, I followed and thus got pounded with fertile wet dirt thrown by the mare's thumping hooves. Nearing woods, we slowed to a canter and then to a trot. While I bounced in the saddle, Sarah smoothly posted—something I'd never learned. It took me back to my youthful days at the horse barn, watching women ride and wondering if their saddle motions stimulated them as much as it did me. Sarah asked her mare to walk, and then stopped near to where the fast moving creek widened into a waterfall over a steep cliff. As I moved up next to her, Lucifer shook his head and blew slobber. It felt heavenly, sitting in the saddle admiring the marshy waterway below and how it dispersed into a beautiful green bottomland dotted with saplings. My gaze moved up to endless skies. Sarah asked, "You okay?"

"Very much so."

"You ride well," she replied while chuckling.

"You too. Are you laughing at me?"

"I'm laughing at all that dirt on you." As I knocked off chunks of moist soil, she asked, "Can we stop a while and talk?"

"Certainly," I replied as she dismounted.

Leaving the horses tied to saplings, we walked to the cliff's edge. Sarah pointed down at a pool which had been formed by the waterfall. "How far down do you think that is?"

Leaning over the edge gave me one of those, way too far down, strange feelings in my groin. "Thirty, maybe forty feet," I guessed.

"Forty-nine to be exact. Can you believe I jumped from here when I was fourteen and three months?"

"You're braver than me. Do you always deal in exact numbers?"

"Mom used to say I'm too much a geek. She fears it will keep her from having grand babies."

"That's bull. Geeks have hormones."

Sarah stared at my comment way too long. It made me uncomfortable, so I changed the subject. "Who owns this farm?"

"My mother."

"How many acres?"

"Two hundred and fifty."

"Exactly?" I joked.

"No. Give or take point three, three, three acres, asshole."

"Thank you. So I'm guessing she bought the farm with all that cash she got for raising you."

"No, she invested a lot of that. The old man left her the farm and a considerable amount of money in his will."

"Wow. Maybe he wasn't such a bad guy after all?"

Sarah's face changed. "Never say that. He was an animal. He left the farm to Mom because she took care of him and they had a, a strange relationship."

"What about his wife?"

"She died three years and two months after we moved here. From then on, Mom and I occupied the upstairs while the old man lived on the first floor."

"You refer to him as the old man?"

Sarah nodded. "His name was Alon. Using his first name denotes respect. I have none for him."

"Did he ever tie you up?"

Without answering, Sarah sat down on a big flat rock and turned her head enough to gaze out over the bottomland. I took a seat next to her and waited for her to look at me. Sad eyes gave it away. I said, "We don't have to talk about it."

"Thank you."

We both sat silent for a moment and it made me uncomfortable. *What next?* I really didn't know what to say. Then she spoke. "Elijah, more than once at Del Junco's, I picked up on you and your friend John talking about climate."

"Can't believe you spied on us."

"Get over it. Your phone knows more about you than your wife does. Has John ever explained Ice Ages to you?"

"Not that I recall. Why?"

"Ice age is a term that describes a period of time when the planet Earth has cooled to the point of having significant ice. Right now we have continental ice sheets and glaciers. Therefore, we are in an ice age."

"Okay, I get that, but why do we call it an ice age?"

"Good question. We call it an ice age because ice sheets and glaciers haven't always been present. We've been in the current ice age for about two and a half million years. Before that, no significant ice. We've had five known ice ages and between each one there were hundreds of millions of years with little or no ice."

"Damn, you just shot the heck out of Preacher Herman's sermon on creation."

"Preacher Herman?" Sarah asked.

"Yeah. I remember telling my mother he was full of it when he said the world got created twelve thousand years ago in about six days."

"Your preacher studied scripture, not science. I studied both. Before you judge him you might consider that the scriptures were magically written in such a way as to allow each reader, then, now and in the future to read them, analyze according to their own level of knowledge and still come up with the same conclusion."

"Which is?" I asked.

Sarah spread her hands like Jesus in paintings I'd seen. "Love, sir. It's all about love."

I sat staring into the distance and trying to analyze the best Bible advice I'd ever heard. It would be worth sharing with Jane.

"Am I losing you?" Sarah asked.

"No. I get what you're saying, but the question is why do we have ice now?"

"This ice age got started after Pangaea. You familiar?"

"We talked about it in high school."

"The land we're sitting on right now was under water before Pangaea, and it was fifteen to twenty degrees below the equator. It's taken about a hundred and seventy-five million years for it to drift north to where we are now, at about the rate that your fingernails grow."

John would love this woman.

Say something smart.

"Bet that changed climate."

"Exactly," Sarah replied. "As the continents began drifting apart, ocean flows and weather patterns changed significantly. Trees began to grow on land masses that were once under water. Trees consume carbon dioxide which affects the greenhouse. All the combined effects slowly began to cool temperatures."

"So when they say lowering greenhouse gases would lower temperatures, are they telling the truth?"

"Yes, that is true, but it's a sensitive situation. Most people don't realize that without a steady supply of greenhouse gases, this planet would be one big ball of ice."

"So greenhouse gas is a good thing?"

"As long as we don't have too much of it."

"Oookay. I see why your mother thinks you're a geek. You're really into this stuff. And why exactly are you telling me all this?"

"It's interesting, don't you think?"

Sounds more than just interesting. "Somewhat."

"Next time you're with John and he brings up climate, tell him that when the dinosaurs were proliferating on Earth, there were no glaciers. That ten thousand foot thick ice sheet that is currently on Antarctica, it wasn't there. The average global temperature was nearly twenty degrees warmer than it is now."

"I'm thinking maybe you shoulda said yes when John hit on you. You two could talk climate change all day long. But since you chose me over him, don't we have other things to talk about?"

"As in?"

"As in, like, how much am I gonna get if I deal with those terrorist guys?"

She tilted her head. "How much do you need?"

Can't believe I'm negotiating with this woman. "You say you're gonna help me, right?"

"Yes. I need to interrogate them." Sarah eyes opened wide. "You need to give them a reason to answer my questions. Can you handle that?"

There were things about Sarah Smith that didn't add up. The girl had been cool as a cucumber when I had her restrained. She was obviously versed at drugging a man, and she insinuated that she has no problem with torture for interrogation. I said, "I don't understand why you need me?"

"What do you mean?"

"Doesn't make sense that you would pay me to do something that you can do yourself."

"My father never took me fishing, and I've never actually tortured a man."

"And you think I have?"

"No," she answered while rising to her feet. Then looking down on me she said, "David led me to believe that you have what it takes to do what I need done, and not fall apart later. Right now, I'm not so sure. Why would he believe such?"

Good question. Lying back on the rock, I stared up and said, "I've been asking myself the same thing. Did he like, tell you that I go around torturing and killing people?"

"No. Not exactly. But let me ask, could you? Could you do what I'm asking?"

Honestly, I don't know.

Then tell her that.

"Those cows out there, you ever butcher one?"

Sarah sort of kicked me, lightly, in the side and said, "Nooo. Those are not Mom's. She leases the pastures to a farmer."

"So then, you don't know what it's like to kill and butcher a steer that you bottle fed when it was a calf."

"No, Elijah. Can't say that I've done that."

"You ever put a gun to the head of an old dog that you fed and loved on every day of its life? Pulled the trigger and watched it stretch out and die?"

"No."

I said, "It's not an easy thing to do."

"My mother suffers daily. In the barn, you mentioned doing her a favor. You think I should do her a favor by shooting her?"

"I didn't say that. But there may come a time when she is suffering terribly and you'll consider it."

"Sounds morbid."

"When your dog becomes unable to protect itself, you do what you have to do."

"Oh, I understand. So, if you end up doing what I need to do to James and Timothy, are you going to be able to live with it? Will you be able to sleep at night?"

"All I can say is that when I was a kid, I shot practically every kind of animal in the woods. Some I ate. Some I didn't. They were all innocent. Only one ever tried to hurt me was a rabid groundhog. Now, you're asking me if killin' a couple terrorists is gonna make me feel bad?"

Sarah turned to straddle my feet. Looking down at me, her head perfectly eclipsed the sun. As I lay there wondering, *What's the odds of that?* she said, "A lot of soldiers talk the talk before they go overseas. Most still come back with PTSD. Are you saying you won't?"

Leaning my head back, I used all my fingers to lightly scratch my neck and chin. "Hell, I don't know."

Sarah rubbed her temples as if realizing that she'd made a mistake in picking me. "Tell me then," she asked, "why does he describe you as psychotic?"

"Cause he's an asshole."

"Seriously. He has to have a reason."

"Why should I tell you?"

She kicked me again, lightly, with the side of her boot. "Because, I asked you nicely."

I grinned and said, "Now I see why you need me to do the torture."

"Oh yeah?" Sarah raised her boot, lowered it down on my crotch, and tried to speak in a manly voice. "Talk, boy."

I almost laughed. Something about the threat and her sweet smile afterwards made me want to get up and kiss her. Instead, I said, "You know, if I grab that leg and flip your pretty ass over the edge, you're gonna fall exactly forty-nine feet and hit the water. Then I'm gonna have to jump down there to save you. We'll both be all wet and staring into each other's eyes and it'll wind up being like one of those romance novel moments, and then you never know what might happen."

"Really?"

"So how about you just let me up and I'll tell you what you wanna hear?"

When Sarah stepped over a couple of feet, I rose and brushed myself off. She said, "This better be good. I was kind of looking forward to that romantic moment."

Yeah right. "Okay. I'll tell you this now because my father's dead. But I still don't want it repeated. When I was a junior in high school, my friend Billy and his sister, Sissy, and me, we were all walking down the road...."

I told her the story of how I ended up skinning Brad Stone's dog. She listened closely. "....by the end of the week, the whole county thought I was some sort of a psycho. The sheriff and his deputies thought by roughing me up, I'd talk. I just grinned at 'em."

"David said those things about the girl?"

"Yes," I replied, "your honorable friend is really a creep."

"So you say."

"What, you don't believe me? I swear to you I'm not lying, and if you think David Weeper is a good guy then he's got you fooled."

Sarah stood there a moment, as if considering my story. "Nothing you just said convinces me that you can handle what I'm asking you to do. Inflicting pain on another human being is not an easy task."

In my mind, I began to wonder what it would be like. "A fish doesn't make noise when you cut it up? What about these guys? Are they gonna scream or cry?"

"Probably."

"Can we gag 'em?"

Sarah shook her head and said, "How are they going to answer my questions if they can't talk?"

"Oh, didn't think about that. Well, it all sounds interesting, but what if I do fall apart? You gonna shoot me?"

Before answering, she raised her right hand lightly touching her fingertips to my cheek. "Not sure why David referred you, but if I come to the conclusion that you can't handle it, I'll find somebody else."

"How you gonna know before the time comes?"

"I'll know."

She'll test you.

"By the way," I asked, "if we get rid of Proctor, won't your father just arrange your marriage to someone else?"

"All the more reason to eliminate Wellington as well. He would probably be my father's next choice."

"And then he'd pick another and another." Sarah started walking. I caught up and said, "Unless you wanna become a serial killer, I'd say your father has to die."

She spoke while continuing forward. "My mother wants you to take care of James and Timothy. Killing my father will not be your job."

I stopped walking. "For real? You wanna waste your own father?"

She turned around and said, "He's a terrorist, and he...."

"And he what?"

Sarah gazed out over the scenery. I couldn't tell if she was mad, emotional, or both. After a few seconds, she spoke. "Elijah, I've missed out on a lot because of my father and that old man. I'm not sure if I've limited my life out of respect for their religion, or because I've always been afraid of them." She turned toward me with a wild look and finished. "One thing's for sure. My life is never going to be normal as long as my father is alive."

That's messed up. "Wow. All I can say is a woman your age shouldn't have to fear her father. And what the hell did that old man, Alon, do to you?"

Sarah's eyes closed. Her lips were tight. When she opened her eyes, she looked into the sky and said, "The clouds really are beautiful today."

This girl's got as many issues as my wife. "I'm glad the man gave this land to your mother, but I'm betting he was an evil person. Something tells me you've been abused. Can't believe your mother didn't kill him."

"She didn't have to."

"You're kidding me. You nailed the old man?"

She took a step, turned and said, "Can we please not talk about him?"

"Sure. Let's talk business."

"We were talking business," she answered. "Seems we got sidetracked somewhere around that romantic moment in the water." Motioning left with her head, she said, "Come on."

Are you really stupid enough to get involved with this woman?

Yes, I am.

Sarah led the way along a narrow path on the ridge. We were like two old friends, out for a hike. I couldn't help but stare at her ass. Suddenly, she stopped, turned and said, "What are you thinking?"

You don't wanna know. Trying to put myself into TV secret agent mode, I thought, *What would I need?* "Can you bring me information on these guys? On paper. I'm assuming, no online communications between you and me. And whatever expenses I come up with, somebody has to reimburse me for it." *You can't spend your own money.* "Second thought, on the expenses, I'll need cash up front so I can pay for whatever I might need. If I decide to do what you want, when it's all over, I'll expect two hundred thousand per man, in cash, and I'll want payment for the first man before I do the second."

"You negotiate as if you've done this before."

"Blame it on television. Man can learn a lot from cop shows."

"So what do you mean by, 'if I decide'?"

"Girl, I believe you hate your father, and if you wanna waste him, that's your business. But I'm not gonna abuse or kill anybody just because you and your mother say they're bad. I'll have to convince myself that they are who you say they are."

"Sounds reasonable, but keep in mind that dealing with them on separate occasions might be problematic. May be better to lure them together and handle both at once."

"In that case, I might need some of the money up front. I'll decide that after we make our plans."

"Works for me," Sarah replied. "I'll share the details with my mother before I take you home. Now, let's talk about something else."

"Oh yeah? What's that?"

"I need a confidant. Someone to talk to."

"About what?"

"You know. Things I can't talk to anyone else about."

Bull. "What about your mother?"

She raised one eyebrow. "Especially not her."

"So what do you need? A girlfriend, preacher, or a psychologist?"

"Something like that. Perhaps we can be of service to one another."

"Excuse me?" I chuckled. "You think I need counseling?"

"Probably. Don't we all? Aren't there things you can't talk to your wife about? And if you decide to be my confidant, shouldn't I become yours as well?"

First day we're together and she wants me to be her BFF?
I'm warning you. Get the hell away from this woman.

"Okay. I have to admit, the idea is interesting, but we're moving kinda fast here."

"You're right," she huffed. "Never mind."

"No. Not saying I don't wanna give it a try."

This might just be her way of prying.

As long as I know that, it can work both ways. I said, "Let's just take it slow, and make sure we keep it professional."

Sarah stopped walking. "Who says it has to be professional? Neither of us is a psychologist."

"You know what I mean. We have to avoid becoming emotionally connected."

"Oh, yeah. That."

"And," I continued, "if it's not professional, what about confidentiality?"

"I thought that came along with being a confidant."

"As long as we both understand that," I agreed.

Sarah grinned and asked, "Can we start right now? Take a little walk and share thoughts? We can call it, session one."

What am I getting into?

Chapter 7

For this woman that I'd barely met to ask me to be her confidant seemed over the top. At first I thought it would be her way of prying, but then, she'd already been spying on me. We began strolling down a path that ran the ridge. I asked, "Is it okay to turn my phone on?"

"No. Mine has to be on, or it'll draw suspicion, but yours, well, it's better that our phones don't show up together. Common denominators are highly used in monitoring. And since it's done by computers, two or three instances can trigger what we call electronic curiosities."

"In other words, you don't want them spying on you the way you've been spying on me."

"Basically."

"Okay then, since your phone is on, tell me what time it is."

"I should be able to do that without my phone." Taking in the sun's position, Sarah said, "I'd guess it to be around twelve thirty." She pulled out her phone, accessed it and showed it to me.

I read, "Twelve twenty-five. Looks like your biological clock is off by five minutes."

"Excuse me! My biological clock? What has my ability to tell time got to do with my reproductive system?"

"Sorry. It was a joke."

"You don't joke about a woman's biological clock. You have no right to talk about a woman's biology, period, let alone her reproductive system."

"Whoa, whoa, whoa!" I said, stopping in my tracks. "Don't you be lecturing me. I made a joke, and in no way was I referring to your reproductive system. I already told you, I don't play that political-correctness crap. You want me to be your comrade, your confidant, you're gonna have to lose that friggin' attitude. Got it?"

The tough girl Sarah Smith stood with misty eyes. I stood monitoring the ridge's edge in case she decided to push me over. She wiped her face and said, "Now perhaps you see why I need sessions?"

"Ask me, you being a geek ain't gonna run men off nearly as much as all that defensive crap. You need to lighten up, lady."

In movies I never recalled an agent with such emotions. This one seemed messed up. She asked, "Can we use our first session to talk about this? Maybe I should hear a man's perspective on the whole hormonal thing."

"Excuse me?"

"You know, do hormones drive guys crazy? And to a man, is it more about biology than psychology?"

This woman is crazy.

And you are too if you keep talking to her.

"You ... you wanna talk sexual stuff with a guy who just tied you up?"

"That was a test, you said. So, yes, please. I'd like your opinion."

"I'm pretty sure people write books about that stuff." She stood there wide-eyed and waiting. After a few seconds to think, I said, "Preacher Herman would say, when I lust for you, it's the devil tempting me. I'd say it has more to do with chemicals. Like a deer in the woods, it's my body telling me we should hook up and make a baby."

"The chemicals you speak of are your hormones. That's biology."

"Call it what you want, but when a man checks out a woman, if he gets a favorable reaction from her, it starts to mess with his brain."

"And then, it becomes about psychology."

"Well, there you are. Looks like we answered your question."

"You lust for me?"

"In a manner of speaking."

"A manner of speaking? So you really don't find me attractive."

"Didn't say that, and we're not married, so don't play games with me."

"In the barn, you were disappointed."

"Why would you say that?"

"After you saw me, you stopped. Your wife has bigger breasts. You were disappointed."

I couldn't help but laugh.

"Please don't laugh at me."

"Lady, you're so full of it. You sound like a child. Surely you're not that insecure?"

"I'm not a child, and I'm not insecure. I'm, curious."

"About what?"

"I told you, I'm looking for a man's perspective. My educated guess is that sexual urges in human beings are brought on by leftover biological instincts to survive. Like you, I don't think the devil tempts us to have sex. I believe it truly is our hormones that drive us crazy. Now, when you say it starts to mess with your brain, what you are indicating is that my favorable reaction feeds your ego. That in turn, releases more chemicals in your brain, endorphins, which makes you feel good."

"Jesus, when I was in school, girl geeks were ugly. You just blew the lid off of that."

"I'm sorry. Have I overwhelmed you?"

"Hell, I've never even had a conversation like this with my wife."

"See there, I told you there would be things you could talk to me about that you can't say to your wife."

"Yeah, well she might not appreciate me talking sex to a perfect stranger."

"I'm an imperfect stranger."

"Good grief." Looking around, I motioned and said, "Come on, let's finish this conversation on our way back to the horses." As we started walking, I considered how I might change the subject. From our elevated position, we could see for miles. Clouds drifting across the sky were heavenly. I asked, "Are you religious?"

Without stopping or looking at me, Sarah said, "Define religious."

"Do you believe in God?"

"I try to."

"That's an honest answer. And your father wants you to follow Islam?"

"Yes. Now I suppose you want to know if I'm Islamic."

I stopped walking and said, "It crossed my mind. Muslim or Christian?"

She turned and began walking backwards while facing me. "To be a child of God, does one have to identify with a particular religion?"

"No, I don't think so."

"Thank you. I studied Christian ideologies while attending Catholic elementary and high school. But there are so many areas where I have doubts that I cannot totally give myself to Christianity."

"We all have doubts." I started walking again, quicker to catch up, and said, "I'm a Christian, but I still have issues with some of the Church's interpretation of scriptures."

Sarah stopped walking so abruptly that I nearly ran over her. "I asked you a question about hormones and you somehow turned it into a religious discussion. Are the two related?"

"If you believe in God, yes. My hormones drive me crazy just like every other man my age. As an American, I'd say I have a right to be bothered or excited or whatever. I have choices. I can be faithful to my woman, or not. If I do mess around, I have to deal with my wife, myself, and my God. But yours is a different story. You also are American, but before you were conceived, your sweet loving mother appears to have sold your soul to a man who believes in Sharia Law."

While nodding at my thoughts, she asked, "You are familiar with Sharia Law?"

"I told you, I work with Islamic women. We talk. And I can almost guarantee that your father's outlook on biological sexual urges wouldn't be very American. He'd be one pissed daddy if he knew I was alone with you, here, right now."

"Are you afraid to be alone with me?"

Maybe. "Not afraid, but cautiously concerned."

"Good. I like cautiously concerned. But what am I to do about myself? My desires. My urges?"

"Hold on a minute. What the...? Why you gonna stand there and talk like you ain't never...."

"Never what? Been with a man? I'll plead the 5th."

"No way."

Sarah asked. "Would it make a difference in our ability to work together?"

"First you say a man can't talk about a woman's biology, and then you bring up stuff like this. You don't know me that well. Your sex life is none of my business."

"I brought it up because, hell, I don't know why. I just did. Do you feel sexually harassed?"

Her comment made me laugh.

"Please, I asked you not to laugh at me."

"Aww." I puffed out my lip. "Did someone laugh at Sarah when she was a little girl?"

Her face distorted and she sort of growled before speaking. It reminded me of Jane. "Elijah, let me tell you something. People do laugh at and make fun of a little girl whose skin is darker than theirs, or not as black as theirs, or who has good hair. Especially if that little girl's smarter than them or skinnier than them."

"You were bullied?"

"Yes, along with all the other stuff I went through. When David told me how ruthless you could be toward someone who picked on your handicapped friend, I wanted you to be the one."

"The one?"

"The one to help me, silly."

"Oh. Can't believe they made fun of you for having good hair."

"It happens."

"Is that why you wear your hair short?"

She hesitated. "Yes."

There I stood with a woman who had spied on me and then mysteriously inserted herself into my life. To make matters worse, she reveals the possibility that her father's Sharia Law beliefs have somehow kept her away from men. *Why? How am I supposed to react to all this?* "You know, I often sit alone at night with a cigar and a bottle of bourbon, while my wife works. It definitely gives me time to think. Sometimes I get caught up in feeling sorry for myself for what I've been through. One night I took a walk downtown, and I stood in a crowd of strangers. Then I realized I'm not alone. They're all just like me. We all have our own issues. It helps me to get along with my wife if I accept that even a doctor, a strong woman, can have her own issues. Now, I talk to you and I can see that like her, despite the strong part of you that makes you who you are, you too are allowed to have issues."

Sarah wiped her eyes and said, "Elijah Haycraft speaks words of wisdom."

"If you say so, but let me ask, what you did to me in the car. Was that less about being a freak and more about curiosity?"

"Oh, my God. I love you."

"No, no, no. You can't say that! If you're gonna say that, we can't work together. You understand?"

"Yes, I understand" Sarah replied, still smiling. "Does this mean you forgive me for my bad behavior in the car?"

That sounded like a confession. Shaking my head, I grinned and asked, "So while I was asleep, Sarah Smith got behind the wheel?"

"Do you forgive me?"

Damn. Can we go back to the car? "Yes. Of course I forgive you."

"Good." She grinned and spoke in a melody. "I-feel-bet-ter."

She's nuts.

And playing you like a fiddle.

Sarah stepped backwards between two saplings, raised her arms and rested her wrists on forks in the branches, as if restrained.

"You okay?" I asked.

"Session one is over." She closed her eyes and said, "I'll have my kiss now please."

Chapter 8

Like a worried mother, Ella met us at the barn. I couldn't tell if it was me or Sarah that she didn't trust. She had dressed in jeans and a flannel shirt, and wore a wig that fell past her shoulders. For a middle aged black woman, I found her quite attractive.

"You let him ride Lucifer?" Ella asked.

"It was his choice. Don't worry, boy knows how to ride."

Boy?

"Y'all were gone so long, I began to worry."

As Sarah dismounted, she said, "We worked out a lot of things."

"I bet you did."

"Excuse me." I interrupted. "Could you two quit talking about me like I'm not here?"

"Mama, he interested, but he needs expense money up front, and he wants two hundred grand per man."

As my boots hit the ground, Ella mumbled, "That's a lot of money."

"Not when you consider what we are asking, Mom."

Ella looked at me and asked, "How much expense money?"

While I considered, Sarah tilted her head. "How much, Cowboy?"

"I'd like ten thousand to start. If I don't need it all, I'll subtract the remainder from what you owe me."

Ella stepped past Lucifer to make eye contact with her daughter. "Can we trust him?"

Sarah grinned. "We seem to have earned one another's trust."

"What's that supposed to mean?" the mother replied.

"It means you should give him the expense money."

Ella flashed me a motherly look. "What if I give you ten thousand and then you decide not to do the job?"

"If that happens, I'll return anything I haven't spent." Ella squinted. I said, "Ma'am, that's the best I can do."

Ella stepped to me and reached for my hand. When I accepted her grip, she said, "I'll front you the expense money. If you do the job, I'll make sure you get the rest later." I nodded my approval.

Before Sarah and I started back toward Louisville, Ella handed me a large, brown envelope and said, "Count it please." Both women watched as I counted the cash in well used one hundred dollar bills. "That's a lot of money, Mr. Jones. Please don't screw me ... or my daughter, if you know what I mean."

Damn. I glanced at Sarah and then back at her mother. "So," I asked, "this money is between you and me, and David Weeper will know nothing about it?"

Ella looked at her daughter. Sarah said, "David wants information. He'll find some funding. I don't want him to know about the money you'll be getting from Mom because I don't want him to know what she's paying you for."

"Works for me," I replied while placing the envelope in my backpack. When I shouldered the bag, Ella gave me a plastic cup of iced tea for the road. I poured the tea into the sink, rinsed the ice and refilled it myself.

Ella frowned. "You trust my daughter but you don't trust me?"

Looking at her mother, Sarah lifted her eyebrows a couple times. "Momma, you may have to get intimate to gain his trust."

"Is that what you did?"

"No, ma'am," I interrupted. "Don't take it personal. I'm just not a very trusting person, and I'm damn sure not gonna drink anything you or Sarah offer me before our drive home."

Ella looked at Sarah and then back at me. "You take care of the bad guys first, and then we'll get as intimate as you want."

Wasn't expecting that.

Sarah looked at her mother and said, "You behave."

Ella reached up to rub my face. "Sarah, honey, don't you think he should grow a beard?"

"I believe you're right, Momma." Looking at me, she asked, "Can you do that?"

"As a disguise?" I asked.

"Yes," Sarah replied.

It made perfect sense.

The drive back to Louisville took right at an hour. Sarah said I had been out for ninety minutes. That meant she potentially had her way with me for thirty minutes in her mother's garage. Back at Starbucks, before I got out of the car, she handed me a small, black flip phone.

"What's this?" I asked.

"It's a burner. You use it to call or text me if we need to communicate. I have one just like it."

"Why's it gotta be a frigging flip phone? I'll look stupid with this."

"That's the point. I don't want you pulling it out in public."

"You guys use flip phones? Isn't that like, outdated?"

"We don't use flip phones, typically. But the burner phones we use are encrypted. They're only traceable and monitored by the agencies. And since we don't want to be monitored, I chose Walmart specials."

"Flip phones suck."

"It works, it's cheap, and I don't have to worry about you accidently using it for a personal call. Only number saved on it is mine. It's listed as 'Ruth'."

"Like the horse?"

"Yes."

"So when I call you is the Caller ID gonna say Lucifer?"

"Close. It'll say Angel."

"Your name is Sarah, but on the phone I call you Ruth, and my name is Angel?"

"Exactly."

"A bit confusing."

Sarah gave me a thumbs-up. "Welcome to my world. I'll get with you as soon as I have the materials you requested. While on this phone, I'm a real-estate agent. When I call, I'll say something that relates to that. You'll figure it out. If I mention the office, that'll be the parking lot of the Holy Name Catholic Church. It's on Third Street across from the University of Louisville baseball field."

"I'm familiar."

"We'll only meet after dark. The parking lot between the old school and the church building is very secluded. That okay with you?"

"Secluded at night could be dangerous."

"We won't be there long."

"Works for me."

When I opened the door to get out, she said, "By the way. Thanks for being nice to my mother."

"She's hot."

"And you're a pervert. Mom's sick, and she's lonesome."

"What kind of cancer does she have?"

"Breast, and now it has spread."

"Then it pleases me to cheer her up."

After getting out of the car, I looked back, and said, "By the way, you still owe me the other five hundred for today."

She pulled out a second white envelope.

On my way home, I considered what I would tell Jane about the meeting. Fortunately, I arrived before she did, hid the ten thousand dollars, grabbed a new unused flash drive and then drove two miles to a Public Library branch. It seemed like the most logical place to do anonymous research. I hung out in the stacks, monitoring computer users. After several minutes, one young lady stood quickly when her apparent boyfriend came into the room. She grabbed her backpack, leaving in a hurry without logging off. Taking her seat, I went directly to the internet.

On Google search, I keyed in James Davis Proctor. There were several items that popped up, but the one that drew my attention was JAMES DAVIS PROCTOR for STATE SENATE. I clicked and waited while the man's campaign website loaded. The sight contained a lot of political propaganda, some of which I found amusing—his testament about American Pride and a detailed plan for immigration reform. *Interesting*, I thought while plugging in my flash drive.

There were several pictures on the sight that I felt might come in handy. While copying them to my drive I noticed Facebook minimized on the taskbar. "Hell yes," I mumbled to myself. Restoring the site introduced me to one Mary Ann Bizwell.

Wow, she sure looks better on Facebook than in person. A Facebook search revealed several men named James Proctor. Sure enough, I found a public Facebook page titled Proctor for State Senate. It had more of the same. Backing up, I clicked on other listings until I found the personal page for James Davis Proctor. Clicking revealed it to be private.

Pulling out my phone, I called John's cell. Recognizing me on the caller ID, he answered, "Just because you're not working doesn't mean I'm not."

"Dude, I miss like one day a year."

"I hear you. So what's up?"

"I need your help. Remember how you said you gain access to the private Facebook pages of applicants?"

"Yes."

"Can you text me instructions on how to do that?"

"Just send me the name and I'll do the research here."

"I can't do that. I really need you to send me the instructions. I'll explain later."

"Okay, but make sure you delete the text. You know it's not legal."

"Neither is driving seventy in a fifty-five, but we do it every day. Just send it ASAP. I'll see you Monday."

In less than a minute, my phone whistled delivering John's simple hacking instructions. I read them, used them, and suddenly had access to James Davis Proctor's private pages. First glance revealed nothing important. More political crap. Scanning through his photos, I did find one of him with Sarah. She wore a rather plain outfit and a fake smile. The odds of me seeing a picture of the back of James Proctor's neck were slim to none. I began sorting through his *friends* list and noticed that there were three whose photos were unavailable. They had generic American names: Larry Smith, Steven Cook, and Mary Wright. Right clicking on Mary Wright took me to her private page. More hacking revealed that Mary Wright was in fact Mambo Hussein. Her site contained enough suspicious activity to scare me away. I soon found more of the same on the pages of Larry Smith and Steven Cook. No doubt, James Davis Proctor had communications with foreigners whose true identities were being hidden. *Apparently the government doesn't look deep into candidates for State offices.*

Facebook searching on Wellington came up short. I tried both Timothy and Tim. He was either more cautious, or did not participate. Googling did bring up his campaign site and more political rhetoric. Before I could absorb his ideologies, I caught a glance of Miss Bizwell returning. I quickly logged out, removed my flash drive, and then leaned back into my chair looking at my phone. When she approached me, I looked up.

"Sir, I was sitting here earlier and I believe I forgot to log out."

"You sure did. Don't worry though," I said while rising, "I logged you out before I logged in. I'm finished here. You can have it back."

As I walked away, she checked to assure I had actually logged her out.

While waiting for the traffic light at the entrance to my condo complex, the burner Sarah gave me vibrated in my pocket. I answered, "Hello."

"Hey Angel, this is Ruth. I found that last inspection on the property you said you were interested in. Can you meet me at the office later?"

"Damn, that was quick."

"Ah, well, it's a listing I'd already been working on."

"What time's good for you?" I asked.

"I have two more meetings this evening. To be safe, let's say around nine thirty. Is that too late?"

"No. I'll be there."

"Thanks. Bye."

Closing the phone, I glanced in the rearview mirror and saw Jane behind me. "Why isn't she at work?" The light changed and we both proceeded to the condo. I parked, got out and waited for her. As soon as she got out of her car, Jane started in on me, loudly. "Who were you talking to on the phone? Was that even your phone? You never hold your phone. You use speaker phone. Were you talking to that—"

"Jane! Stop it already. We can talk inside."

Her jacket flopped over a chair as her purse hit the kitchen table. "Okay. We're inside, now talk."

Instead of talking, I pulled out my phone and whispered, "Give me yours."

"Excuse me?"

I held an index finger to my lips and held out my other hand. When she handed me hers, I took both phones to the bedroom, placed them plus the flip phone on the bed and covered them with pillows. Closing the door, I returned to the kitchen.

Jane asked, "What the hell's going on, Eli?"

"All I can say is that I suspect the stalking I talked about earlier was being done with my phone. At this point, I prefer not to talk in front of it. Does that make sense?"

"Yes," she replied, "but I don't like it."

"Neither do I."

"So now we're alone. What happened today?"

Instead of answering, I asked, "Why are you at home? Shouldn't you be working?"

"My stomach was upset. Dr. Brooks came in for me."

"Are you pregnant?"

"No, Eli. I'm worried about you."

"Really? Are you worried about me cheating? Come on, Jane?"

"Don't come on me. I've got that gut feeling again. This feels like when we first got married. The way you used to disappear. It's like you're hiding something from me."

"How can you say that? As soon as I got out of the car you started in on me."

"You spent the whole day with this woman. Why would you be talking to her on the way home?"

"Oh.... That's why you're upset. She called to tell me she has some information I requested. We're gonna meet later so she can give it to me. Honey, I'm excited about an opportunity to make some serious money. I'm talking enough to pay off your student loans, a nice down payment on a house, and then some. Do you understand what that means to me? I'm dying here in this jail cell we call home, and all you can think about is me cheating on you!"

"Well, if you think I'm going to quit thinking about that, you're crazy. Now, go ahead and explain your day and why you need information."

Ugh. I took a deep breath. "It's not a permanent deal, but a great opportunity. Problem is I'm not supposed to talk about it with you."

"Why not?"

"If I do speak to you, anything at all about this, you have to promise not to repeat it to anyone. Understand?"

Don't. You'll regret it.

"No, I don't understand. How can I when you haven't told me anything?"

"I'm not supposed to. It could put lives in danger. Mine, maybe even yours."

"Damn, Eli," she replied while settling into a kitchen chair. "What have you gotten yourself into?"

"You know me. I'm bored to death with my job. When these people offered me excitement, yes it did get my attention."

"These people? Spit it out Eli."

"Homeland Security."

"Do what?"

"They want me to do work for Homeland Security."

So much for secrecy.

"Eli, why would they want you? You're not a cop."

"No, but I do have skills. And I'm not on anyone's watch list. That's why they want me. I can work covertly."

"You have skills? What the hell kind of skills do you have that Homeland Security is interested in?"

Jane's always been a tough girl. I get that. But for her to downplay my ability to take care of myself felt insulting. I went to the cabinet and pulled out a bottle of bourbon. She stared as I pulled the cork and took a long swig. "Ahhh," I exhaled. Leaning back against the cabinet, I said, "Dammit Jane. You and I sit here every night watching the news and bitching about how our country is going to hell. This is my chance to make a difference, and a lot of money."

"No. This is a chance for you to get killed."

"I could get killed driving to work. Honey, I keep my job, and I have a ton of sick days built up to use whenever I need to travel. And if it works out, you can go off the birth control. Like, real soon."

"Just because you make a bunch of money doesn't necessarily mean I'm going to change my mind about having a kid."

"At least it makes the option more doable," I reasoned.

"So are you going to be hiding stuff from me?"

"Probably. The less you know the better. And like I said, you can't mention a word of this to anyone. Period."

"What if something happens to you? Then what? Who do I talk to?"

"No one. If something happens to me, they'll probably make it look like an accident, and you'll just have to leave it at that. Otherwise my life insurance might not pay off."

"No. No. No." She stood shaking her head. "I don't want you getting into something like this. I can't handle it."

"You can't handle it? Are you kidding me? Like I don't worry my ass off when you come home late? We made an agreement. I don't question what you do. I live with it, and I don't complain. So you have to give me the same respect. I can't believe we're even having this conversation."

"It's not fair, Eli."

I took a swig. "If you think it's not fair, I'll make you a deal. I'll turn this down if you promise never to go out again at night without me. How's that? Deal?"

Jane frowned and said, "You know I can't say that."

I didn't reply, but stood staring and tapping my foot on the floor.

"Stop that dammit," Jane huffed. "I'll worry every time you leave the house."

"Yes you will. I know exactly how that feels. Honey, I really wanna do this. What they want from me is a temporary deal. I'm thinking two, maybe three months at the most. That's why I'm not quitting my job."

Jane reached for the bourbon bottle, took a swig and made a face. "You know we don't need the money."

"Yes we do. You're not exactly a specialist. It'll be years before you can pay off those student loans. I want a house now."

"Will you be working with Miss Excitement?"

"Some. And like I said, I may have to travel a little, but the majority of my work is gonna be right here in Kentucky." I stepped closer, straddled Jane and squatted down onto her lap. While sliding my hands up under her hair and gently rubbing the back of her head, I whispered, "Come on, baby. Support me on this. We'll do it together."

"Together?"

"I'll keep you informed as much as I can."

"I don't know."

When I began kissing her face, she whimpered, "This isn't fair."

"Honey," I whispered, "you *are* my Miss Excitement."

When she nibbled my bottom lip, I felt we had an agreement.

Chapter 9

At 9:10 p.m., I lowered the volume of cable news. Jane appeared to be snoozing on the couch. Instead of carrying the small .380, I put on my elastic waist band holster and slid in my 10-shot 9mm. The small amount of whiskey remaining in the bottle on the kitchen counter drew me like a magnet. I finished it off and dropped the empty into the trash. When I opened the door to leave, Jane said, "Behave."

In close proximity to the Churchill Downs Horse Racing Track and the University of Louisville athletic facilities, I slowly approached Sarah's office—a small parking lot nested between a cathedral style church, the old school building, a convent, and a deserted priest's rectory. Sarah's Toyota sat waiting. Parking next to her, I got out of my car and into the Camry, noticing that her interior lights still did not come on.

"Thanks for coming," she said while displaying two folders. "This is everything I have to date on each of them."

"How about a little light?" I asked.

She lowered the window on my side allowing in light from a nearby street pole. Her features became beautifully highlighted. She made a face. "I smell liquor. Let's get something straight. I don't mind that you drink, but please, not when we're doing business."

My first thought was to snap at her, but I did understand her concern. "I hear you. But the way I see it, every time you spied on me at Del Junco's, you knew I was drinkin'. I'm not likely to sit around sober waitin' for you to call me out for one of these little meetings. When we plan to go somewhere, it won't be a problem."

"Good," she replied. Opening the first folder, she handed me a document. "Here are your FMLA papers already signed by a doctor. They're your ticket to get off from work whenever we need to meet. You have a half-sister living in Cincinnati. She's dying of cancer. You'll need to help care for her on occasions. Your employer knows what this is and will not have a problem since you never miss work—"

She knows that?

"—Tell them that it'll only be for a short while and that you'll be using up your sick days to keep from losing money. If they have questions, they can call this number and leave a message for Dr. Shomoni. He knows how to cover you."

"You already talked to a doctor?"

"No. I had these forms with his signature on file. I'll call the doctor in the morning."

"Thought you were doing this behind their backs?"

"This is standard procedure. Happens so often that these doctors don't even question."

Sarah then began shuffling through photos of Timothy Wellington and his residence. When she handed me the folder, I sorted through information and asked, "What's all this stuff you marked out?"

"Those are redactions. Things you don't need. Mostly phone numbers that I need to make sure you don't call. If you did there would be a permanent record that could get you connected down the road. Understand?"

"Yeah, boss, I get it."

"Don't take this stuff lightly. I'm being serious."

When I nodded she began describing photos and details written on several pages of type written notes. "You'll find a lot of information here describing his educational background, a little about his social activities, and his campaign."

I nodded my approval as she handed the folder to me. Then she opened the second folder to sort through Proctor's photos and notes. "Remember now, no matter what, nothing happens to either one of these guys before I have a chance to interrogate."

"Only way that'll happen is if I decide to kill them and you."

"That's not funny."

"Didn't mean it to be."

She sat silent for a moment and then said, "Remember in the barn when you talked about having a party with my mother?"

"Yep."

"Please keep in mind that you're not the only party animal in this car."

I stared at her comment. "What's that supposed to mean?"

"It means you shouldn't be throwing around remarks like the one you just made. How would you feel if I threatened to harm you or Jane?"

"Threaten me all you want, but if you talk about hurting Jane, I'll kill you."

"Kind of the way I felt in the barn when you talked about my mother."

"Oh," I replied.

"So how about we make a pact that regardless of what occurs, my mother and your wife have some sort of diplomatic immunity."

"You're saying they're both off limits, no matter what?"

"That's exactly what I'm saying."

I winked and said, "I'll protect your mother no matter what. You protect my wife. Works for me."

"Good." While raising my window, Sarah said, "If we're making a pact, shouldn't we at least seal it with a kiss?"

Would the kiss become our handshake, our ceremonial seal of approval?

Remember, no emotional involvement?

Sarah spread her arms and closed her eyes.

Why am I doing this?

On my drive home, I wondered if it would be cheating to have sex with Jane while Sarah lingered on my mind.

Yes.

"Who asked you?" I thought aloud.

Nearing home, I turned my phone on and saw where Jane had texted, **Let me know when you are on your way**.

Too late now.

From the parking lot I could see that lights were on inside the condo, and for a short second it looked like Jane peeking out between blinds. *Bet she's pissed.*

Upon opening the door, my senses were stimulated by perfume. Stepping through the doorway between the kitchen and living room, I found my wife lying on a quilt in front of the fireplace, naked, with her back to me. She had a white bath towel draped over her bottom. A wine glass and a half empty bottle of chardonnay sat nearby on an end table. I began to feel what Sarah would term a biologically-induced sexual urge. "Be right back." I hid Sarah's folders and then buried both mine and Jane's phones before returning to my beloved. Inch by inch, I slowly removed the towel.

Nearly an hour later, Jane finished off the chardonnay while I had bourbon. She said, "What am I gonna do with you?"

"Excuse me?"

"You never kiss me like that."

"I'm sorry. Was it that bad?"

"I didn't say it was bad. Just wondering why my husband is suddenly so romantic?"

"I come home to a naked wife stretched out on the floor, and you don't expect me to be romantic? What's up with that?"

"Never mind."

As she spoke, I turned on the big screen TV over the fireplace and then relaxed into the recliner.

She continued, "So tell me about your meeting."

I turned the volume up on the TV and spoke quietly, "Not much to tell. We met. I got the information, and I came home."

"I can't lie about this, honey. I'm already struggling with what you've gotten yourself into."

"If what I just experienced is a byproduct of what I've gotten myself into, I should change careers."

Jane huffed and said, "You're so full of it."

The TV news flashed NEWS ALERT followed by:

Another street bomb has caused three deaths and numerous injuries in the province of Bonzinic, 15 kilometers inside the southern border of Vitora, Africa.

"See that," I said. "Do we really wanna live in such chaos?"

"It's on the other side of the world."

"Yes, but it'll be here eventually if we don't stop it. Actually, it already is. Nine eleven. The Boston bombing. San Bernardino. Who wants to bring a child into that kind of fear? Am I wrong to wanna do my part?"

"You want the money, Eli. I'm not stupid."

"Yes I do. Hell yes. But I also would like to make a difference."

Jane stared for a while and then said, "You already know I'd prefer not to bring a child into this world, period."

"Come on, Jane. I'm excited about this."

"I can tell. You had better be excited about the job and not Miss Excitement. You know what I'll do if you screw up."

I grinned and said, "Don't tease me."

Chapter 10

On that following Monday morning I arrived a little early for work. Pulling into the parking lot, I noticed that John had backed his car into the furthest row from the building—an area surrounded on three sides by trees. His windows were down. The temperature was a pleasant 74^0F. Before I had even backed in next to him, John got out and started tapping on my passenger side window. He had a blunt in his hand. I lowered the window, receiving wind, weed, and a chill, and said, "Don't bring that stinky stuff into my truck."

"Then get your ass out. You're gonna want some of this."

"Not now. It's too early."

"Boy, there's two things in this world a man never turns down early in the morning, and they both start with the letter P."

I climbed out and asked, "You got my breakfast?"

Mondays suck, so we alternate buying breakfast. It was John's turn to buy. He reached back into his car and came out with a bag and two large coffees. I lowered my tailgate and took a seat. Handing me a cup of coffee, he said, "You look rough. What's with the whiskers?"

Rubbing my three day beard, I said, "Got lazy this weekend. Decided to let it go. See how it looks."

"Okay. Well, check this out. I found this cool site this morning with diagrams that have to do with climate change." John held his phone in a shadow so I could see it. "These charts are called the Milankovitch cycles."

"Dude, it's too early for all that, and I'm not interested in somebody's global warming rhetoric."

"But I think you might like this guy's theories since they indicate that climate change has a lot to do with things man cannot control."

"Haven't I been telling you that all along?"

John let me hold the phone so I could see as he explained. "This guy figured it out back in the 1920s. He says there are three cycles that continuously affect climate on Earth. Eccentricity, obliquity, and procession." Pointing at the first diagram, he said, "Eccentricity is when the orbit of the Earth around the Sun changes over time from a circle to an ellipsis and back. Takes about a hundred thousand years for one cycle."

"Too long for me to worry about."

"I hear you," John replied. "Scan down." I did, revealing another display that showed the planet Earth on its axis. John continued, "This is obliquity. That's how the planet has a change in its tilt of just a few degrees that occurs back and forth over a forty-one thousand year cycle. It's a small change in the angle of the Earth to the sun."

John and Sarah are like two peas in a pod. "Let me guess," I sassed. "It's just enough to change temperatures."

"Exactly," John replied. "You get it. Now move down again." I did and it revealed a diagram labeled, PROCESSIONS. "This shows a change in the Earth's rotation. It gradually changes at what point in the orbit of the sun we experience the different seasons. In other words, the first day of winter moves approximately fifteen days every thousand years. Eventually, what is now the first day of winter will be the first day of summer. It never stops changing."

The display looked confusing. I handed John's phone back to him. "So you believe all this?"

He held up his thumb and said, "It makes good sense. Crazy part is that when all three of those cycles line up just right, we have an ice age."

"Really," I replied, "then they must be lined up now, because haven't we been in an ice age for like, millions of years?"

"Nooo. Ice age is when the ice spreads down from the North Pole over Canada and into the United States. It just ended around fifteen thousand years ago."

"Did you research that?"

"Don't need to," John replied with confidence.

"Are you sure about that?"

"Elijah, I think I know what an ice age is. Why you asking?"

"Never mind." Reaching for the bag, I asked, "Now, can I eat my breakfast?"

"Sure," John answered as I pulled out a sausage, egg and cheese biscuit. Then, when I handed the bag to him, he said, "Speaking of research, what's the deal with the Facebook stuff?"

"Nothing really. My cousin's worried about her daughter. Wanted to take a look at the girl's Facebook to see if there's anything that might keep her from gettin' a job with the company she's applying for."

"And what company is that?"

"Hell, I don't know."

John took a sip of coffee while backing off a couple steps.

"What?" I asked.

"I thought we were friends."

"Excuse me?"

"Look man, I ain't no stupid nigga. I took a chance sending you that Facebook stuff and now you start lying to me?"

"Ask me no questions, and I tell you no lies."

After a sip of his coffee, John asked, "Why do I think this has something to do with the woman at Del Junco's?"

"What makes you think that?"

"Because, that lady doesn't have herself and some man stalking your sorry ass just because she wants to get laid. What'd she want?"

"Didn't I tell you to ask her that?"

"Don't mess with me Elijah. I gave you that formula in confidence. You gonna sit there and tell me that woman wanted you to look up someone's Facebook page?"

"No. I wanted to look at hers."

"Oh. Damn bro. You didn't really—?"

"I told you I liked the car."

John hesitated again. "That's where you were Friday. Isn't it? You spent the day with that bitch."

"She's not a bitch."

"Kiss my ass. You really are messing up. I knew this was gonna happen."

"Stop it, John."

"Better keep it on the down-low bro. Jane catches you, man she'll cut your nuts off."

"Perhaps you should have thought about that *before* you went over and talked to the lady."

"I told her you were married and she needed to leave you alone."

John relit the blunt and blew smoke into my face. I waved it away. He took another draw and again blew it into my face. I asked, "What the hell are you doing?"

"Call it smoke boarding. I'm gonna do this until you tell me all the dirty details."

"Forget about it. All I'm gonna say is that even though my car doesn't have all the bells and whistles, I still like it better."

"Well you know me bro. I prefer a lease so I can turn it in for a new one every couple of years."

I took a bite of my sandwich and replied with my mouth full. "You ain't right."

After work that day, I stopped at another branch library. John's questions that morning had triggered a curiosity. Why hadn't I researched Sarah? It took me a while to get an open computer that had not been logged out. When I Googled Sarah Smith there were a number of articles involving a multitude of Sarah Smiths. Needing Facebook, I quickly created a false identity and a Facebook page for a woman named Debra Jones. It took a few minutes to create the page, complete with a profile pic. I used a photograph I found online; some woman in England.

Searching for Sarah Smith on Facebook turned out to be a joke. There were dozens of women with the same name. None even remotely reminded me of the Sarah Smith I knew. Then it dawned on me that Homeland Security employees might not do social media, and Sarah Smith might not be her real name. It wouldn't be easy to research her.

That evening, while taking out the garbage, I called Sarah's phone. She answered, "Ruth speaking."

"Hey Ruth, this is Angel."

"Well, hello there. Did you find a property you like?"

"Possibly," I answered, "but it's out of state. I'm looking at a job in Virginia. I'm assuming you're not licensed in Virginia, but I'd still be willing to pay you to accompany me there to look at the property. You know, to advise me."

"Depends on when you plan on going."

"As soon as you can," I replied.

"Let's see then," she asked, "Can it be this week?"

"Certainly."

"How about Friday? That way we can spend the night if necessary."

"Oh." *Hadn't really thought about that.* "Friday's fine."

"Good," she replied. "We should leave early, say around seven, so we can drive back that day if at all possible."

"I'll be ready whenever you want."

Sarah seemed to be thinking. "If you can find your way back to my mother's place, we can leave from there. I'll spend Thursday night with her."

"No problem, I can find it."

"Good. See you on Friday. By the way, do you have a casual suit jacket?"

"Ah, yeah."

"Bring it with you Friday."

"Okay. Can I still wear jeans?"

"Sure."

"Good."

She said, "Bye," and hung up.

For a moment, I stood staring into the sky at what few stars were visible and thinking about how easy it would be to screw up with Sarah. Her looks, her mind, her spunky attitude, and of course the kiss, all turned me on. "Boy, what an exercise in discipline?" I thought out loud on my way back into the condo.

One step inside the door, Jane jumped me. "Who were you talking to on the phone?"

"Excuse me?"

"I looked out the window and you were talking."

"Are you spying on me?"

"No," she replied, "but I'm not stupid. You took out the garbage when it wasn't even full."

"This is not working."

"Excuse me?"

"I have to communicate with this woman, and it looks and very well may be disrespectful to you. How can we do this?"

"*We* are not doing this. *You* are and it is making *me* uncomfortable. It still feels like I'm being cheated on."

"But you're not."

"Can I be sure of that?"

"Come on Jane. Do you really think I would—?"

"Are you a man?"

"Oh, so now all men cheat."

"Well that *is* what they say."

I stared for a moment and then said, "You know they say the same thing about women."

"Mr. Haycraft, I'm not the one who is hanging out with a beautiful woman who happens not to be your wife, and who offers you excitement. What would you say if I told you I was going to be spending time with a tall, dark, and handsome man who offers me excitement?"

"Ouch. I have to admit, that's a tough one. So how do I do this? I wanna make this work, but I don't want you to have to worry the whole time I'm gone."

"Gone? Gone where?"

After a deep breath, I said, "I have to go out of town on Friday. To another state, and it might be an all-day affair." Jane's eyes grew. *Wrong word, dumb-ass.* "I mean, it might take all day, and if so, I might have to drive back on Saturday."

"Are you going alone?"

"No. My boss will be going with me."

"By boss you mean, Miss Excitement?"

"Yes, but can't we call her something different?"

"Her name would be nice."

"I'm sorry, but I can't reveal her name. Besides, she probably gave me a fake name."

Jane shook her head. "Eli, I swear to God, this is going to be the end of us."

"How can you swear to God if you don't believe in God?"

Chapter 11

Before Friday morning arrived, Jane had nearly driven me crazy. She'd already put in four 12-hour shifts in the ER. Each night she came home tired and took her frustrations out on me. My lovely wife just couldn't get over the idea of me traveling with a beautiful woman. One she had never met and likely never would. I understood but didn't know what to do. With no one else to turn to, I called Ruth.

"Hey there, I'm having some difficulties at home about my time away on this issue."

"You mean your wife doesn't want you to go?"

"Precisely."

"Jesus, Angel. Grow a pair."

"Excuse me?"

"You have to learn how to overcome obstacles."

"That's easy for you to say. You've never been married."

She hesitated a moment and then said, "Just give her money before you leave."

"Money?"

"She's a woman. It'll make her happy. Drop her a grand. Consider it an expense."

Sarah's idea seemed shady, and expensive, but what other choice did I have? Before leaving the house, I stuffed $1,000 into an envelope. As I stood in the kitchen, licking the flap, Jane's alarm radio began blaring. Country music lasted ten seconds before she hit the snooze button.

Inside the bedroom, I placed the envelope on the dresser and then stood staring. Just when I was sure she had fallen back to sleep, Jane rolled over to look at me. Her gravelly morning voice said, "You leaving now?"

"In a minute."

"I wanted to get up and have a cup of coffee with you."

"You got in so late. Figured I'd let you sleep."

"I didn't expect you'd be leaving this early."

"I insisted on an early start. It's a six hour drive. Hoping we can get done today and return home sometime tonight."

"Can't believe you're going away on my only night off this week."

"I had no way of knowing that before we made plans."

"Are you getting paid for today?"

"I took a sick day."

Then she surprised me. "Six hour drive. Damn, Eli. I'd rather you guys spend the night than to chance nodding off on the way home. Just behave, please."

Did she just tell me to spend the night with Sarah? Maybe I don't need to leave the money?

Pitching the envelope onto the bed, I said, "I'm leaving you a little something."

Without raising her head, she asked, "What's this, a butter-me-up note? Did you buy me a Hallmark card?"

Stepping close, I said, "If I do make it home tonight, it'll be late. Treat yourself. Call Lisa, or your cousin, Melinda. Go out for dinner and drinks, on me."

Jane lifted herself up on one elbow. "What? You left me money?"

"Yes."

"How?"

"They gave me an advance. For expenses."

"Oh, so now I'm an expense?"

"Well, it wasn't my idea."

"You mean she said you should give me money?"

"I told her you were having difficulties with this arrangement."

"Arrangement? And so she suggested you buy me off."

"She said I should give you a night on the town. That you would appreciate it. That's all."

"So how much did she suggest?"

"A thousand."

"Do what?" Jane sat up in the bed, exposing her perky tits. "Are you serious?" She ripped open the envelope like a kid at Christmas and removed all 10 one-hundred dollar bills, spreading them on the bed. "Jesus, Eli. You want me to spend all this."

"You don't have to spend it all in one night. And by all means, don't flash money."

Gathering the bills, she said, "You know this would nearly cover next month's college loan payment."

"No!" I said. "This is for you. It's been a while since either of us had money to blow. Enjoy yourself." I kissed her on the forehead, avoiding morning breath, and said, "Gotta go now, and please, if you're gonna drink, get a cab or Uber. No matter what, do not mention my project."

"I'm not stupid," she said while leaning back against the headboard, both hands behind her head, looking all sexy.

Damn. Maybe I should stay a while.

On my way out the bedroom door, Jane spoke loudly, "Eli!"

When I stuck my head back in, she said, "Separate rooms, by the way."

As I left the parking lot, I pondered the idea of Jane going out on the town, without me, and having a couple drinks. *Hmmm. Can I trust her?*

What, so you're afraid she'll kiss somebody?

"Shut up," I replied to myself.

An hour and a half later, I drove down the gravel lane toward Ella's farm and from a distance could see the garage, its large door open. Sarah leaned into the open trunk of her Camry, parked in front of the house. She wore a black ankle length skirt, tan pullover blouse, and ankle boots with thick 1.5 inch heels. During approach, I lowered my window. "Good morning, Miss Smith."

Grinning, she said, "Nice beard."

"Glad you like it. Jane says it scratches her when I—"

"Please, don't." Sarah suddenly had an odd look, as if I had offended her.

"I'm sorry."

"Don't be. It's not your fault. My private issue."

"Session material?"

"At some point," she replied, staring into my truck. "If that's your bag, hand it to me and I'll put it in the trunk with mine." As I opened the door and passed it out, she said, "Leave your truck in the garage. I'll close the door when you're out."

Sarah used her remote to lower the garage door and then joined her mother on the porch. They were both sitting in rockers as I stepped closer. Ella had on jeans and a light jacket and wore her wig. She smiled as if happy. "Nice beard, Mr. Haycraft, and I like the sunglasses too."

I bowed. "Ella, you and I will never make it to intimacy if you continue to call me Mr. Haycraft. Elijah will do."

"Very well. But don't go getting any ideas before you get the job done."

Sarah shook her head, scanned my attire and asked, "You gotta gun under that jacket?"

"Yes."

".380?"

"9mm."

"Nice conceal. You any good with it?"

"Yes."

She took a second look at my jeans, western boots, and dark tee-shirt under my jacket and said, "You'll do."

Ella stood on the porch waving goodbye as Sarah accelerated down the lane. It suddenly felt as if I were living a double life. Like one of those husbands who have a secret second wife. Through the side mirror I could see the dust cloud Sarah's speeding car left behind. In five years of marriage, Jane had only driven me a handful of times. It usually occurred after I had consumed too much liquor.

"You always drive so fast?" I asked.

"Look, I let you stay awake this time, so don't go all front-seat-driver on me."

"No problem. How long will it take us to get there?"

"Not as long as you think. We're not going to Virginia after all."

"What?"

"I did some thinking and decided you should meet James before we go snooping around in Virginia. This way we might not have to hide our intentions so much."

"I don't get it."

"To get my father here in the States, I agreed to the wedding. He, James, and Timothy Wellington will all be there at the same time."

"So now you plan on killing 'em all at the wedding?"

"That's what I'm thinking. But first I needed to come up with a way for you to be there. Trust me when I say this will be a closed event. Privacy is big with these people. My plan is to introduce you now, so that everyone involved will be comfortable with your presence by the time the wedding gets here."

"And when exactly is that?"

"We'll probably set a date today."

"Can't believe I'm going with you to meet your fiancé."

"Why?"

"Won't he be jealous?"

"James knows I work for Homeland. I told him I had a threat on my life and that the agency won't let me travel alone until the issue is settled. He thinks I'm not happy with the arrangement, but must follow orders nonetheless."

"I'm gonna be your bodyguard?"

"That's it. Your name is simply, Jones. And the genius is that as an escort, you won't be expected to carry on conversations. All you have to do is follow my leads. Also, he wants me to join him for a swim."

"Nice. So, I get to see a lot more of Sarah." She shook her head. I said, "Maybe we'll get a look at your boy's neck. See if he has the tattoo."

"Exactly."

"Cool. Sounds interesting. I'll be your bodyguard. Just don't expect me to take a bullet."

"Aw. You wouldn't do that for me?"

"Would you take one for me?" I asked.

"Probably."

"Really?"

She glanced into the rearview mirror and said, "I will definitely have your back, at all times. And yes, I'll expect the same from you."

"That's an agreement I can live with."

Sarah hit the brake, pulling to the side of the road. After putting the car in park, she spread her arms, closed her eyes and said, "Let's seal the deal."

Bet this is her way of checking to see if I've been drinking.

Chapter 12

Driving into Morganville, Kentucky felt like going home. It's one of those quaint communities where the town square involves a courthouse and a dozen small shops along the one way street that circles the stately building. Traffic management consists of stop signs and local citizens who actually know what is meant by the term, 'complete stop'. Imagine that.

On the small courthouse lawn, two statues of Civil War era Confederate soldiers stood guard while two more loaded their cannon. They all appeared to be protecting Old Glory, waving high atop a ten degree less than vertical flagpole. Aged gentlemen sat on benches, tipping their hats and caps at those passing by. A middle-aged woman swept the sidewalk in front of a shop on the town square. It took all of sixty seconds for Sarah to drive through the business district while unexpectedly abiding by the twenty-five mph speed limit.

"You ever check out the shops?" I asked.

Sarah replied. "How many African Americans do you see walking around this town?"

Glancing back over my shoulder, I said, "Ah, like, none right now."

"Exactly. And I'd say it hasn't been too long since a Confederate flag flew on top of that pole. So don't expect to see me shopping there."

"But there were a few black folks here when I was a kid."

Sarah ignored my comment.

For several miles past Morganville, the roads are bordered with stone walls—layers of flat limestone rock stacked waist high. I said, "Always did love the walls."

"Where'd all the rocks come from?" Sarah asked.

"Farmers pulled 'em out of those fields when they cleared for pasture and crops."

"Then I'd say it was slaves that built the walls," Sarah replied.

"You forget this is where I grew up. I do know the history. Back in the day, there were a few farmers around that had slaves. And maybe some got to work on walls, but for the most part, all these walls got built by my ancestors, the Irish and the Scots. They were stonemasons when they settled here in the late 1700s."

Sarah gave me a sly look and asked, "Your people own slaves 'back in the day'?"

"Would it make a difference?"

"Maybe," she replied, trying to glance at my eyes while navigating the erratic road.

Sometimes less said is better. I changed the subject. "Were you listening in this week when John and I talked about climate?"

"Nooo."

"He showed me some charts. Called 'em some kind of cycles. Started with an M."

"Milankovitch Cycles?"

"That's it."

"Excellent. You guys are learning about climate change."

"Yeah, well his truth and yours aren't the same. He says an ice age is when the cycles line up and the ice spreads down over North America. Is he wrong?"

She rocked her head. "Technically, he's wrong. But he's not alone. Most people you ask, including a lot of teachers and some scientists call what he is referring to, an ice age. Truth is, what he described is a glacial period within an ice age. As the Milankovitch Cycles do their thing the glaciers extend down over the northern hemisphere. Around twenty thousand years ago, the ice peaked at between one and two miles thick over most of what is now Canada and all the way down to right above Kentucky. Just a few hundred miles or so from where we are now."

"Okay, but I seem to recall my high school science teacher, Mr. Billingsworth, calling that an ice age."

"I'm guessing your Mr. B had a Bachelor of Science with a master's degree in education. If he had a master's or a PHD in one of the earth sciences, he might have taught you about glacial periods and interglacial periods and their significance in climate change."

"What's interglacial?"

"That's when the ice is melting. Tell John that he should be able to go online and find charts describing the glacial and interglacial periods of the past that correspond with his Milankovitch Cycles."

"Do *you* have a master's degree in earth science?"

"I have a master's in environmental science. That's what I studied at Oxford."

"What'd you study at Dartmouth?"

"My bachelor's is in chemistry with a minor in psychology."

Why am I attracted to women who are smarter than me?

Better question is why are they attracted to you?

Five miles out of town, rock walls gave way to wire fences. Scenes from my youth lay as a reminder of who I am. Hills and valleys blanketed with fescues, clover, and bluegrass, groomed by herds of fat Hereford and Angus cattle. Eventually, Sarah took a left, and we entered a different world, that of the upper echelon of Wilson County. A place I rarely visited even as a teen. Instead of wire and cattle, we began seeing black four-board fences and thoroughbred race horses. There were several large colonial mansions, some old, some new.

Three more miles down the road, Sarah slowed and announced, "Here we are!" She turned left again onto a tree-lined lane that provided an awesome view of the Proctor Estate. A large, white, two-story residence with six pillars and shaded by ancient pin oaks, sat at the end of the drive that circled around a fountain in front of the entrance. To the left, the drive forked off to a four bay garage. Beyond the right side of the house, I could see the end of a new horse barn.

I said, "Ritzy."

"Exactly what I thought the first time I came here."

Four thoroughbreds grazed nearby in the field. "They own race horses?"

"Yes, but James told me the ones they keep here are retired. They treat them better than you can imagine. Hope you get to see the inside of their barn. Much nicer than ours."

The closer we drove to the house, the more anxious I became. Not out of fear, but excitement and a bit of uncertainty. Something had been bothering me, so I asked. "Before we go in, I'd like to know, do you really work for Homeland Security?"

"Excuse me?"

"You heard me. Do you work for Homeland or is it just a front?"

"Why would you ask such a question?"

"I think you know. It doesn't add up. Your education, your travels. Your bi-cultural upbringing. You speak Arabic. I'd expect you to be recruited for something bigger."

"By bigger, you mean?"

"I mean you're a spook, aren't you?"

Sarah let off the gas, stared at my eyes way too long, and said, "You got no problem calling a black person a *spook*?"

"I don't think of you as a black person."

"Then what the *hell* do you think I am?"

"You're a person, Sarah. That's all that matters to me. I'm not afraid, intimidated, or ashamed of the color of your skin. Do you see my eyes close when we kiss?"

"I don't know. I close mine."

"Yeah, I noticed. So, you don't like the color of *my* skin?"

She tilted her head and asked, "Do people really kiss with their eyes open?"

"I do."

"Then I'd say there's something wrong with you. Besides," she continued, "I like the color of your skin."

"So what's your problem, then?" I asked. "Why do you always have that chip on your shoulder, like you're gonna catch me in some kind of racial slur and then give me hell about it?"

"I do that?"

"You should listen to yourself. You gonna go through life not stopping to shop because you don't see someone that looks just like you? That's ridiculous. I bet if you stop in that town and behave well, you'll get treated well."

"Behave well?" Sarah asked.

"Yes. I'd say it's those who act badly that get treated badly. And then, assholes that act badly expect society to treat them better *because* they act badly. It pisses me off."

"Calm down—"

"Calm down! You ask if my people had slaves. Sure they did. Now does that mean *I* have to treat black people badly? Hell no! I'm just glad I wasn't born during those generations when my ancestors felt they legitimately had the right to possess another human being. You can write it down. There is no part of slavery that I condone. Not now. Not in the past. Not ever. Period."

128

"Elijah, I believe you. Now, could you please calm down?" Sarah urged while slowly progressing into the circle driveway and stopping in front of a three step landing. My adrenaline peaked about the time large double doors opened and out popped an elderly black, grey bearded man, cloaked in all white with black buttons down the front. He wore a head covering that hung past his collar. The man looked native African. "Just stay calm," she repeated.

I whispered loudly, "No wonder you wanna kill 'em. They've got black servants."

"Shut up."

"So are you a spook?"

Sarah squinted and said, "Yes, dear, I am. And if you repeat that, I'll have to kill you. These people only know me as a Homeland agent, and you best not screw that up."

"Jesus," I mumbled as the old man opened Sarah's door.

"Good morning, Miss Sarah."

"Good morning, Charles."

I sat first contemplating the idea that I had no idea what I was getting into, and secondly that I would have to open my own door. Stepping out, I squinted at the sun while putting my sunglasses back on. Sarah passed me without a word, her purse hooked over her arm. As she walked up the steps, the old guy passed me, observing nonchalantly through the corners of his eyes. I stepped in line. At the entrance, I stopped to scan the property, and then noticed that the old man stood holding the door.

"Thank you," I nodded on my way in.

The great room had stairs on both sides that led up to the landing of the second floor.

Sarah said, "I'm going up to change." When I followed her onto the steps, she glanced back, saying, "You may wait down here."

Ignoring her comment, I followed to the top.

"Really?" she sassed as I caught up.

Reaching the second floor landing, I began scanning the ground floor from a better perspective, and then the second floor. Between the two stair landings, separating a pair of bedrooms on either side, three huge windows provided a view of the glassed-in four season swimming pool below. *Wasn't glassed-in back in the day.*

The roof system for the pool area consisted of several large glass panels, each currently mechanically opened into a forty-five degree position. Slightly downhill from the pool sat the fancy horse barn. Beyond that, a wooded area separated the Proctor Estate from the back of the Burton farm. I thought, *Wow. Sure looks different from this side of the woods.*

A door to the right opened and out came one James Davis Proctor, black hair slicked back, wearing a robe tied around his waist and carrying a small calico cat. Man looked just like his photo. Sarah said, "Hello James," and then turned to me, pretending to be upset. "No matter what, you're not following me into my room."

When she stormed in and shut the door, Proctor said, "She's high-strung," while holding his hand out for a shake. "I'm James Proctor, and you must be Mr. Jones."

Guy sounded gay to me. I raised my elbow to him and said, "Yes, sir. Good to meet you Mr. Proctor."

"Shelly's a clean cat. You afraid of germs?"

I nodded.

He said, "Oh my," while lowering his hand. "And you're supposed to protect Sarah?"

"That is my assignment, sir."

"Well. You can call me Jimmy."

I nodded again, thinking, *She calls you James and I'm supposed to call you Jimmy.*

"Would you like a drink?" he asked.

"Coffee would be fine."

"Cream and," he asked and then whispered, "sugar?"

Jesus. "I like my coffee black."

"Charles!" he spoke over the balcony. "Fetch Mr. Jones a cup of coffee! And make it *black!*"

Turning to me he asked, "Mister Jones, do you prefer your women like your coffee?"

I decided to mess with him. "Don't prefer women."

"Oh ... dear. Well then," he mumbled while starting down the stairs. Speaking loudly he said, "Sarah darling, I'll be by the pool!"

And I'm supposed to kill this guy?

I heard what I assumed was Jimmy closing the door on his way out. Two seconds later, Charles started up the stairs with my steamy cup of coffee.

"Thank you, sir," I said when he handed me the cup. Charles stood as if waiting for my comment on his java. After a sip, I said, "Excellent."

"Thank you, Mister?"

Oh, I get it. This where I am supposed to give up my personal information. "I'm sorry, sir. It seems we were not properly introduced. People call me, Jones."

"Just Jones, sir? No first name?"

"Just, Jones."

"Then Mr. Jones it will be." Apparently satisfied, Charles turned away.

By the time Sarah came out of the bedroom, I had finished my coffee. Wearing a robe as did her fiancé; she stood for a moment, and then asked, "What are *you* looking at?" When I didn't reply, she turned to the stairs and I followed her silent descent. Sarah knew her way through the dining area to the foyer that leads to the pool. When she opened the exterior door, Shelly the cat dashed in and across the floor. Sarah began ranting, for her fiancé to hear, I'd say. "I'm not in danger here. You can give me a little room, please."

Jimmy looked up from his phone. Turning to close the door, I heard a noise. Charles stood on the other side of the dining area in the doorway to the kitchen, steeling his knife and observing. *Better watch that old man.* I lowered my glasses to make eye contact before closing the door.

When Sarah sat down at the table with Jimmy, I strolled around to opposite side of the pool and leaned against the fancy four-foot tall, white aluminum rail that separated the pool from the glass enclosure. A sense of approval floated my way. Sarah and Jimmy kept their voices low enough to prevent me from hearing their conversation. I stood for over fifteen minutes waiting for them to swim. I wanted to see James's neck, and I wanted to see Sarah in a bathing suit. Behind me, outside the glass, the ground sloped to a narrow blacktop drive. Beyond that, the horse barn sat attached to more four board fencing. No horses were visible, but I did hear one blow from the barn.

Finally, Jimmy stood up facing me, removed his robe, and dived into the pool. He swam a few yards and then looked back.

"Come on in," he pleaded.

When Sarah stood and began loosening the tie around her waist, I could hardly wait. Then came a slight let down. She wore a one piece bathing suit. One like I would expect from my grandmother's generation. Honestly though, she still looked stunning. Her shapely legs were a mile long. She made a point to look my way before diving into the pool like a champion swimmer. *Hmm. Bet the government put your ass through a lot of training. Bet you can fight like a man. Bet there's a lot I should know about you. Bet there's a lot I don't wanna know about you.*

Without coming up for air, Sarah swam the full length of the pool, passing Jimmy half way. She stood at the other end wiping water from her face as he joined her. I turned and continued inching along the railing, checking things out.

Jimmy raised his voice, "Mr. Jones, you have an interest in my barn?"

Your barn?

Sarah said, "He's like, the horse whisperer."

"You know thoroughbreds?"

"Show horses," I replied.

"Saddlebreds and Standardbreds?" he asked.

"Yes."

Moving on down the rail, I tried to get a glimpse of James's neck, but could not. Thinking back to the last time I hung out with a girl in a pool, it seemed odd that with Sarah and James there was no kissing, no hugging. They weren't even touching. James's glances suggested he found it uncomfortable, me watching. I turned and began checking out the stand of trees about 30 yards from the north side of the barn. A tall tulip poplar marked the spot where three of us had stood with our rifles, checking out the topless woman. Back then they had a different barn, smaller and less fancy.

The sound of Jimmy and Sarah splashing back toward the far end of the pool drew my attention. When they began walking up out of the water, I wondered if Sarah had gotten a glance at Jimmy's neck. As his first foot touched the deck, Charles magically appeared with two towels, a comb and a mirror. He handed Jimmy and Sarah each a towel and then assisted Jimmy with his robe. Then the old man held the mirror while his boss groomed every hair back into place.

Noticing my stare, Jimmy raised his voice. "Might as well join us for lunch. Charles will serve pea salad with crackers, followed by a grilled turkey BLT. And merlot of course."

While vigorously drying her hair with a towel, Sarah said, "I'm sure Mr. Jones would enjoy lunch, however, he prefers surveillance from a distance, and *no* wine. Isn't that right, Mr. Jones?"

I nodded my reply.

Five minutes later, Charles served salad to the charming couple and then to me. I had taken a seat at another table. He asked, "And what non-alcoholic drink would Mr. Jones prefer?"

Not trusting the little man, I said, "A bottle of water. Unopened, please."

My first ever grilled turkey BLT turned out to be fantastic. I picnicked alone at the opposite end of the pool, watching. Jimmy chattered away between bites, while his black widow spider fiancé contemplated consuming his ass on their wedding night. It became hard to tell if Sarah's giggles were real or fake. She finished off her third glass of merlot just as Charles arrived escorted by a medium sized white man in a suit. He looked fiftyish and reeked of Secret Service. His earbud lead me to believe he wasn't alone. Getting to my feet drew a stare. When I took a step in that direction, Sarah spoke loudly. "It's okay Jones. I need to go inside. Won't be long."

As she and Jimmy walked toward the door, I continued that way. The suit stepped between me and the woman whose back I was supposed to have. He stood with his legs apart, chest out, shoulders high. Instead of looking at the man, I watched Sarah disappear.

"Who are you?" the man asked.

"Believe you already know."

"She'll be okay."

"So you say. What if I stepped between you and the Senator?"

"You're assuming I'm with the Senator?"

After stepping backwards a few steps I said, "I'm assuming that my assignment is out of my sight and that if she's not back in ten minutes, I'm gonna go introduce myself to your partner."

"Now you're assuming I would let you go in."

"At this point I'm assuming we're on the same side. Ten minutes from now, if you don't allow me to go in, I'm gonna assume we're not."

The man grinned and said, "Relax. We're on the same side."

I took a seat facing the door at the table formerly being used by Sarah and Jimmy. Suit guy followed my lead, sitting across from me. "How long you been with Homeland?"

"Too long," was all I could think to say.

"Strange we've never met."

I picked up the wine bottle to read its label and said, "Strange doesn't even begin to describe following Miss Smith."

The man gave me a funny look. Seconds later, he said, "Agent Smith is an attractive young lady. Hope you're not inappropriately involved."

Agent. I called her Miss Smith and he noticed. "You sleeping with the Senator?"

The man leaned back and replied, "Kind of a wise guy, aren't you boy?"

"Nope. Just don't play. You ask a stupid question, I'll give it right back."

"Good enough."

I leaned into the chair, scanned the area and said. "Agent Smith talks like she might get married here."

"That's why we're here."

"Really?"

"They're in there talking details as we speak."

Sitting up straight, I asked, "Will you guys be doing the security?"

"Yes. Us and you and that big fellow who follows the Wellington boy."

"Boy?"

"I've known him since he was a kid. Still a boy to me."

"You knew Ambassador Wellington?"

"Yes. Knew him well."

"His wife?"

"Vaguely. She died when the boy was young. Tragic accident."

Yeah right. Accidents, assassinations. Why would anyone want to be in politics?

He asked, "Are you familiar with the Wellingtons?"

"No," I replied. "But I do recall the assassination." After an odd moment of silence, I said, "You guys do your thing on wedding day. I'll just blend in."

"Or vice versa."

"What's that mean?"

He frowned and said, "Means you do your thing and we'll blend in. That's what we do. We blend in."

"How do you blend in wearing that suit and earpiece?"

The man shook his head and said, "I'll introduce you to the team that's on that morning and then we'll leave you to your work."

Your work? Does he know what Sarah's planning?

As I sat trying to figure out what to say next, the door opened and Sarah stepped back out, alone.

Short meeting. When I stood, the suit rose also.

"Jones, I'm going up to get dressed," Sarah spoke without approaching. "Meet me at the car!"

As I started to walk away, the suit said, "See you around, Mr. Jones."

Chapter 13

Everything seemed to move fast at the Proctor Estate. We came, we ate, the senator came, we left. Somehow, Senator Proctor remained out of sight as I stepped through the house and toward the front entrance. Charles accompanied me to the door. I said, "Thanks for the lunch. It was excellent."

"You are welcome, Mr. Jones. Perhaps I will see you again."

I nodded and said, "I'd say there's a good chance of that."

A black SUV sat behind Sarah's Camry in the driveway. Leaning against the car, I lit a cigarette and took in the awesome view. *Hard to believe I grew up only a mile or so over the trees.* I'd seen the Proctor Estate often from the air, in my father's plane. It looked more impressive from the ground.

The house door opened again. Charles escorted Sarah down the steps. *Why didn't her fiancé walk her out?* I opened the door and she slid in. Charles said, "Please take good care of Miss Sarah."

"Will do, sir."

Sarah remained quiet as she started the car and drove up the driveway. When she glanced into the rear-view mirror, I asked, "Okay, what's the deal?"

"The deal is James's father came home but wouldn't come outside where you were because he doesn't know you."

"The Senator's that paranoid?"

"Apparently."

"Hope you told him I don't trust him either?"

"Don't be funny. I told him to check you out with Homeland."

"And how's that gonna work?"

"They'll acknowledge you."

"Really? They know about me?"

"When they call to inquire about you, the point of contact is David. He'll take care of it."

"Is he the only one at Homeland who knows about me?"

"Yes," Sarah said. "And we need to keep it that way."

"How about that creep I was just sitting with? And the CIA? Do they know who I am?"

"Like I said, Elijah, I told them to check you out. At this point, I'm hoping they haven't already. They at least acted like they didn't know who you are. But you can be sure that after today they'll be checking. Those guys are pretty thorough. As for the Agency, I can only hope they're not onto us."

"So you're actually trying to pull something off behind the backs of the CIA?"

Sarah took a deep breath and her cheeks puffed out like a balloon. When she finally exhaled, she said, "You ask too many questions."

As we drove back around the courthouse in Morganville, I spotted a small restaurant called BLUEGRASS DINER. "That's new. Bet they have good, country cooking. Wanna stop for coffee?"

"No thanks. I'm not going in there."

Looking back over my shoulder, I said, "Jane would like that place. She's all about country cooking."

Sarah focused forward. "We'll do the drive through at Mickey D's."

"Hard to believe the Senator doesn't know you work for the CIA?"

"If he did, I'd be in big trouble. And you need to quit using those acronyms. They'll draw attention to you and then to me."

"If you're with the ... the Agency, why are you working for Homeland? Why aren't you working overseas?"

"For starters, you need to understand that my work for the CIA is not official. I'm not a CIA officer. My work for them is entirely covert."

"We've already established that you're a spook."

"So you do understand what that means. The importance of secrecy. The threats to my wellbeing if you run your jaws."

I nodded.

She yelled. "You're the one who said 'no nodding' dammit! Say it, Eli! Tell me you understand the importance of keeping my positions private!"

Whoa. "Yes, ma'am. I do understand completely. Now you can settle down, please."

Sarah suddenly went silent. *Honeymoon's over. Girl just got serious.*

Sitting at a light, within eyesight of McDonald's, Sarah spoke calmly. "When Mom drew the correlation between the tattoos on those terrorists and the one on me, it worried me. If my father is indeed somehow related to a terrorist group, and the agency finds out, they'll tag me as a double agent."

"I thought we already covered that. Question is, *are* you a double agent?"

"No."

The light changed, Sarah accelerated, and I asked, "So they assign a spook to Homeland Security. That in itself seems suspicious."

"Not really. I wanted to stay stateside, close to Mom, and they were looking for a volunteer. The Agency had already been watching suspicious activities. Homeland is my cover."

"Why not the FBI? I thought the CIA only operated outside the United States."

"That's a rumor. We're here all the time. We monitor international issues inside the states."

"We have terrorists operating here?"

Pulling into the drive through line, Sarah said, "You have no idea. You want sugar in your coffee?"

"I'd like bourbon in my coffee."

"I hear you. Now listen. Before I roll my window down, I want to advise you again to not say anything that could be heard over the restaurant speaker. You need to be constantly conscious of the fact that there are cameras and microphones everywhere these days. If you keep mentioning the CIA and the FBI or even Homeland you'll get us both in trouble. Understand?"

"I understand."

"Good." She reached to run her fingers along my cheek and said, "I was impressed with your performance today."

This feels like a movie. "Sarah, am I like, the expendable operative? The guy you use and then eliminate?"

"I promised you excitement. Are we having fun yet?"

"You didn't answer my question."

"And today, I felt like you had my back."

"You're avoiding my question."

She grinned and said, "I pick my words carefully."

"You should be a politician."

"Hell no," she said while lowering her window. "They're all a bunch of liars."

I waited while she ordered two cups of coffee and then pulled forward, raising her window. "Speaking of liars, in the barn you said you would not lie to me. I'm thinking that was a lie?"

"In my line of business, sometimes you have to lie. Especially when bound up by a crazy person."

"You think I'm crazy?"

"When you tied me up, there were moments when I wasn't sure."

Sarah lowered the window, received our coffees and then pulled away. After several hot sips and too much silence I asked, "Do you really want me to kill your fiancé?"

"Wouldn't be wasting my time or yours if I didn't want him dead."

"Has your father ever even met the man he wants you to marry?"

"I would assume."

"Well, I wouldn't. The guy's gay for Christ's sake. Aren't Muslims adamantly opposed to homosexuality?"

"Maybe he's just a metrosexual."

"Yeah right. So has Jimmy-boy metro-sexed your sweet-ass yet?"

After some hesitation, Sarah said, "Believe we already eliminated that possibility in session one."

For the next mile or so we were both silent. I sipped my coffee while attempting to read Sarah's mind. Finally, I spoke. "I know it's a personal thing, but since you brought it up, I have to ask. How does someone who looks like you manage to remain a virgin? Are you like, a lesbian?"

"No, I'm not. I would've told you that. I've been through a lot. And my father put so much pressure on me as a child that I was afraid to touch a boy."

"Until last Friday."

"That's not funny. I never should have admitted that to you."

"But you did, and it arouses me. I close my eyes and picture the details of you touching me."

"Elijah, please don't tell me you masturbate while thinking of me. We can't get caught up in fantasies. Professional. Remember? We have a job to do. If you get attached or caught up in the details, it'll cause problems."

"They teach you that at the Agency?"

When she said nothing, I put on my sunglasses, leaned back into the seat, and said, "In answer to your question, no I haven't."

But you made love to your wife while thinking about her.

For the next several miles, I sat silent, considering how the old man may have abused Sarah. Was she really a virgin, or had she just never made love?

Are there those who somehow, emotionally consider themselves still a virgin after being raped?

"Thought you wanted to stay awake on the way home?" Sarah asked.

Straightening my slouch, I said, "Sorry. Did I doze off?"

"Don't know if you were asleep, but you were non-communicative."

"Damn. Who says non-communicative?"

"I do, and now that we're talking, I'd like to hear your thoughts on Islam."

It wasn't a subject that I really wanted to talk about. My grandmother always said to avoid politics and religion. At that moment, it appeared I had no choice. "My thoughts on Islam? Is this about to be a session?"

"Yes, please. I think you already know I struggle with faith."

"When it comes to religion, I might not be the one you wanna talk to."

"Why's that?"

"Didn't I already tell you? My beliefs are nontraditional. I have my own elucidation."

"Damn!" Sarah mocked. "Where does a country boy like you get a word like that?"

"You like that? Did I use it rightly?"

"Rightly? You go from elucidation to rightly. You are a mess, and yes, by the way, you did use it correctly." I felt myself grin as she continued. "So Preacher Haycraft, do you have an elucidation on Islam?"

"Maybe. I'm not sure. But why do you care what I think about your religion? It's your religion. You're in America. You can believe in anything you want, and to whatever level you want, providing it's not harmful."

"It's not so much that I care what you think as it is that I'm interested. Like me, you seem to live according to your own set of rules, to an extent. We abide by the laws of the land yet our instincts often lead us in a different direction. While I struggle, I do know what I think. What I believe. I just never get to discuss these things with another person."

"Wow," I replied. "Since you put it that way, let me say, religion is a funny thing. It's like, well, look at you and me. Though we both went to Christian schools, our beliefs are different. Our levels of faith are different."

"That's not a bad thing," Sarah replied.

"Agreed. As Americans, we have the God-given and Constitutional rights to believe any damn way we want, providing, as I said before, it's not harming someone else. Religious freedom and separation of church and state has allowed Americans to evolve religiously. We tend to tolerate and respect one another's faiths. Even Christians and Muslims get along in this country. At least for the time being."

"You fear the terrorists will change that?"

"They're already trying to. Sarah, my co-workers are practicing Muslims. They're good people. But I'm afraid they're gonna get hurt if these crazy terrorist groups from the Middle East and Africa don't stop killing people and cutting their heads off because they're not Muslims. If they keep doin' that stuff in the name of Allah, some crazy Americans might start taking it out on anyone who worships Allah."

Sarah's look ensured me that she truly had an interest in my thoughts. She asked, "How do we fix it?"

"We? I hope you say that in general, as in we humans. Because *we* as in you and *me* ain't gonna fix it. We're just gonna talk about it. I don't give a damn if those people overseas wanna keep living and worshiping like they did thousands of years ago. That's their business. But when they try to bring their old-fashioned beliefs and practices to America? When they try to force Sharia Law on American women, they're gonna be in for a rude awakening. American women fought long and hard for their rights."

"Why did American women have to fight for their rights if it was their Constitutional Right?"

"Good point. You have to remember that early settlers in this country were from Europe, where at that time nearly every society, regardless of religion, thought men had some God-given right to dominate women. They treated their women like second class citizens. Just ask your mother if she, as a black woman, is willing to give up her Constitutional Rights because some man says she belongs to him."

"She would cut his throat in his sleep."

"Exactly, and she would have my blessings in doing so. Muslim or not, in this country, a woman has the exact same rights as do men. A wife has the same Constitutional rights as her husband. Americans will have mercy on women who resist religious slavery."

"Sounds like I need a good sharp knife."

As I sat there thinking, *bet she already has one*, Sarah left the interstate and began driving down a small country road. "Where we goin'?" I asked.

"Just looking for a place to stop." After a mile or so, she pulled off the road into a gravel parking lot. A small drab structure sat 40 feet away, guarded by two dusty pickup trucks and four Harley Davidson motorcycles. A hand-painted sign over the door read: PEAT'S POOL HALL.

After putting the car into park, Sarah stretched her arms wide and said, "Thank you for the session. I feel better now."

Chapter 14

Sessions with Sarah were strange yet interesting. I couldn't tell if she truly needed advice, or might be using the sessions as a way to learn more about me. One thing for sure, they ended well. As she fixed her lipstick, Sarah asked, "Does your wife think we're going to be staying overnight?"

"I told her that was a possibility."

"So we like have until sometime tomorrow to get you home."

Here we go!

I said, "Didn't you just tell me that we couldn't get carried away?"

"I'm not getting carried away. I was just thinking that since we had some time, we could make an outing of it. You know, go somewhere we wouldn't normally go. Become someone we've never been."

Hmm. "Someone we've never been? How does that work?"

"It's easy. In my line of work, it happens all the time."

"I bet it does."

"We could make a game of it. I'll let you decide one place to go, and then you can let me decide one place to go. Before we start, I'll show you how to become someone new." She used the lever next to the seat to release the car's trunk lid. "Sit still, I'll be right back."

Seconds later, the driver side back door opened. Sarah slid in a medium sized piece of luggage, and then climbed into the back seat.

"Now what?" I asked.

While unzipping the luggage, she said, "This is my disguise kit. I'm about to become someone else." She drew out a curly red wig, blue jeans, and a white button blouse with ruffles. "Honey, I'm about to become a country girl,"

After grinning at her fake twang, I said, "I like country."

"Good. Now you just keep a lookout while I change clothes."

As she started, I glanced back a couple times. Sarah never looked up and despite my adjustments, I could see very little while she squirmed out of her skirt and into the jeans. That changed however, when she twisted enough to face her back to me while pulling her blouse over her head. She turned to catch me looking.

"You're supposed to be keeping watch."

"I'm a multitasker," I replied while checking out the edge of her right breast.

"Multitasker?" she asked. "Is that even a word?"

"It is for me."

"Must you ogle?"

"Sorry. I don't get many opportunities to look at another woman's bare boobs."

"You've already had your hands on these, twice." Sarah slipped into the white blouse. As she buttoned up, she asked, "So you're not one of those married guys who run off to the strip joint to see other women?"

"Nope. Don't see the point of teasing myself. If I look, it makes me wanna touch."

"You just looked at me," Sarah stated while adjusting the wig. Did it make you want to touch?"

"Yes."

"Ouch. So the married man's not so loyal after all."

"I have discipline. Nothing says I have to act upon my desires."

"You desire me?"

"You said we were gonna pick a place to visit. You go first. What's your pick?"

Sarah stared into my eyes. "Elijah Haycraft, you are a rare bird." Glancing around, she said, "Perhaps we should go into Pete's Pool Hall. Do you like to play?"

"Play?"

Sarah smiled, and then said, "Pool, silly."

"I've been known to on occasion. Not all that good at it."

"Same here, but it might be fun to go in and experience the atmosphere. Pretend like we're a couple traveling and just wanted to stop and have a glass of sweet tea."

"Sweet tea? Sarah, this is a beer joint. They'll laugh at us."

"Who cares? I don't get intimidated easily, and you shouldn't either."

"You are one crazy girl."

Sarah stuck out her bottom lip and begged, "Pleeeeze. Shoot pool with me."

"Are you gonna turn me into a country boy?"

"You're already a cowboy. You just need a..." Sarah reached into her luggage and produced a green cap with a John Deere logo on it. She squeezed the bill into a good curve and then handed it to me. "With what you're already wearing, this should be sufficient."

"You want me to wear someone else's hat?"

"Don't worry, cowboy, I'm the only person who's worn it."

Outside the car, Sarah laughed when I smacked the cap into a dusty spot next to the parking lot. I said, "Country boys wear dirty hats." As we started across the parking lot, I slowed down to admire Sarah's stride.

"Stop staring."

"Hey, you started this. Right now I'm a country boy, and this is what we do."

"Honey, I believe this is what you always do."

Nearing the entrance to Pete's Pool Hall, I asked, "What exactly do you expect to get out of this little adventure?"

Reaching for the door, Sarah replied, "Excitement, sir. I promised you excitement. So far our day has been rather uneventful."

Hope this is not my test.

Sarah entered first. I followed to the sound of pool balls banging. There were three tables and to my satisfaction, none were vacant. They were being used by five burly looking dudes with beards and beers, and one wild ass looking, full figured woman. All eyes were on Sarah as she strutted across the room to the bar. It was as if I didn't exist, and I kind of wished I didn't when she ordered. "My partner and I will have sweet tea please."

The bartender grinned and said, "Well Sweetie, we don't have sweet tea here, but if you don't mind the wait, I'll drive into town and get you a real big glass of the sweetest tea I can find."

I stepped up and said, "She's driving, sir. Give 'er water. I'll have Jim Beam on the rocks."

The man glanced at her hands and then mine. "Ain't neither one of you wearin' no ring. Reckon that means you're not married."

I adjusted my cap and said, "Where I come from, bartenders don't meddle in other people's business. If you don't mind, she'll have water, and I'll have Jim Beam. And I believe now, I'd like that to be a double."

By then, the sounds of the games had ceased as five men and the one woman monitored our conversation. The bartender's face distorted and he growled, "Mister, I own this place and I say the lady can speak for herself. If you don't like that—"

"I'll have water, please," Sarah interrupted.

The man stared at her, then me, then ran her a glass of water. As he poured my drink, the wild ass women approached Sarah, patted her on the butt, and said, "Relax sweetie. Pete don't mean no harm."

Sarah turned and said, "Didn't figure he did."

"You and your boyfriend ain't from around here, are you?"

"No ma'am. We're just hanging out."

"My name's Darleen. I live a short piece down the road. Where y'all from?"

"Like I said, we're just hanging out."

"Ooooh. I gets it. Y'all's up to a little hanky-panky. He does look fine. And you, well that's a nice ass you got there. Y'all wouldn't wanna hook up for a little threesome would ya?"

I stepped past the ladies, with the water glass and my drink, just as Sarah said, "Probably not. You see, he's gay, and well, I'm not."

Sarah joined me at a booth near the door as the wild woman returned to the furthest pool table and began talking with two men. I said, "What was that all about?"

Shrugging her shoulders, Sarah said, "I figured you'd rather be a gay guy than to hook up with her."

"Thank you," I admitted. "Looks like the pool tables are all full."

"That's okay. I just wanted to come in and see what it's like."

"There ain't a black person in here. Sure you wanna hang out?"

"Probably not. But we can stay long enough for you to finish your drink." As she spoke, a burly looking dude accompanied by Darleen, headed our way.

I said, "Here comes excitement."

When the big guy reached our table, Sarah relaxed back into the booth. Darleen stood behind the guy. He tipped his hat to Sarah and then turned to me. "Mister, this ain't no gay bar. Recon it'd be best if you moved on."

"Ain't no gay bar," I mocked. "So what is it when your lady there makes a pass at my friend?"

"That there's different. She ain't no lesbian. She just likes a threesome now and then."

"Is that right. Well don't you two ever have a threesome with another man?"

"Hell no! I ain't no homosexual."

"Truth be told, sir, neither am I. My friend just said that for fun. She knows better."

"Well I don't know that. And they's somethin' funny about your woman too. Darleen says she's wearin' a wig." Turning to Sarah, he said, "Spent a little time overseas myself. Ask me, she looks like one of them sand niggers. You from the Middle East, lady?"

When I stood up, Sarah said, "It's okay, Jones. I'll handle this." She slid out of the booth to address the man. "First of all, sir, I detect that you might have served in the military."

"I did."

Pete leaned over the bar listening and several other men moved our way as Sarah continued. "Then let me say thank you, sir, for your service. And might I remind you that American soldiers fight for the US Constitution and all it stands for. Therefore, how dare you criticize my heritage or my friend's sexuality? He really isn't gay, but if he was, I'll be damned if I'd stand here and let you down him for it. We were all born in America and we're all under the jurisdiction of the same Bill of Rights. That said, I'd appreciate you giving us the same respect we give you."

"Damn lady, you sure are a feisty one." Then looking at me he asked, "So what's your story? You a cop?"

I glanced at Sarah. She said, "Go ahead. Tell him."

"Mister, this lady here is about the most spoiled little bitch I've ever met. She goes where she wants and does pretty much what she wants. My job is to make sure she doesn't get into any trouble, and if she does, then I do what I have to do."

"What? You sayin' you're some kinda bodyguard?"

"I'm prefer escort, sir, unless it goes too far."

"Well no offense boy, but just what the hell you gonna do if I decide to show her a good time."

What are you gonna do?

Sarah stood grinning at the mess she'd created. Again, it felt like a test, so I gave it my best shot. "Mister, I'm not gonna do anything. Just came in here to have a drink, but that doesn't seem likely now. Hope you and your friends have a good rest of the day. You ready, Ruth?"

As Sarah turned, burly guy stepped in front of her saying, "Sweet boy ain't gonna do nothin' so how about me and you…"

I didn't know whether to reach for my 9mm or the silver spoon in my pocket. It had been handed down from my granddaddy to my daddy and then to me. Sarah seemed to be reading my mind. She shook her head. As the man reached for Sarah's arm, she leaned away and said, "No thank you." When he put his hand on her shoulder, she went off. Her hands were so quick it startled him and me as she hit him fast, left, right, left, right, about four or five times in only a few seconds. The room erupted into laughter as blood flowed from his nose. She kicked him between the legs and he was pretty much done, all bent over and in shock.

While Sarah used napkins from the table and hand sanitizer from her purse to clean up, I downed the rest of my drink, sat the glass down hard, and said, "I tried to warn you, sir."

No one said a word as we walked out. When the door shut behind us, Sarah began childishly spinning her way toward the car, dancing and singing, "That was sooo much fun!" She stopped short of the vehicle, spread her arms and closed her eyes.

"That wasn't a session. Just get your ass in the car before he comes out with a gun."

Chapter 15

We survived Pete's Pool Hall, Sarah's choice for entertainment. What I thought would end up being a test for me, didn't. Instead, I got to see the real Sarah Smith in action. Whooping up on a Harley guy seemed to be something she needed to do. Sarah's cockiness reminded me of Jane. *Man oh man.*

The red headed country girl version of Sarah caused a cloud of dust as she sped across the gravel parking lot. In the side mirror, I monitored biker dudes streaming out the pool hall door. "Glad those are pool sticks they're holdin' and not guns."

When she hit the blacktop, Sarah said, "I believe we should have smoked a cigarette before we got in the car."

"Is that your way of telling me you got off on beatin' up on some old drunk ass, war veteran?"

"He was drunk?" Sarah replied, while starting to pull off the wig.

"Leave it on." I said, "It's my turn to pick a stop."

"You like the red hair?"

"Yes."

"Does that mean you don't like my hair?"

"Didn't say that. I just happen to be enjoying the red haired girl."

"Oooow. That excites me. So, where does Mr. Jones want to go?"

"Instead of getting back on the highway, I'd like to continue on this road until we get to the Red River Gorge."

"Red River Gorge? Heard of it but never been there."

I said, "Just follow the signs. We'll take a little hike. There's a special place I'd like you to see."

"Special. I like special."

Twenty minutes later, Sarah parked near the hiking trail that leads uphill to the rock formation that has been named Natural Bridge. Still dressed country, we gazed at the long steep incline. Sarah said, "Didn't we just pass a chair lift?"

"I've gone up both ways. Rather not do the chairlift. Let's walk it, please?"

We met other hikers coming and going. About 2/3rds of the way up, Sarah stopped, looked around and said, "This better be good. These boots weren't made for walking."

"Sorry," I replied. "Didn't think about that. You wanna turn back?"

She grinned and said, "No. I want to see your special place."

I took a deep breath and asked, "Would you like me to carry you?"

Sarah gave me a childish look. "You would do that?"

"On my back, maybe. You know, piggy back."

She gave me a 'Darlene' pat on the butt, started walking and said, "That's sweet, but no thanks. I can do it."

We climbed another ten minutes before reaching the top. Sarah took in the area and then had to explain how softer rock substances had eroded away over thousands of years, leaving the natural bridge above. When we stepped up onto the wide surface of the bridge, Sarah turned full circle and said, "This is it, your special spot?"

"Oh no," I answered as other hikers passed us. "But we're almost there. Follow me."

A pathway led from the bridge, around the ridge towards the upper station of the chairlift. At a familiar turn, I hesitated to make sure we were alone. "Now let's go this way."

"You sure you know where you're going?" Sarah asked as I led her into the foliage. Thirty seconds later, an opening answered her question. We stepped out onto a flat rock ledge overlooking the forest. Our eyes were blessed with nothing but trees for as far as we could see. Sarah stood in a trance. "Oh my. This is awesome."

"Yes it is," I replied. "Have a seat."

I sat down first, on a spot that provided a natural foot rest. Sarah slowly lowered herself next to me. "I've seen forests in several countries. This is a gem. Nothing manmade. Not even a power line. It really is special, this place of yours."

I said, "Close your eyes and listen. Tell me what you hear."

"I hear the wind ... and a bird."

"A crow."

"And something sad," Sarah replied.

"You hear something sad?"

"No. I feel something sad. Something sad about this place. Why does this beautiful place make you sad? And why are you breathing funny?"

I am breathing fast. "After that long hike up here, aren't you a little out of breath?"

"No, I'm not. What happened here? Why did you want to come here?"

You've never talked about this. "On my 16th birthday, I came here with a girl. Kelly Francis."

"Hold on!" Sarah gave me a look. "Are you about to tell me how you lost your virginity?"

"No. I held her in my arms."

"That's all?"

"She was special. I had wanted her to be the one, and it should have happened that day."

"But it didn't? Why?"

"We ate lunch together, at the campground, with our parents. Afterwards, Kelly wanted to come up here. She and I had walked up here the year before. But on that day, she couldn't walk it, so we rode the chairlift."

"Why couldn't she walk?"

"She could walk, but not all the way up this hill. Kelly had leukemia. On the way up, she got sick. While she leaned over the handrail of the chairlift, throwing up, her wig fell off. When we reached the top, the park workers wanted to call for medical help, but she talked 'em out of it. She told 'em it was a daily experience. We came here, sat down just like you and I, and smoked a joint. It made her feel better."

"Good."

"She wanted me to have sex with her, but I couldn't. So, I just held her."

"Why couldn't you do it?"

"I was afraid I would catch her leukemia."

"You can't catch someone else's cancer."

Staring forward across the forest, I said, "I know that now. And to this day, I feel like I let her down. Kelly stretched out right here and laid her head in my lap. While I held her, she cried."

"What color was her wig?"

151

"Red."

Sarah removed her wig and tossed it over the ledge. "Eli, did we come here so you could do for me what you didn't do for her?"

"No. Hell no. That wasn't my intention. I see how you might think that. I'm sorry, I—"

"Stop!" Sarah said, while pointing the palm of her hand at me. Before I could comment, she scooted up against me and said, "Come here," while urging me down into her lap.

"Really?" I asked.

"Please, Eli. I want to hold you the way you held her." It seemed odd at first as I adjusted and put my head into Sarah's lap. She held and caressed me the way I had Kelly in that exact spot. In fourteen years, I had never allowed myself to grieve. In Sarah's arms, I cried. When I gripped her wrist, she asked, "How long did you hold Kelly?"

"A long time. Until the sunset."

While running her fingers through my hair, Sarah said, "Eli, you didn't let her down."

* * *

"Wake up, Eli. I want you to share the sunset."

I opened my eyes and realized that the sun had dropped behind the trees. Shades of red streaked the western sky. Sitting up, I said, "I must have fallen asleep."

"You did."

"Why didn't you wake me?"

"I was enjoying the view."

I rubbed my face and said, "Sorry about the crying."

"Don't be. You needed it." Holding up my cigarette pack, she asked, "Want one?"

"How did—"

"I looked to see if you might have a joint hidden in there."

"Why would you think that?"

Sarah tilted her head. "I've seen you smoke pot."

"Really. You know, I still don't like you spying on me."

"Get over it. We're all being spied on every day of our lives."

I stood up, stretched and inhaled the clean fresh mountain air while thinking, *Why was she looking for a joint?* "Were you wantin' to get high?"

"During your nap, I sat here thinking how beautiful it is and how nice it would be to get a buzz."

"You didn't tell me you get high."

"You didn't ask."

"You don't get tested?"

"I work covertly. Sometimes taking a hit or two helps maintain my cover."

"That's interesting. Well, hell. I can fix you up right now."

Sarah looked surprised. "No way! I checked you all over."

I pulled my one hitter and a small bud tied into the corner of a plastic baggie from the watch pocket in my jeans. "You didn't check here. It's not a lot, but it'll do the job."

She seemed shocked. "Why did you bring that with you?"

"In case we spent the night somewhere. Sometimes I need it to sleep."

As we sat enjoying the pot and the sunset, I took Sarah's hand and said, "I'm not sure why you did this for me, but I do want you to know that you've made my day. This has been *my* session."

She stared into my eyes for a moment and then asked, "You okay?"

Instead of answering, I spread my arms.

If I said my time with Sarah didn't excite me, tease me, I'd be lying. By the time we got back to her mother's farm, I could feel a physical need for Jane. Sarah stood at the garage entrance until I backed out. With my window down, she said, "I know you've had a day and you're tired. Please be careful. Text the Ruth phone when you get home so I don't worry."

She's getting attached and so are you. I drove away thinking, *It's okay.*

My drive home proved uneventful. It felt like one of those left brain right brain situations as I turned into our neighborhood and couldn't remember driving the expressway into Louisville. I had been on autopilot while thinking of the day's events and how I planned to spend the rest of the night in Jane's arms, providing that is, that she had made it home from her evening out. Pulling into the complex, I could see Jane's car parked crooked. *Jesus, Jane. Thought I told you not to drive after drinking.* There were no visible lights on, so I figured she would be asleep. "Damn!" Before going up, I texted Ruth.

When I opened the entry door of the condo it worried me that the alarm warning didn't go off. We always set the alarm before bed. After dropping my bag on the couch, I stepped into the kitchen and laid my gun and keys on a placemat on the table. Jane's shoes were in the middle of the floor. It had been a day, so I decided to reward myself with a drink. As I pulled a bottle of bourbon from the liquor cabinet, a noise drew my attention. It sounded like Jane, but it sounded intimate. *What the...?* Suddenly my chest tightened and my stomach ached. Three steps later, I found her dress in the hallway. Cupping a hand over my ear guaranteed it was Jane, and that she was making noises only I should hear. I nearly threw up.

Back stepping, I quietly returned to the kitchen to grab my gun. For a second, I thought about leaving, but the more I listened, the more enraged I became. I'm sure every married man considers what he would do in such an event. Inch by agonizing inch, I snuck down the hallway. Nearing the door to our room, I stopped and listened. It made me sick as her moans heightened in pitch. She hadn't even bothered to close the door. *Wasn't expecting me home tonight, were you?*

When I peeked in, what I saw rocked my world. Jane was alone. I stood there becoming aroused and thinking, *I didn't even know she had that.* As she finished, I quietly retreated to the kitchen, stepped back outside and then came in again, noisily as if just arriving. I tossed my keys onto the table to make more noise. As I began taking my shoes off, Jane walked in wearing nothing but a nightshirt. "You're home?"

"Just walked in."

"Wasn't expecting you tonight."

I straightened up in my chair and said, "Told you I would try to come home if I could. I didn't really wanna spend the night."

"Why not?" she asked quickly.

Oh my. Interrogation. "Really. Come on Jane. You know if it were you going out of town with a guy, I'd be concerned."

She stepped close, grinned, and said, "I bet you would." When I slid my hand up under her shirt to rub her bare bottom she backed up and said, "If I can't trust you away, I can't trust you here. Might as well get rid of your Romeo ass."

"Romeo?"

She gave me a look and said, "Romeo, Romeo, hast thou been behaving, or not?"

"Wow. Someone's been drinking."

"I'm not drunk," she replied.

"Why's your car parked crooked?"

"I don't know, but I'm not drunk."

Yeah right. "Did you guys have a good time?"

"We went to eat and then to a party."

"A party?" I asked.

"When I called Melinda, she said she was going to a party and I could come along."

"What kind of a party?"

"Some friend of hers was selling stuff."

"What kind of stuff?"

"You know. Women's stuff."

"Oh? Did you buy anything?"

"Nooo." Jane's eyes squinted as she noticed the bourbon bottle on the counter.

Chapter 16

When I began a covert relationship with Sarah, I suspected it would cause friction within my marriage, and it did. As September rolled around, Jane began to question every moment I spent away from home. In my mind, I compared her and Sarah. How they walked, talked, dressed, and even their fragrances. It wasn't something I did on purpose. It just happened as if by default. Both were beautiful women and in some ways similar, yet very different, and that became intriguing. But was it fair? Was it fair to Jane for me to be around a woman who possessed different, interesting characteristics?

On a Saturday night, Jane and I joined friends at GORDY'S, a local nightspot. With midnight drawing near, drunken karaoke filled the room. My mind analyzed how booze and karaoke were like bread and butter. Many wannabe singers require adult beverages before singing, and listeners often need alcohol to survive the awful sounds of those who probably should never sing outside the privacy of their own shower.

I'd been married to Jane long enough to know that while she loves to put 'em down, after a certain point, she simply needs to go home before she says or does something stupid. On that particular night, she drank one too many Long Island Teas and then felt the need to butcher a Katy Perry song on the karaoke stage. Midway through the song, while listening, I multitasked between an email on my phone from John and wondering if Sarah could sing. Suddenly Jane stopped her performance to call me out, loudly, through the microphone.

"What the hell? Are you texting her while I sing?"

It spoke volumes that Jane in her inebriated state would assume I had been communicating with Sarah. When I laid my phone down, Jane stumbled off the stage. Background music continued as she shuffled my way. The whole room watched when she began to shout. "How could you? Can't you forget about her while you're out with me?" When she snatched my phone, turned it over and saw that it was on John's email, her lips drew tight and I knew she was not happy with herself.

Rising from my chair, I said, "Come on. Let's go home."

In the car, I tried to address the issue. "Jane, I'm not mad that you called me out like that in front of everybody. Embarrassed a little, but not mad. What concerns me is that you automatically assumed I would be texting with her while you sang. Believe it or not, I was paying attention to every note you slurred."

"I wasn't slurring! You're an asshole."

"Don't be that way, Jane. I knew you couldn't handle that last drink."

"What I can't handle is this, this relationship you have with some mysteeeerious, beautiful woman. Someone who offers you lots of excitement!" If Jane could cry, she would have at that moment. I pulled into a gas station, put the car in park, and reached for her. She backed away, opening the door and stepping out. "You want excitement! I'll give you some excitement!" As she spoke, she lifted her blouse up over her head.

"Stop it Jane!" I shouted as she began unclasping her bra.

Too late.

"Come on baby!" she shouted with her boobs bouncing. "Let's get exciting!"

Before I could exit the car, I spotted a guy in a hoodie, using his phone to video. It infuriated me. Climbing out, I told Jane, "Get your ass in the car." When I stepped toward hoodie guy, he put the phone in his back pocket and asked, "What's your problem?"

"Problem is, that's my wife you just videoed."

"And?"

"And I'd appreciate you deletin' it right now."

"Mister, you need to tell your wife not to undress in public."

"She's drunk, sir. I'd prefer you don't put her through something embarrassing."

"Hell, she's got nice tits. Maybe I'll put 'em on Instagram. Let the world have a look."

I held up my index finger and said, "Shsssssh. I've got a secret for you. If I see that video on the internet, or anywhere else, I'll find you."

"And what are you gonna do?"

"I'll come to your house in the middle of the night. I'll drug you so you can't move, and then I'll butcher your sorry ass alive like a fish."

"Like hell you will. I'll—" When he stepped into me, I surprised him an uppercut to the chin. With his head high, I busted him low. His belt buckle cut my hand. He bent over, and I double fisted him in the back of his head. That put him face down on the pavement. I reached into his back pocket, removed his phone and stomped it. He looked up weakly. I said, "Sorry about the phone, but I did ask you nicely."

As we left the parking lot, the man struggled to his feet. He had his crushed phone in his hand. I drove while sucking blood from my hand.

That night ended with Jane hugging the commode.

The next morning, as we had coffee on the balcony, Jane said, "My head hurts." Then she asked, "What happened to your hand?"

"You don't remember?"

"Remember what?"

"I kicked a guy's ass for videoing you."

"Why would you do that?"

"Damn, Jane. You really don't remember? He said he was gonna post a video of your boobs on Instagram."

"My boobs! How could he do that?"

"Jesus." For a second, I felt like screaming. Instead, I took a deep breath, exhaled slowly and said, "You were dancing in a parking lot without your blouse or bra."

"You're lying. I wouldn't do that!"

"Never mind. I told you not to drink so much. Jane, I kicked a man's ass and stomped his phone because of you."

"Oh, my god." Jane lit a cigarette. "What else did I do?"

"You know you're the only doctor in the world who smokes cigarettes. It's gonna kill you."

"I smoke less than a pack a day. Most doctors die from stress. Not me. I'd rather take my chances with the cigarettes. Now, what else did I do last night?"

"You're so full of it. You're stressing right now."

Jane stood up and yelled, "I asked you a question!"

I almost laughed at her. "Do you remember calling me out during karaoke?"

"No. Yes. I think so. You were texting your, your whatever lady."

"I was not. I was reading an email John forwarded me about work while you made a fool of yourself on stage. I should have videoed you trying to roar like Katy Perry. It was pretty sad dear. Then you started screaming at me through the microphone."

"Ouch."

"I'm sure all our friends think I'm having an affair. Now, what the hell am I supposed to tell 'em? Honey, you can't blow my cover on this thing. You'll get me, or Sarah, or—"

"Sarah?"

"*Damn.*"

"Her name is Sarah?"

"Now you've got *me* acting careless."

"I don't like her name being Sarah." Jane sat back down, took a draw and then began smashing out her cigarette. "It sounds sexy."

"You're being ridiculous."

Jane huffed, "This whole thing is ridiculous."

"You know what. You don't trust me. Probably never will. I think you should get an attorney and divorce me now. Get it over with. Then, if I make a bunch of money on this thing, I won't have to share it."

"Oh, so now it's about the money. Not the woman."

"Are you kidding me? It was never about the woman."

Are you sure about that?

Jane stared for a moment, stood again and said, "I trust you, Eli. It's her I don't trust."

"That's a lie. You don't trust me. You said so just the other day. And how can you not trust her? You've never even met the woman."

"Exactly." As she stepped inside the apartment, Jane mumbled, "It's a woman thing. We sense stuff."

At work on Monday, I got slammed by John. "Tell me you're not hooking up with that black chick!"

"Why would you say that?"

"My cousin was at Gordy's Saturday night."

Here we go. "And?"

"She said Jane went off on you."

"She thinks I'm messing around, but I'm not."

"You're my friend, so I'm gonna believe you. But if you're getting some action, you best be filling me in on the details."

"Define action."

"See there. You are messing around. I just know it."

"Damn John, you sound like Jane." I threw him a fake smile and then started walking away. Glancing back, I said, "By the way, what you called an ice age is really a glacial period within an ice age. Google glacial periods of the last 450 thousand years. Check out the charts."

For several days, I heard nothing from Sarah. This seemed to please Jane, yet I knew that time was becoming a factor. Impatient, I texted the Ruth phone. **What's up?**

Five minutes later, her simple reply said volumes. **Shhhhhh!**

Great, I thought.

What's the deal? You miss her?

Maybe.

Are you falling in love?

I'm not falling in love.

So what do you call this infatuation you have for another woman? Remember last time?

Last time? Oh boy. I was 27. Had only been married a couple of years. Woke up every morning with a hard-on and an exhausted wife who spent more time on med school than me. During my Saturday midday run in the Jefferson Memorial Forest, I felt an immediate lust for a woman who turned out to be 15 years older than me. The whole universe must have come together to make that moment in time occur. Running at a seven minute mile pace, I used earbuds to listen to classic rock on my phone. When I drew near to the lake, there she stood on the bank, dressed more like a homeless hooker than a fisherman—plaid man's button-up shirt, a short black skirt, and red Converse shoes. But she was fishing. I swear she was. Her long dark hair danced in the wind as she bounced around on that bank excitedly reeling in a fish. From the arch on the rod, I decided she was either snagged or she had a good one hooked.

"You need help?" I asked on approach.

"Please!"

She backed up on the bank as I held the tight string and reached into the water to secure a good size catfish. "Thank you so much," she said, while looking me over.

A little out of breath from running, I said, "It's a nice fish. You plan on eating it?"

"No. But it's so big. I'd love to have my picture with it before letting it go. Problem is I left my phone in the car, way down there." She motioned toward a red Volvo some seventy-five yards away.

What woman leaves her phone in the car?

She asked, "Could you take a pic and then text it to me?"

She wants your number.

Or she wants me to have hers.

"No problem," I replied.

She wrapped line around her hand to hold the fish up while I took several shots from different angles. The ends of her fingers turned red as the weight of the fish tightened the line around them. Standing close, I allowed her to see each pic. She wore an unfamiliar fragrance.

"I prefer this one," she stated while leaning against my sweaty shoulder. Then she passed the fish to me. "Could you unhook it and put it back in the water for me?"

Her shadow covered me as I knelt to reach the water. After releasing it, I said, "Have a nice day Mr. Fish, and thank you for providing so much excitement for..." I glanced up to ask her name. The angle of view took my breath.

"I'm sorry," she said as though comfortable with my position on the ground, looking up. "My name is Margaret."

I sat on my heels glancing back and forth between the woman's blue eyes and her long shapely legs. It took me back to a moment in time when I was young:

  ....I was maybe five or six years old. Mother stood at the kitchen sink in her short summer robe. Sitting at the table, I somehow knocked over a toothpick holder. "Pick 'em up, now," she had ordered.

  I crawled around gathering the toothpicks and drew closer to her. At some point, I looked up and saw more of my mother than a son should see. When I made a comment, I had wound up with a bar of soap in my mouth....

"Are you okay?" the woman asked with a grin.

"I'm fine. You always wear a short skirt to fish?"

"I'm taking a break from work. Don't have time to change, but I do cover my blouse with this old shirt so I don't get dirty. Nothing relaxes me like the park, and fishing. Are you comfortable down there?"

"I, well, I was just noticing your legs. They're like, perfect. Do you run?"

"Thank you," she replied. "I don't run much, but I work out at the gym." Margaret glanced around and said, "You're not some kind of a pervert, are you?"

She even sounds like Mom. "No, ma'am," I replied while standing up. "It's just that you remind me of—*Don't say your mother, dumbass*—someone special."

She smiled and said, "That's sweet. But I told you my name is Margaret. If you keep calling me ma'am, I'll start feeling old."

"Sorry, Margaret."

"And you are?"

"Elijah."

"I like that name. It's biblical," she replied while picking up her fishing rod and a small tackle box. "Would you like to walk with me to my car?"

"Sure. Let me carry your stuff."

As we walked, Margaret said, "When the world I live and work in gets too crazy, I come here, among the trees, the water, the ducks, and find myself. The real me that was before chaos. Does that make sense to you?"

"Hell yes," I replied. "More than you can imagine. I grew up in the country. Like you, I come here to get away." I used the fishing rod to motion around the area. "All this takes me back home for a few minutes. It's like therapy."

We were nearing her vehicle. Margaret stopped walking and said, "For a moment back there, I was afraid you were going to put your fishy hands on my legs."

I shook my head. "No. Wouldn't do that. But it sounds like if I had some hand sanitizer, it might be okay?"

She stared at me and asked, "Are you married?"

Whoa. Straight forward. Don't lie. "Yes, I am."

She reached for the tackle box and said, "In that case, bad as I'd like to throw your young ass down in this grass and have my way, I think we best not."

I wondered, *Is this what John calls a Cougar?*

She opened the tackle box to retrieve her keys and her phone.

Noticing my stare, she opened the hatch on her Volvo SUV and said, "Yes, I lied." While placing her fishing stuff into the back, she added, "Don't worry about sending me the pic. You should delete them all. Wouldn't want your wife to see me or my number on your phone."

As she settled into her driver's seat, Margaret asked, "Does Elijah like to fish?"

"Yes. I used to quite often. Not a lot since I moved to the city."

"That sucks." She closed the door, started the engine, and lowered the window. "I'll be here same time next week."

We became friends.

Chapter 17

Sarah Smith and her mother wanted me to believe that Sarah's father had created a plot to infiltrate the American government. Was it true or could it be a big lie designed to get me to kill her fiancé, his friend, and the father she says arranged her marriage? Inheritance didn't make sense as a motive. She would soon be getting her mother's estate and at least a portion of daddy's eventually. You would think if these guys were truly terrorists, the government would have already captured and interrogated them. Amor Saline Al-Riase had paid a lot of money to conceive, financially support, and religiously influence Sarah's upbringing. And I'd say he spoiled the you-know-what out of her every summer throughout her youth. What girl doesn't want to spend summers traveling the world with her rich daddy? As the biological daughter of a Middle Eastern business man, all Sarah had to do was play the part. By speaking Arabic in transit, she could accompany her father into countries that few Americans are allowed to or would even feel safe to visit. The girl had it made until her father began implementing his long-term plans. When he scolded her for hugging a male friend, and then revealed that he had arranged her marriage, that must have become the line in the sand for Sarah—the moment when she became Super American Chick and privately said, "Hell no!"

Apparently, Al-Riase did not have an open relationship with Sarah in the United States. But that wouldn't keep her off the CIA's watch list. My guess is they were watching her from childhood. Between Sarah's travels, her education, and her fluent Arabic, it made perfect sense that she would be recruited by an agency. In my attempt to grasp the overall picture, I struggled with the idea that she would be trying to hide her deadly intentions from the Agencies. That alone would make her look like a double agent. There was something shitty about the whole situation, and I'd stepped right in it.

From the beginning, I found Sarah's ability to plan an execution of one, two, or even three men somewhat outrageous, yet interesting. It didn't appear that James Proctor had abused her. Being gay and spoiled didn't make him a bad person. My hope was to connect him to the terrorism angle. I began to consider that the answer might lie in the other guy, Timothy Wellington.

For over a week, I tried to find something, anything about Wellington, but could not. In late September, I decided to get a firsthand look at the man we already knew had the tattoo on his neck. Sarah had provided me with an address for the Wellington Estate. Using GPS to get there might leave a digital trail. Therefore, I decided to visit yet another random branch of the Public Library in order to print out directions. This time I disguised myself, parting my hair and putting on fake eyeglasses from the past Halloween. They were black, thick framed and had one lens cracked. Add worn dirty jeans, old tennis shoes, plus a dirty striped sweater from years ago, and I looked homeless. *Sarah would be impressed.*

The library bustled with an unusually large crowd for a Sunday morning. It took longer than expected for me to get a computer not logged out by its last user. Hanging out in the stacks drew attention from the librarian. Fortunately, the computer I wound up sitting at gave me a view of her desk. Without wasting time I did a search for Wellington's address in Covington, Virginia. Zooming in with satellite view revealed a colonial mansion and several out buildings. On the directions tab, I used the library location. Written details and a map appeared. While preparing to print, I noticed the librarian glancing back and forth between her computer screen and me.

She's monitoring. Don't print.

I used my phone to take a shot of the screen and then quickly searched Milankovitch Cycles. Several graphs came up. When I began printing, the Librarian stood and walked to the printer. She headed my way and handed me the copies. "I see your interests have evolved from Virginia to astronomy, sir?"

Using my best hick accent, I said, "Excuse me?"

"I noticed you were researching Virginia. Thought you might need some help. But you seem to have moved on to the environment."

"Do you monitor all your patrons?"

"Only those who hide in the stacks waiting for a computer someone forgot to log off from."

Ouch. "If I told you why I did that, you might call ICE."

"While it's not our policy to turn in undocumented individuals, we do monitor strange internet activity."

"Well, ma'am, I actually came to research climate change. We all do need to understand the environment."

"Yes we do," she replied.

"But while I'm here, figured I might as well check out Virginia. When I lost my job, my wife and child went there to live in the hills with a friend. Thought I might be a good daddy and go visit."

When I logged off and stood up, the librarian said, "Sir, your accent doesn't seem foreign. Why would you be afraid of ICE?"

"I'm not an illegal, ma'am. My wife is. I can't bear the idea of losing her or my daughter."

"I see. In that case, please do visit them. But if she is your wife, why would she be afraid of being deported?"

"She was smuggled into the country, escaped, and then we met."

"Was she here over a year before you married?"

"Yes." I replied.

"It's complicated, but I'd say considering her circumstances she can still get citizenship without being deported. Especially if she has a child that is a citizen. You need to see and attorney."

"Thanks," I said while stepping away. "I'll consider that."

The woman watched me to the door. Exiting, I turned to observe her logging onto the computer I had been at. One thing for sure, I wouldn't be going back to that library branch.

At work, I had begun wearing a ball cap with my hair tucked up under it. As we stood in the parking lot on a Monday after work, sharing a buzz, I removed the cap. John asked, "When you gonna get a haircut?"

"Not sure," I replied. "Jane says she likes it."

"So why do you hide it under the cap?"

"It's at that length that looks sloppy right now. Maybe when it's longer I'll get rid of the cap."

"And the beard?"

I stared at John and said, "Thought we were friends."

"We are."

"Then why you worrying about my hair?"

"Truth is I'm worried about you."

"Don't worry about me pal. I'm fine. Does me good to get away from this place. Gonna take off again this Friday."

"You're gonna get fired, Elijah, if you keep missing."

"No I won't. Got a ton of sick days built up."

"Yeah, but you're not sick."

"I turned in FMLA papers. Told 'em I have a terminally ill sister who lives out of state, and I need time off now and then to help care for her."

John shook his head. "And they bought that?"

"They had no choice. A doctor signed it."

"You're committing fraud with a federal agency. You could do time."

"I'm not taking any money. They're paying me with my sick days. I'd say they're glad I'm using 'em up."

"But you're only taking off on Fridays."

"Told 'em I have to travel and it gives me a long weekend. Plus, I explained that it'll all be over soon."

"You worry me dude. This whole thing you're into is changing you."

"I haven't changed. I've broadened my horizons."

"When you gonna tell me what it is you're into?"

"When it's over. Maybe."

"Does it have to do with environmental issues?"

"Why would you ask that?"

"Just a guess since you suddenly became interested in climate after you started hanging out with the woman."

Good question. Why is she teaching me about climate?

After work that day, I stopped by a rental facility next to the airport. It would make no sense to drive my own vehicle to Virginia—might break down, might be recognized at a later date.

"Can I help you?" the lady at the counter asked.

"Yes. I'm going out of town on business this Friday. Don't trust my truck. I'll need something reliable for a week."

"Well, mister," she replied, "you came to the right place. Once you decide what vehicle you want, all we'll need is your driver's license and a credit card."

"I have a card, but my wife doesn't like me to use it. She'd prefer I pay cash."

"While we do accept cash, we'll still need the card for collateral. As long as you return the vehicle on time, undamaged, nothing will show up on your account."

"That'll work."

Not knowing exactly where I might wind up in Virginia, I wanted a 4-wheel drive SUV. I left the rental facility with a receipt for $212.50 cash in advance for one week's rental and insurance. The vehicle I wanted would be ready on Thursday.

Before I could get home, Jane called me from work. "What's up?" I asked.

"I'll be on supper break in thirty minutes. Can you pick me up a grilled chicken sandwich and a diet?"

"Sure. See you in a few."

Jane and I sat at a concrete table in a small park next to the Hospital. She liked eating there so she could smoke afterwards. Opening the bag, she looked up. "You're not eating?"

"No."

"Why not? Did you already eat?"

"No, dear. I had chicken for lunch. I'll pick up something else later."

"So what are you in the mood for?"

"Honey, I'm in the mood for a few minutes with you. Just eat please so we can talk."

She took a bite and spoke with her mouth full. "You have something you need to talk about?"

I laughed, thinking, *She's the one who asked me to stop by.*

"What? What are you thinking?"

Grinning, I said, "I'm thinking how much I love you."

"Liar."

As Jane finished her sandwich, I took in the area and found it amusing that a hospital patient had crossed the street with an IV stand on wheels in order to smoke. When Jane pulled out hers, I said, "Give me one, please."

She handed me a cigarette and offered a light. After lighting hers, she said, "You're smoking. Now I know there's something on your mind. Spit it out, Eli."

"There is something I need to tell you." I explained about renting the vehicle and my Friday travel plans.

She got upset. "Another Friday? I don't like you running off all the time."

"I'm not running off. I'm going to do some research."

"Where exactly are you going?"

"Somewhere in Virginia."

"Is she going with you?"

"No. I'm going alone."

"Oh, so now I have to worry about you being out there alone—"

Jesus, there is no winning with this woman.

"—and who knows what you're researching. Eli, I'm not stupid."

"I didn't say you were stupid."

"I know you're into something illegal."

I glanced around at the people sitting at nearby tables. "Jane, stop talking so loud. I already told you who I'm working for."

She growled for several seconds. "I don't believe that. You're going to get killed or, or put in jail. Then I'll have to live alone. I don't want to live alone. I don't want you to be in jail. I don't want to marry someone else. I, I've been thinking about this and I—"

"Dammit Jane! Would you shut up, please? You have no idea what I'm doing."

"Then explain it to me. I'm a good listener." When I hesitated, she barked, "Eli, I'm waiting!"

"Jane, I love you, but we shouldn't be having this conversation here and now." I held up my phone and pointed at hers as if someone might be listening. She didn't seem to care.

"You're going to get caught. You're not good at this."

"You worry too much. We can talk about this when you get home—"

"I wanna talk about it now."

With no better alternative, I put out my cigarette, stood and walked away.

"Eli, don't you walk away from me!"

I crossed the street without even looking back. By the time I started my truck, she'd sent a text that read, **ASSHOLE!**

Chapter 18

Demetrius, the bartender at Bart's Bar and Fish House, prepared my second bourbon and coke as the waitress arrived with two plates of whole baked fish and fries. One for me and one for the woman seated three barstools to my right. She had arrived just after me and sat there drinking a martini while entertaining on her phone without so much as a glance my way.

Bart's is my favorite place to have fish and booze. I typically wind up there when I'm pissed at Jane. While I watched the waitress walk away, my attention strayed back to the woman at the bar and her preparations to eat fish with chopsticks.

Demetrius moved up and down the bar as he talked. "Been a while. You doin' okay?"

I glanced his way, scarfed down a french fry and said, "I'm good. How about you?"

"Okay. Ready for cool weather. Tired of fightin' the heat."

"Heat don't bother me," I replied.

"Yeah, well I'm guessin' it's guys like you that's heatin' up the planet."

Thinking about what Sarah had told me about ice ages, I said, "Demetrius, how long you reckon man's been on this planet?"

"Modern man, as in Homo sapiens?" he asked while stepping left to wash and dry glasses.

"Well, yes."

"I'd say a few hundred thousand years. What's your point?"

"When the dinosaurs were here, there was no ice on this planet. Therefore, I'd say it was a lot hotter before man came around." My comment seemed to grab Martini Mamma's attention. She took a break from her fish and stared.

Demetrius scratched his head and said, "Never thought of it that way."

My phone started quacking, Jane of course, and I decided not to answer. When it quit, Demetrius said, "Whiskey drinkin' man don't answer the phone, has to be his wife calling."

"You're a wise man, sir."

"Not so wise, just observant."

"Yeah, well, right now I'm observing this lady eatin' fish with chopsticks."

Demetrius, flipped his towel over his shoulder and asked, "You've never used chopsticks?"

"No, sir."

Seconds later, I had a set of chopsticks. Demetrius laughed at my clumsy attempt. The woman at the bar, dropped her phone into her purse, shouldered it, and then slid her plate and martini while moving to the stool next to me. "It's really quite simple," she said, "but you need to do it correctly from the start."

So, she has been paying attention. My attention suddenly went to her full figure, full lips, and beautiful eyes, in that order.

"May I," she asked while pulling my plate in front of her.

I guess so, since you already put your hands on it. "Sure."

First, she tore off the tail and dorsal fins with her fingers. Next, she demonstrated how to use the chopsticks to pick at and remove the meat from the left side of the fish. She had a system for pulling the skin and meat away from the bones. She then somehow pulled the entire backbone and most of the rib bones away and laid it on the plate. "Now," she said, "it'll be easier to eat."

"You're pretty good at that," I replied.

Demetrius, watching, said, "It's not hard to do if the fish is baked well."

Having shown me the proper way to hold the chopsticks, the woman went back to eating her own fish. I did my best to pick apart and eat some of the flaky flesh. While watching my efforts, she said, "I'm Brenda." When I didn't immediately reply, she said, "And you are?"

"Elijah," I answered while savoring my first decent bite. Turning, I said, "Demetrius? Give this lady another drink on me."

She said, "That's not necessary."

"Please," I replied. "It's my way of saying thank you for teaching me something."

Finishing off the drink she had, Miss Brenda said, "Perhaps you can teach me something in return."

What the hell? "Sorry, but I'm not much of a teacher."

Turning back to her fish, she said, "I'd say you just taught the bartender something about ice."

When Demetrius brought her drink, she looked my way, gave me a wink, and then focused on her phone.

While shaking out hot sauce onto my plate, I spoke to Demetrius. "Can you get me a live catfish? I'd like to cook it on the grill."

"Have some back there now?"

"Can't take it now. Got no place to keep it. I'll let you know a day or so in advance."

As some old dude sat down two stools to my left, Demetrius headed his way while speaking. "Elijah, you the only man I know who would buy a live fish to cook. Most wouldn't wanna deal with the guts."

"Cleaned a lot of fish when I was a kid."

Eventually, I gave up poking at the fish with my chopsticks and began eating it with the fork which had been wrapped in my napkin. I turned to see Brenda staring with a smirk. Showing her my fork, I said, "Turns out I just don't have the patience for chopsticks." She stared as if I should say more. "And I can't think of anything to teach you."

She said, "You could teach me how to clean a catfish."

"It's a nasty job."

"Oh, my." Looking into my eyes, she asked, "Is Elijah a nasty man?"

"Sorry, I didn't mean it that way."

"No need to be sorry. I happen to like nasty. So, let me ask, why didn't you want to talk to your wife?"

Nasty and nosey. I suddenly began to consider why this woman was sitting next to me in the first place. "Can't see how that would be any of your business."

She finished her drink and said, "Might be if I'm considering taking you home with me."

This time, I squinted, gave her an up and down scan, and said, "Lady, I'm flattered. Seriously, I am. But I'm afraid my wife wouldn't approve."

"What she doesn't know won't hurt her."

"Yeah, well I've heard that line before, and it wound up hurting my wife and me." Holding up my drink, I added, "Thanks, but no thanks."

Brenda waved down Demetrius and handed him a fifty dollar bill. "Whatever's left, you can split with the girl that brought my food, please."

He replied, "Will do. Thank you very much."

As Demetrius walked off, she turned my way and said, "You did teach me something."

"Really?"

"You taught me that you are a good husband. I like that."

She walked out, leaving me confused. When Demetrius returned, I asked, "You know that woman?"

"Never seen her before tonight."

"Why would she ask me to cheat on my wife and then compliment me for being a good husband when I turned her down?"

Demetrius shook his head and said, "I don't try to figure 'em out. Woman gives me a fifteen dollar tip, she can say anything she wants."

After spending four hours and too much money on fish, fries, chit chat, and bourbon, my loyal bartender, Demetrius, cut me off. "It's almost midnight. How about I call you a cab?"

"No, I'm good."

"Listen my friend, you got no business driving."

As I paid my tab, I said, "I'll take a nap in the truck. Then I'll be okay."

Demetrius shook his head. "Famous last words." I dropped twenty for a tip and shuffled toward the door. "Don't be a stranger, Elijah. Let me know when you need that fish."

Without looking back, I gave him a thumbs-up and said, "Thanks."

Outside, I stumbled a little stepping off the curb. Reaching the truck, I popped the hood, laid my keys and wallet on top of the engine breather, and then closed the hood. Inside the cab, I locked the doors and snuggled up against the driver side window. Before dozing off, I checked my phone in hopes that Jane had called or texted. She had not. I sat there a moment, wondering if my wife's rants were more about worries for my wellbeing and less about jealousy.

Some forty yards away, at the corner, a stoplight cycled from northbound to southbound and back every couple of minutes. Red. Green. Yellow. Red....

Around 2:30 in the morning, a fire truck siren and its air horn startled me awake. I had somehow slid down in the seat. When I rose up, a cop car waited at the light. I needed to pee really badly. The signal changed and the cruiser drove away. I popped the hood and got out as the fire engine noises faded. Other than distant traffic sounds, that particular part of the city had become eerily quiet. Across the street, a huge rat hugged storefronts in a hurry to go somewhere. I lit a cigarette and was just about to take a piss right there next to my truck, when two man-sized silhouettes appeared out of the shadows a half a block away. It seemed like a good time to leave.

Despite my nap, I got home still feeling woozy. A grinding sound filled the night as I somehow backed into the only parking spot left, a very narrow one next to the dumpster. Lights were still on in the condo. I slumped over the steering wheel, wishing for more sleep.

Gotta pee.

I'd already pulled myself out of the truck when I noticed my Ruth phone lying in the front seat. "Oh no! Did I use that?" Leaning against the truck, I opened the little phone and tried to focus on a small font text. **Call me**.

"Damn. It's too late now." As I put the burner away, the iPhone in my other pocket began quacking. "Damn!" When I pulled it out, the screen lit up with Jane's picture. Closing the truck door, I started walking while answering. "I'm on my way in, and I gotta pee."

Keys seem thicker and less cooperative when alcohol is involved. Jane opened the door for me and I stumbled in. "Look at you. You're drunk. What the hell were you thinking driving home like that?"

"Gotta pee," was my only reply as I made my way toward the bathroom. Jane followed. She pushed the door open, stared a few seconds, and then asked, "Who were you talking to on the phone down there?" When I turned to answer, pee went on the floor. "Dammit Eli, watch what the hell you're doing!"

Adjusting my aim, I asked, "Were you spying on me again?"

"Spying! I looked out when you hit the dumpster, asshole! And don't think for one second that I'm going to clean up your pee. Now, who were you talking to?"

Without answering, I finished pissing.

Jane growled. "I asked you a question."

"Hold on, dammit. You have no idea how long I waited for this."

"You shouldn't hold it so long. It's hard on your bladder."

"No shit. I was cramping."

When I had finished, she asked, "How many times you gonna shake that thing?"

"Jesus. Can't a man take a piss in peace?"

"You're done. Now, tell me who you were talking to."

I took a deep breath, exhaled, and said, "No one, Dear. I was reading a text. She wants me to call her."

Jane growled and said, "Probably wants to go with you to Virginia."

"She doesn't know I'm going."

"Really. And why would that be?"

"I need to go to bed."

"No you're not. I'm gonna go start the coffee. Bring your sorry ass in the kitchen so we can talk."

I'm gonna start coffee. Bring your sorry ass in. I mumbled, "Blah, blah, blah."

"Don't blah, blah me mister," Jane sassed as she walked away.

Moments later, the coffee maker hissed out a healing aroma, luring me to the kitchen. I'd barely slid into the chair when Jane started bitching. "What took you so long?"

"I cleaned up the floor. That alright with you?"

"Good. Now we have a lot to talk about."

"Like what?" I asked while Jane set me out a mug and filled it.

"Like, how come she doesn't know you're going to Virginia?"

"She wants me to do a dirty job, but I'm not stupid. Gonna check things out on my own."

"Dirty job? What the hell does that mean?"

"Did I say dirty?"

"I hate when you drink too much. You make a fool of yourself."

"At least I didn't show my tits to anyone."

"Don't you try to change the subject. Eli, I'm tired of being left out in the cold on this job, project thing of yours. You say you're gonna make a lot of money, but where is it?"

"Damn girl. Already gave you a grand. You spend it all?"

"No, I didn't spend it all. That's not what I'm talking about. I want to know what you have to do for all this money you say you're gonna get."

"I already told you it has to do with Homeland Security."

"In other words you're dealing with terrorism." She read my drunken silence. "You're gonna get yourself killed."

"I'm not the one."

"You're not the one what? Gonna get killed? You're not the one gonna get killed? Does that mean someone is?" Backing off, she asked, "Elijah James Haycraft, are you planning on killing someone?"

"Shhhhhh," I hissed. "Stop talking so loudly."

Jane pushed my shoulder. "Don't you play games with me. Are you or are you not planning to kill someone?"

You can't tell her that.

Instead of answering, I pulled myself up and said, "I'm through talking about this. Gotta go to bed."

"Don't you walk out on me, Eli." When I'd reached the hallway, she asked, "Where'd you go tonight? Were you with her?"

"No dear. I was just out having a drink."

I continued down the hall without looking back. She followed me and stood in the doorway watching as I emptied my pockets onto the dresser. When I kicked my shoes off and flopped across the bed she asked, "Eli, where's your gun?"

"What do you mean?"

"Where is your gun? It was on the dresser this morning."

"I don't know. Did you move it?"

She picked up a pillow and slammed me with it. "Look at me!"

I rolled over and said, "What?"

"I didn't move your gun. Where is it?"

"It's ... in the truck."

"In the truck. You're sure of that?"

"Yea I'm sure. I think. Under the seat."

"Did you lock the doors?"

"I usually do."

"Oh, my God."

"There you go again. I must be a holy guy. I make you pray a lot."

When she growled, I asked, "You coming to bed?"

"No. I'm awake now."

"Well, wake me up in a couple hours. Don't wanna be late for work."

"You'll still be drunk. You should probably stay home."

"Can't miss today if I'm taking off on Friday."

Jane growled again. She does that when she's not happy. She stood there so long I began to think she might be getting ready to clobber me. When she finally walked away, I could feel myself drifting off, until the outside door closed.

What the hell? Where's she going? "To my truck?" I mumbled aloud while rolling off the bed.

By the time I got up and made my way to the front window, the door of my truck was open. She had the back of the seat forward. "I said under the seat. Not behind it." *Damn, I thought, She stares out the window at me. I stare out at her.*

Jane put the seat back and crawled up into the truck. "Now she's snooping." I nearly dozed off watching. The dome light went off when she finally got out and closed the door.

My feet left the floor and I landed into the pillow just as Jane reentered the condo. When her silhouette darkened the entrance to the bedroom, I pretended to be asleep, moving only in my loud breathing. She set my gun on the dresser. My eyes, already heavy, closed and...

* * *

"Quack, quack! Quack, quack!" filled the room. I reached for the night stand but then realized my phone was on the dresser. "Ugh," I mumbled while being forced to rise. "Hello."

"Wake your dead ass up," Jane's voice demanded.

"Why you calling me?"

"You told me to wake you up."

"Where are you?"

"I'm on dayshift today, which you would have known if you'd answered your damn phone last night."

"I swear, you change shifts more than I change underwear."

"Oh well. It's just one day."

My head hurt as I tried to focus on the time. "Jane, it's only five-thirty. Where the hell are you?"

"I left early. Had to make a stop."

"Where?"

"I'm at the drugstore. That time of the month."

"Already? You sure of that?"

"No dammit. I haven't been cramping and bleeding for days. I'm sitting at the park smoking cigarettes and making out with my boyfriend."

"You should quit smoking." She hung up on me.

Chapter 19

It wasn't easy, but somehow I made it to work. I tried to call Sarah on the way in but she didn't answer. That afternoon John and I had lunch in the parking lot. The burner rang. When I pulled it out, John said, "What the hell is that?"

"Shhhhh," I said while opening it and answering. "Good afternoon."

"Sorry I couldn't answer your call this morning," Sarah replied. "I was talking to my mother."

"No problem. So, what's up?"

"Where are you?"

"I'm at work. Why?"

"You're at work and your IPhone is at your condo?"

"I forgot it this morning."

"I need you to carry your phone, Angel. Anyway, I got a date for the closing. Can you meet this evening at the office to discuss?"

"Should be able to," I said. "What time?"

"It'll be late before I'm free. How about nine o'clock again?"

"Works for me."

"Great. See you then. Gotta run."

She hung up before I could say goodbye. As I closed the phone, John started. "What in the hell are you doing with a flip phone?"

"It's a burner."

"You're talking to that black bitch."

I slid the phone into my pocket and said, "Look man, you can't keep calling her that."

"Why you gotta use a burner? You're up to no good. I can tell."

"Damn John. Quit hounding me about this. You're beginning to sound like Jane."

"I don't think you have a job. I think you're sleeping with this girl and using the job thing as an excuse."

Standing to go back to work, I said, "Listen to me. I'm not having sex with her. We're working together and if you breathe a word of this to anyone, I'll kick your ass. And I'm not kidding."

After lunch, all I could think of was Sarah and what John had said about her and me. No, I wasn't sleeping with her, but thinking about it sure made work go by. Before the shift ended, I'd already lusted myself into a frenzy. My groin ached for relief.

You need to take care of that before you go to this meeting tonight.

When Jane got home, I had already started dinner, and was on my second glass of merlot. "I smell garlic," she commented while dropping her purse onto the couch. "What's the special occasion?"

"You, baby," I replied in the act of wrapping my arms around her waist and giving her a kiss.

Pushing away, she said, "Jesus, Eli. After last night, I can't believe you're drinking again already."

Ignoring her comment, I said, "We're having baked pasta with meat sauce, and garlic bread."

"Are you trying to butter me up, Mr. Haycraft?"

"No Dear. Can't a man show his love? I know you didn't get much sleep last night. Figured I would surprise you." Opening the cabinet, I removed another wine glass and poured it half full. "Might as well join me."

Before I could hand it to her, she began sniffing the air. "Are you burning the bread?" When she bent over to open the broiler, I instinctively leaned into her sweet ass.

"Stop that!" she complained while bumping me backwards so hard that I spilled some of her wine. She used a glove to pull out the bread and then turned to see me on my hands and knees, wiping up the floor. Stepping close, she looked down and said, "You're not yourself, Eli. What's going on?"

Still on my knees, I began spider crawling my fingers up the inside of her leg. When I passed her knee, she said, "Already told you that's out of order. Why you so tore up?"

Damn. I stood, downed the rest of my wine, and said, "Never mind. You ready to eat?"

"Can I smoke a cigarette first?"

Taking a deep breath, I replied, "Go ahead. I'll put everything on the table."

As she stepped out onto the balcony, I rubbed myself and thought, *Should have taken care of that myself.*

Maybe you can talk her into a ... you know.

"Yeah. That'll happen."

When dinner ended, I washed pots and pans while Jane loaded the dishwasher. Afterwards, we spent an hour on the deck, sharing a blanket and finishing the bottle of merlot. Jane relaxed and began talking shop. "This guy comes to the ER in an ambulance, escorted by cops. He'd carjacked an old woman. He apparently threw her ass on the street and took off with a Beemer. They caught up with him down on Main Street and blocked him in. Asshole gets out shooting and one of the cops plugged him in his right quad. Whole time we were working on him, I was thinking how I'd like to finish him off."

"But you didn't, right?"

"Nooo. But I'll never forget his face."

"Let me guess. He came in wearing a hoodie."

"He did, and…"

Patiently, I waited until Jane's story ended before announcing, "I have to go out for a few minutes."

"This late?"

"Have to meet with you-know-who for an update."

"Update? What does that mean?"

"I'll know more about it after the meeting. She's always vague on the phone."

"When did you find out about this meeting?"

"During lunch. She called."

"And you're just now telling me." Jane got that *uh huh* look. "So that's why you were in such a mood when I came home."

"What's that supposed to mean?"

Jane stood up, glaring down at me. "You know what it means. You were all frisky when I came in. Is it because you're going to meet with her?"

"Are you kidding me?"

"Believe you want her and I just happen to be here."

Rising from the chair, I thought, *damn, is that right*, and then threw the blanket at her anyway. "I can't believe you just said that."

Jane shook her head slowly back and forth. "Swear to God, Eli, I catch you messing around with this woman…."

Sliding open the door, I looked back and said, "Do me a favor. Tomorrow at work, ask your coworkers how many would like to come home to a nice cooked meal and a horny husband. Then come back and tell me what they say."

Jane followed me in, growling. "Eli, hold on." She plopped down on the couch, and said, "Bring your sorry ass over here."

Really?

Told you not to underestimate her.

After freshening up in the bathroom, I joined Jane on the deck. She sat chewing her nails and smoking a cigarette. Stepping out with two cups of coffee, I said, "You look stressed."

She looked up and said, "Thought you had a meeting."

"She can wait."

"Who can wait?"

"You know who."

"I'm not sure I do. Who's Ruth?"

"Excuse me?"

"You heard me. Who the hell is Ruth?"

What the? I set the coffee cups down and asked, "Why do you ask?"

"You got a text," Jane snapped while holding up my flip phone. "Ruth wants to know where you are." I reached for the phone. Jane drew back. "I want to know who Ruth is."

Looking around I said, "Keep your voice down."

Jane whispered loudly, "Who the hell is Ruth?"

I bent over to her ear. "Sarah is Ruth when we communicate on the phone."

"Now you know I don't believe that!"

I took a seat. "You might as well. It's the truth, and that's all I'm gonna say."

"And she's just patiently waiting on you?"

"Apparently not too patiently. She texted. She knows I'm married. She'll just have to understand."

While handing me the phone, Jane asked, "You gonna tell her why you were late?"

"You want me to?"

Jane shook her head to say no.

When I left the building, Jane spoke to me over the balcony rail. "Tell Ruth I said hello."

I stopped, looked up, and quietly said, "I don't want her to know you know anything about her."

"Yeah right. She's a woman. She knows I know."

Before leaving the parking lot, I texted, **On my way!** Sarah gave no reply.

Minutes later, I arrived at the church parking lot. Two hooded characters, seated in the shadows behind Sarah's car, rose to their feet. Sarah sat at the wheel, window down, seemingly unaware of their presence. My headlights apparently blinded the hoodies as I pulled in next to the Camry. Covering their eyes, they moved on. I got out and watched them walk away before getting into Sarah's car. Once seated, I asked, "Did you know those two guys were sitting back there against the building?"

"One's a girl."

"Really?"

"I was here when they came along. They probably thought my car was empty. I've been monitoring them in my mirror. They're junkies. Dumb asses just shared a needle."

"Are we safe here?"

"We won't be here long." Sarah pitched an envelope into my lap. "This is from David."

Inside the envelope, I found five-thousand in used currency. "Nice. You said he would come up with something."

"David referred you. He wants information. It's protocol. I'd appreciate it if you subtract anything he gives you from what my mother owes you in the end."

Up front money? This should make Jane happy. "Works for me."

As I slid the envelope into the inside pocket of my jacket, Sarah said, "You should know, the date has been set for the wedding. Saturday, October thirteenth."

"Damn, that's quick. At the Proctor Estate?"

"Yes."

"How many people are gonna be there?"

"Charles says James has a short guest list which includes Timothy Wellington since he's the best man. The Senator will invite a few, and of course my father will be there, but he probably won't bring any guests."

"Your mother?"

"No. I'll tell them she's too sick."

"Good. What about your friends? They gonna be there?"

Sarah sat silent for a moment. "I really don't have any friends."

Wow. This is a lonely woman. The whole thing seemed odd to me. "How we supposed to deal with these guys at a wedding? We just gonna invite 'em out to the barn for a chat and then kill 'em?"

"Look, Eli, I know what you're thinking. It's complicated, and there's no guarantee it'll work." When I didn't reply, she said, "I'm not happy about the plan, but it probably is our best chance to get them all together at one time."

The plan? Who's plan is it? "And what if the plan doesn't work?"

"If it doesn't, we'll decide on another day. But I do have an idea. What if I set up a rehearsal and dinner for that Friday evening? If my father gets here in time for that, we have them all three there for the night. No guests involved."

"What, if your father doesn't come that night?"

"Then maybe we take care of James and Timothy and I'll have to deal with my father later."

Suddenly, I felt sick. Like I'd gotten into something I couldn't pull off. "Open the window. I need a cigarette."

"No. You can't smoke in my car."

"Then I'm getting out."

Sarah said, "Eli!" as I pushed open the door and climbed out. By the time I lit a cigarette, she was coming around the front of the car. "What's your problem? Are you falling apart on me? I thought you said you could handle this?"

"You know you're pissin me off," I blew smoke at her. "You're supposed to be smarter than this." I looked around to make sure we were alone and then got close enough to whisper. "We kill them two and your father is alive, as soon as he finds out, I'm a dead man. He's got time and money and probably a whole army of thugs to come after me."

"So what are you saying, Eli? Are you dropping out on me after all we've been through?"

"Girl, we ain't been through shit. We've been hanging out like two teenagers trying to fall in love. I'm going through this crap thinking you've got some fail proof professional plan and now I find out you're, you're, you're probably not even calling the shots."

Whop! She slapped me. I grabbed her wrist, drew back my fist, clinching the cigarette, and damn near let her have it. Then I saw a tear. *What the hell?* I released her and took a step back. After one last draw of the cigarette, I dropped it, stepped on it and asked, "Why'd you do that?"

Sarah wiped away her tears. "Because, it got your attention when I smacked you at Del Junco's. I need you to focus. Believe it or not, this mess I'm in is very stressful. In a way, I'm sharing the stress with you and it makes things much easier. There's a side of you that I enjoy. I'm sorry if I've been using you like a teenager. It's something I've never experienced before. But now, you're confusing *us* with what we're doing. I warned you about that."

You let this get carried away. "Why are you crying?"

"Don't ask me that."

"Why not?"

"Because, if I answer, you'll have to smack *me*, and right now that's not what I need. Eli, you know I'm trying to pull off something few in my position would even attempt. All I want right now is for you to focus and tell me what it takes to fix this."

Jesus. In the movies these people always have their act together. I crossed my arms and thought for a few seconds. "Let's get back into the car."

When we were seated, I continued. "I'm saying it only works if your father is there that night. He has to die and anyone who is associated with him who knows I'm there will have to die. And then there's Charles, and whoever else comes for the rehearsal. A preacher, I'd guess. Are you willing to turn this thing into a friggin' massacre?"

"Yes, Eli, if that's what it takes, I'm willing. If it becomes necessary, I'll kill every one of them myself." The real Agent Smith seemed to be coming out. When I scratched my head, she said, "I'll do everything I can to make sure that my father is there for the rehearsal. If he doesn't show up, we scrap the whole thing. You can hang out and watch me get married. And you won't be involved in my next attempt."

"You would go through with the wedding?"

Sarah nodded. "If it happens, it'll be temporary until I can kill his ass. So, can you just let Jane know that you'll be away for that weekend, Friday, Saturday, and possibly Sunday, depending on how things work out?"

"I'll do that, but let's get one thing straight. I'm not spending a penny of this money from David until everything is over. If I decide to drop out, I'm giving him back his money. Don't want it hanging over me."

Sarah nodded. "Good thinking." While wiping her face, she said, "By the way, if you can get away on this coming Monday, James and I are flying out to see Timothy Wellington. You should go with us to reinforce the idea that you are my protector. It would give you a chance to meet Timothy and for him to meet you."

"Seems like a lot of trouble for something that might not happen."

With her right hand Sarah touched my cheek. "My father will be at that rehearsal."

The more I tried to talk myself out of the situation, the more she kept drawing me in.

If this all turns out to be a big lie, you may have to kill her.

If it turns out to be a lie, I may have to kill myself. "Covington, Virginia is only about a six hour drive. By the time we get processed through the airport, we could be halfway there if we drive."

"We fly private," Sarah replied. "James is a pilot. He has his own plane."

"Oh. That does sound interesting. Jane won't like it, but you can count me in."

"If she has reservations about you going, tell her that our time together will soon be over."

Damn.

You're getting too attached.

"Maybe," I spoke aloud.

"Maybe what?" Sarah asked.

"I'm sorry. Just talking to myself."

Sarah stared at me for a few seconds and then asked, "Eli, do you hear voices?"

For a moment, I faced the side window, considering. Turning back, I asked, "Do we have time for a session?"

She glanced around and said, "Not here. We could find another spot."

"Okay."

She started her engine and said, "You follow me."

Chapter 20

Country music played on the radio as I followed Sarah out of that small church parking lot. A minute later, we were passing barn after barn on the backside of the world famous Churchill Downs horse racing facility. I questioned my own judgment. *What have you gotten yourself into? Does this woman even know what she's doing?* It only took a few minutes to reach the 300 acre inner-city forest known as Iroquois Park.

Jane wouldn't like this.

Sarah led me to the far end of the woods before backing into a rather private, dark spot. I backed in next to her. It was very secluded. When I had gotten into the Camry, she asked, "This okay with you?"

Scanning the area, I replied, "It's private."

"Have you ever been here before?"

Instead of speaking, I nodded to say yes.

"With a girl?"

"You ask too many questions," I replied.

"You're the one who wanted a session."

"Not about this park. Can you lower my window?"

"How about this," she asked while opening the sunroof.

The sounds of crickets and distant traffic dropped in. "That's fine."

She asked, "Are we here to talk about the voices?"

Voices? "I talk to myself. Sometimes I get answers."

"So you do hear voices."

"No, not voices. Only one. I've decided that it's my conscience. She keeps me in line."

"You talk to your conscience?"

"Yes," I replied.

"Well, it's good to know you have one."

"Already told you I'm not psychotic. How about you? Does Sarah Smith have a conscience?"

"Yes. But it doesn't talk to me."

"Then how do you know you have one?"

Both of Sarah's eyebrows rose. "Good question. I've always thought of my conscience as a feeling that tells me not to do something, or that I'd already done something wrong. Never thought of it as a conversation."

"Years ago, my grandfather told me that when I had something to say and there was no one around to listen, I should say it to the North Star. I took his advice."

"You talk to a star?"

"It's symbolic. Like my conscience, the North Star is always there, day or night, in the same spot. When we talk, I just call her Star."

"You named your conscience Star. I like that."

Suddenly the night got interrupted by small engine sounds. I stopped talking as a passing trio of hoodie guys on noisy mopeds slowed down to check us out. Sarah watched until they disappeared and then turned to me. "You speak of your conscience as though it is female."

"Yes."

Reaching for my hand Sarah said, "Do you think I should name my conscience?"

"Why not? It works for me. If you know someone's name, aren't you more likely to listen when he or she speaks?"

"Interesting."

"Just pick a name."

She said, "Believe I'll have to think about that. I want it to be a special name." Looking around, she asked, "Is this session over?"

"Yes."

Sarah pushed me away and said, "We have a visitor."

A marked Metro Police cruiser slowly approached, stopping in front of the Camry. Its spotlight nearly blinded us as while scanning both our vehicles.

Sarah said, "Damn. He can't see my plates."

"And?"

"If he ran my plates, he probably wouldn't bother us."

A second cruiser showed up. Red and blue lights began to flash.

Now what?

Guess we'll see what she's made of.

Both officers exited their cruisers at the same time. One remained at the front of the Camry. The other approached Sarah's door. He carried a flashlight and had his second hand resting on a holstered handgun.

Sarah lowered her window and asked, "Is there a problem, Officer?"

"That's what I'm trying to figure out, ma'am. This vehicle matches the description of one that was involved in a robbery earlier this evening."

"Well I can assure you it wasn't my car."

"I'm gonna need to see your license and registration please." Leaning down to glance at me, he said, "Gonna need to see your ID, sir."

Sarah – apparently observing the officer's name tag – said, "Officer Braxton, my driver's license is in my wallet, in the console. Would you like me to get it?"

"Ma'am, is there a firearm in the console?"

"No, sir. It's inside my jacket."

Backing off, the officer's voice loudened. "Ma'am, keep both hands visible! I'm gonna need you to exit the car keeping both hands visible!" Leaning down again, he said, "You too, sir! Keep both hands visible while exiting the vehicle! Now!"

The second officer had his gun up.

"Is this necessary?" Sarah pleaded. "If only I could show you my ID."

"Ma'am, I said get out, and I mean now! Both of you out and step to the front of the vehicle."

Sarah and I opened the doors and climbed out. The second officer recognized me. "Elijah Haycraft, what the hell are you doing here?"

Oh hell. It's Lisa's husband. Now what? "Hey Bill, I can explain. Or maybe I should let her explain," I said, nodding toward Sarah.

Officer Braxton barked, "Ma'am, I need you to slowly open your jacket to show me the weapon!"

"Easy, Kevin," Bill spoke, "I know this guy. His wife and my wife went to college together."

"Is that right?" replied Braxton. "And he's out here fooling around."

"I'm not fooling around, sir. This is a business meeting."

"Sure it is."

Sarah said, "Officer Braxton, may I suggest you be careful with your comments until you see my ID. Anything you say can and will be used against you. Do *you* understand?"

The officers glanced at one another. Braxton asked, "Ma'am, are you a police officer?"

"Not exactly." As she spoke, Sarah opened her jacket, exposing her shoulder holster and her badge attached to her belt. The officers were no more surprised than me to see **HOMELAND SECURITY INVESTIGATIONS—SPECIAL AGENT**.

Well, now it's official.

Sarah continued, "Sir, I showed you this, not to gain a favor, but to let you know that I am on official business. You have my permission to retrieve my wallet from the console. However, you may not say my name out loud since I am undercover and this man does not need to know my real name. Do you understand what I am saying?"

"Damn Elijah," spoke Bill, "what the hell have you gotten yourself into?"

While we stood at the front of the car, still at gunpoint, the first officer retrieved Sarah's wallet from the console. He brought it to her and said, "ID please?"

Sarah opened the wallet. As Officer Braxton inspected her credentials, Bill stepped to the back of the car. "Nice ass!"

"What the hell?" the other officer mumbled.

Bill returned and said, "That's one hell of a license plate."

Braxton handed back Sarah's ID and said, "You two can relax. Why didn't you tell me this to start with?"

"Because," she replied, "as I stated I'm carrying out official business. And by the way...." She hesitated while reading Bill's name tag. "Officer Tibbs, you already said your wife knows this man's wife. For the record, may I respectfully remind you that if you breathe a word of this meeting, it may cost you your job?"

"I get it, ma'am," Bill answered in a smartass tone. Turning to me he grinned and said, "Damn, Elijah, you messin' with that?"

Before I could say a word, Sarah stepped toward Bill. "Excuse me. I believe you already know that a comment like that could get you in front of HR."

"Hell, lighten up lady. I've known this guy for a while. Just messin' with him. Sorry if I offended you."

Sarah said, "Apology accepted, but like I said, if your wife, Lisa, breaths a word of this meeting to Jane, I'll be sending out a couple suits to see you."

"You know my wife?"

"Five foot, six. Blonde. Cute as a button."

"How do you know that?"

I said, "She saw her at Starbucks, Bill."

"Oh. Well don't worry, ma'am. I don't tell my wife anything about my job."

Sarah nodded her approval. Officer Braxton reached to shake her hand. "Sorry Agent, ma'am, for the inconvenience, and I apologize for this asshole's mouth. You two go ahead with your meeting. We'll make sure no one disturbs you."

The two cruisers left in opposite directions. Though we couldn't see the vehicles, lights flashed through the woods. They were obviously blocking the road in both directions so we were not disturbed. I asked, "You think Bill's gonna keep our secret?"

"If he wants to keep his job he will. They'll tell their comrades about us, but they won't mention names."

"Hope you're right. Jane already has a problem with us meeting. She finds out we were in this park, she'll blow up."

Before we parted for the night, I asked Sarah, "Do you happen to know a lady name Brenda?"

"No last name?"

"No. Met her last night at Bart's Bar and Fish House. She came in right after me and sat three stools away, at the bar."

"Were there plenty other seats at the bar?"

"Yes there were. I kind of got the feeling she had followed me there."

"Describe her."

"Oh, I'd say five foot, nine. Full figure. Dark hair with streaks of blond. She had green eyes and long eyelashes."

"Damn. Elijah boy checked her out."

"She made me a little paranoid."

"Really. So, she just introduced herself to you?"

"Somewhat."

"Did she say what she wanted?"

"Among the chit chat, she said she wanted me to go home with her."

"Oh my. So how'd that turn out?"

"You already know. I didn't go."

"Good. But I'm glad you told me. I'll look into it. Meanwhile, it's good to pay attention to those around you. Don't be getting drunk in a bar and running your mouth. Hope you didn't talk about anything we talk about."

"No. I didn't"

You talked about climate.

Oops.

As I got out of Sarah's car, she said, "By the way, Eli, considering what happened with your parents, are you going to be okay with going up in a small plane?"

"That's been years. I'm all right."

"Good."

Sarah left in one direction while I took the other. Officer Braxton's flashing lights went out when I passed his cruiser. He followed me a block or two outside the park before turning. When I got home, Jane appeared to be asleep. I quietly crawled into the bed, kissed her on the shoulder and then dozed off thinking about Sarah's tears.

Chapter 21

A few hours later, I woke in a panic, fearing that I would spend the rest of my life in jail. It only took seconds to realize that the chaos had all been a dream. Details faded on my way to plug in the coffee pot. Back in the bedroom, I snuggled against Jane's warm fetal position, trying to continue the dream. After a nine minute snooze that seemed more like nine seconds, I went to the balcony to wake up with a cool breeze and a hot cup of coffee. While I watched a momma raccoon and her two little ones trot away from the dumpster, Jane surprised me, stepping out wrapped in a comforter and carrying her cigarettes. I asked, "You still on day work?"

"No. You don't listen. I told you it was a one day deal."

"So why you up?"

"Thought I'd spend a little time with my husband before he goes to work. It's not like we get much time together."

"You got that right."

Jane eyeballed me while lighting a cigarette. "Your meeting went kind of late."

That's why she's up. "Yes. Longer than I expected."

"So how was it?"

"Intense."

"Intense?" Jane sat staring at me, waiting. "What's that mean?"

"Our first choice of a meeting place was already occupied by a couple heroin addicts. Then our second choice got interrupted by the police."

"Police?"

"Yes, and one of them was Bill."

"Lisa's Bill?"

I could feel myself getting into trouble. "Yes, and whatever you do, don't mention it to Lisa."

"I won't."

"And if she mentions anything to you at all about my project, you tell me right away."

"You think Bill's gonna talk?"

"If he does, he'll lose his job."

"Why?"

"Because what we're working on is apparently a National Security issue. He knows better."

"Where were you when you saw Bill?"

"He first thought Sarah and I were having some kind of an affair."

Jane took a deep draw from her cigarette, the way she does when she's upset. She blew smoke at me and asked, "Why would Bill think such a thing? Where were you?"

"Why wouldn't he think that? I was with a strange woman and you weren't with me."

Jane mashed her cigarette into the ashtray. Rising, she said, "You said she's vague with you. Now you're doing the same thing with me. I asked you twice, where were you when you saw Bill?"

You have to lie.

I can't. "We were in the park."

"Park? What park?"

"Iroquois Park," I mumbled.

"What the hell, Eli? Are you kidding me? How could you—?"

"We were just sitting there talking."

"Of all the places. You should never go into that park. That's *my*.... Dammit!" Jane jerked the sliding door opened. "You were sitting there in a car in the dark. What were you doing?"

"I already told you. We were talking."

"Sure, and that's why Bill thought you were messing around on me. Because you were talking?"

"We were talking ... about Monday. I'm going out of town with her and her fiancé."

Jane's head tilted as she asked, "She has a fiancé? Why didn't you tell me that before?"

"You didn't ask. Didn't think it was important."

She squinted at me while sliding the door closed. "And you've already met him?"

"Yes." Jane's face twisted as she lit another cigarette. I said, "So now you're chain smoking."

"No, I'm not a chain smoker. I'm pissed. This guy, it doesn't bother him that you're spending time with his fiancé?"

"No. He knows it's a business relationship."

Jane appeared nervous, puffing, and asking, "Eli, I don't know how long I can take this. I mean, I trust you, but I don't."

"Well you don't have to worry much longer. It's just about over."

"About over? As in?"

"She says it'll be over in a couple of weeks"

"Really?" Jane looked more concerned than relieved.

"October thirteenth, fourteenth, and fifteenth."

"You'll be out of town all those days?"

"That's what she says."

Jane puffed hard and exhaled. "So you're going out of town tomorrow, and then Monday too? This is unfair, Eli. Where're you going on Monday? What's so important?"

"We're going to meet somebody."

"Oh. Another woman?"

"Noooo. It's a man. You're killing me."

Jane straddled me in my chair and spoke in a much more civilized tone. "So in two weeks when it's over, you get the money and then you and I can take a little vacation and spend some of it?"

"Sounds good to me. Can you get off from work?"

"I'll sure as hell try. How much money are we talking about, Eli?"

"Ah. I really can't say. The exact amount isn't concrete. It'll depend on how things turn out."

While nibbling on my neck, Jane said, "You're being vague again."

When I didn't answer, she straightened up and asked, "Are you staying over tomorrow night?"

"No."

"What about Monday? You know it's my only day off next week."

"She didn't say."

Slowly grinding on my lap, Jane whispered, "You know I'm broke as hell until I get out of residency. I was just wondering if I get to go out and spend more money."

"Best save some for the long weekend in October."

Jane's lips moved slowly from my neck to my earlobe. "Aww, I'm guessing she gave you a bunch of expense money."

And I'm not about to tell you how much.

After nibbling and then biting my ear, Jane asked, "Are you meeting John for breakfast?"

"No, not breakfast. But he said he'd pick me up a coffee this morning." *And we're gonna get a buzz.* "Why?"

"I just thought if you weren't like spending time with him, you could spend a little time with me."

"I thought you were, you know?"

"It's pretty much over. I showered before bed."

You sure are getting a lot of action from Jane since you met Sarah.

Weird, isn't it.

Competition?

You think?

Sliding my hand up under Jane's gown, I said, "Screw John."

"Me first," she replied.

When I entered the parking lot, John slammed his door. He had my coffee in his hand. "It'll be cold now," he snapped as I lowered my window.

"Sorry!"

"Sorry? That's the exact word I was thinking of to describe you this morning."

Feeling bad for leaving John hanging, I said, "Okay. Should have texted you."

"But you didn't, asshole."

"I was busy, man, with Jane."

"You expect me to believe that. This time of the morning?"

"Trust me, it surprised me too. But I sure as hell wasn't gonna turn her down."

"You white people kill me. You time everything out and still can't make a baby."

"It's not like that. We're not trying to make a baby. Not right now. I guess she was just in the mood. You know?"

John lit his joint and said, "Hit this."

I took a good draw and said, "So you're not mad at me for passing up coffee with you to get it on with Jane?"

"You had me worried, and yes you should have texted. But I'd be more worried if you passed up pussy."

At lunch that afternoon, John and I sat outside of work at picnic tables provided for smokers. Looking at the sky, he said, "Can't believe it's not raining."

"Give it a few minutes. It'll start."

John focused on me. "Doesn't it worry you that September is typically our driest month of the year, and this year we're setting record rainfalls?"

"No, not really. Don't worry about things I can't control."

"All this rain," John continued, "it's just another example of climate change."

"Dude, we're getting the leftovers from Hurricane Florence. It happens."

John tends to get quiet when I scold him about his obsession with the climate. Over soup from his thermos, and a sandwich, he asked, "Do you know the difference between a buddy and a friend?"

"The way they're spelled?"

"No dumbass, a buddy is someone you spend time with because you have to. School, job, church, etc. Might even hang out now and then."

"Sounds like a friend to me," I reasoned.

"But there's a difference. A friend gets his butt out of bed at one o'clock in the morning to come to your rescue. A buddy's gonna say, "Are you nuts? It's one o'clock in the morning!""

I sipped sweet tea while scanning the area for strangers, and replied, "I get it. So you wanna know if we're friends or buddies?"

"Exactly." John sat quietly as if waiting for my answer.

When his head tilted, I said, "Dude, I'd interrupt sex if you were in dire straits."

John held up his soda for a toast. When I bumped his cup with mine, he said, "Friends."

"Friends," I repeated while watching his eyes.

He really means it.

As we sat eating, I observed the sky and then our surroundings. John asked, "Are you becoming paranoid?"

"No. Why?"

"You're always looking around."

"Just being, you know, cautious."

"Cautious?" John questioned. "What do you need to be cautious of?"

Waiving my arm, I said, "There's a lot going on out there in this crazy world."

"Never seemed to bother you before." John crumbled his trash, shot it into the garbage can like shooting a basketball, and then lit a cigarette. "You've been this way since you met that girl. We need to talk?"

"Can't."

"Sure you can. Friends talk to friends about what's bothering them."

Was he building up to this? "Friends try not to involve friends in things that could get 'em hurt."

John shook his head and said, "And I'm not supposed to worry about what danger you might be in?"

"Worry if you wish," I said while rising. "I'll take your concern as a compliment."

Staring up at me, John said, "Look in the mirror, pal. Don't know what you're into, but with all that hair and beard, you're beginning to look like some kind of a terrorist."

I put my hand on his shoulder and said, "You don't have to worry about me. I'm one hundred percent American." John said nothing, but appeared to be eyeing one of the office blondes who had stepped out for a smoke. I asked, "What's with you and the white girl?" He stuck his fist up for a bump.

After work, I went home and then took an Uber to the rental place to pick up my shiny red, 4WD SUV. Before going home, I stopped at Walmart and bought a white GoPhone under a fictitious name.

Chapter 22

Taking off from work on Friday and Monday would create a potentially awesome long weekend. My travel bag had been prepared on Thursday night. When I picked it up from the bedroom floor, I noticed that the zipper wasn't closed as tightly as I'd left it. Jane had obviously been snooping. The bag contained pretty much the same items as on the day I spent with Sarah at the farm—nothing that needed to be hidden from my wife.

Leaving at 5:00 a.m. would prevent getting caught in the Friday morning rush hour traffic. After taking the garbage out and putting my bag into the SUV, I stepped back into the condo and heard the toilet running. Jane walked into the kitchen. I asked, "You up early again?"

She yawned. "Wanted to see you off." As her eyes focused, she stared at my disguise and said, "There's a stranger in my house."

"Like it?" I stood there in black slacks, black Converse shoes, a long sleeve plaid dress shirt and a solid black bowtie. My beard, though long, had been trimmed. I wore my hair in a ponytail under a wide brim straw hat. I also wore the black-framed fake eyeglasses.

"You look like some nerd attorney on his way to the Kentucky Derby. This Sarah woman is having an interesting effect on you."

Don't comment. No matter what you say, she'll make something out of it. "If you're going out to smoke, I'll stick around a few minutes. Have another cup of coffee."

"Ohhh, my man loves me."

I poured two cups while Jane grabbed a comforter. She slid the door open and we both went out. "Damn, it's cool," she complained. We settled into our chairs.

I replied, "At least it's not raining."

"What's the temperature?"

"My phone says sixty-five. Supposed to warm up into the mid-seventies." As Jane lit her cigarette, I said, "Let me have one of those."

She passed hers to me and lit another. "When did you start smoking again?"

"Lately, why?"

"Just wondering. Are you nervous about this trip today?"

Savoring my first draw, I said, "Not sure if it's nerves or being excited about doing something different."

"I still don't like this thing you're doing," She replied. "You're gonna get yourself killed."

"I'll be fine."

"Eli, look at me."

When Jane says look at me, it means she has something important to say. I faced her and said, "Yesss, dear."

The look on her face was so serious it almost made me laugh. She said, "I can't live without you."

"Oh yes you can."

"I don't *want* to live without you. No one else understands me like you do. If something happens to you, I want to die."

"Damn, Jane. Stop talking like that."

"I'm serious. I should go with you today?"

"Hell no."

"Why not? If you get into trouble, I can either help you or die with you."

"We've been through this. You're not supposed to know what I'm doing."

"But I do. I'm not stupid, Eli."

Hmmm.

Don't even think about it.

"You'd have to take off from work."

"So? I've only missed two days in almost three years. I could use a little excitement too, you know."

Damn.

Don't let her talk you into this.

Jane gave me her best sensual grin and said, "You say we don't get enough time together. It could be like a date. Just you and me, baby, driving to wherever. I can be ready in fifteen minutes."

You know she can't be with you. Sarah would have a fit.

Sarah doesn't even know I'm going.

Don't say I didn't warn you.

"Can you disguise yourself? Don't want anyone to recognize us."

Jane didn't give me a chance to change my mind. She put out her cigarette, stood, and said, "You stay here. I'll be right back."

When she slid the door closed behind her, I leaned back into my chair to finish my smoke and began thinking about how long it would take to drive to Virginia. Then it dawned on me, *Do I really wanna drive six hours each way when I'll be flying there on Monday with Sarah and James?*

A few minutes passed. As I checked my email, the door slid open and a stranger walked out. She said, "My bag's packed. You ready?"

"Wow!" was all I could say.

"Recognize me?"

"Only because you're my wife. I thought we agreed the wig never left the house."

"Honey, the wig is for fun. Today, I plan on having fun."

For a few seconds, I sat admiring my dark haired bombshell. She looked sharp and very much my mate for the day. Instead of contacts, she wore her designer eyeglasses. She had on a white dress with red lilies pasted all over it that she had bought a couple years ago for Oaks Day at the Downs. It struck her about eight inches above her knees. I enjoyed the way it zipped all the way up the front. Like me, she wore sneakers. She purposely left the zipper down enough to reveal most of her perfect cleavage.

She looks like a hooker in that wig and dress.

Or a cop disguised as a hooker.

"Well?" she asked.

"You resemble a high-priced hooker. I like it."

"I don't want to be a hooker."

"You don't have to be a hooker. Honey, today you can be whoever you wanna be."

You're going to regret saying that.

Before leaving, I placed my iPhone on the coffee table. I put the little burner phone Sarah provided onto my nightstand in the bedroom. Then I said to Jane, "Do me a favor. Leave your phone somewhere in the kitchen. Don't want Sarah to know where we are. With our phones and our vehicles here, she'll think we both stayed home today."

"Aren't you the smart one?" She grinned. "But what if we break down?"

I pulled out the white burner I'd bought at Walmart. "Bought this one yesterday."

As we left the parking lot, Jane shined like a kid going on vacation. I said, "Since I'm going to Virginia on Monday, how about we just take a nice drive in the country?"

Now you're talking.

"But I was looking forward to seeing the man you're going to be involved with."

"Honey, there's no guarantee that we'd even see him. What if we drive all the way up there and he's out of town? I only wanted to drive there without Sarah to check the guy out before things happen. If I'm gonna meet him on Monday, that may be enough."

"You know this disappoints me. I wanted to see something, anything, to do with your project. Can you show me where she lives?"

"Hell no. Actually, I'm not sure where she lives."

"Really. So where did she take you on the first day?"

"That was where her mother lives."

"You met her mother?"

Stop talking dumb ass.

"Yes. I'm not certain, but Sarah could be living there for now."

"You didn't tell me any of this."

"I'm not supposed to tell you anything."

Jane sat quietly for a few seconds and then asked, "So where are we going?"

"Not sure now."

"Take me where you went to meet her fiancé."

"No I can't."

"Please," she begged pitifully.

Don't even think about it.

"Well, maybe we could, you know, just ride by there. Let you see the place."

Jane said, "I'd like that."

"Okay then. We'll just ride through." Jane suddenly looked happy again. I asked, "Having fun yet?"

"Yes indeed." She grinned.

As I maneuvered thru traffic, Jane got acquainted with the radio, searched for country music and then lit a cigarette. I said, "You shouldn't be smoking in here."

While opening the sunroof, she said, "Now that we're on the road together, alone, is there anything else about this project of yours that you can tell me?"

"Nope."

"You know, I think the reason I am so anxious these days is because there's just so much you don't tell me. I don't like it when you keep things from me."

"You don't tell me everything. I don't tell you everything."

She blew smoke in my face. "What the hell's that supposed to mean?"

After lowering my window a couple inches to help suck out her smoke, I said, "That night you went to the party with Melinda. You said you didn't buy anything. Did you lie?"

"You've been snooping, haven't you?"

"No."

"Then how'd you know?"

"You didn't hear me come in that night. I heard you from the kitchen. To be honest, I about had a heart attack. Thought you were in there with a man."

"Oh, my god. You really don't trust me!"

Stopping at a red-light, I turned and asked, "If you came in and heard me in the bedroom making intimate noises, wouldn't you think the same thing?"

Jane remained silent for a moment. "Wasn't that noisy, was I?" When my eyes widened, she blew smoke out the window and without looking at me she asked, "Did you see me?"

The light changed. I could feel myself growing as I gave it the gas and merged onto the interstate. "See you what?"

Turning back to me, Jane snapped, "Are you gonna be an asshole about this?"

"It was interesting."

"Interesting! I guess it turned you on."

"You wanna know, do it when we're together?"

"It did turn you on, didn't it?" Jane sassed in a sexy tone while sliding her hand onto my right leg. I think it's turning you on just talking about it. Oh my. What have we here?"

I jerked and nearly left the road. "Stop it. You'll cause me to hit somebody."

Leaning against the passenger door, she smiled and said, "Bet you wouldn't tell Sarah to stop."

"What the hell, Jane?" I slowed down and pulled over in the emergency lane. "Why would you say such a thing?"

"Well, would you?"

"Would I what?"

"Would you tell Sarah to stop?"

"That's a stupid thing to say. How about we turn around and go back home?"

"No. I don't want to go home. I'm just playing, dear. It's the wig. I thought we were going to have fun."

Merging back into traffic, I said, "There is a difference between fun and frustration."

"Oh, but honey, I like seeing you frustrated." Leaning against the door, she pulled the zipper of her dress down further, revealing even more of her boobs. "I'm gonna try and keep you frustrated all, day, long."

"Well, you're doin' a good job of it so far."

Half a mile down the road, Jane lit a cigarette and said, "You still didn't answer my question."

Just after leaving the highway, I read the sign with my best country accent. "Welcome to Morganville, Kentucky."

Jane said, "Why are we getting off here?"

"This is the way to where we're going."

"Isn't this where you grew up?"

"Pretty close." Jane got quiet and I could feel her thinking. "Come on," I asked. "Don't go silent on me now. We're out to have fun. Remember?"

Looking out the door window, she said, "Don't know about you, but I'm starving."

"Me too," I replied. "There's a place here I'd like to try." Three quarters of the way around the town square, I parked on a side street near the corner, directly across from the Bluegrass Diner.

"Are we overdressed?" Jane asked as we got out of the SUV.

"Maybe."

"You go check it out while I smoke a cigarette. If you don't come back out by the time I finish, I'll come in."

"Sounds good," I replied while locking the vehicle.

During my short trek across the street, Jane wolf whistled. "My man's still got that walk!" I shook my head and continued.

Inside, the place bustled. It wasn't fancy and we probably were overdressed, but I didn't care. All but two tables in the back were occupied. To my good fortune, as I stood there scanning, an elderly couple rose vacating a table next to the window. I took a seat and waited for someone to clean things up. While doing so, I monitored Jane across the street. She stood there all sexy looking in her short dress, purse hanging on her shoulder, smoking. A busboy broke my trance. "Got a couple clean tables in the back."

"Saw that, sir," I replied, "but being partial to the window, I hoped my wife and I might keep this table." As I spoke, I handed the young man a ten dollar bill.

He smiled and said, "No problem." Then he glanced around the room. "Your wife, sir?"

I pointed out the window and said, "That fine looking woman standing across the street there smoking her cigarette."

Leaning to see below the blinds, he said, "Oh no!" sat down his dish tub and dashed toward the door. Across the street, Jane stood facing me, smoking. Behind her, a scraggly, street-looking fellow approached. The busboy shouted something. Jane turned to see the other man approaching. Purse on her shoulder, she waited. The busboy was arriving as the man reached for Jane's purse. She leaned back, grabbed his wrist with one hand and gripped his bicep with her other. In one smooth motion she took him to the ground, put her knee into his back and punched him three or four quick times in the head. He was done. She stood, arranged her dress, and then sashayed across the street, purse on her shoulder as if nothing had happened. Busboy leaned over the shocked scraggly person.

A dark haired twentyish waitress arrived at the table just ahead of Jane. She had milky skin and a bit too much fragrance. She began filling the dish tub and asked, "Where'd Josh go?"

"He's out there," I replied.

When she leaned down to see below the blinds her breasts were bulging out of a dress she must have purchased at a younger age. By then the boy had started back across the street. "Why's he out there?" the waitress asked.

Jane said, "Excuse me."

"Sorry," the girl replied while moving out of Jane's way. My wife took a seat across from me, tilted her head, and grinned.

She saw you looking.

The waitress had already begun wiping our table when the busboy returned. She asked, "What's the deal Josh?"

"Don't worry about it," he answered while lifting the dish tub.

"Y'all want coffee?" the waitress asked.

"Yes please. Both of us," Jane answered.

With the waitress walking away, Josh spoke quietly. "You some kind of cop, lady?"

"No." Jane grinned. "But I do appreciate you giving me the heads-up. Guy might have gotten my purse."

"You hurt him pretty bad."

"Oh well," Jane replied. "Maybe he'll think twice about grabbing a lady's purse."

As the boy walked away, he mumbled, "You're a cop. I can tell."

Jane stared out the window at shabby guy limping away. "Saw him coming before the boy came out. Pretty much knew what he was up to."

"You got off on that. Didn't you?" I asked.

"Why do you say that?"

"Because, I see it in your eyes."

"Well, I saw where your eyes were when I came in."

Jane turned, looking for the waitress. "Where's my coffee?" When I refused to reply, she got the message and said, "Told you I wanted to have fun today."

"You call that fun, beating up a scraggly old man? Just because you've been trained, doesn't mean you have to use it."

"He's not that old." Jane gave me the stare and then said, "Honey, you call it excitement. I call it fun. Same thing."

"The kid thinks you're a cop."

"Oh well. It's the wig. It lets me be someone else."

"Not sure I like that."

"You like it when we're at home."

"But we're not at home."

Jane turned to see the waitress approaching, coffeepot in hand. "Here she comes. Eli, relax Baby. It's just for fun. Besides, you said today I can be whoever I want to be."

"So who do you wanna be?"

The waitress arrived apologizing. "Sorry, was waiting on this fresh pot." She poured two cups and turned saying, "I'll be right back to take your order."

Jane watched me watching the girl walk away. I anticipated she would comment on the waitress. Instead, she said, "Today I want to be Sarah."

Good God.

I told you not to bring her.

Breakfast at the Bluegrass Diner is worth bragging about. We had biscuits, scrambled eggs, and real fried potatoes, all smothered in white gravy. Bite after bite, my mind wondered into uncharted territories while trying to decide how Jane might imitate Sarah.

Dude, you just saw an example when she kicked that guys ass.

As I stood at the counter paying for our meal, Jane flagged down the busboy. He seemed reluctant to go her way.

Then I saw her hand him money. *What the hell?* The kid passed me with a grin as I returned to the table. "What's that all about?" I asked Jane.

Glancing out the window, she said, "The guy is his cousin. Has mental issues."

"I suspected that."

"I gave him a twenty. Told him to buy the man breakfast and keep the rest."

Outside the restaurant, Jane lit a cigarette and then stepped in front of the window of a small butcher shop. She motioned and said, "Would you like to go in there?"

As she spoke, karma kicked my ass. Charles, the house attendant from the Proctor estate, stepped out with a bag full of what I assumed to be fresh meats. He stopped, facing me and stared. "Mr. Jones? Almost didn't recognize you."

So much for the disguise.

"Charles. How are you?"

"I'm, well. Having some back issues, but other than that, I'm just fine." While checking out Jane, he asked, "Protecting someone new today?"

"Uh, not really."

Jane jumped in to rescue me and only made things worse. "My name is Jackson, sir. I work with Jones. On occasions when the agency feels I might need assistance, they send him along."

"Oh, I see," replied Charles. "Might you be accompanying him on the fourteenth for the wedding?"

Jane smiled and said, "That's his gig. They might ask me to help out if it's a big crowd."

"Senator Proctor plans for a rather private event. I'd say no more than fifteen."

My wife's eyes widened at the mention of Senator Proctor. She said, "In that case, my assistance may not be needed."

"Very well." Then he turned to me. "May I ask, Mr. Jones, why are you not protecting Miss Sarah?"

"She's in the office today, so I'm working with Jackson."

"What exactly then is your business here in Morganville?"

This better be good. "No business here at all. Our work today is on down the road in Mason County. Jackson said she wanted country cooking. I remembered seeing the Bluegrass Diner."

"You ate at the Diner?"

"Yes sir," replied Jane, "and boy did I love them homemade biscuits."

"Believe mine are better."

"You don't say." Speaking with a heavy country accent, she asked, "Do you also make those real fried potatoes and white gravy?"

The old man grinned at Jane's version of Southern Charm. "Yes ma'am, I do."

Jane winked and said, "Well sir, if I wasn't so busy, I'd trade you my best back massage for a lesson in your kitchen."

Charles looked at me and said, "I should have your job." Then, he turned to Jane. "Ms. Jackson, Mason County's just down the road. Is there something going on there that I should know about?"

"Probably not. Some teenager posted threatening stuff on social media. I'm the lucky person who gets to check it out."

"You stick close to Mr. Jones. I trust he'll protect you."

I said, "More like she'll be there to protect me."

The old guy grinned at Jane. "Something tells me he's right about that. He started to walk away, but turned and added, "Ms. Jackson, I'll add you to the security list for the wedding. I can only assume Mr. Jones will accompany Ms. Sarah on that Friday. If you could join us on Saturday morning, say seven o'clock, I'd be honored to have you join me in the kitchen as I prepare my version of a southern country breakfast."

Jane saluted Charles and said, "I'll check my schedule, and at the very least I'll take a rain check on the kitchen."

"Likewise on the back rub, ma'am."

For a moment I stood there silent, watching Charles shuffle away and wondering if he always wears the head cover. Jane lit a cigarette and asked, "When he said Senator Proctor, was he referring to George Proctor, the senator?"

I sort of nodded.

"Dammit, Eli. What has Senator Proctor got to do with the wedding?"

"Her fiancé is James Proctor, son of the Senator."

Jane covered her face with both her hands and began shaking her head. Slowly, she slid her hands down to her chin. "Eli, are you out of your mind?"

"Yes, I'm out of my friggin' mind ... for bringing you along."

"Are you pissed at me?"

When Charles turned the corner out of our sight, I stepped off the curb and toward the SUV. "Sarah's gonna kill me."

"What was I supposed to say?"

"You could have told him you're my wife."

"But I'm not. I'm Sarah."

"Jesus," I mumbled from the middle of the street.

Catching up, Jane asked, "So what's in Mason County?"

"A graveyard full of my ancestors." As I opened the door on the vehicle, I added, "And it feels like it's calling my name right now."

When I started the engine, Jane stood on the curb to finish her cigarette. I lowered the passenger side window and said, "You do realize how you appear standing there on that corner, dressed like that."

She stepped around to my window, leaned in with her ass sticking out and said, "Wanna date?"

"Get your ass in the car."

"I'm not cheap," she shouted while walking around to the passenger side.

Chapter 23

On our drive towards the Proctor Estate, Jane quietly took in the scenery while I slowly gave up worrying about our encounter with Charles. When I turned left off the main road, she looked back and said, "Can't imagine how long it took to build those rock walls."

"Sarah thinks it was her ancestors."

"Really. Her people own property here?"

"Her ancestors were slaves."

Leaning against the door, Jane looked surprised. "She's black?"

"Half."

"You didn't tell me that."

"You didn't ask."

Focusing on me, she asked, "Didn't you once tell me you'd never been with a black woman?"

I nodded my reply.

"Can you still say that?"

"Yes."

"How about a half black woman?"

"We're nearing the Proctor Estate, up here on the left. I'm gonna drive past without stopping."

"Don't ignore my question, asshole."

Making a face, I said, "Not to my knowledge."

As we passed the long, tree lined drive, Jane said, "It's hard to believe."

"What, that someone can be that rich?"

"No. It's hard to believe you don't know if you've ever been with a half-black woman."

"Okay, I haven't. Unless of course there's something in your ancestry you're not telling me."

Way to turn that around.

What're you gonna do if she asks if you've ever kissed a half black woman?

The road curved left providing a good view of the back of the elaborate horse barn. An entry door there sparked my interest. Jane

213

also seemed to be taking in details. The barn soon disappeared as we drove into a wooded area. Just ahead, the road sloped downhill to a narrow bridge that crosses Todds Creek. Clear water ran swiftly, splashing over rocks. Local fishermen had created a small parking spot just off the road. About two hundred yards downstream would be the spot where the Barton twins and I had crossed on our way to the Proctor Estate some sixteen years earlier. As I slowed down to take in the view and old memories, Jane asked, "Can we pull in there? I'd like to smoke a cigarette."

"No, not here. Someone might see us."

After we'd crossed the bridge and started uphill, Jane scanned the woods. "Doesn't this thing have four-wheel-drive?"

"Yes," I replied.

"Then pull off the road. Out of sight."

"You that desperate?"

"No. I want to have fun."

Letting off the gas, I asked, "What kind of fun?"

"You say you've never had a black girl. Today, I'm Sarah. I want you to take advantage of me as though I am her."

I said, "That's insane. You know I wouldn't—"

"You have to pretend, asshole."

Your wife's a freak.

She has my attention. "You're kidding, right?"

"No. I want you to pretend I'm Sarah. I'll do the rest."

Aroused, I asked, "Are you sure about this?"

"Positive. Find a spot."

Nearing the crest of the hill, to the right, a broken down mailbox and a small opening in the woods indicated an abandoned drive. I knew the place well. A family from our church had lived there until the house burned down. The only person home at the time of the fire was the grandfather. It had been said that he fell asleep while smoking a cigarette. He died and the family chose to move rather than rebuild. "How's this?"

"Works for me," Jane answered changing her voice.

"That's not the way Sarah sounds."

"Really? So how does she sound?"

After thinking, I said, "Actually, a lot like you."

Brush drug across the side of the vehicle on my drive back the tree covered lane. "If it scratches the paint, I'll have to pay extra."

"Don't worry honey. It'll be worth it. Besides, you have plenty of expense money."

I glanced at Jane. "How do you know that?"

"You wouldn't have given me a grand if you didn't get a lot."

A hundred feet or so off the road, the lane turned. Weeds and vines grew over remnants of the burned down house that lay around a stone chimney. No one could possibly see us as we were hidden by trees and underbrush. When we got out, my senses were aroused by the surroundings.

"You like this, don't you?" Jane asked.

"I feel at home. This is where I belong."

Jane scanned the area. "I don't get it."

Way in the distance, I could hear a farm tractor. Other than that, the only sounds were a symphony of birds and wind blowing through the tree leaves. When Jane reached for her cigarettes, I said, "Give me one."

She grinned, handed me one and said, "My man's nervous."

"Or excited."

While smoking, I opened the back of the SUV. From my bag, I extracted a ten foot length of rope and my hunting knife. Jane asked, "What's that for?"

"You said you wanted to be Sarah."

Careful. You'll give yourself away.

"Oh. Am I going to be your slave?"

"No. That's one game I won't play." Without further explanation, I cut the rope in half and created a slipknot on one end of each. When we'd both finished our smokes, I said, "Unzip your dress enough to pull your arms out."

"Really?"

"Unless you want me to cut that pretty dress off of you."

She did as told and then zipped back up over her breasts. I slid the rope loops over each of her wrists. "Should I struggle?"

"Do you think Sarah would struggle?" She didn't answer. "Back up please." I eased her backwards until she was close enough to a couple small saplings for me to loosely tie the ropes; spreading her arms the way Sarah spreads hers. Jane played along nicely. When I began kissing her, her breathing shortened and she whispered, "There you go again, kissing me that way. Did she teach you to kiss like this?"

"Quiet, Sarah," I whispered back. Calling her Sarah brought a whimper. When I began unzipping her dress, she leaned her head back, and it excited me.

"Please, sir," she whined. "Don't hurt me. I'll do anything. Just don't hurt me."

"I'm gonna take you, naked in the woods."

"Please?" she spoke louder.

As I slowly unzipped the dress all the way down, Jane moaned. When it dropped to the ground, she stood naked other than her thong and sneakers. After hanging the dress on a branch, I stepped behind my wife and imagined her hard ass was Sarah's. The pressure was killing me so I loosened my belt and began to unzip.

"Mister, if you touch that woman, I'm gonna unload this birdshot in your sorry ass!"

I turned to see a teenager in bibbed overalls and a blue cap with a UofK logo, stepping from behind the SUV. The only thing more impressive than his size would be the shotgun he held. "It's not what you think," I pleaded.

"I'd say it's exactly what I think. Some damned deranged fool about to do bad things to this, this. Lady, are you a hooker?"

"No," she whined. "But this awful man apparently thought I was."

She's going to get you killed.

She's enjoying it.

The boy said, "Heard y'all comin' in the woods from the house. Lucky for you lady, I came a lookin'. Seen it all mister. Her beggin' you not to hurt her."

"I can explain."

"You alright," he asked Jane.

She stood there, boobs perked out, nipples hard as rock in the cool morning air, making a face as if she'd been crying and said, "Yes. Thanks to you. Can you make this asshole step away while you untie me?"

"You heard her mister. Step on back there where I can keep an eye on you while I let her go. And if you try to run, I'll shoot you in the back."

I did as told, backing up several feet. Holding the gun in his left hand the boy used his right to untie one of the ropes. Jane turned enough to give me a wink. When he'd untied the second rope, he stood staring at her breasts as she slid the ropes off her wrists. She looked up into his eyes.

"Sorry. Can't help but look."

"That's okay. Touch them if you want. Least I can do for what you've done for me. Hell, you might have saved my life."

"Lady, I'd like to touch you all over, but I'm not sure I—"

As he spoke, Jane grabbed the shotgun out of his relaxed hand. Backing up a step, she said, "Boy, you interrupted a little game we were playing. That man there wasn't going to hurt me."

"Holy Ghost, Mother of God," the boy mumbled.

As I walked up, Jane said, "Now you run along so we can get our stuff and get the hell out of here. I'll leave this gun up against that tree there and you can come back to get it when we're gone. Okay?"

"Okay, I guess."

"You guess?"

"Well, I mean, if this is all games and all that, I'd like to take you up on feelin' them boobs. That is if you don't mind."

Jane nodded my way and said, "Don't believe he'd go along with that."

In a weird moment, both the boy and Jane stood looking at me as if I should make some executive decision allowing a stranger to touch my wife's body.

Don't act like you never wanted to see someone touch her.

Sure, but I never actually...

Jane grinned and said, "Cat got your tongue? Remember what you said last time I wore this wig?"

But that was bedroom fantasy.

Maybe this is her fantasy.

I took a deep breath and said "Boobs only, boy. That's it."

Jane's face lit up. She said, "Awe." Handing me the gun, she added, "Maybe a little more than boobs. You've got the gun. You tell him when to stop."

Oh my, she's getting off on this.

And so are you. Be careful.

The boy tilted his head and said, "You ain't gonna shoot me are you, mister?"

I raised the gun and said, "When she says stop, it means stop. If you don't, I'll shoot your ass. Got it?"

Country boy stood there nodding.

Jane whispered, "You sure you're okay with this?"

I stepped forward for a better view. "You said you wanted to be Sarah. How far you go is up to you."

"Would she do this?"

"Don't ask me? You decide."

She grinned and turned back to the boy. "Gently."

As the boy reached, my heart skipped a beat. He followed Jane's order as he lightly cupped both her boobs and then rotated his large rough looking hands. His thumbs slid over her hard nipples as he moved his hands to her shoulders and then slowly down her arms to her hands and back up. I watched Jane's eyes. She seemed frozen. The boy kept contact with her body as he slid down her sides to her hips. Jane's eyes rolled back in her head as he brushed over her buttocks and squatted on his way down the back of her legs all the way to her shoes. He gripped her ankles and then started back up on the insides of her legs. When he reached her knees, Jane's head tilted back and her left leg moved sideways opening herself up.

"That's enough, boy," I ordered.

Face to face with Jane's bulging thong, he looked up at her face and asked, "Can I see it?" Jane glanced at me.

By then, I had begun to wonder what she would let him do if I were not there. "Hell no," I said. "That's enough. That's all you get."

"How about you, lady? You want me to stop?"

"Boy, she ain't the one holding this shotgun. I say you got about two seconds to get your ass up, or I'm gonna bury your body parts all over these woods."

He stood, took a deep breath and said, "Sorry, mister. You gotta understand. I ain't never seen or touched anything as pretty as this woman."

"Well I'm sure she appreciates the compliment, and you got your feel. So, now it's time to move on out of these woods. And don't you dare come back until we're long gone."

Before walking away, he turned to Jane and said, "Thank you, lady." Every few steps, he kept glancing back. From a distance, he shouted, "I hope you know I ain't never gonna forget you."

"Good grief," I mumbled.

"That's my daddy's shotgun!"

"It'll be here when we're gone."

Jane stood watching the boy until he disappeared in the woods. Considering that he might be standing out there watching, I said, "Get dressed. We need to move on."

As Jane redressed, I gathered the ropes. She went to the vehicle to get her cigarettes. "Want one?" she asked.

I shook my head to say no while breaching the shotgun and discarding the shells. After wiping away mine and Jane's fingerprints, I leaned it against a tree. When I got in behind the steering wheel, Jane stood in front of the vehicle, finishing her smoke and staring into the woods.

Neither of us spoke a word on our way back out to the blacktop. When we got to the bridge at Todds Creek, I stopped a moment to look at the path that ran downstream on the bank. "What are you looking at?" Jane asked.

I accelerated and said, "My past, Honey. Lookin' at my past."

A minute later, as we drove back by the Proctor Estate, Jane asked, "You okay?"

Don't lie.

"Yeah, I'm good. You?"

"What happened back there in the woods ... that was weird."

My mind dwelled on how she might have gone further, had I been okay with it. That idea tortured me all the way back to and through Morganville. On the highway, Jane seemed to have a case of restless leg syndrome.

She's as tore up as I am. I said, "You know, what happened back there, like you said, it was weird, but I can't say it didn't turn me on."

"Really?"

I nodded.

Looking at me, she said, "I've been sitting here thinking you're upset with me."

"Hell no, not at all."

When I turned on the radio to country music, she opened the sunroof to smoke a cigarette. Afterwards, she leaned back and closed her eyes. A few miles later, I figured she might be sleeping, but then noticed more movement in her hips. Reaching over, I ran my fingers along the inside of her left thigh. When she opened her eyes, I said, "Go ahead. Finish what the boy started."

She squinted. "You want me to do that?"

"Sure. I'd like to watch."

"I feel bad that you didn't get to complete your Sarah fantasy."

"Well, you're still wearing the wig."

"You've seen Sarah touch herself?"

"Noooo. But I thought we were pretending."

"Can you keep your eyes on the road?"

Grinning, I said, "I'll try."

Chapter 24

All weekend I wondered what time I was supposed to meet up with Sarah on Monday. Around 6:30 Sunday evening she texted. **Meet me at Starbucks 8:00 tomorrow morning. Don't be late.**

Jane rose before me. I joined her on the deck for coffee. She smashed out her cigarette and said, "Wish I could go with you today."

"Me too," I lied. "Hoping we're going directly to the airport this morning. If we go to the Proctor Estate first, Charles will likely mention you and I'm screwed."

"So what will you tell her?"

"Haven't quite figured that out."

Jane said, "Just tell her the truth. Tell her we were together and I played on what Charles was saying without really knowing what he was talking about."

"And when she asks why we were there, what do I say?"

"Stick with the story you told Charles. Tell her we were on our way to Mason County and stopped for breakfast."

"Probably wouldn't work. She's too smart for that."

"Seriously," Jane replied, "stick to the story. It'll work out. Honey, she's not stupid. She knows I have to be curious about what's going on. I'd say it's too late for her to get someone to take your place anyway. If she gets mean about it, just say, adios. I'm out of here. She'll be okay."

"We'll see," is all I could think to say.

Jane looked disappointed, standing at the door as I left. In a way I wished she could accompany me. But then, I could only imagine what might happen if she and Sarah were together.

Don't act like you haven't thought about that.

"Shut up."

It sucked getting into my old truck with the shiny red SUV sitting there next to it. On my way to Starbucks I wished I'd brought along a pack of Jane's cigarettes. When I arrived, Sarah's vehicle sat empty. Pulling in next to it, I waited for her to come out. She carried two cups of coffee. "Yeah right," I mumbled.

Stepping out of the car, I reached for a cup. Sarah handed me one and said, "You trust me?"

I shook my head and said, "Not sure."

Inside her car, I sat the cup in the console while fastening my seatbelt. "Where does he keep his plane?"

"It's at the Lincoln County Airport."

"Are we picking him up?"

"He'll be there already," Sarah replied. "He has to do all that preflight stuff. Inspection, fueling, etc."

"How big is this plane?" I asked.

"It's seats four."

Four? "Anyone else going with us?"

"Not unless Charles comes along."

"Charles, the butler? Why would he come?"

Sarah seemed to be analyzing my question. "He worked at the Wellington estate before Ambassador Wellington died. Doesn't really care for the son, so James hired him."

As she pulled out of the parking lot, I asked, "Why would he wanna go back?"

"Maria. His old girlfriend. She still works there."

Damn. Old man's still chasing pussy.

Sarah accelerated up the freeway ramp while I sat quietly considering the coffee. I waited for her to take a couple of sips. When she sat the cup into the console, I made sure it was less than full and then switched mine with hers.

"You okay?" she asked.

"There's something I need to tell you before we get to the airport."

"Does it have to do with Jackson?"

Great. "You already know?"

"I know you showed up in Morganville with another woman. Someone named Jackson."

"You talked to Charles?"

"No. James told me. Was Jane with you in Morganville?"

She already knows it was Jane. "Yes. We stopped there to eat at the Bluegrass Diner on our way to Mason County."

"Why were you going there?"

"Just spending time together. I've been ignoring my wife a lot lately."

"Why did you both leave your phones at home?"

"I think you just answered that question." I took a sip of my coffee and said, "If I'm gonna be out with Jane, I don't need you monitoring our every move."

Sarah hit her brakes while swerving into the right lane. I fell forward. Half my coffee went on the dash. Just ahead, there were road workers standing beyond orange caution cones. They all spread out as we skid to a stop only a few feet from them. One guy raised his hands as if to say, "What the hell?" Sarah glared back, offering no apologies. Traffic flowed by slowly, drivers and passengers staring. When the construction guy turned away, an interrogation began.

"Why did you introduce her as Jackson? Why'd you tell Charles that she works for Homeland? Why did he invite her to the wedding? Why did—"

"Hold on dammit. For starters, I didn't tell Charles any of that. Jane did. She's not stupid. When Charles mentioned the wedding date, she knew that was the same date I told her I'd be with you. She knows I'm into something with you that's not on the up and up. She didn't necessarily want him to know that she's my wife. So, you can thank her for not blowing our cover."

"She's not going to that wedding."

"I know that, and you know that, and she knows that."

Sarah sighed. "But Charles doesn't know that."

"Just tell him she can't make it. Tell him she's on another assignment."

"He likes her. Wants to cook for her."

"Oh well. He'll get over it. My wife's not going to be at that wedding. Period! I don't want her involved in this stuff."

"Good. At least we agree on that."

Sarah raised her console and pulled out paper napkins. She handed them to me. "Would you mind?" While I wiped up the coffee, she said, "Your wife's pretty sharp."

"Yes she is." I threw the wet paper at her and said, "You should keep that in mind."

Sarah dropped the napkin into the floor behind her seat and then replied, "There is something more I should tell you about Charles. Remember when I told you a friend of the old man helped him with my tattoo?"

"Yes."

"It was Charles. I recognized him the first time I went to the Proctor Estate."

"And he knew you?"

"Yes. He knew my name."

"Then there's no doubt these people are all in this together."

She patted my leg and said, "Thank you, Sherlock Holmes."

"By the way. Does Charles wear that head covering all the time?"

"I'd say he does. Why do you ask?"

"Old man probably doesn't have much hair. Figure he might be concealing a tattoo on his neck."

Shifting the car into reverse, Sarah said, "Another good observation, Inspector Haycraft." She backed the car up enough to rocket her way into the flow of traffic. Half a mile later, construction ended and Sarah found the fast lane.

A half an hour later we left the highway. For the first time, Sarah turned on the radio. Hip hop played. "You like rap?"

"Some."

My chauffeur began rocking behind the wheel and then surprised me when she started adlibbing her own lyrics.

"Woke up this morning, fell out of my bed,
Last weird dream rolling round in my head,
Feeling kind of guilty from the things that I said,
In my head,
In my bed,
Can't believe I'm not dead,
Amen!"

I stared, impressed with her beats. Sarah winked at me and then continued.

"Jump into the shower,
Leaving in an hour,
Drink a pot of coffee so that I can have some power.
Get in my car, drive real fast,
Burning up a whole lotta high dollar gas,
People don't like it they can kiss my—

Amen!"

When she hesitated, I said, "Damn girl. You're pretty good at that."
"Can you rap?" she asked.
"A little, maybe."
She reached over, turned my hat and said, "Go for it big boy."

It took me a few seconds to absorb the beat, and then I began:
"I, I, I get to work, pull my hammer out,
Hit my thumb, start to shout.
Take a deep breath, then I let it out,
Change my mind cause there's no doubt
While other people let this stuff drive 'em insane
Elijah boy kinda like the pain.
Amen!"

I stopped and looked at Sarah for her approval.
She said, "Keep going!"

"Oh boy, boy, boy, I get back to work, it's starting to rain.
Thumb still hurting, ignoring the pain
Gettin' all wet while I thump, thump thump.
Get the job done and now I'm pumped.
Amen doobie, doobie, doobie do."

When the song on the radio ended, I quit rapping. I expected Sarah would wait for more beats, but instead, she reached and turned the power off.
"Was I that bad?" I asked.
"No. You were actually good."
"You too."
"Eli, I want to ask you about your outlook on pain. I've heard David Weeper's version, but I'm more interested in your thoughts."
"It's not something I talk about."
Sarah glanced my way and asked, "Couldn't we consider it a session?"
Why not? "I, I used to hate my father for how he disciplined me. He almost always got carried away."

8888y

"You said, 'used to.' Did something change?"

"After I left home, I came by the house one night. My parents were watching a movie. It involved slavery. At a point, some slave owner had a black man tied to a post. He was using a strap to give the man lashes on his bare back. It turned my stomach. I looked over and noticed my father's wet face. I wanted to say something, but Mom shook her head as if to say, don't do it."

"Your father had empathy for the black man?"

"My father felt sorry for himself. Not long before he died, Dad and I got drunk in the barn. He apologized for things he'd done to me and then explained that his father had done the same to him."

"Things?"

"My grandfather whooped my father the same way the man in the movie did his slaves. Stripped down and tied to a post."

"OMG."

I continued, "You asked before if my people owned slaves. I told you they did. And when it ended, that mindset that allowed them to beat another human being didn't easily go away."

"So they took it out on their kids?"

"I'd say, and their wives. Apparently the abuse got handed down for generations."

"Your father did the same to you?" My silence said it all. "I'm so sorry, Eli. Now I understand what you went—"

"No! You don't understand! Unless you've been through it, you have no right to say that." When tears began running down Sarah's face, I realized that she too had somehow been abused. "Oh." I lowered my voice. "I'm sorry." I reached for her hand.

For a while, we sat in silence, Sarah driving with one hand as I held her other. My mind drifted to the last time I saw my father's face when he looked out the window of the Cessna. *What level of self-hatred and pain does one have to meet to do what he did in the plane that day?* Grandpa did his best to convince me that Mom was either unconscious or already dead before the crash. For several years, on the anniversary of their deaths, I returned to the scene. I would sit alone on the ground behind the barn, drinking whiskey and reliving a scenario in which my father had accidently killed my mother in an argument. I chose to believe that he couldn't live with what he had done and therefore tried to make the crash look like an accident, for me.

My eyes remained closed as I began to consider the woman sitting next to me. *What kind of pain is Sarah in to consider killing her own father? What did he do to her?*

Thoughts were interrupted when Sarah squeezed my hand and asked, "Eli, do you abuse your wife?"

I pulled my hand away. "No. Why would you ask?"

"You said it gets passed down. Will you abuse your children?"

"Hope not," I quietly replied. "Guess I'll have to have one to find out."

We were driving through a small community on a State road. As I pondered how much I miss the country, Sarah asked, "Does Jane abuse you?"

"I ... I don't know." Turning back to Sarah, I said, "John says I'm weird. Maybe I am. Things that others find painful somehow bring me pleasure. What can I say?"

"So you don't just ignore pain, you enjoy it?"

Why are you talking about this to a stranger?

I turned away, staring out the window and spoke softly. "No one else wants to talk about it."

"Excuse me?" Sarah asked.

"I ignore pain. I enjoy sensations. Sometimes there's a fine line between the two. When something itches, most scratch for relief. I scratch because it feels good. When poison ivy caused me to itch, my mother would say, 'Stop that. If you break the blisters, it'll spread.' I learned that dragging a tissue across the blisters allowed the sensation without fear of breaking the blisters."

"I've never heard anyone say they enjoyed poison ivy."

"I can't describe it perfectly, but for me it became stimulating. Over time, my desire for sensation got stuck somewhere between the poison ivy's itch and my father's beatings. In my mind, I could flip the switch and one became the other. His belt became my tissue. The sting became the itch. When my father said, 'This is going to hurt me more than it will hurt you,' he had no idea."

Sarah watched the road while speaking. "It would be nice if I could learn to ignore pain from the past long enough to enjoy passion in the present."

"That's a tall order. I find it easier to ignore pain in the present, than that of the past. Pain from the past lives inside. There's a difference between pain on the outside and pain on the inside."

"Please, tell me the difference."

"Not sure I can describe it properly. For me, pain on the outside comes from getting hit, smacked, punched, or whatever. It's shocking and typically short in duration. If you can handle the initial shock, it becomes interesting. Pain on the inside is more about a disease or a broken part, or something emotional and when it goes on for way too long, it hurts."

Shaking her head, Sarah said, "Pretty deep stuff for a country boy."

"If you say so." *Deep stuff? Jane never says that about me.*

Fence posts flying by nearly hypnotized me. I could feel myself dozing off when Sarah spoke again. "Tell me, Eli, do you consider loneliness to be a pain that hurts?"

"Hell yes," I replied. "Loneliness lives on the inside."

"How would you know that?" she asked. "You're not lonely, are you?"

"Not as much as in the past. But there are times when Jane's at work and I'm by myself at the condo, and I get to feeling lonely and sorry for myself. Reckon I get it from my mother."

"Your mother was lonely? Tell me about that."

Sarah was beginning to sound like a psychologist. "You don't wanna hear about my mother?"

"Yes. Please tell me about your mother."

Just thinking about it made my eyes swell. *How do I say this?* "Even though my mother had a husband who cared about her, she lived a lonely, uneventful life. To my knowledge, she never got to experience things like you and I do together. Pete's Pool Hall. The ledge at the Red River Gorge. Or anything remotely exciting. After I left home, she took a job at the Library and ended up meeting a man there. She said he showed an interest in what she had to say."

"They had an affair?"

"I'm not a hundred percent sure, but I'd say he took advantage of her loneliness. Mom called it passion. She thought the man cared. When I confronted him about his intentions, he spoke disrespectfully of her. I busted him and told him that my father might kill 'im for what he'd said. Man got scared, I guess, and left town. Not sure my mother forgave me for that. Her life ended soon after."

Sarah drove on a ways and then asked, "Do you think your mother was a bad person for trying to experience passion outside her marriage?"

"My mother was not a bad person."

Again, Sarah reached for my hand. "I agree. Everyone deserves passion. Like you, Eli, I've watched my mother go through years of loneliness. It makes me sad just to think about it. I doubt she's ever experienced a truly passionate kiss."

"Sarah Smith, you and I seem to have a lot in common."

She pulled to the side of the road to end our session.

Chapter 25

About five minutes before we reached the Lincoln County Airport, Sarah sent James a text. When I said, "Shouldn't do that while driving," she ignored me.

On arrival, I thought, *Ain't much here.* There were two runways crisscrossing, a few hangers and a multipurpose building with the tower room on top. Several single engine prop planes sat near the building. One had its engine running. James stood next to it as we parked. *No Charles. Good.*

When we approached, Sarah went to James. As they talked, I observed the plane, a Piper Warrior with registration numbers N6921J. As if by default, I began a visual check of the plane. James came to me. "You fly?"

"Grew up in a rebuilt sixty-three Skyhawk."

"Rebuilt?"

"Yeah. Reinforced so we could play. Looks like you've done the same with the Piper."

"Excellent observation." James had the door open. Sarah stepped up onto the wing and crawled in. As she took the back seat, he patted me on the ass and said, "You'll be my copilot."

After James, I climbed in. To my shock, Charles sat in the back with Sarah. *Here we go!* Settling in, I closed the door. Sarah said, "You never told me *you* were a pilot."

Let them think you have a license. "You should have known. It's in my profile."

"Good morning, Jones," Charles rang in.

"Morning. How are you?" I asked.

"Good," Charles replied.

Turning to look at him I said, "Jackson said to tell you hello."

He seemed surprised that I mentioned her. *That's interesting.*

Before throttling, James handed me a headset. "David Clark. Nice." I commented.

"Yeah. Latest, greatest," James replied.

As James began to throttle, I put on the headset and adjusted. They were much better than anything I'd ever used. Charles and Sarah put on sets also. "Can they hear our conversations?"

"Yes," Sarah replied. "I can hear you, so don't be talking about me."

"Don't worry, boss. You're not my choice of conversation."

James said, "We're all one big happy family up here." Turning to the back, he added, "Unless of course, you guys choose to mute or bluetooth your phones and listen to music."

When the plane started moving, James began radio contact with the tower. "Lincoln traffic. Piper Warrior six niner two one Juliet, requesting permission to taxi. Will be flying due East to Ingalls Field Airport, Hot Springs Virginia."

"Piper six niner two one Juliet, take Secretariat to runway two, north. You've got clear skies with winds from the south at 10 knots."

"Roger traffic. Any company up there today?"

"Piper, no. Closest traffic thirty miles due west. Slow coming in. You'll be clear."

"Roger that."

Reaching the runway, with the plane pointed north, James announced, "Lincoln tower, Piper Warrior six niner two one Juliet, ready for takeoff."

"Piper six niner two one Juliet, you're good to go."

Seconds later we were in the air. The sky ran blue and clear forever. I commented, "How can anyone look at these skies and say America is polluted?"

"That's a pretty deep subject," James replied. "For the most part, America's air is clean. Definitely a whole lot cleaner than it was when all these folks around here burned wood or coal for heat. While we have a ways to go, a lot of the pollution rhetoric is pure politics."

For the first time, James had begun to sound like a politician. Figuring I should at least try to sound knowledgeable about the subject, I asked, "If the whole world lived by the same pollution standards that we do here in the United States, would that solve the problem?"

"No doubt it would help," he replied. "You do know I'm running for office."

"Yes."

"Then don't go quoting me on political issues."

"I hear you."

While James changed the subject and began rattling on about aeronautics, I looked back on Charles and Sarah. It became obvious that neither wanted to talk. After giving me a wink, Sarah closed her eyes and relaxed. Charles monitored his cell phone. In my mind, I knew Sarah would be listening.

Around a half hour into the flight, James's chatter got interrupted by his phone ringing. "Take over, Jones. I need to grab this call."

I'd been wishing for the opportunity and gladly took control. James had his phone connected via bluetooth to his headset. When he answered, I could hear his voice, but not that of the caller. "Hello, Tim.... Yes, we're about an hour out...."

Glancing back, I could see that Sarah's eyes were still closed. *She's not hearing our conversation.*

James said, "Hold on a second, Tim." Looking my way, he asked, "You comfortable?"

"I am."

"Enjoy yourself. Have a little fun if you wish. I'm back, Tim."

Have a little fun if you wish. Have a little fun. I closed my eyes for a second and could feel my father next to me saying, *Have a little fun if you wish.*

The Piper seemed to have plenty power. With clear skies ahead and cruising 115mph at 5,500 feet, my mind drifted into Dad's Cessna. There were occasions when he'd do an aileron roll or a loop and then let me take over to do the same. Ignoring James's phone conversation, I full throttled, lowered the nose and waited for 135 mph. As soon as I started pulling up, I believe James knew. "Are you gonna...?"

At 20° I banked hard left taking the Piper into an aileron roll. It surprised me how well I executed having not flown in years. Before I could stop myself, I went again.

Charles shouted, "What's going on?"

"Ooooooweee." James squealed. "Damn, Jones, you da Man! Gotta go, Tim! My man's doin' rolls in my plane!"

Finishing and leveling off, I turned to James. "You said have fun."

By then, I figured Charles had soiled his pants as he shook Sarah screaming, "Wake up. We're gonna crash!"

I asked, "James, can this thing do a loop?"

"Damn right, it can! Go for it big boy. I got your back."

"What the hell?" Sarah screamed while I climbed into a full loop. As I finished and leveled out, she yelled, "Stop it, James, you'll kill us all!"

As I went for a second loop I decided to turn it into a full barrel roll. James said, "I'm not doing anything, darling! Jones is all that! He's up here showing off."

"Then stop it, Jones!" she yelled.

For a second, Sarah's voice took me to my parents and their fatal crash. I nearly stalled the engine before finishing the roll, leveling out and then banking back into our original flight pattern. My heart thumped as I slowly let out a deep breath and said, "You can take it back now, sir."

"Told you man, it's Jimmy to you, and you can fly my ship anytime, boyfriend."

Boyfriend? Jimmy? James? "Your Piper handles well," was all I could say.

We landed at an airport even smaller than Lincoln, just outside of Covington, at a little past 12:00 noon. James taxied in to where Timothy Wellington stood next to a huge black SUV. A slightly shorter, younger version of Sarah in high heels and a tight-ass, black leather miniskirt stood with him. The driver—I assumed—all six foot two, 250 pounds, stood behind them in his dark suit and cap.

When James shut down the engine, Sarah said, "I'd say that's Maria's daughter?"

James replied, "Yes it is. She's become quite the woman. Hasn't she Charles?" Charles did not answer. "How about you, Jones? You think she's hot?"

I said, "Looks like your fiancé with longer hair."

James frowned and said, "You been checking out Sarah?"

"Just an observation, Jimmy."

He raised his eyebrows and said, "Oh yeah, that's right. You've no interest in girls. So what'cha think of Timmy, or do you like his driver?"

"Timmy looks like he'd go down in one punch. The driver might take two or three."

"Damn, Sarah. Your boy Jones talks like he's a real badass."

"It's his job," she replied to Jimmy while staring at me.

There were no more words as I opened the door and climbed out, followed by James. He jumped off the wing and hurried toward Timothy and the girl. I helped Sarah down. Big guy stood like a sentry watching. When I gave Charles a hand the old man seemed surprised. I said, "Didn't mean to scare you earlier."

"I'm okay."

"So if I may ask, why don't you like the girl?"

"No, you may not ask," the old man replied as he moved on.

I caught up with Sarah. She asked quietly, "What the hell happened to you up there?"

"What do you mean?"

"You know what I mean. The flying. What were you trying to prove?"

"James told me to have fun. I was having fun."

"You could have killed us all."

"I've done those moves many times, Sarah. James's plane has been modified to do stunts. He knew it. I knew it. I went somewhere I needed to go."

When I stopped walking and stood staring at the group. Sarah bumped me. "So you're okay?"

I nodded.

"Do we need a session?" she asked.

"Maybe later. Right now I'm thinking about that girl with Timothy."

"What about her?"

"How old is she?"

"Who knows?" Sarah replied.

Trying not to stare, I said, "Girl looks Middle Eastern."

"I've never officially met her. Her photos are in my file. She was at the pool with Timmy the day I took pics."

"Oh. So how come you didn't show 'em to me?"

"Probably because she was nearly naked. Wouldn't want to tease you."

"Damn. Feel free to tease me anytime."

"Yeah right," Sarah frowned. "Just so you know, being Maria's daughter makes her half Latino."

"What's the other half?"

234

"Rumor is she belongs to Charles."

Belongs? "Ohhhh. You sure she's not your sister?"

Sarah quietly replied, "No wonder I love you." Turning toward James, she added, "We think alike."

She loves you?

As Sarah and I approached the group, James said, "Timmy, you know Sarah, and this is Jones, her badass bodyguard."

"Already heard about him," Timothy replied while giving me the look over. "How come she needs a bodyguard?"

"Someone made a threat on her life," James replied. "Homeland won't let her travel alone for now."

My attention remained on the girl as Timothy asked, "Can we trust him?"

"Jury's still out," James answered, "but I tell you right now, boyfriend can sure fly my Piper. He was doing rolls and loops while I talked to you."

Timothy reached for my handshake. When I accepted, he gripped and said, "Mr. Jones, notice you've been checking out my woman. Are you to be trusted?"

"In my line of business, sir, it's best not to trust anyone."

Asshole winked at me and said, "Maybe I will like you." Turning to his driver, he said, "Jones, meet Bo. Bo's the guy who will kill you if you repeat anything you hear while in my company. Understand?"

After a deep breath I replied, "Mr. Wellington, I'm here for one reason and that's to protect Sarah Smith. Your business is not my business unless it involves injury to her. If that occurs, I'll eliminate whoever is involved. Even you, if necessary."

"Well," Timothy huffed. "I believe Bo would have something to say about that?"

Bo stood at attention, wearing an earpiece and looking like a secret service agent. I grinned and said, "Bo already knows."

Turning to Bo, Timothy asked, "Knows what?"

Bo said, "He'll kill me first, and then you."

James interrupted. "Would you boys get a grip on your hormones? Nobody's going to kill anybody today. Let's all be friends. Timmy, Jones is a good boy, and you'll be happy to know he's not into ladies. So you can relax your guard a bit."

Timothy's head tilted. He turned and walked toward the vehicle. The girl scanned me from head to toe. When her eyes met mine, she squinted before following Wellington.

You saw that, didn't you? Neither one believes you're gay.

Chapter 26

Riding shotgun in the Suburban, I tried to adjust the visor mirror to see Sarah, squeezed in between Charles and the young girl, two seat rows back. Bo seemed to be watching me watching them. James sat directly behind Bo with Timothy behind me.

While I tried unsuccessfully to monitor conversations, Bo said, "Yes, sir," and I knew he was talking to someone remotely through the headpiece. Seconds later he turned his attention to me and said, "Benson filled me in on you."

"Benson?"

"Senator Proctor's security."

"Oh," I replied. "The suit."

"Yeah. Said he checked you out."

"Checked me out?"

"With Homeland. They say you're good to go."

I glanced back at the others and then replied, "That's good to know."

Bo asked, "So who's Jackson?"

The earpiece. Someone may be monitoring this conversation. "Homeland didn't tell you?"

"They said they couldn't elaborate on her. What's that mean?"

Staring forward, I said, "It means just that. They can't elaborate. She's not a part of this assignment. Therefore, they choose not to compromise her identity."

"But she's been invited to the wedding."

"Your man Charles met her by happenstance. First thing I knew they were talking about food and cooking and all that. I believe he invited her so he could cook for her, if that makes any sense."

Bo glanced into the mirror and then said, "Charles loves to cook. Old man used to work for the Wellingtons."

"Really. So, why'd he leave?"

A short silence preceded Bo's reply. "Why would you care?"

Someone on the earpiece told him to ask that. "Don't care. Just noticing how you guys all seem to know one another. Like the Proctors and the Wellingtons are one big happy family."

"They are. And you best keep in mind what Mr. Wellington said. If you repeat what they say, it could get you into big trouble."

I replied, "I'll keep that in mind," and then remained silent for the remainder of the drive. It took longer than I expected to get to Covington, Virginia. The small town nests inside of recently logged forests. Logging roads zigzagged through the steep mountainsides. It took all of three minutes to drive through the developed area of town. We passed some industry and then were back on a country road that wiggled through a rare section of flatland lying between the road and the Jackson River. A few miles later, the Suburban's engine quieted as Bo braked and turned left into a private drive. He hesitated as a decorative mechanical gate opened. I had an idea what to expect having seen it all from Google Earth at the Library. As we proceeded down the drive, to the left, a line of trees ran along the river's bank. Beyond the river, mountains. To the right, across the road, mountains. Straight ahead, past the buildings, more mountains. Staring up at the crests, I said, "Bet the days are short here."

Bo answered, "Yep, especially in the winter."

Lights and surveillance cameras were attached to tall posts scattered about the property. "Looks like they make their own sunshine."

Bo didn't reply as he circled in front of the mansion and parked. A Charles lookalike and an elderly Hispanic woman stood at the top of the stairs waiting. She had 'Maria' written all over her. Bo opened the door for James as I did the same for Timothy. He said, "Thank you, Jones."

I was opening the door for Sarah. "You're welcome, sir."

When I raised the seat, Timothy's little hottie slid out first. Our eyes met as I offered her a hand. When she leaned over to exit, it took an effort not to stare into her cleavage. As her feet hit the ground, before releasing a soft grip, she purposely used her middle finger to scratch the palm of my hand.

That was weird.

Sarah came out second, giving me a look and was followed by Charles. The old man barely exited the SUV when the woman hurried down the steps. The two of them embraced for a moment. I watched Timothy's lady up the steps. Her short skirt suddenly seemed shorter.

The whole rich folk thing was something I had never been exposed to before meeting Sarah. For the opportunity, I felt grateful. The butler fella held the door for me as I followed everyone else. I found the Wellington mansion to be much like the Proctor estate. Everything old looked new and everything new or old looked expensive. My scan kept landing on the young lady. Her tight dress, high heels, and long, dark, wavy hair didn't make sense in what I had presumed would be a pro-Islamic environment. I kept wondering, *How come no one mentions her name?* And why had she accompanied Timothy to meet us?

As things got cozy with Sarah, James, and Timothy Wellington, I watched the girl disappear down a hallway. Looking back, I could tell that Wellington had watched me watching her. Sarah raised her voice. "Jones, could you join Bo out by the pool for a while. We'd like a bit of privacy."

"As long as you don't leave," I replied. "Is Charles gonna join us?"

James answered. "Charles is preoccupied for the moment. He may come out later."

He's gonna nail Maria!

Poolside at the Wellington Estate had a slightly different theme. Lots of greenery surrounded the walkway in pots and in sections of exposed earth. I liked it better. More natural. Bo sat at a glass top table with a tall drink, smoking a cigar. "Cuban?" I asked on approach.

"No. Something local. Timothy knows the guy who makes 'em. Would you like one?"

"Sure."

Bo cut the tip on one and handed it to me. I asked, "You call him by his first name?"

"Called his father Mr. Wellington. Called him Timothy. Can't get used to anything else."

As I lit the cigar, Timothy's lady popped out the door carrying a tall glass like Bo's. She was hot and knew it. Had that model walk thing going on, even more so than Sarah. "Mr. Jones, Sarah said you might like a glass of sweet tea."

"Thanks," I replied.

"Join us," Bo ordered while cutting another cigar. Miss Hottie sat down across from me. It seemed odd to watch her accepting a Madura.

She wet the tip between her lips before lighting. The waves in her hair seemed natural. Bo watched me watching her.

After lighting her cigar, the girl asked, "So Mr. Jones, are you married?"

"Jones is gay," Bo answered for me.

She grinned and said, "But don't they have gay marriage in your state?"

Beginning not to like this gay thing.

"They do. But I don't have time for a relationship. You could say my work is my partner."

As I spoke, the door opened. Timothy asked in a commanding tone. "Bo. Could you join us?"

Thank you, I thought as the big man placed his cigar into the ashtray before walking away. The girl sat, relaxed with her back to the door, across from me. Through the glass tabletop I could see her bare legs. She watched to see if I was looking. Our eyes met. Hers were mysteriously dark and distant, maybe disturbed. When I took a toke on the cigar, she spoke.

"It's a shame, a guy like you being gay."

Instead of commenting, I just stared.

She seduced a toke of her cigar before continuing. "The Koran and the Holy Bible both say it's not right, you know, being gay and all that."

I could see Sarah at the door, watching. Had her meeting ended, or was she checking out mine? Rising from the chair, I said, "Been sittin' all day."

"Would you like to take a walk while we finish our cigars?"

No.

Yes. "I'm here to watch Sarah."

"You don't have to worry about her here. Let me go see how long they'll be."

Before I could say a word, she added her cigar to the tray and wiggled her way into the house like an excited child. The Madura and Iced tea occupied me for the three minutes it took her to return. She had replaced her heels with running shoes. I stared at her approach. "Sarah says she's fine for a while."

"Nice shoes."

"I run every other day. Keep them handy."

Opening the gate, I said, "You can lead the way."

"Timmy said we shouldn't leave the estate grounds."

Figured that. He wants to watch the video later. "I agree."

We walked downhill a piece and then began up a short rise. She made a point to walk faster uphill than me. Her butt cheeks were visible below the short dress. Halfway up, she spoke without looking back. "Mr. Jones. Are you checking out my ass?"

"Not on purpose." I lied. "But you must know how revealing your short skirt is."

"I was hoping it might tease you. At least a little. You know."

I stopped walking. When she stopped to look back at me, I said, "Apparently you've never participated in work-place sexual harassment training."

"You really are gay." When I didn't reply she said, "Okay. Come on. I'll show you my favorite spot on the property."

We were walking an asphalt sidewalk, similar to a cart path on a golf course. Halfway around the property, it crested again and then started downhill, "Is this your running path?"

"That's what I use it for. Goes completely around the estate. Lacks a little bit being a mile." After continuing slightly downhill for about another 25 yards, the ground leveled. "See that big tree up ahead."

"Yes."

"As we pass it we will be out of the camera's view. To the right will be an opening in the brush. Follow me exactly as I walk. We'll be back out before they become concerned."

It seemed risky but I followed nonetheless. Her secret pathway opened up at a small pool formed by a twelve inch wide waterway that must have been dug as a feeder from the river. On the far side, a small spillway allowed the water to continue through the woods. Trees surrounded it and the whole thing looked like something out of a fairytale. "Wow! I've never seen anything quite so perfect."

"I've been coming here most of my life. I analyzed the terrain and dug that waterway myself with a spade to form the pool." Producing a joint, she said, "This is where I get high. Sometimes I skinny dip. Would you like to—"

"No. I'm not taking my clothes off and neither are you, please."

"No silly. I was asking if you would like a hit off my joint. It's good stuff."

Hell yes, I'd love too. "No. You go ahead. I can't. I'm subjected to random drug testing."

"Sucks for you," she said while using her cigar to light the joint. "I only need a hit or two. Then we'll move on."

As she hit the joint, I toked on my cigar, admired the surroundings and could see how it would be her favorite place. Away from the cameras. All alone. The water. The birds. The joint. When she took her second hit, I focused back on her. "Funny," I said, "haven't heard anyone mention your name."

"I'm, Doris."

"How old are you?"

"Doris is nineteen. Come on," she said, grabbing me by the hand. "We have to keep moving or they'll get suspicious."

We exited the way we came in, staying out of camera until reaching the tree. Turning right, we continued as if we had never stopped. "Did you get a buzz?" I asked quietly.

"Sure did. Shame you can't smoke. Have you ever?"

"Yes, but not since joining the Agency."

"Tell me, how well do you know Sarah?"

Here we go. Interrogation. "Well enough. I mean, we work together. Strictly professional."

"You two would make a great couple. That is, if you weren't gay."

"She's engaged to be married."

"Not by her choice."

"Really. What's that supposed to mean?"

"Nothing. Just saying, I think she would be happier with you."

"That's sad. I hope the best for her and James. He seems nice."

"You're not a good liar, Mr. Jones. You and I both know Jimmy's more gay than you are."

Our cigars were done by the time we completed our walk around the estate. Nearing the pool gate, Doris said, "Mr. Jones, I won't threaten to kill you, but I would appreciate you not repeating anything we've spoken about. My existence here is unique, and when I mess up it's hard on my mother. Okay?"

So things aren't perfect in paradise. "Roger that."

Sarah, James, Timothy, Bo, Charles and Maria were all waiting at the table. I noticed Maria's eye contact with Doris. James said, "Hope you two have been behaving."

Sarah's eyes widened when Doris replied, "Life's no fun if you spend it behaving."

"So Mr. Jones," Timothy asked, "what did you two talk about on your walk?"

"I taught her how to breathe."

"Excuse me," Timothy huffed.

"She's a runner. I taught her my three steps in, one step out breathing technique. Basically breathing in slow and out fast. Keeps you from running out of breath on a distance run."

"You're a runner?" James questioned. "Are you fast?"

"Not really. Takes me eighteen minutes to run three miles."

"Six minute miles," Doris interjected. "Pretty fast by my standards."

Timothy gave me a look and asked, "So that's all you two talked about?"

Not liking his attitude, I asked, "Is there something you would prefer she and I talk about?"

"Actually, Mr. Jones, I would prefer you two didn't talk at all."

"Then you shouldn't have arranged for her and me to be alone."

"Excuse me?"

"Mr. Wellington, this is not my first day on the job. I'm here to accompany Sarah Smith. That's it. Your business is yours and mine is mine. If you don't trust me, perhaps the agency can send someone else next time. But for now, you need to cut the crap, because I'm not impressed and I'm not here to kiss your ass."

"That's enough, Jones," Sarah ordered.

I spread my arms and smiled.

"What's that all about?" James asked.

Sarah shook her head and said, "He's being silly. Can't you guys come to some sort of truce here?"

Timothy stood and offered a fist bump. "I'll say it again, Jones. Believe you and I can get along just fine. You ever decide to leave Homeland come see me."

I said, "Thanks. I'll keep that in mind," and then turned my attention to the silent Charles. I grinned and asked, "You feeling any better, sir?"

Everyone laughed.

The day went well from that point on. It seemed odd to be buddying up to two men I was expected to eliminate in a few days. Bo drove us back to the airport by himself. Like earlier, I rode shotgun. James and Sarah sat behind us. Charles sat alone in the back. As we drove off, Doris stood behind Timothy, waving and giving me a wink.

At the airport, James began his preflight inspection. Sarah and Charles climbed into the plane before me. Bo said, "Hey Jones."

I turned and stepped back to him. "What's up?"

"Between you and me, when Timothy said he likes you, believe he was lying. Man doesn't like anyone who talks back to him."

"Thanks. I'll keep that in mind."

James seemed tired, having had a few glasses of wine. After takeoff, he asked me to fly home. Sarah insisted, "No funny stuff please. Charles and I will be napping."

Ten minutes into the flight, only I remained awake, which was fine with me.

James woke as I began communicating with the Lincoln County Control. "You want me to land?" he asked.

"Might be better. Never landed a Piper."

James took over the communication and the landing. On the ground, he and Sarah said their goodbyes while I spoke with Charles. "Just want you to know, I consider myself a good judge of character and found both Maria and her daughter to be pleasant people."

"Mr. Jones, my relationship with Maria and her daughter is unusual, to say the least. Private sort of thing that I don't discuss with anyone. Without being rude, I'd like to keep it that way."

"I understand sir, and I'll never bring it up again."

"Thank you," the old man replied. "Will I be seeing Ms. Jackson on the fourteenth?"

Lie, lie, lie.

"Haven't seen any threat to Sarah's wellbeing around the Proctors or the Wellingtons, so my gut feeling is they'll only send me. But if she could get away, I'm sure she would like to experience your cooking. Hell, I look forward to it myself."

The old man frowned and spoke quietly, "But you didn't offer me a back massage." He turned and started walking. Hesitating, he looked back and added, "Tell Ms. Jackson that she is on the list, and that I'll be in the kitchen at seven a.m. sharp. Brunch will be served at ten."

Chapter 27

As soon as Sarah closed her car door, I said, "Glad you're driving. Now it's my turn to nap."

"Not so quick. We need to talk first."

"What, you need a session?"

She started out the drive, glanced in her mirror and said, "You know what I'm talking about. What *did* you two talk about on your walk?"

"Now you're beginning to sound like Timothy Wellington."

"Don't mess with me."

"Doris," I began, "is an interesting subject. Doesn't offer much information. Felt like she was the one looking for information."

"Doris?" Sarah mumbled. "Thought her.... And?"

"And what?"

"What information did you give her?"

"I didn't offer any. You know, I'm thinking she might be a better girl than my first impression suggested."

"Oh really. Better at what?"

Typical female question.

When I didn't answer right away, Sarah continued with, "What was your first impression?"

Now she sounds like Jane. "Her appearance, you know. The way she dressed and all. Just gave her a promiscuous look."

"And she's not?"

"Not what?"

"Promiscuous? Are you saying you didn't find her to be promiscuous?"

"Is there a particular reason for this line of questioning?"

Sarah hesitated and then said, "Like you, I noticed how Timothy called Bo in to leave you alone with ... Doris. He spoke briefly with her at the door when she was changing shoes. To you, he said he preferred you two didn't talk, yet I'd say that's exactly what he sent her out there to do. We both know he had an agenda."

"Yes, I agree. She tried to feel me out. Probably trying to decide if I'm trustworthy."

"And what did she find out about you?"

Go ahead and mess with her. "I told her that you and I were having a secret affair and that my wife was probably going to kill us both."

"Stop it, Eli. I'm serious."

"Okay. She didn't get shit from me, but I'd say Doris is a lot like you. She seems to be stuck in a situation there at the Wellington Estate. She confided in me about certain things and then like you or Jane or any other woman, she asked that I not share what we talked about."

"And?"

"And what? You want me to tell you everything she talked about?"

"Yes I do. We weren't there on a vacation, Elijah. We too were there on a fact finding mission. That's the way it is in my world. We seek information about the people who are seeking information."

"So" I replied, "it's spies spying on spies."

"Exactly. No better way to put it. Therefore, I couldn't care less about her privacy. I'm trying to decide if she's a frigging terrorist. Does she need to be interrogated or killed or whatever, and you sit here talking like I need to be concerned with her privacy."

"Jesus."

Sarah pulled the car over, stared at me and said, "Look, I didn't hire you to care about people. I hired you for your ability *not* to care. Not to become emotional, or fall apart in the end if things don't go the way *you* might want them to."

So this is the real Sarah Smith! "You wanna know what she talked about. Okay, I'll tell you. She talked about you and me. She thinks it's a shame that I'm gay because she thinks you and I would make a better couple than you and James, who by the way she says is gayer than me. Sounds like she thinks he's only marrying you out of some sort of an arrangement."

"She said all that?"

"Yes. And she says her existence at the Wellington's Estate is unique. Says when she screws up it's hard on her mother, whatever that means."

When I stopped talking, Sarah asked, "Is that it?"

"That's it. That's all we talked about."

Sarah merged back into traffic and mumbled, "Much better, Eli."

"Much better than what?"

"A couple minutes ago you said Doris didn't offer information. Now you tell me all this. I'd say she offered a ton of information. And you weren't going to share it with me. I pretty much knew most of what you just said. It's good to know you picked up on her situation, and even better that you were willing to share it with me. We seem to have come to an understanding." Offering me a fist bump, she said, "Much better."

Are all women manipulators?

I closed my eyes for most of the way home. Basically thinking about the mess I'd gotten myself into, and how Sarah's true personality had begun to surface. Talking about killing Doris added an all-new perspective to things. I had never before considered going off on a woman.

It seemed like déjà vu when I felt fingers in my hair, nails lightly scraping my scalp. "Wake up Eli. We're home."

"Could you just continue that for about an hour?"

"I would love to, but after ten minutes or so I might get carried away!"

"Me too," I mumbled, opening my eyes and rising in the seat.

"You drove your truck this morning."

"Yes. Parked almost right next to you."

"But isn't that your car in the front?" Sarah replied while pointing out Jane's Honda.

"What the...!"

"Look inside. Is that her sitting near the window to the right of the door?"

"Sure is! And Lisa's with her."

"Is Jane stalking you?"

"Or just here to have coffee."

Sarah sat silent a few seconds and then said, "My guess is Lisa saw your truck here and called Jane. That's when Jane came to join her. She doesn't trust you after all."

"You're wrong," I stated. "I'd say she's just curious. Wants to see you. What you look like."

"Well, that's not going to happen," Sarah replied while pulling away. She left the parking lot and started down the street.

"Where we going?"

"Out of sight. I'll drop you off and you can walk back to your truck."

"Oh."

As she parked on the side of a convenience store, Sarah said, "This should do."

I replied, "You know, Agent Smith, this was sloppy work on your part."

"Excuse me?"

"You already knew our meeting at Starbucks had been compromised last time."

"You're right. I should have picked another spot. Will next time." When I opened the door, she said, "Hold on a second."

I closed the door and leaned back into the seat. "What?"

"We've had a good day. I hope adding Doris to the situation doesn't upset you."

"Not sure yet. Hadn't really thought about goin' off on a woman. And it's like you just keep adding to the equation."

Sarah rubbed her face for a moment before speaking. "I understand your concern. I'll talk to mom about more money."

"It's not just about money. I won't be layin' a hand on Doris unless I'm convinced she's a bad character. At this point, I'm not."

"Fair enough." Sarah spread her arms.

As I left the car and started to walk, Sarah lowered her window. "Hold on a second."

I stepped back to the car and stood watching as she wrote something on a piece of paper. She folded the paper, handed it to me and said, "Before you start trusting her, her name's not Doris. Don't know why she told you that. I'm giving you her phone number. If she's using an alias, you may need it for research. Look at me, Eli." I looked at her eyes. "It's for research only. Do not call that number."

"Gotcha."

She raised the window while pulling away. I opened the paper. It read, Itzel Elizabeth Victoria Mendoza and had a phone number.

Damn, that's a mouthful.

It only took a couple minutes to walk back to the Starbucks. I thought about slipping into my truck and driving away but then decided differently. Lisa spotted me as soon as I walked in the door. Jane, seated facing my truck, turned and said, "Hey there. Back already?"

"Yep. Crazy day. How are you, Lisa?"

"Fine and dandy. Just catching up on gossip with your lovely wife."

Catching up on catching me with Sarah. I asked, "How's Bill?"

"Working as usual."

"Cops do work a lot," I commented for lack of something else to say.

Jane tapped on the table and said, "You look tired, Honey. Have a seat. I'll get you a latte."

"No, that's okay. Believe I'll go on home and take a nap."

Rising, she insisted. "No. Seriously, I have someplace I want you to go with me."

"Really? I was hoping to go home and crash. What's so important?"

"I want to show you a house. One of the girls at work is thinking of moving out of town."

"Seriously?" I replied. "You wanna buy a house?"

"It's nothing concrete, but I want to take a look, just in case they do go. Honey, it has a garage, and a fenced in yard for a dog."

"Or a swing set."

"Don't get carried away," Jane sassed while leaving the table.

"Damn," I mumbled. "Isn't that a surprise?" I sat down, checking out my wife's ass as she walked away. Turning back, I noticed Lisa's stare. "You and Bill doing okay?" I asked.

Glancing towards Jane, Lisa said, "We're fine. Better question is what's up with you two?"

Here we go? "Excuse me?"

"Elijah, are you having an affair with that lady I saw you here with a while back?"

"Why would you ask that?"

"You got into her car."

"And that means I'm having an affair?"

"If I saw Bill getting into a car with a beautiful woman, I'd think something was up."

"What if you saw him getting into a car with an ugly woman?"

"Don't mess with me Elijah. Jane's my BFF and I don't want you hurting her."

"Obviously you didn't talk to Jane about this."

"No."

"Well, you don't have to worry."

"Then what are you doing with that woman?" she asked while glancing again at Jane.

"Excuse me?"

"I'm sorry. Being nosey, aren't I. Guess that's what happens when you're married to a cop."

I could see Jane watching us as I asked, "Did Bill put you up to this?"

"No. Why would he?"

"Then why are you using him as an excuse for prying into my business?"

Returning with my latte, Jane winked while sitting down, and then asked, "So, Eli is your butt sore from taking that ride with Ruth?"

She's helping you out.

"Not really. We didn't get to go that far. Aunt Martha needed me to help her repair a stall door."

"Ruth?" questioned Lisa.

"Yeah. Eli's cousin is in Kentucky for a while, taking care of her sick mother. The two of them used to ride horses together when they were kids. She invited him out for a ride today."

"Oh. I see."

As she spoke, I tilted my head as if to say, "I told you."

That evening, as we prepared dinner, Jane said, "Lisa got kind of nosey about your friend."

"Yes she did. Thanks for the help," I replied while rinsing out a colander. "By the way, why were you at Starbucks that time of day?"

"You got a problem with me going to Starbucks on my day off?"

I turned to face her, leaned back against the sink, and said, "No. Just wondering if maybe Lisa called you because she saw my truck there."

Holding up her kitchen knife, Jane said, "Actually, I called her to see if she wanted to meet for coffee."

"Because *you* saw my truck there?"

Pointing the knife at me, she said, "No. I didn't see your truck until Lisa pointed it out."

"And you stuck around waiting to get a peek at Sarah. Didn't you?"

"Maybe."

"Well, Sarah nailed you as soon as we entered the parking lot. Drove away and made me walk back."

"Damn. She looked in the window?"

"After she spotted your car."

"She knows my car."

"Yep."

Jane set the knife down, moved close and began rubbing up against me. "Come on baby, can't you take one little pic of her for me? Just want to see what she looks like."

"I'm surprised Lisa didn't take a pic last time. Didn't she describe her to you?"

"She did see a whole lot more than I did the day we were walking."

"Well, she would never let me take a pic. It would be entirely against her protocol."

Turning her back to me, Jane started aggressively dicing tomatoes, tap, tap, tapping the cutting board, and said, "Damn her protocol! Woman gets to see me but I don't get to see her. It's not right, Eli!"

Didn't I tell you this would happen!

I put my hands on her shoulders and began massaging. "Calm down. It'll all be over soon."

She turned quickly and said, "Bull! If you do a good job for this woman, she's going to want you again and again. It'll never end until you're dead."

Chapter 28

Itzel Elizabeth Victoria Mendoza had no social media footprint. At least not that I could find. After a week of searching, John became my last resort. We were having breakfast in the parking lot. While he chewed a bite of sausage biscuit, I asked, "How the hell do you research someone who doesn't do social media?"

"How old?"

"She's nineteen."

John took a sip of coffee and said, "At nineteen, unless she's Amish, she's on social media. She got a phone?"

"Yes, of course."

"Then all you need is a phone number or an email address."

Sliding off of John's truck tailgate, I said, "I've got her name and phone number, but I really don't know how to go about—"

"Want me to try?"

If he researches the girl, and then something happens to her, they'll connect the dots.

"I'd love you to try, but I can't let you associate her name with you."

"Why not," he asked, "she in some kind of big trouble?"

Easy.

"No. Not exactly. I mean, she's like associated with some high powered people."

"So why do you need to research her?"

"You see, John, this is the reason I can't come to you. You ask too many questions."

John lit a cigarette, blew smoke my way and said, "Got something to do with that woman, doesn't it?" When I shrugged my shoulders he continued. "Dude, how long before you let me in on whatever in the hell it is you're doing?"

"I can't. Dealing with some private kind of people. People who get really upset if you share their information."

John held up his coffee cup like a toast. "All the more reason why I should check 'em out. You do it, you'll get caught. I do it, ain't nobody gonna know."

"You saying you can research this girl in a way so no one can trace or associate you with her?"

"You give me her name and phone number and I'll figure it out."

"If I do, you have to swear on your life that you won't call the number or let any of this out. And don't call or text anything to me that could be tied to it."

During that week, each time I saw John, I asked if he had anything for me. All he would say is, "Not yet." On Friday, he said, "I took a look. Just enough to know I need to go on a little road trip this weekend to do my research."

"Road trip?" I asked.

"Some things you don't do in your own neighborhood. Everything leaves a digital imprint. People that don't even understand what you're doing are collecting your data. They sort it by different categories and then sell to those interested. If their data sorter is sophisticated enough, it may kick out my stuff as suspicious. At that point it might even get picked up by a government agency's computer."

"So then they'll know what's going on. They'll connect Doris, and her mother, and maybe even... Damn John!"

"Who the heck is Doris? That's not the name you gave me."

"No, but it's the name *she* gave *me*. Her real name is the one I gave you."

"You didn't tell me she was using an alias."

"Thought all you needed was her real name and number. Can you do this or not? And can you do it without getting us in trouble?"

"Chill, bro. I got you covered. Ain't nobody more careful than me. Problem is the way I want to do this ain't cheap."

"You need money?"

"Yesss."

"Will a thousand be enough?"

He hesitated. "I doubt it. Not for what I'll need to do."

"Are you kidding me?"

"No I'm not. Dude, when I research this stuff, I don't intend to log on with the same internet source twice, or in the same city, or with the same computer, or for more than a few minutes. I'll buy a new laptop, with cash, from a different store chain, in a different city for each time I log on. When I log off, I'm gonna destroy and then trash the computer."

"Damn. That is careful."

John tilted his head and gave me that questioning look. "I'd say some of those government boys are gonna retire trying to figure me out."

"How much money do you need?"

"Bring me two grand now for expenses? Later on, if you can afford it, give me something for my time."

My man John is a good salesman. He made two thousand dollars seem cheap. "I can do that."

Early the following Monday morning, Jane and I made our sleepy way outside to savor our first cups of coffee. A mysterious dense fog hung just below the balcony. Birds chirped from every direction. Just as Jane lit her cigarette, my phone, lying on the table between us, alerted a text message.

We both looked down at the same time. I picked it up and read: **It's your turn to buy breakfast. Don't be late.**

"John?" Jane asked.

"Yea. Worrying I won't have his breakfast."

"You guys are gay."

"Excuse me?"

"You know what I mean."

As I stared at the phone, waiting for more, Jane asked, "You and John eat together every Monday don't you?"

"Yeah."

"So why the need to text you today?"

"Good question. I'd say he has something he needs to talk about before work. I'll leave a little early."

Even before reaching the parking lot, I could see John standing next to his truck, smoking a cigarette. He opened my passenger door as I turned off the engine. "You that hungry?" I asked.

Closing the door, he said "Your girl, Mendoza. You got no idea who she is!"

Handing him his coffee, I said, "If I did, I wouldn't need your help."

"She lives with a rich guy named Wellington. Man's running for Congress."

"Timothy Wellington. Yes, I already knew that."

John's face crunched as he reached into the breakfast bag. "Believe it or not, she draws a disability check."

"Really? Doesn't seem disabled. Maybe it's a front."

"But there's more, bro. The Wellington guy talks with some really interesting people."

"I'd say that makes sense. His father was an Ambassador, and he's running for office."

Talking with a mouthful of breakfast, he said, "Not talking politics. I'm talking NASA. Man knows a lot of people who work for NASA."

"Really. That's interesting." *Sarah didn't mention that.*

"And another thing, whoever told you the girl was nineteen is lying."

"She did. I'm sure she told me she's nineteen."

"Well the bitch is twenty-four. Started college but lasted less than a year."

"Bad grades?"

"No dude. She has an assault record. Apparently beat the crap out of somebody."

I about choked on my coffee. "I think you got the wrong girl."

"That's what I thought at first." John ate fast, seemed nervous. As he removed a second sausage biscuit, he said, "Reason you couldn't find her on social media is because she doesn't use her real name."

"She uses Doris?" I asked.

"No, she has a Facebook account, which is kind of weird for her age, but she goes by the name of Rosa Hernandez."

"No way? Another alias?"

"And there's more. While she was born an American citizen, this girl is somehow financed by a major sugar daddy in Dubai. Some real-estate monster name of Amor Saline—"

"Al-Riase," I finished for him.

John started shaking his head and said, "Brother, you are into some deep stuff. You're messing with people way out of your league. Good way to wind up dead."

He's right, you know.

Could Doris actually be Sarah's half-sister?

"So" I asked, "do you think someone from the government knows you've been looking?"

"Oh yeah. You don't look at these kind of people unnoticed."

"Great."

John sipped his coffee and said, "Don't worry. They might know someone's been looking, but they don't know who or why."

"I'm still confused about the girl, Itzel, Doris. People don't go around using fake names for no reason."

John asked, "Could she be a mole, you know, like spying on the guy running for office?"

"Doubt it. Girl's mother is the Wellington's maid. They've been living there for her whole life."

John finished his biscuit and lit another cigarette. "Guess I'm gonna have to keep looking. I'd say there's something going on between the politician guy and the NASA people he's been talking to."

I said, "Maybe they're financing his campaign."

"If they are, it should be public knowledge. These guys are all attention grabbers. If they have anything to do with the man from Dubai, dude, this is one crazy mess you're stepping into."

"Damn."

As I finished my sausage biscuit, John said, "Talk to me Bro."

"About what?"

"Tell me what the hell you've gotten yourself into."

"At this point I'm not a hundred percent sure. But I'm damn sure gonna find out."

John reached for my forearm, griped it and said, "Listen to me. My instincts tell me someone's using you and you're gonna get hurt. Jane too, maybe. Remember, I ain't your buddy, boy. I'm your friend."

I opened a second sausage biscuit, took a bite and said, "The other day, you mentioned something about me paying you for your time. You keep quiet on this thing, when it's over, I'll take care of your ass."

"Now we're talking. How much?"

"All works out, I'll give you five thousand beside the expense money I already gave you."

"Damn, you must be getting paid a shitload."

"Don't worry about what I'm getting. You okay with five grand?"

"Works for me," John replied with a grin.

"Now tell me, is there anything else I should know about Doris?"

"That's it for now. Are you going to keep calling her Doris?"

"Yes, for now. Don't want her to know I know her real name. There's a reason she gave me an alias. I'll talk to Sarah about it. She's the one who gave me her real name."

"Sarah?" John asked, leaning back against the passenger door. "Is that the woman you've been messing around with?"

I shook my head, partially in anger, breathed deeply and said, "Look *friend*. If we're gonna work together on this, we have to get somethin' straight. As much as I'd like to, I'm not doin' Sarah. It's all about business."

"Okay boss. I believe you."

Looking at my phone, I said, "It's gettin' late. We need to go in. Do me a favor and see if you can find out why Timothy Wellington is talking to NASA people."

"No problem. Especially now that I'm getting paid."

"And while you're at it, check out the connection between Wellington and a guy named James Proctor. Proctor is running for a seat in the Kentucky Legislature. He's the adopted son of Kentucky's U.S. Senator, George Proctor."

"Name rings a bell. Believe he's on the list of people who worked for NASA before the Obama administration cut their program. I'll look again and let you know."

Sarah's not been telling me everything.

As I sat there thinking, John opened his door. Before getting out he said, "Elijah, you're getting in deep bro. Best be watching your back."

I said, "Do me a favor. See what you can find out about that Amor Saline Al-Riase guy."

Chapter 29

On Tuesday I saw John in the hallway at work. He avoided me and I'm like, what the? Then it dawned on me that he didn't want to be seen with me anymore than normal. On Wednesday, I beat him to Del Junco's. Though the air felt cool whenever passing clouds blocked the early October sun, I hung onto our traditional outside table. A new waitress named Charlene delivered my shot and a tall mug of dark draft beer while I waited for John. I downed the shot. As I chased it with a sip of beer, a blonde across the way caught my attention. Her homely appearance seemed unnatural. Instead of putting my phone on the table, I shoved it into my front pocket.

A minute later, another lady joined the first. She too had blonde hair, a little shorter. I began to consider: *Sisters? Lovers? Cops? Or?* None of the options satisfied my paranoia. Someone tapped me on the shoulder. I turned so quickly that my elbow knocked my drink off the table. The mug shattered and beer splattered. Looking up, John's face appeared more like a shadow in the glare of the overcast.

He said, "Sorry man. Didn't mean to startle you."

"Damn," I complained, while lowering to gather large broken pieces of glass. "That was almost a full beer!"

"Why you so jumpy?"

"I'm not jumpy," I mumbled as Charlene stepped up with a hand brush and a dustpan. When she squatted to help me, her clean fragrance seduced me. "You don't have to do this," I said. "It's my fault."

"No problem," she replied. "I'll clean it up, and I'll get you another beer." Our eyes met and we were suspended for a few enticing seconds. "You okay?" she asked.

John answered for me. "This guy hasn't been okay for a long time."

I forced myself to rise, and said, "Thanks John."

"You're welcome," he sassed.

When Charlene had finished sweeping up pieces and then disappeared, John asked, "Are you like the horniest man on Earth?"

"What?"

"Dude, you just laid that girl with your eyes, and she knows it."

"She smells good."

"You're a mess." Taking a seat, John said, "We need to talk."

I sat down and spoke quietly. "Before you got here, it felt like I was being watched."

Expecting John to laugh, it surprised me when he started scanning the area and asked, "Who is it?"

"Now look who's paranoid."

He looked back at me. "Bro, if you'd seen what I've been seeing, you'd be paranoid too."

I said, "Look over my shoulder. Two blondes sitting together. One had already been eyeing me before the other joined her."

"Now they both are," John replied. As he spoke, his phone rang. "How can I be calling myself?" John mumbled.

I said, "Don't answer that!" After another glance, I added, "We shouldn't be talking here."

John agreed with a nod. We stood up to leave just as Charlene returned with a fresh beer. She looked at John. "Sorry, I forgot to ask if you wanted one."

"That's okay," he replied. "We're about to leave."

"When I handed Charlene a five dollar bill, she said, "No, it's on us."

"Then that's for you. Hold on a second." I turned up the mug and chugged nearly half of it. I handed it to John. He finished it off.

Charlene took the empty mug and said, "Thanks guys," as we walked away.

John had parked close enough to see the outside tables at Del Junco's. When we got to his car, he pulled his backpack out of the back seat, placed his cell phone in it, and then held his hand out for mine. Before handing it to him, I used Pandora to find bluegrass music and turned it up loud. John put the backpack in his trunk, under a blanket. He said, "Can't be too careful," as we got into the car.

With the faint sound of music leaking in from the trunk, I scanned the area. John seemed to be doing the same. "Okay." I asked, "Whatcha got?"

"Dude, your man, Al-Riase, he's lousy rich, and he's talking to rocket launch people."

"Rockets? You mean, like, missiles? Terrorist stuff?"

"No. I'm talking actual launch em' up rockets. The kind that go into space."

"There's the NASA connection," I assumed.

"Bingo mofo. This guy is a real-estate mogul who's doing three-way calls with guys who used to be at NASA. These are the same guys who once worked on putting drones into orbit."

"Drones, as in unmanned?"

"Yep."

"So what's the big deal?" I asked.

"Big deal is that these people also communicate with big business guys in China."

"Chinese! And you know this how?"

"Don't ask," he replied while staring past me. "Look." The two blondes from Del Junco's were approaching from my right. They passed in front of the car, both glancing our way. While John and I watched them walking away, the flip phone in my pocket began vibrating. John glanced back at the sound. I pulled the phone out and then held my fingers to my lips before answering. "What's up?"

"We need to talk."

"Okay, talk."

"Not now," Sarah replied. Can we meet me at the office?"

John turned his attention to the two blondes, standing at the corner bus stop.

"What time?" I asked.

"Can you be there at seven thirty?"

"Sure."

"Good. See you then." Sarah hung up before I could say bye.

When I folded the phone, John turned to me, shook his head and said, "Why do I feel like I'm living in a novel?"

I grinned before replying, "And the book just keeps getting better."

John rubbed his forehead with both hands. "Elijah, this is dangerous stuff we're messing around with, and look at you. You're getting off on it."

"If it's too much for you John, you can drop out anytime you want."

"I'm not worried about me, Bro. It's Jane I'm thinking of. How's all this going to affect her?"

For as long as I'd known John, it seemed like he knew more about Jane than he was willing to share. "John, we both know Jane has issues. She's told me very little about her past. It feels like she's holding back."

"That doesn't surprise me. She's always been a private kind of person."

"Do you know things I should know? Was she like, attacked or molested or something?"

John frowned. "No! Hell no. Don't think that for a second. If that happened, I would know."

I bet you would.

"Why'd you ask me that, Elijah?"

"I don't know. It's like she worries too much."

"Dude, she's a woman."

"I get that, but it's like she's overly protective of me? Like she doesn't think I can take care of myself. Jane gets all pissy if I go to the park without her?"

"What park?"

"Iroquois?"

"Elijah, I feel where you're coming from. It's not what you think."

"Then what is it?" I snapped. "There's something you're not telling me."

Rubbing his temple, John asked, "Did Jane ever tell you about her father?"

"Yes. He was in the Army."

"Special Forces."

"I know that."

"Dude, when he was overseas, she spent every minute of every day longing for his return. Jane loved her momma, but it was her daddy she needed the most."

"I gathered that they were pretty close."

"Darn right, they were close. When that man was home, they were always out running or hiking. He took her to the movies. I remember seeing them in the back yard. Him showing her self-defense moves. It was actually interesting to watch. Jane's daddy turned her into a bad ass."

"I knew he trained Jane. He didn't teach you?"

"Hell, no. Believe me, I wanted to go over there and learn the moves, but when her daddy came home, Jane wanted him all to herself. Captain Darrel Higgins was his daughter's hero."

"Until he died." John gave me a look and then pulled out a joint. I said, "You can't do that here."

"Then we'll take a ride," he replied. As John pulled away from the curb, he handed me the joint. "Light it up."

I did and took a hit. When I handed it back to him, John took a toke and then spoke while holding it in. "Jane ever tell you how her daddy died?"

"Got ambushed."

He blew smoke out the window. "She tell you *where* he got ambushed?"

"He was in the Army. What the hell, John?"

We passed the joint as John explained. "After Jane's momma died, her father finished his second tour overseas. Wasn't back home long. While me and Jane were at school, her old man was taking a woods run up in Iroquois Park. He came up on two boys who had grabbed a girl runner off the road. They'd drug her into the woods. Girl said they beat her to the ground, stuffed a rag in her mouth and had already pulled her clothes off when Jane's daddy came along. He went after 'em, but he didn't know there were two more bad guys in the rocks watching. One got him in the back with a knife. The girl said Captain Higgins reached back and grabbed the guy's hair and held on while he stuck a finger in the man's eye. She said the punk screamed and dropped the knife. Jane's dad used that knife to kill three of them hoodie guys—"

Hoodie guys?

"—while the one who stabbed him ran off into the woods."

I held my hands up. "And Jane's dad died?"

"Oh yeah. Even though he was bleeding like a stuck hog, he carried that little girl out to the road. She survived, but he didn't."

"Damn. Jane never mentioned none of that. Did they catch the one that ran away?"

"Nope."

"How come you didn't tell me this before now?"

"Didn't figure it was my place."

I hit the joint again and just sat there thinking about how close John and Jane were as kids. *They still are.*

John stared and asked, "Guess who Jane's hero is now?"

"You?" I replied.

"No, dumbass. Elijah, *you* are Jane's hero. She worships the ground you walk on. And you damn near killed her when you hooked up with that older woman. Jane needs you, man. More than you can imagine."

"I appreciate you telling me that."

"If something were to happen to you now, I'm not sure she could survive it. You gotta be careful and make sure you let her know you're not messing around with this woman."

As John drove me back to my car, I considered all he had said. Suddenly, I had a buzz and a better understanding of why my wife didn't want me hanging out in Iroquois Park. Her dislike for bad guys wearing hoodies made better sense.

I avoided going home and possibly having to deal with Jane before heading to my rendezvous with Sarah. Arriving early, I parked in the middle of the lot and sat observing an unusual amount of suspicious activity. From a white step-van positioned near the west alley entrance, a lady wore surgical gloves and passed out clean needles to the addicts. With the sun dropping behind buildings, shadows darkened obvious drug deals occurring in the south alleyway. A hooded character with an unlit cigarette approached my lowered window.

"Gotta light?" he asked.

Careful. Keep an eye on his hands. "No. I don't smoke."

"What are you doin' here?"

Before speaking, I turned to look toward two other creeps, assumedly his comrades, who had paused from their business to observe. My guess put them around 45 feet away. When Hoodie-man glanced in their direction, I slid out the silver spoon from my right pants pocket. "I'm waiting for someone."

Looking back at me, he asked, "You a cop?"

"No, sir."

"Sir? I ain't your daddy, motherfucker."

Sarah arrived in her black Camry. She stopped ten feet from me and idled with her window remaining up. Hoodie-man stood between us. He glanced her way and asked, "Who's that?"

"That's who I'm here to meet."

"Cop?"

"Hope not."

"Is it a woman?"

Don't answer.

"Hope so."

"Y'all gonna get it on?"

"Nope."

"You best not be doin' business in my hood."

As the thug spoke, Sarah lowered her window. "Is there an issue here?"

When the guy turned, I opened the door of my truck and slid out. Hearing my exit, the man turned back around, stepped up into my face and pulled the unlit cigarette out of his mouth. "Mister, don't you come up behind me!" Sarah opened her door. "Bitch, you stay in the car!"

"Sir," I said, "you need to calm down."

"You call me sir again, I'll calm *your* honkey-ass down!"

Holding the spoon up in front of me, I said, "I'm trying to be nice, but you seem to have a problem."

He smiled, then huffed out, "What the hell is that, and whatcha gonna do with it?"

His two buddies heard him and began walking our way. I could see Sarah monitoring them. Glaring at the thug, I quietly said, "Way I see it, you either don't have a gun, or if you do, you weren't smart enough to go for it before I pulled out my spoon. Now, by the time you reach for it, I'm gonna knock the shit out of you and then I might use this spoon to pull your left eye out and show it to your right eye. And if that don't calm your black-ass down, then I'm gonna rip your nasty tongue out and let you watch yourself lick your left eye. Do you understand me, *sir*?" As I spoke, the man went for his waist. I punched him square in the chest and then began whaling his head, avoiding hitting him with the spoon because I didn't want to draw blood. He sunk to the ground as his friends arrived.

Sarah crawled out of her car, holding up her Glock .40 and said, "First one tries to interrupt, dies."

The step van drove away quickly as I drew the thug up by his collar and pushed him back against the hood of my truck. His shirt came up enough to reveal a revolver tucked under his belt. Holding him with one hand I snatched out the gun, pitched it into the back of my truck and then gently laid the spoon's edge against the bottom of his left eye. Several addicts were by then watching to see what would happen.

While monitoring them and Hoodie-man's two friends, Sarah's clinched jaw relaxed and her thick lips threw me a sweet hint of a smile.

"Don't do it mister!" begged one of his buddies.

"Let him go," the other stated. "We'll take him home. You won't see him again tonight. I promise."

I held the spoon out enough for him to see how the tips curved edge had been sharpened and said, "You know what it makes a man when he butchers a fish alive?"

He shook his head.

I said, "It makes him a fisherman. I am the Fisher Man. You ever come near me again, I'll butcher you like a fish." Piss dripped from the thug's sagging jeans onto the asphalt next to my front left wheel. Backing off, I let him slide down onto his own waste. Turning to his friends, I said, "Get him outta here."

As they helped their buddy into the shadows, the crowd dispersed. Sarah focused on my spoon and said, "That was interesting." She reached into the bed of the truck to get the handgun. After putting it in the trunk of her car, she said, "Now, let's get in so we can talk."

"Not until I'm sure they're gone." Still watching, I put my spoon away and asked, "What is it you wanna talk about?"

"Your research."

Leaning against Sarah's car, I asked, "What about it?"

"Who's doing your research?"

"Me," I lied. "Why?"

"So you're doing a lot of traveling without your phone."

"There are times when I need my privacy. You would do the same."

After a look of disbelief, she said, "Okay. But I do want you to know you're kicking up red flags. If it's you, you're good at it, the way you change locations and equipment. Never using the same IP address. Good use of the expense money."

She thinks John is you.

"I try to be careful."

"That's good," she replied, "but slow down a bit. They're watching and eventually they will figure you out."

"By then it'll be over."

Scanning the area, she said, "I'd say it's safe to get in the car now."

When I closed the door and turned toward Sarah, she had her Glock pointing at my face. Without blinking, I said, "If you wanted a session, all you had to do was ask."

"See how quickly things can change? You keep snooping, someone's going to come after you. Is that what you want?"

"No."

"They don't know who you are, yet, but they definitely know what you're looking at."

"Is that right?"

"I suggest you stop before you get hurt."

What's she afraid of? "Who should I fear the most, them or the one pointing a gun at me?"

Sarah lowered the gun and said, "I don't want to lose you."

"You don't want to lose me?" Reaching over and stroking her arm, I asked, "Is my comrade getting attached?"

"I don't want to start over, and I don't want to lose my confidant. I like our sessions."

"I like the sessions too, but I have to ask, are you keeping things from me?"

"As in?"

"Don't play with me. You already know. There's more about your boys Timothy and James than you're telling me. Doris too. My question is why? Why do you wanna hide stuff from me?"

Staring at my eyes, she said, "It's for your own good. The less you know the better. Does it make a difference? I hired you to do a job. The link or links between James and Timothy, and Doris for that matter are for me to worry about. Not you."

Things have changed. "I told you before that I would have to be convinced."

Sarah leaned closer, put her fingers in my hair, and asked, "What's your litmus test, Elijah Haycraft? What does it take for you to want to kill someone? You first agreed to do the job simply because they were part of a covert effort to infiltrate our government. Now you need more?"

"I need to know what their NASA connection is."

Scanning the area, Sarah said, "It's getting too dark. I'm not comfortable here. Those assholes or someone they know could return." When I nodded, she asked, "Can you follow me to the park?"

Not a good idea. She's gonna kill you.

"Don't like having my truck seen in the park after dark. Not fair to Jane."

"We can drop it off at that Mexican restaurant down from the park. Pick it up later."

Chapter 30

Streetlights positioned every 100 feet illuminated the park's entranceway. Going there a second time with Sarah felt like playing a game of Russian roulette. I leaned against the passenger-side door, wondering why I hadn't thought of a better place to meet. Sarah drove the same route as before, beyond the lights and around the same curvy roadway. This time however, she asked, "Have you ever been to the top?"

"I'll plead the fifth."

Sarah frowned at my answer as she hesitated at the stop sign and then turned left. After winding uphill, we emerged from the trees at a spot overlooking the city. Sarah parked facing the view. "Let's sit on the wall."

We took a seat on the waist high stone structure. To our left, beyond the treetops, downtown city lights sparkled like stars on a dark country night. Straight ahead, we had a good view of the Louisville International Airport. Watching Sarah's gaze seemed like déjà vu. Margaret and I had sat in the exact same spot. Noticing my stare, Sarah said, "You plead the fifth. That's twice you've been elusive about this park. Did something happen here that I should know about?"

You don't need to talk about it. "Something almost happened here that you shouldn't know about."

She took a deep breath, exhaled and said, "Okay." Looking back out over the lights, she added, "It is a nice view." Lights could be seen from UPS cargo jets lined up like stair steps coming across the Ohio River to land. Sarah started counting. "Wow. It's like one every minute. If we sit here an hour—"

"If we sit here an hour, you best fill me in on a few things."

She stared for a few seconds and then said, "Okay." She says okay a lot. "We've already talked about some of what causes climate change. So let me ask, do you try to keep up with the ongoing political debate on climate?"

John said this was about climate. "John talks about it. I see it on the news, but most of it goes in one ear and out the other."

"Well, that's about to change. Lesson one. For millions of years, life forms on this planet have evolved and survived or not according to their ability to adapt to changes in climate. Humans are one of those life forms. To survive on this planet, we have in the past and must continue to adapt. Sometimes the change is rising temperatures. Sometimes it's getting colder."

"Now you sound like John. When it's hot, he bitches about global warming. If it's cold, he calls it climate change."

"It's a lot more complicated than that, but climate changes are directly related to global warming and global cooling."

"I get that. It's called winter, spring, summer, fall."

"Eli, I'm going to assume that other than what you and I have already talked about, you've never really researched the environment."

"That would be true, but don't act like I'm stupid. Between John's charts and Jane's nightly news, I've seen enough. And are you saying the NASA connection with James Proctor and Timothy Wellington has something to do with climate?"

Sarah took a deep breath as if analyzing my comments. "I'm not making fun of you. You asked me to fill you in. That's what I'm trying to do. Before we proceed, I'd just like to make sure you fully understand what I'm talking about. And yes, the NASA connection has to do with climate. Okay?"

I nodded.

"For starters," she began, "if you get your education about climate from the news media, you may be doing yourself a disservice. The media tends to tells us what they want us to know."

"So Professor Smith, are you saying you know more about the subject than all those professional guest speakers on the news?"

"I can't say how much the news media or their guests actually know, but I'm sure I know more than they're telling you."

"Oh. In that case, let me have it. I'm all ears."

Sarah turned to face me with her legs crossed on the wall. "Like I said, climate change is complicated and can be very boring. Therefore, I'm going to give you my condensed version."

"Good."

Sarah started, "This planet's been around for billions of years. During that time, it has evolved nonstop from a hot lifeless ball of mass to its present state that is bursting with millions of life forms, all of which have become somewhat codependent on one another. The formation of continental plates is a complicated science but can be simplified by imagining the outer edges of molten materials hardening when exposed to a cold atmosphere. Once formed, the surface exposed to the cold became frozen. Hot liquid elements below the plates rotate causing said plates to move slowly. Over billions of years, cracks and gaps in the plates allowed lighter molten materials to come to the surface forming volcanoes. Those volcanic eruptions helped form much of our land masses as lava cooled into solids. Volcanic steam pumped moisture into the atmosphere providing water. Does any of this make sense to you?"

"It makes sense to you, and apparently you're gonna make sense of it to me. I'm listening."

"Thank you. Understand that as early continents moved and collided, plates cracked and got pushed up forming mountains, ocean currents changed, and volcanoes continued to erupt all around the globe spewing steam, carbon dioxide and other greenhouse gasses into the atmosphere. The greenhouse effect eventually trapped enough heat to create a warm atmosphere. Carbon in the air enabled plant life which in turn created oxygen. While the Earth's atmosphere has evolved to the point of supporting life, its physical structure never stops changing. Continental plates, moving at about the rate your fingernails grow, are a major player in what causes an ice age. For hundreds of millions of years between ice ages, the average daily temperature is around twenty degrees warmer than now. Little or no ice. No glaciers. No—"

"Time out," I interrupted. "We've been through this before. Why you gotta keep talkin' about ice? Can't you just get to the point?"

"Boy, someone's in a bad mood."

"Are you kidding me? We just confronted bad guys with guns. I came within an inch of popping a man's eye out, and all you wanna talk about is ice ages."

Sarah's face distorted. "Listen mister! We didn't come here for a date! We came here because you asked for details. If I hired an operator to do this job, he'd just do what he's told and wouldn't ask questions! But no, needing someone off the grid, I hired you, a guy who wants to know everything. So, Elijah Haycraft, if you want details, you have to shut up and listen."

I'm back in high school. "Go ahead ... professor."

Sarah sat up straight like some proud high school teacher that just put a student in his place. "Now that I've covered early Earth, let's move on to man. Keep in mind that mankind's earliest ancestors began to develop around the beginning of this current ICE AGE..."

Now she's being a bitch.

"...That means there's been ice on Earth throughout the evolution of Homo sapiens."

"Human beings, right?"

She nodded yes and continued. "We've only developed into modern man in the last one hundred thousand years. During that time, there have been several global temperature swings of fifteen to twenty degrees. We somehow survived those changes in climate."

"Hold on," I interrupted. "Are you saying that all that temperature change happened before man started burning oil and coal?"

"Correct. The whole freezing and then melting cycle has taken place over and over without human interference."

"If it's all a natural process, why's everybody so worried about it?"

Sarah leaned back with her hands on the wall behind her. "It's about survival. We've managed to overpopulate this big ol' planet and now we have to be concerned about how future generations will survive as earthly changes occur. We worry about it getting hotter because we don't want ice to melt causing sea levels to rise. When mankind began building civilizations and cities on coastal properties, no one understood what I'm telling you."

"Are you saying sea levels will rise?"

Sarah nodded and said, "If we don't do anything about it, yes. The hot truth about climate change is simple. If there wasn't a single human being on this planet, over the next ten thousand years, temperatures and sea levels would continue to rise. Geologists have developed records of glacial and interglacial periods. We know how high temperatures and sea levels were at their peaks and we're not at all comfortable with the idea of relocating large populations. Sea level has already risen about 400 feet in the last twelve to fourteen thousand years. Powers to be say we need to somehow keep it from going any higher. To do that, they believe we must stop the melting of glaciers. And of course, the climate change debate is about whether or not the burning of fossil fuels is causing global temperatures to rise faster than they would otherwise."

"What a mess," I mumbled. Sarah said nothing. My mind drifted to an old saying about knowledge being a curse. It seems the more you know, the more you worry. "So," I asked, "what exactly do the scientists say we need to do?"

"The current reasoning being sold worldwide is that by reducing greenhouse gases we can lower temperatures and halt the melting of glaciers."

"Do you agree?"

Sarah sat up straight, turned to face the city, feet dangling and said, "Think of greenhouse gases as being nature's thermostat. If you want more heat, add more greenhouse gas. If you want less heat, theoretically speaking, you cut greenhouse gas emissions."

"Can we do that?"

"Anything's possible. But it always has a cost. Many environmentalists blame excessive methane and nitrous oxide levels on farming activities. The big focus lately is on livestock, cattle in particular. We have around one-point-five billion head of cattle on Earth. Their digestive systems apparently produce a significant amount of methane. This is why we have the push to quit eating meat. Certainly, eliminating cows would have some effect. Personally, I don't see that happening. The cattle industry is too lucrative. Big money typically makes big decisions. And besides, cows are not the only methane producing animals on Earth. I wouldn't count out the methane produced by human feces. Multiplied by 7.5 billion humans pooping every day, one would think it has to be significant."

I asked, "Isn't that what comes out of the vent pipe on top of every building that has a toilet?"

"Pretty much," Sarah nodded. "So you know what I'm talking about. It's said that in addition to methane, when you consider the burning of fossil fuels, which creates CO_2 and nitrous oxides, we're possibly emitting enough greenhouse gases to cause temperatures to increase at a faster rate than they would otherwise. Therefore, without other means of controlling global warming, some in Congress want us to eliminate cows, become vegetarians, transition to fuel sources that don't involve the burning of fossil fuels, and reproduce less."

Like most Americans, I'd heard all the talking points. "Okay professor, you've been telling me what everybody else thinks. What do you think? Is it gonna get hot? Will the water rise? Are we all gonna die?"

"Those are sixty-four thousand dollar questions."

"Then I wanna hear your sixty-four thousand dollar answers."

"All I can say is the powers that be have decided that global warming and the climate changes involved needs to be controllable."

Chapter 31

Warm wind blew hair into my face as a distant ambulance siren echoed through the night. Would its unfortunate occupant wind up under Jane's care? Would her skillful hands fix another broken body? Restart a heart? Patch a gunshot wound? Perform an emergency C-section on a dying mother-to-be? I sat there wishing Jane could have been with me for my lesson in climate. She would ask questions I might not think of.

"Have I overwhelmed you?" brought me back to Sarah. For a few seconds, I stared at her features the way I often do Jane's when we sip coffee on a cool morning on the balcony. Drifting back to reality, I wondered why spending time with such a beautiful woman had to involve so much uncertainty. "Are you okay with what I've been saying?" Sarah asked. "Does it frighten you?"

"Can't say it frightens me, but now that you've infected my mind with all this global warming and climate change crap, I'll be sittin' around like everybody else, worryin' about it."

Sarah crossed her arms, exhaled a big breath and said, "Don't worry about it. Just be concerned."

Yeah right, I thought, and then said, "You still haven't told me what the hell it's got to do with why you hired me?"

Sliding closer, she reached and used her fingers to brush hair away from my face. Moonlight glittered in her wet eyes. "You okay?" I asked.

"Yes."

"You look like you're crying."

"The wind makes my eyes water."

Sure it does.

"Eli, if I share something important with you, can you keep it to yourself?"

"Depends on what it is."

Sarah stared as if trying to read me. "This is about to be our most intense session."

"I thought sessions were supposed to involve things other than business."

"What I need to say crosses that line."

"Wow."

She said, "I'm thinking maybe we should seal it with a kiss before I tell you."

"And another afterwards?"

With a smirk, she replied, "If you're still in the mood." Sarah released my hand and spread her arms.

This is getting out of hand.

Shut up.

I leaned in. This time, when our lips touched Sarah wrapped her arms around me and I felt trapped in a feeling I'd feared. This was no ceremonial kiss. It lasted too long—became too passionate. Her tongue took me into another universe. While her fingers gripped into my back, mine ran up her neck and into her soft thick hair. She slid her lips off of mine and I began tasting her salty, wet cheek. Sarah's breathing shortened into puffs of warmth. My conscience had disappeared. A dark demon emerged and there would be no turning back. She bit my earlobe lightly and I felt my own breathing shorten.

This woman's not a virgin.

When Sarah bit harder, I let out a moan. She pushed me away and said, "What the hell? You really do like pain!" She began palming her hair back into place.

My desires ached, and I said, "Excuse me?"

She replied, "That's enough of that. We need to talk."

I stood up, uncomfortably aroused and looked down on her. "You are one cold-hearted bitch."

Sarah stood also and whispered, "Easy boy," as she tapped her finger on my lips. "It's about discipline. Keeping secrets is all about discipline. If you want to survive in my world, you have to be able to stop on a dime."

"Well, you've sure got that down pat."

"Thank you."

Backing away, I said, "If that's your idea of an exercise in discipline, you're an asshole."

"You can handle it."

"You were crying."

"I'm still crying, inside. Eli, I want you like I've never wanted a man in my life, but that can't be. When it matters most, cur minds will be blinded with passion and we'll lose. Something happens to you, I can't stop to cry. If something happens to me, you can't stop either. Yes, this is an exercise in discipline."

"Screw you."

"No. Not now. And besides, consider this payback for the way you teased me in my mother's barn."

"Ouch. I was afraid I hadn't heard the last of that."

She gave me a look, hesitated and said, "Never mind. Are we ready to sit back down and talk?"

"No. Yes. I mean I'm ready to talk, but I don't wanna sit down."

Sarah jumped off the wall and reached for my hand. "Come on then, we'll walk and talk."

As we stepped away, she used her key fob to set the alarm on her car. Moonlight provided enough light to see. Trees on both sides of the inclining road ahead looked like creepy characters lurking over our pathway, casting shadows that moved about with the wind. I tugged the cigarette pack from my pocket and tapped one out.

Sarah asked, "How long have you been a smoker?"

"Started in high school. Quit a couple years ago. Now, here I am smoking again."

"Do you smoke one after sex?"

"Excuse me?" I complained. "Don't tease me like you just did and then talk that way."

"Sorry."

I stopped walking and said, "You know what, I apologize for teasing your little butt in the barn. I guess we're even now. So, can we just get on with the secret?"

"You think I have a little butt?"

"It's a figure of speech. Get over it."

Sarah made one of her geeky expressions and said, "Eli, I've never experienced love, but if what I just felt back there is an example, believe I could learn to like it."

"You can't say that. It's not fair."

"Okay then, I take it back." She winked, grinned, took my hand and encouraged me along.

This woman is messing with my mind.

And that's why you like her.

As we walked uphill on the road, Sarah asked, "Do you remember in 2009 when former Vice President, Al Gore, said there's a seventy-five percent chance that in five to seven years the entire polar icecap will be melted away?"

"Yes, I remember. But it hasn't."

"Correct," she replied. "At least not anything near the extent he predicted."

"So Al Gore lied? Or is he just full of it and he wants a carbon tax?"

"Or we're fixing it and he still wants a carbon tax."

"Fixing what?" I asked.

"Global warming. Either Al Gore and his scientists lied, or we're fixing it because the polar icecap is still there."

"I'd say he lied."

Sarah said, "I wouldn't."

"Whoa!" I stopped walking again. "I'm no scientist, but I'm no dummy either. Are you saying someone came up with a way to stop the stuff you've been talking about?"

Instead of answering verbally, Sarah tilted her head and opened her eyes wide.

I said, "Wouldn't that be cool?"

"Trust me. They're working on it."

As I stood there enjoying my cigarette, Sarah made a face and said, "Damn Eli, did you pass a little methane gas?"

"Excuse me?"

"Smells like doody."

Before I could reply, the sound of a vehicle climbing the hill caught our attention. We turned to see headlights shining over the top of the Camry. Seconds later a spotlight zigzagged and we knew for sure it was a cop. After focusing on Sarah's license plate, the cruiser turned our way.

I dropped my cigarette, stepped on it and asked, "Now what?"

"First, pick up that butt you dropped. As for the cop, I'll handle it."

When the officer reached us, he stopped and rolled down his window. "Ma'am, is that your car down there?"

"Yes, sir, it is."

"You got some kind of ID to show that?"

Sarah presented her badge to the officer. "Looks good." Glancing around, he said, "Smells like shit out here."

"That's what we thought," Sarah replied.

The officer spotlighted white paper nearby next to the road's edge. "Damn drug addicts crap wherever they want up here." Then focusing on me he added, "You must be the man Braxton was talking about."

Sarah said, "No, sir. He's the man Braxton shouldn't be talking about. You tell him I said that."

"I understand ma'am, but with all due respect, can't you two find a better place to meet?"

"No, we can't," Sarah replied while leaning to see his ID tag. "Officer Goodman, this park is dark and it's not wired, and this man's married. If he and I meet in public, it could cause him undue scrutiny. Here, we know that you and your fellow officers understand the importance of our privacy and the repercussions should any one of you deny that privacy."

"Okay. If you say so. Just be aware, ma'am, there's more activity up here at night than you might think."

"What kind of activity?" Sarah asked.

"Buncha junkies killin' themselves with heroin and fentanyl. And we got bad guys killin' bad guys. Couple months ago, we found a dealer up here all mangled up. Had the sleeves of his hoodie tied around his neck. Found another one about a year ago. Same MO."

"Same as in?" Sarah asked.

"Guy was all butchered up with his hoodie sleeves tied around his neck. Ask me, it's like some kind of a calling card."

"Interesting," Sarah replied. "Sounds like a possible serial killer. Wonder why I haven't heard anything?"

The cop huffed and said, "We'll get the guy eventually. but as long as that sick son-of-a-bitch targets nothing but these low life dealers, it might stay on the hush."

Sarah said, "I see. Well, thanks for the heads up. We'll keep our eyes open."

"Pretty sure you two can handle yourselves, but bustin' up someone in this park might cause attention you don't want. And you sure don't need to draw blood. They're all prime candidates for HIV."

"Affirmative," Sarah replied while pulling latex gloves from her pocket. "I assume you carry these."

The officer grinned and said, "Yes, we all do."

Sarah stuffed the gloves back into her pocket as the officer drove away. We remained in the middle of the road, watching while the cruiser disappeared over the crest. I said, "This all gets back to Jane, she'll kill me in my sleep."

"Why would she do that?"

"Guess you'd have to be married to understand. I'm like, hanging out in a park at night, with a beautiful woman and talking to cops that know my wife's best friend."

Sarah grinned and said, "Come on, let's get away from that smell."

We continued walking uphill. Despite the hue of city lights, a multitude of stars were visible. "Look up Eli. One of those tiny lights is the International Space Station. You have any idea what's going on up there?"

"Does anyone?"

Sarah said, "If you visit NASA.gov, it'll name fifteen countries involved and a whole list of mission statements."

"That's cool. Everyone gets to know what's going on."

"To some extent. Now let me ask, considering today's political climate, no pun intended, what do you think would be the first and most important mission of the International Space Station?"

"Duh," I replied. "You just said it. Climate. Climate change."

"Exactly. That's what any educated person would anticipate. Yet if you read the list of missions, you'll not see the titles Climate Change or Global Warming."

As I gazed into the sky, considering, she added, "Same goes for the U.S. Air Force drones that continuously orbit the Earth. No mention of climate or global warming."

"That makes no sense. Are you saying climate's not that important?"

"I would never say that. It's very important."

"Then what are you saying? Come on dammit! At what point do you realize you're losing your audience. Get. To. The. Point!"

Sarah looked like she wanted to scold me again, but didn't. Believe she knew my patience had run out. "What I'm saying is that no one outside of our government is supposed to know exactly what our space program is doing to fix global warming and climate change issues. In conjunction with the International Space Station, we have unmanned drones orbiting the planet. One comes down, another goes up. They call it the FIX program."

"No one is supposed to know," I replied, "but your boys James Proctor and Timothy Wellington are out there talkin'."

"No doubt in my mind. That's why I need you to help me get information from them. Truth be known, part of why Obama shut down much of NASA's operations is because of what we're talking about. NASA is an independent agency of the U.S. government, but it's operated by civilians. They tend to talk. That got cured by shifting the FIX program from NASA to the U.S. Air Force. Another reason the program got moved is money. Al Gore and Obama were pushing for a carbon tax to fund the FIX program."

"And to think, people hated on Obama for cutting NASA. So, why couldn't they get the carbon tax?"

"Most Americans feel they're already overtaxed. Plus, scientists are in disagreement as to carbon's effect on climate. Right now, atmospheric CO_2 is over 400 parts per million. At the end of the past three interglacial periods, when temperatures and sea level were much higher than today, CO_2 maxed at around 275 parts per million."

"Okay then, without a carbon tax, who's paying for the FIX program?"

Sarah gave me a thumbs-up and said, "The American taxpayer, of course. By shifting the program to the Air Force, we now use the military budget to pay for it."

"Really? Is that why Trump raised the military budget soon after he got into office?"

"Exactly," Sarah replied

"Shouldn't this all be public knowledge?"

"Powers that be are still trying to hide the FIX program."

I thought for a few seconds. "When Trump backed out of the Paris Climate Accord, didn't he say our money could be better spent on our own efforts? Was he talking about the FIX program?"

"What do you think?"

"I think you're telling me the government's trying to fix climate in a way that allows us to keep burning fossil fuels?"

"Then I'd say you're paying attention," she answered.

"But why? They keep saying if we don't stop using fossil fuels, the whole damn world's gonna end."

"Eli, everyone in politics knows a transition to renewable energy won't be easy. We're going to have to continue using fossil fuels for some time. Yet, we still want to keep temperatures from rising. And...."

"And what?"

"There's something else that I caught wind of recently. I overheard a conversation between a high level agency official and a U.S. Congresswoman. What they spoke of rang a bell. One of my professors had lectured briefly on his concerns, but then abandoned the concept. When I began a paper involving his theme, he seemed uncomfortable while advising me to find another subject. Now, it seems some in our government have the same concern. Before man started burning fossil fuels, volcanoes were the main culprits in climate change. Millions of people died because of the short and long term effects. That hasn't been the case in recent history."

"Why then and not now?"

She held out her hands and said, "My professor, the Congresswoman and whoever inspired her seem to think there is some correlation between our removing fossil fuels from the earth, and volcanoes becoming less active ... less volatile."

For a moment, I stood there rubbing my chin. "Are you saying if we quit burning stuff out of the ground, volcanos will?"

"No. I'm pretty sure volcanoes don't burn fossil fuels. And even if we completely quit mining fossil fuels, it would take millions of years to replace what we've already taken. Yet the question remains, what is the effect of removing three hundred and sixty five billion barrels of crude oil and around eight-point-five billion tons of coal from the earth year after year after year? Crude oil removed is replaced by water. Water is less of an insulator than oil. It would seem that coal too is an insulator. The question then becomes, does the removal of fossil fuels somehow allow more heat to escape from the layers below? Does it amount to significant changes in subsurface temperatures? And if so, how much effect do these factors have on volcanic activity?"

"You're asking the wrong guy if you're asking me."

Sarah continued. "Did you know there are around fifteen hundred potentially active volcanoes on Earth? Maybe twenty are active at any given time. What if that doubled? What if it tripled? While I remain skeptical on the whole concept, there are those who apparently think that if we had never mined fossil fuels, volcanos would have remained more active and more volatile, resulting in more greenhouse gases and higher temperatures. And that would be without burning an ounce of fossil fuels."

"Damn," I mumbled. "Volcanoes don't have scrubbers. Maybe us burnin' fossil fuels with clean technologies is better than volcanoes pumpin' a shitload of those greenhouse gasses into the air."

Sarah grinned and said, "You might have just answered your own sixty-four thousand dollar question."

Chapter 32

If someone had told me a year earlier that I'd be taking a walk in the park, with a beautiful woman, a spy, talking about climate, I would have laughed. Like it or not, she did educate me. She at least had me convinced that the world's concern about the greenhouse was real. Understandably, nobody wants our properties flooded by the melted glaciers. But then, she seemed to be hinting that our government had a plan to fix it. I stopped walking, thinking about how tough it must be on a President when presented with such chaos.

Sarah took several more steps. Looking back, she asked, "What?"

"This stuff you know about. It's amazing, but not as amazing as how you look standing there in the moonlight."

"You're so full of it." She started walking again. I caught up and stepped in front of her. She stopped. I stared. "What?" she asked again.

"Do you seriously believe we can control temperatures?"

Sarah pulled out her cell phone and held it up in front of me. "Eli, if we can do this," pointing the phone at the sky, she finished, "we can probably do that."

"I'll take that as a yes."

She let out a deep breath and said, "Good. Does that mean we're done with this conversation?"

"Ahhh, no. You haven't told me how this FIX thing works."

Sarah stood there shaking her head. "Jesus, Eli. First of all, I'm not a hundred percent sure. Secondly, you're asking me to reveal Top Secret information. Don't you realize I'm trying to protect us both? If I tell you what you want to hear and you talk about it, they'll come after us."

"At this point, if you don't tell me, I'm gonna think it's all a big lie, and you're just trying to talk me into killin' some people you don't like."

"I don't think you believe that at all."

"If you wanted a regular op, you should have found one. You came to me. I am who I am. Now that you've gotten me interested in all this climate crap, I'm curious. I wanna know how it works."

Her eyes squinted like she wanted to hit me. "I'll tell you what I know. You breathe a word of it, I'll kill you."

She's probably gonna do that anyway. I smiled. Sarah put her hands together, as if praying. "Okay Eli, I want to make this as simple as I can. Let's say you and I are going to the beach. How do we prevent sunburn?"

"Don't know about you, but I'd use sunscreen."

"Exactly. You'd block the sun's ultraviolet rays from heating up your skin."

"Yes. I get that."

"So if we want to lower temperatures on Earth, might we simply block ultraviolet rays from reaching the Earth's surface?"

I nearly laughed. "Let me guess. We're using Air Force drones to spray sunscreen into the atmosphere."

"That's actually a good guess. In 1815, Mount Tambora erupted as a level-7 volcano in what is now Indonesia. Ash that spewed into the atmosphere blocked ultraviolet rays, lowering global temperatures by more than five degrees. People living in the Northern Hemisphere called 1816 the Year Without a Summer. The overall effects were devastating. I've read that a million people died of famine. Today, drones orbit the Earth for various reasons and studies. My sources say that while doing so, the drones are releasing crystals into the atmosphere. Those crystals are intended to reflect UV rays away from our planet. Thus, lowering temps."

"That's it? It's that simple?"

"Apparently," Sarah replied. "The crystals are less dense, yet more reflective than volcanic ash. Serves the purpose. We only need to lower temps by a degree or two."

"Then I ask again, if this is such good news, why aren't we talking about it?"

"They're still trying to tweak it. How much and where to release crystals to make the greatest difference for our money. Currently, they concentrate on lowering ocean temperatures."

"Why the ocean?" I asked.

"Last year, Atlantic hurricanes caused over three thousand fatalities, with a damage cost of nearly $300 billion. Harvey, Irma, Maria, and Nate, devastated the Caribbean and Texas. If we can lower the ocean temperatures by a couple degrees, we should be able to greatly lessen the severity of hurricanes. That alone could save enough money to supplement the FIX program."

"Is it working?"

"Time will tell. Right now it appears to be. This year, while we've had a ton of rain, we're having fewer hurricanes hit land and the severity of those that have has been down. Last I heard we're at 181 deaths and less than $50 billion in damages."

"That's a hell of an improvement."

"Yes it is," she continued. "Think about how much the United States has spent in the last twenty years on hurricane damage. Fixing the problem could save billions annually. Trillions in the long run. I've heard it predicted that in 2019 the hurricane numbers will be even better. We'll just have to wait and see."

"You keep throwing out all these numbers, but you still haven't answered my question. Why keep it a secret?"

Sarah had that look that a mother has when her seven-year-old asks about sex—trying to figure out how to satisfy my curiosities without giving me all the information. "We don't need other countries blaming us for their bad weather."

"That's it. That's the best you can do, and you want me to whack these guys because they leaked information? Maybe I should talk to them instead of you, seeing as how they're willing to spill the beans."

Sarah squinted again and said, "Now you're pissing me off."

"Oh really? Well, maybe that's what I need to do."

At first it looked like a slow dance, but then I decided her arms out, slow turn in the middle of the road might be a nonchalant scan of the area, making sure we were alone. She surprised me with, "May I have a cigarette?"

Tapping out two, I asked, "You smoke after sex?"

She grinned and said, "Probably would."

"Oh yeah," I mumbled while giving her a light.

She took a long draw, let it out like a seasoned smoker, got close and spoke quietly. "What I've been trying to tell you is that an ability to control temperatures equates to an ability to control weather patterns, which equates to an ability to use the FIX technology as a weapon."

"Weaponizing weather?"

Sarah put her finger to her lips. "Not so loud."

GAMBRELL

I lit my cigarette and said, "Sounds like sci-fi to me."

"But it's real, Eli. Changing temperatures in either direction to excess causes havoc. Now do you see what we're up against?"

"I'm not sure. Are you saying someone's using James and Timothy to steal the FIX technology so they can use it for terrorism?"

Sarah got close again. "Yes ... but I'm also saying that when it comes to climate change and global warming, we're probably not being totally up front with the American people. It might just be a ploy to get us all to agree to a tax that will provide the cash to build, implement, and maintain the latest greatest weapons technology since nuclear arms."

I backed away from her fragrance and asked quietly, "Is it really that great a weapon?"

"Only if you think destroying a region with devastating hurricanes, floods, tornados and blizzards without stepping a foot onto foreign soil, all conveniently implemented from space, is worth the investment."

The idea seemed extreme. I asked, "Do you think it'll work?"

She said, "Doesn't matter what I think. But my guess is you'll be seeing a lot of crazy weather in the near future, and they'll blame it all on climate change."

"You think they'll use it on Americans?"

"Yes I do. Can you think of a better way to convince the taxpayers that the threats of climate change are real?"

For a moment I stood there imagining our own government causing floods, tornados and blizzards. I asked, "What kind of psychos would use Americans as guinea pigs?"

"Eli. I'm the first to admit that there are times when it's hard to determine the good guys from the bad guys. But you can't go there. We have to concentrate on the job at hand."

"Which is to make sure the Chinese don't get their hands on it?"

Sarah exhaled a draw from her cigarette and said, "Or the Russians, or anyone else for that matter. Eli, if the wrong people start perfecting this technology, it'll be an all new arms race and we'll need a U.S. Space Force to prevent their using it on us."

"Seems too big, Sarah. You and I are not gonna fix any of this."

For a moment, Sarah stood quietly while finishing her cigarette. I finished mine, put it out and gave her a look. She said, "Eli, this is

287

exactly why I didn't want to tell you everything. Now you've lost focus. We're not trying to fix FIX. It is too big for us. So can we just focus on my problem? Those leaking information appear to be working for my father."

"A frigging one-percenter with financial ties to space exploration, who supports Sharia Law and is working hard to infiltrate our American government with his offspring."

"Thank you." Sarah spread her arms, "Now, do you still want to kiss me?"

Before I could, she lowered her arms and stared past my head. I turned to see blue and red lights flashing over the road's crest ahead of us. "Guess I'll take a rain check on that kiss." While we stood there watching the lights, I thought about how messed up it was that I had gotten involved in such a mind boggling situation. "By the way, I've decided this all does need to be kept secret."

Sarah said, "Well, that's good. You sure you're not just afraid I'm going to kill you in the end to keep you quiet."

"That crossed my mind."

"Awesome. As long as you continue thinking that way, I probably don't have to worry." Sarah dropped her cigarette and stepped on it. When she bent over to pick up the butt, I felt myself wanting to lean up against her from behind. "More harassment?" she asked while straitening up.

"You reading my mind?"

"I'm wondering what your conscience has to say about you lusting over my butt."

"I'm wondering what *your* conscience has to say about you teasing me."

Sarah stretched her neck as if monitoring the lights on the hill and then glanced at the sky. "Speaking of, I named my conscience."

"That's cool," I replied.

"Aren't you going to ask me what the name is?"

"I see it as a private thing."

"Well, Eli, you told me yours, so I feel I should. I named my conscience, Poly. It's short for Polaris. And Polaris is—"

"The north star."

"Are you mad at me," she asked, "for copying your star?"

I touched the side of her face and said, "It's okay. I'm honored. Only thing is, now when I speak to my conscience, I'll think of you."

Lights over the crest quit flashing. Officer Goodman's cruiser headed our way. When he reached us, his window already down, he said, "Like I told you, there's some crazies up on the hill. If I were you guys, I wouldn't go any further than this."

"Thanks for the heads up," Sarah replied. When the officer pulled away, she said, "Almost as if he doesn't want us to see what's going on up there."

"Or he doesn't want us to get hurt," I replied.

Seconds after the cruiser passed Sarah's car, turned downhill and disappeared behind trees, high pitch sounds of engines echoed like chainsaws from somewhere at the bottom of the park. Sarah said, "We should probably go back down."

Ignoring her, I asked, "Does the government know about your father's connections to the space program?"

"They know he has financial ties."

"Do you think they know he's a terrorist?"

"I hope not." Sarah's eyebrows lifted. "Now you know my dilemma."

"This is nuts. How can a person's life be so screwed up?"

"What person?" Sarah asked.

"You! Do you seriously think you or me or both of us together can kill these people and get away with it?"

Without answering she said, "Listen." The small engine noise grew louder and more in strain. Turning that direction, I said, "Sounds like mopeds, and they're coming up the hill."

"Interesting," Sarah mumbled. "Cop leaves and suddenly they come along."

Seconds later, three hoodie guys pulled up to Sarah's car. Their headlights shined on her 100-ASS license plate. Dismounting, they used flashlights to inspect the car. When they began shining their lights through the windshield, Sarah said, "These guys are pissing me off."

That's what Jane would say. I said, "Let's step into the woods."

"Can't let them break into my car. My wallet is in the console. Too many IDs."

"You've got to be kidding. So, you wanna just walk on down there?"

She stared, cold faced. "Yes, Eli, I believe we should go down there. Are you afraid?"

Maybe. "No, I'm not afraid, but yes I am afraid if we go down there, someone's gonna get hurt. This ain't what I signed on for."

"Then just let me handle it."

"Are you out of your mind? Those are the bad guys the cop was talking about."

"I get that, Eli."

"So what do you wanna do? You want me to shoot 'em?"

"Noooo, not if we can avoid it. Are you packing?"

"Yes," I replied.

"Don't use it. We can do this."

Chapter 33

Sarah never ceased to amaze me. She had no fear of encountering three men we'd already been warned about. Walking down that hill would be like walking into war. In my mind, I began visualizing scenarios. None were good.

"Let's approach like a couple of lovers," Sarah suggested quietly. "Maybe they'll let us get in the car and leave."

"You know that's not gonna happen. We go down there, it's gonna get physical. You can bank on that."

"You think they have guns?"

"Does a bird have wings?"

Sarah said, "Then the trick is to get close before they draw. Can you hold my arm and act blind?"

"Did Weeper teach you that?" When she grinned, I shook my head. "They won't buy it for a second. They're either gonna think we're cops or that we're trying to move in on their drug business. Regardless, they'll assume we've been up there with the zombies."

"And?"

"And by the time we get close enough to protect ourselves, they'll have their guns out."

"So what does Elijah Haycraft suggest?"

Talk to me.

It's a test.

"Am I being tested?"

Sarah sort of laughed and said, "If you want to call it that."

I started thinking, *What would my father do?*

What would Jane do?

She would be more prepared. I said, "My grandfather always said he was a fixer. That's what I need to do."

"Fixer?"

"Yeah. When somethin' bad happens, you don't worry about *what* happened until after you fix it. Think quickly. What do I have to do to fix this? And then you proceed to do so. If that doesn't work, you keep fixing according to what's happening."

Sarah said, "Sounds like OODA. I'd say your grandfather practiced it as a pilot in Vietnam."

"What's OODA?"

"Basically what you just described. Quickly and continuously reanalyzing a situation and acting accordingly. So, Private Haycraft, what's your fix?"

"Do you have two pairs of those gloves?"

"Yes."

"Okay. Let's put 'em on."

The smell of feces drifted into my brain as I pulled on the gloves. Sarah said, "They're going to know we're up to something."

"That's fine. We just have to confuse 'em. Even if it's only for a few seconds. Convince 'em that I'm not a threat." I buttoned the top button of my shirt and then pulled out my silver spoon and held it upwards in my right hand. "You're my nursemaid. If they ask, tell 'em I have issues."

"What's with the spoon?" Sarah asked.

"I think you already know."

"Can't you keep it in your pocket?"

"If I reach into my pocket for the spoon they'll think I'm going for a gun. Just holding it up's gonna confuse 'em. Trust me."

"Okay. I like it," Sarah replied. "I'll do the talking. One of them pulls out a gun, I'm going off. You do what you have to do. I'd prefer no gunshots, but if it gets to that, oh well. They are the bad guys."

"Is this the excitement you offered?" With no reply, I prayed at a whisper. "Lord, protect us, and forgive me for what I might have to do."

"Amen," Sarah whispered back. Reaching for my hand she said, "Let's do it."

"Hold on a second." Walking over, I stepped in the nasty pile of human feces and then used the grass to clean the sides of my shoe. When I returned to Sarah she said, "That really stinks."

"Good. Let 'em think I had an accident."

As we began our stroll hand in hand me on the right, walking like I had pooped my pants, Sarah said, "You seem comfortable with this."

"I'm not. I'm counting on you. If we live through this, you owe me big time."

From that point, I remained silent. My heart began to pound and I felt shortness in breath. It reminded me of two other events in my life. The first time I successfully stalked and shot a deer, and the first time I successfully crawled under the sheets with a woman. Both were exciting, life changing events. In my mind, I saw my sweet Jane, purring, growling, excited, and breathing hard like me. *Wish she was here*.

The hoodie guys turned at our approach. Two of them hopped up and took a seat on the trunk lid of Sarah's car. The third one, taller, stood between them, his ass leaning against the car. The man's right hand hung at his crotch. At fifteen feet away, the guy sitting on the left appeared to be Latino. One on the right was black. The one standing looked white. He had a scraggly beard. His hoodie shadowed most of his face. His right hand moved and I saw the gun.

Sarah squeezed my hand again. We stopped. While I stood with my legs separated and staring upward over their heads, she spoke timidly. "Gentlemen, if, if you could move off my car, I'll put Henry in and we'll leave."

The guy standing raised his revolver and spoke. "You got any money, lady?"

"Just enough to fill up my gas tank."

"Nice." Glancing at both his partners, he said, "Or fill up our bikes."

Sarah started walking and I moved with her like a dancer following lead. The two men came off the trunk. All three stood between us and the car. Sarah stopped, facing the guy with the gun. He stared at her and then me and asked, "What's wrong with him?"

"He has issues, sir."

"Like what?"

"Henry is low functioning and somewhat OCD."

The black guy in front of me said, "This guy smells like shit."

"He's had an accident, sir."

The one to Sarah's left asked, "Why y'all be wearing de gloves? And what's with de spoon?"

"Henry's a germaphobe and the spoon is, well, it's like his security blanket. He carries it all the time."

While I kept my eyes upward, moving my head slowly, the man in front of me stared and said, "That's a lotta issues. What kind of germaphobe shits his pants?"

Sarah ignored him while I squirmed.

The white guy asked, "What exactly are you two doin' up here in the dark?"

"We were taking a walk. Henry likes the stars. We would like to leave now. I want to get him home and clean him up."

"Oh dama," chimed the Latino. "I bet he like it when you cleans him up more dan he likes de stars."

The one staring at me asked, "You fucking this creep, lady?"

Sarah said, "I'm his caretaker."

"Caretaker!" All three began laughing as the tall man lit a cigarette and then asked, "What's your name?"

"Mercedes."

"Mercedes. So while a beautiful sister like you spends all her time with this retard, who takes care of your needs?"

Sarah didn't reply. The Hispanic guy said, "Hey jefe. I think maybe dis hot senorita like da ride a horse an den spend un minuto wid one of us."

The white guy slid off his hood exposing a skinned head and a damaged left eye. My chest began to tighten. *Could this be the guy who killed Jane's father?*

He asked, "How about it lady? You like to get high and spend some time with a real man?"

Which one do I kill first? I began to see those three men the way Jane would—hoodie guys. Nasty ass flies that would eat the dung off my shoe. Bugs. I squeezed Sarah's hand slightly and then spoke slowly, "Reeall mannn. What is reeall man?"

The black dude got in my face and said, "I'm a real man motherfucker, and you ain't nothin' but a stupid white boy."

Quick as he spoke, I let go of Sarah's hand and came up with the spoon. Its sharp edge caught him under the chin. Blood squirted. He fell backwards, bounced off the car and was stumbling as the tall guy raised his pistol. Sarah's right leg came up to kick his wrist so hard that the gun flew out of his hand and over my head. As that happened, the hombre launched onto her. When I glanced that way, the white guy busted me up side of the head and then rolled past me onto the ground to retrieve his gun. His blow felt like electricity. By the time I reached him he had the revolver and turned to fire. I grabbed his gun wrist with my left hand while burying the spoon into his temple. Blood sprayed and he released the pistol. I picked it up as he sat on his heels moaning like an injured deer. One swift kick to his chin flipped him onto his back. He went quiet and no longer moved.

The black guy had slumped against the rock wall. His head hung forward and blood filled his lap and the ground around him. His arms and shoulders were limp. Turning, I saw Sarah with a bloody face, stumbling backwards. The Latino had a knife. When I raised the revolver, he looked my way. Sarah said, "No!" as she stepped forward and kicked him between the legs. The guy bent over and she began wearing his head out with her fists. He made one last jab with the knife, missed, and never got in another lick. She pounded him unconscious.

I went to my knees in shock at the mess I'd made. One man looked dead, the other was out, but breathing. Sarah leaned against the back of her car, arms folded against her ribs, catching her breath.

You have to finish this. I pulled the handle off the spoon and shoved its silver blade into the white man's chest. As he gave up his soul, I thought, *How could all this happen so fast?* In an instant, I had gone from being that guy who always wondered how hard it would be to kill a bad man, to doing it. Twice. I mumbled a prayer for both their sorry souls.

Sarah stood over me. "Are you praying for them?"

"Yes. It's the least I could do." Looking up, I said, "You look rough."

"Thanks," she replied while rubbing her face. Then, motioning toward the Latino, she asked, "How about you do him too?"

I pulled the knife out of the white man's chest and offered it to Sarah. "These are my fish. That one's yours."

As she stood there staring at the knife, I said, "Be careful. Even the spoon's edge is sharp."

Instead of shoving it into the man's chest as I had, she sliced his throat. *That was easy.* When the blood stopped pumping and the body lay still, she wiped the blade and seemed to be inspecting its craftsmanship. "If that cop comes back and finds these guys, he'll know it was us."

"So, you just gonna call it in. Tell your superiors you had to kill three bad guys. In the movies you people leave dead bodies everywhere."

"This ain't the movies, honey. You already know I don't want my superiors to know I'm working with you. If they investigate this, the cop will tell them we were together." As she spoke, I handed her the wooden handle. She slid it on the spoon and said, "You know, we could just tie their hoodies around their necks and call it a night."

"Hell no!"

"And why not?" she asked while handing me the spoon.

"Just ... not a good idea."

"Seems perfect to me."

"Sure then, let's just do that thirty minutes after a cop told us about it. Jesus. Do we have any idea how the serial killer guy mangles his bodies? Would he elevate from one victim to three all of a sudden? I think it's a bad idea. But if that's what you wanna do?"

Sarah stared and said, "No, you're right. Good thinking actually. So, what do you suggest?"

Another test? "Well, we sure as hell can't bury 'em."

"Then I guess we need to get them out of this park. Let's go get your truck."

"Are you serious? You want me to drive around with dead men in my truck?"

"If it's not too much trouble," she replied as if we were somewhere else debating on whether or not I should open her car door.

You got a better plan?

I said, "Not exactly what I wanted to do tonight. We get caught, I'm puttin' it all off on your ass." Staring uphill, I asked, "What about the zombies?"

"Too dark down here," Glancing around, she added, "If they're still up on the hill, they couldn't see a thing. And besides, they would think we're cops." Looking around, she said, "Until we come back, let's put the bodies and the bikes behind this wall."

Only the big guy had a gun. The others had knifes. Sarah put all three weapons into her trunk. We rolled the mopeds first and then carried the dead men around to avoid getting blood on the wall. Sarah removed a blanket and a windshield scraper from her trunk. Handing me the scraper, she pointed out a garbage can. "Look in there for a food bag. Find me some dirt while I get up as much blood as I can."

I managed a good size bag of dirt. The blanket soaked up most of the blood. Spreading dirt over the area and pushing it around did a good job. Things actually looked as if nothing had happened. Sarah put the blanket into her trunk and then peeled off her gloves, tossing them in. As I removed mine, she climbed up and stood on the wall. Reaching for my hand she said, "Join me."

We stood side by side for a minute, silently taking in the lights. An uphill breeze lifted a slight odor of death. "You smell that?" I asked.

Sarah said, "A little. No worry. We'll be back shortly." Turning to face me, she said, "So far so good," and then spread her arms. "I'll take that kiss now."

Chapter 34

We left Sarah's car at the Mexican Restaurant. While I pulled into traffic, she put on my Red Man cap and spoke like a hick. "Ridin' in this here pickup, I feels like a country girl."

I lit one of Jane's cigarettes, glanced at the rearview mirror and said, "You grew up on a farm. You *are* a country girl. Don't act like you're not."

"Smoking again?" she replied. "You nervous?"

Instead of answering, I took a draw and then blew smoke at her. She grinned and began scanning the radio until she found Garth Brooks, singing about thunder. When she began to sing along, I wondered if she was crazy or if perhaps singing was her cigarette. Either way, listening to her somehow calmed me, and I too began to sing as we cruised down the New Cut Road. It seemed odd that in such a moment, my mind would drift to Jane, wishing she could be with us, enjoying the music and the excitement. Sarah slid next to me. I said, "Gonna be bad enough if someone sees you in my truck, let alone sittin' up against me."

She ducked her head down to my lap and said, "This better?"

It kind of pissed me off and I said, "Knock it off. No more tests in discipline."

She rose up, adjusted her cap and said, "Can't a country girl have a little fun?"

"Really? You wanna have fun?" I reached over and put my hand between her legs. Her jeans were warm. I gripped expecting her to move away. She shocked me by leaning back and opening her legs. When she began pushing herself into my hand I looked. Her eyes were closed and her full lips were pressed together. She looked more frightened than passionate.

Watch out!

Ashes fell from the cigarette in my mouth as I jerked my hand to the steering wheel and braked to avoid the car stopped in front of me at the traffic signal.

"Multitasking not your forte'?" Sarah asked as she straightened up and reached for the cigarette in my mouth.

"Jesus," I mumbled.

She slid over, leaned against the passenger door and took a draw. "Isn't this where I'm supposed to smoke a cigarette?"

Looking in the mirror I noticed the approaching vehicle had lights on top. "Great, it's a cop."

Sarah checked it out through the outside mirror and said, "Just don't panic." Three blocks seemed like ten miles with the cop on our tail. Sarah advised, "If he stays behind us, pass the park up and pull into the first gas station." There were several cars in front of us as we neared our turn. The cruiser moved right, passed us all and went on. Sarah gave me a nod and said, "You did well."

Driving into that park to pick up cold dead men didn't make me as nervous as the hot body sitting next to me. Something didn't add up. She seemed different. Suddenly less careful. Woman just sliced a man's throat. Now she's singing, playing around like a hot teenager and smoking a cigarette. Couldn't tell is she'd gotten off on killing a man, or might be trying to make me feel better about what I'd done.

"You okay?" she asked on our way up the hill.

Rolling down the window, I spit my suspicions out to the side of the road and said, "Yep."

One thing for sure, Sarah had brought excitement into my life. Nearing the top, she said, "Guess you already know we should back in."

"Yessss," I answered. "Got a couple small tarps and some bungee cords behind the seat. Hopefully they're big enough to cover 'em."

"We'll make it work."

"So" I asked, "where you planning on dumping these guys?"

"Someplace close preferably. Any suggestions?"

"Be nice if we could dump 'em behind the high school. Then they'd think it's one gang sending a message to another."

"Can't do that," Sarah replied. "Schools have cameras."

"Well then, let's just get 'em in the truck and drive out of the city, south towards Fort Knox. Lots of wooded areas out that way."

She mumbled, "Works for me," while opening the door and climbing out.

I suggested we get the mopeds first, and then asked, "You got more gloves?"

"Sure."

We worked together, first shutting off the gas lines of each unit and then lifting them up onto the lowered tailgate. We pushed them forward overlapping the wheels to leave room for bodies. I spread the first small tarp on the truck bed to avoid blood stains.

Sarah had no problem handling dead men. While carrying her end of the black guy, she talked freely. "Be nice if we could get this done and get back before daylight."

"Back where?"

"Here."

"Are you crazy? Why would you wanna come back here?"

After we lifted body #1 up and onto the tarp, Sarah said, "Just thinking once we get rid of these creeps we could sit here and watch planes and the sunrise."

Turning to get #2, I shook my head, thinking, *Girl ain't right.*

"What?" she asked.

"Nothing." Again, I felt uncomfortable.

Told you dumb ass.

Something was wrong and I couldn't put my mind on it. By the time we loaded all three bodies, Sarah's voice had become distant, like a wife rambling about work. My replies were somehow acknowledging her small talk, but my thoughts ran in another direction.

I've been warning you all along, but you wouldn't listen.

Warning me about what? What am I'm missing?

"Eli. Eli. Elijah!"

"What?" I replied, leaning against the closed tailgate.

"The other tarp."

As I leaned down to pick it up from my side of the truck, she asked, "Are you sure you're okay? You seem odd. Don't tell me this is getting to you."

Snap out of it dude. "No. I, I'm just thinking about Jane. She has no idea where I'm at. Didn't tell her I was meeting up with you tonight."

"Should you call her?"

"My phone's turned off. You said I shouldn't use it when we're together."

"That's right. Use the flip phone."

Mercedes is careless too.

"Really? Now we get sloppy all of a sudden?"

"One time won't hurt."

Don't use it. Why ping a phone you're using at the scene of a crime.

"That's okay. She's probably sleeping by now anyway. I'll fill her in later."

Sarah frowned. "What exactly does 'fill her in' mean?"

While throwing open the tarp, I said, "It means by the time I get home I'll have an alibi for where I've been."

From the opposite side of the truck, Sarah grabbed the tarp and began tucking it. "What kind of alibi will you give her? How does Elijah account for a random night out on the town?"

I closed the tailgate and said, "First of all, she's gonna assume the worst. She'll think I was with you. That means I have to come up with a good excuse for being out so late. Got any ideas?"

Sarah seemed stumped as I got in behind the wheel. She slid in, closed the door and said, "Tell her we got into a confrontation with druggies at the office and they were chasing us. We had to hide out for a while before coming back to our vehicles."

I put the truck in gear and said, "I warned you about Jane on day one. Don't underestimate her. She has an IQ of one-forty."

Sarah seemed to ignore my comment. Instead, she said, "Hope we don't meet up with Officer Goodman on our way out of here."

It neared midnight by the time we drove out of Metro Louisville. My goal was to find the first dark road that we could turn onto without cameras or anyone seeing us. A few miles before the Fort Knox Military Reservation, I took a side road that led into trees and had no lighting. At a half mile off the Dixie Highway we came to a flashing railroad crossing. The train sat still. Looking in both directions, I couldn't see the beginning or the end. Stopping I said, "Now what?"

Sarah motioned to the right and said, "Down there. Is that an open car?"

"Yep."

"How about we send these boys on a trip?"

"Works for me, but what if there's a bum or two in that car?"

"Oh well." Sarah replied. "If there's a bum in there, might have to deal with it."

"You maybe, not me."

"Really?"

"Not part of my deal."

Sarah glanced back. "And these guys in the truck were?"

"They were gonna kick my ass and rape you. They needed to die."

"Turn off your headlights and pull down there. I'll look inside."

I left the road. While I drove along the tracks toward the open boxcar, Sarah removed a black head covering from her purse and started pulling it on. It had holes for eyes and nose. About 30 yards from the open door, she slipped on black gloves and said, "Stop here. I'll be right back."

I sat watching as she dashed to the train car. It felt like watching a movie. She stood at the opening shining her phone light inside. I figured she would run back but instead, she climbed in. For over a minute, my fingers tapped on the steering wheel. Finally, she reappeared at the doorway, waving me to come. "Ooookay."

When I got close, she said, "Back in and hand them up to me."

Standing in the truck bed actually made it easy to maneuver the bodies into the train car. Sarah dragged each of the first two guys as far from the door as she could. I saved the big white dude for last. Using both hands, I grabbed his hoodie at the collar and lifted him up against the edge of the opening. Moonlight hit his face and it was the first time I got a good look at his eyes. Both remained open. As I had noticed earlier, they were odd. The right one pointed straight up as if looking at me. The other one seemed damaged and off center. An incision from my spoon ran vertical about an inch and a half behind the eye. Sarah returned and saw my stare.

"There a problem?" she asked.

"Nope," I replied, "just checking out this guy's eyes."

While grabbing his shoulders to pull him in, she said, "Yeah. One's messed up. I noticed it as soon as he took off his hood."

With my arm wrapped around the man's legs, I lifted his ass up into the train. "He's heavy. You need me to help you?"

"No. I'll get him back there. You start with the mopeds."

It took less than ten minutes to get rid of three bodies, three mopeds, two tarps and bungee cords. Together we pushed and pulled on the large door until we had it shut like all the other cars. We were in the truck and about to leave when I noticed headlights coming through the trees from the road the way we came. I said, "Looks like we're getting company."

"Great. Can we make it to the woods?"

Keeping my lights off, I drove quickly across the short field of tall grass, circled and backed in between trees, facing the train. Sarah pulled off her head covering, began straightening her hair and said, "Best kill the engine. Pisses me off."

"What?" I asked.

"Thought we would get out of here quickly."

"You still wantin' to go back to the lookout?"

"Noooo. I'm trying to get you home before the genius wakes up."

"Well thank you. Mercedes must have gone home. Sounds like I'm talking to Sarah again."

Headlights morphed into a Sheriff's department SUV. "Not good," Sarah mumbled. The vehicle stopped perpendicular to the train about 150 yards from us. Exhaust trailed from its tailpipe. We were well hidden. Staring up at the sky, she asked, "You got any more of those cigarettes?"

We both lit up, keeping the flash below the dash. I leaned against my door, Sarah against hers, still staring out. I could see a slight shaking in her hands. "You okay?" I asked.

Without looking at me, she said, "Yes, I'm fine."

"Did it bother you killing that hoodie guy?"

She didn't answer, but shook her head to say, "No."

Then I noticed her wiping her eyes with her knuckles. *Whoa. Is tough girl crying?*

She looked back at me and said, "Worried about that moon up there. Hoping it doesn't reflect off your truck enough to give us away." After staring at my silence, she said, "Those guys wouldn't sit there like that unless they knew the train was going to move soon." When I acknowledged with a nod, she added, "Good time for a session. Anything you want to talk about?"

"Maybe."

"Maybe what?"

"There's a lot I'd like to know about you, but I'm a little hesitant to ask."

"You can ask anything," she replied. "I don't have to answer."

"Okay then, the old man. What did he do to you?"

Sarah took a draw, exhaled out the window and then stared toward the SUV while speaking. "I had just turned eight. It was summer and school had let out. Mother was to be admitted to the hospital for her mastectomy. She agreed to let my father keep me for a month providing the old man and woman would accompany me on the flight and stay with me until my return. A man I didn't know at the time came to our house, drove us to the airport and flew with us to the Middle East. The day after our arrival, my father and the other man left. Sometime later, two more women came to his house. I watched as they spread plastic and then a white sheet on the floor. They told me to sit on it. I had no idea what they were doing. It seemed we were going to play a game until the two women and the old man began to hold me down. The old woman removed my underwear. They all chanted in Arabic while she...."

"No, don't tell me they...."

"Yes, they mutilated me. They performed a clitoridectomy and infibulation..."

I could only assume that the big words Sarah used meant they had circumcised her.

"...The old man held his hand over my mouth. I tried to scream, to bite him, but nothing worked. He told me it would be over quicker and hurt less if I didn't move. It scared me so much. I could feel the cuts and the blood running from my body as they stitched me."

"They didn't numb you?"

"No, not at all.... When it was over, they tied rope around my legs so I couldn't move. I was like that for almost two weeks."

"What did your father say about all that?"

"He and the other man did not return until the last day of my stay. By then I was walking. When I tried to speak to him about what they had done, he put his finger to my lips and said, 'A girt never speaks of these things to her father.'"

"Jesus. Did you talk to your mother at all, like on the phone?"

"They didn't let me call her until after the ropes came off. I wanted so badly to tell her how much I was hurting. They warned me not to speak of what had been done because it might hurt her recovery. When I got home, it didn't take long before she knew something was wrong.

I waited until we were alone and told her. She inspected me and started screaming and cursing. I'm telling you, Mom cried more than I did."

"I can only imagine."

"That night, from my room, I could hear her arguing with the old couple. She came back to me and slept in my bed, holding me all night. The next day, she told me what they did was a religious thing, and that I was never to tell anyone what had happened."

"Why didn't your mother go to the police?"

"I'm smart enough to know that when a mother remains quiet about her child's abuse, it's likely out of fear. Two weeks later, Mom took me to Louisville. A lady doctor there put me to sleep and did a defibulation surgery."

"I'm sorry Sarah, but I have no idea what that means."

"Infibulation means that after they circumcised my clitoris and inner labia, they stitched me up to close off the vaginal opening, leaving only a small hole to urinate and menstruate. The defibulation surgery opened me back up. I had to hide the pain of that surgery from the old couple."

"Oh my God! My mother would have killed em'."

Sarah turned to look in my eyes. "They said the old woman died of natural causes. Between you and me, I'd say Momma helped her along."

"Oh."

Sarah finished her cigarette in silence. When she put the butt in the coffee cup I used for an ashtray, she turned back to me. "As time passed the old man began to include me in his daily readings. He taught me the peace and love aspects of the Muslim religion and it seemed to reassure my mother's words. My circumcision had been a religious thing. A purification of sort. At that time, I suppose I was too young to think differently or to understand what they'd taken from me."

Not knowing what to say, I sat staring out the window and wondering, *How many American Muslim girls have been through this?*

Sarah said, "I shouldn't have told you."

Instead of speaking, I shook my head.

"Do you think differently of me?"

I looked at her and asked, "Is this why you're still a virgin?"

She turned away. After a few seconds, she spoke and her voice told me she was crying. "It's not my body that keeps me from it. It's my mind. The memories. The trauma and the fear instilled in me by the adults around me."

She stopped talking again. It felt like someone had hit the pause button. *What should I say?*

Leave it alone.

Somewhere in the woods nearby, a hoot owl hooted. A cool breeze blew in Sarah's window and out mine. The essence of her pain brushed my mind. I put my cigarette out and sat silently with a chest full of anger and disgust. It made me think of my Muslim co-workers at Indirect Cable. Like me, they work in the call center. How could I ever look at them again without wondering, *have they been mutilated?* Because of my time and conversations with them, I had developed a comfortable acceptance of Islam. I would think no less of them as individuals; however, my feelings for their religious culture had been scarred with a festering wound that may never heal. My heart ached in the same way it did when I first heard that my Catholic friend had been abused by his priest and that such behavior was a common problem within Catholicism.

A loud noise interrupted and the freight train began clanging into motion. One by one, boxcars passed in front of the Sheriff vehicle's headlights. "At least it's heading away from Louisville," I mumbled, not knowing what else to say.

Eventually the noise lessoned and the last car slid by. When I reached for the ignition, Sarah said, "Wait. Not until they're out of sight."

The train's air horn blew in the distance as the SUV accelerated across the tracks and down the road. When it disappeared beyond trees, I started the truck and pulled back into the field. Wasting no time, I bounced without headlamps to the road. Sarah remained against her door as I turned on the headlights and drove away from the night's worries. Not a word got spoken until we were on the Dixie Highway at 55mph heading back toward Louisville. Sarah looked my way and said, "Over time, I began to accept what had been done to me as nothing more than a religious ritual. Something that happens to most girls in my father's culture. The insanity of it all sank in during the summer when I turned thirteen. While overseas I got introduced to a couple. Like me, the girl was covered up, but still, I could tell she wasn't much older than me. At first I assumed the man to be her father. After a while I figured out that they were man and wife. When the girl said something her husband didn't like, he struck her. I looked to my father. He raised his finger to his lips and shook his head as if to say, it's none of our business."

"Has your father beaten on you?"

"No. I try not to give him a reason."

"Did he say anything to you about the girl that got mistreated?"

"He didn't have to. The fact that he accepted the man's behavior said it all."

"Wow."

"Upon my return to the states, the old man began his preaching about boys. I found myself being indoctrinated into the male dominant aspects of the Muslim religion. A religion I had previously understood to be about peace and love had suddenly in my mind become about imprisonment. To make it worse, I heard girls at school talking about themselves and their bodies. With my father's culture, I think the men believe girls won't miss what they never experienced. That's not true in America. I went to a sleepover with several girls. Things were said. Things were done. Girls were messing with girls, you know, touching and stuff. That's when I realized what the old woman had taken from me. From that day forward, my anger grew. At home, alone, I rubbed myself, desperately trying to imitate the feelings my friends had shown. It didn't happen and it made me feel ... incomplete. I've always feared no American man will want me for his wife."

"I don't know what to say. This is like crazy, uncivilized stuff from the past."

"It's not the past, Elijah. Millions of women living in the world today are victims of Female Genital Mutilation."

"I don't see how anyone can take that away from a woman, from their daughter. It's insane."

"Each year in High School, I grew to hate that old man for how he tried to control me. The way he meddled into my personal business. One day we were trail riding Lucifer and Ruth. The old man said he had seen me walking alone with a boy at school. He called my behavior improper, and said that he would have to communicate that to my father. I became furious."

"How old were you?"

"Sixteen. It angered me to think that he had been spying on me at school. He had no reason to be there. I said, 'You will not tell me who I can talk to.' Never before had I spoken to him in such a way. He pulled Lucifer close and backhanded me in the face. I nearly fell off my horse. For the rest of our ride, I remained silent while he preached the ways of Sharia Law. Suddenly, I knew how my mother's ancestors felt when they had become the property of the white man. The words coming out of that old man's mouth were telling me that I would spend my adulthood as some man's slave. So—"

No wonder she hasn't been with a man.

"—when we got back to the barn, he pulled off his saddle and like always, expected me to put it away. I waited for him to take Lucifer into the stall. He pulled the door most of the way shut before taking off the bridle. With his back to the door, I closed it all the way and then latched it. I came back to the window with a metal bucket and began banging it on the bars. Lucifer got agitated immediately. 'Stop!' the old man shouted at me. He struggled to open the door but could not. 'Let me out, I demand you!' My heart raced as I continued beating the bucket on the bars. Lucifer kicked him and he hit the wall. 'Don't do this!' he screamed. I said, 'It's payback old man! You people had no right to take away part of my body? You have no right to tell me who I can talk to? And you will never hit me again!' All the while I kept banging the bucket. He screamed, 'I only do what your father orders. I teach you and speak for him in his absence.' Lucifer reared up and came down on him and he quit begging. It was over. I dropped the bucket, and Lucifer calmed down. When I felt certain the old man was dead, I put Ruth in her stall, put away the saddles and unlatched the stall door. I left him there and went to the house."

"Was your mother at home?"

"She was. As soon as I walked in, she knew something had happened. She asked, 'What have you done?' I said, 'He will never put his hands on me again.'"

Chapter 35

Hot water felt like heaven while I stood in the shower wallowing in the night's events. Sarah's mutilation bothered me more than the killing of three men. Memories surfaced of my own mother's submissiveness to my father and I thought, *How sad is it that men in the world still feel a right to control their women.* In my mind, I wished for an opportunity to be with Sarah. To hold her. Comfort her, and to show her that a man could still appreciate her beauty and could still enjoy being with her. Make love to her.

Somewhere between shampoo and soap, my mind got stuck on the kiss on the wall. Sarah's tongue, her hands on my neck and in my hair, and how I had wanted it to go much farther. As always, my promiscuous mind pulled Jane into the final moments of an otherwise unfaithful fantasy. All ended well, my breathing slowed, and I finally felt relaxed. When I shut the water off, the sound of the exhaust vent in the ceiling filled the room. I pulled the shower door open to grab my towel, and there sat Jane on the closed toilet in her night shirt. "What the hell!"

She stared at my manhood and said, "At least I know you didn't fuck her."

Reaching for the towel, I said, "Can't a man have a little privacy?"

"I didn't interrupt."

I began drying and said, "I hope you got off asshole."

"Don't asshole me mister. My text said, wake me when you get home."

"Maybe I didn't wanna interrupt your sleep."

"Maybe I wasn't asleep! Maybe I laid awake for the past six hours worrying about you! Maybe I—"

"Maybe you should calm down while I dry off and then maybe we can talk about it over a drink."

When I walked into the kitchen, wearing nothing but a towel, Jane sat at the table. She had two short glasses with a couple ice cubes in each and had already opened my bottle of Single Barrel Kentucky Spirit Wild Turkey. "Dammit, Jane, Jimmy Russell signed that bottle!"

"And?"

"And I didn't wanna open it."

"How do you plan on drinking it if you don't open it?"

I took a deep breath and said, "Never mind. It's opened now. Might as well enjoy it."

Before taking a seat, I poured two fingers into each glass, pushed one to Jane and said, "Can't drink too much of this or I won't make it to work."

She picked up her glass, and said, "You may not make it anyway."

Jane made a face upon her first ever sip of Wild Turkey. "Jesus," she complained. "This is supposed to be special?"

I took a sip and swished it around in my mouth before swallowing. "Yep. Pretty damn good, if you ask me." As Jane took another sip, I asked, "So where do I start?"

"Start with why I shouldn't be pissed after you spent the night with your girlfriend."

Glancing at the clock, I said, "She's not my girlfriend, and we didn't spend the night."

Jane shook her head at the bourbon and said, "Okay, then tell me what you've been doing for the last six hours."

"You sure you wanna know?"

"Don't mess with me."

Don't do it.

Believe she already knows.

"We were up at the park, and—"

"Again? I asked you not to go there."

"We had to go somewhere private. There was a drug thing going on where we normally meet and I had to whoop up on some dealer guy and we were afraid his buddies would come back and—"

"This woman is going to get you killed!"

I stopped talking, took a breath and then a sip. When Jane gave me the look, I said, "Are you gonna let me tell you what happened or are you gonna keep interrupting?"

She growled. "Okay, okay, I get it. So you went up to the park. What does *up* mean? Did you go up to the lookout?"

"Yes we did. But I didn't wanna sit in the car with her, so we got out and started walking and talking and when we turned back to the car, there were three hoodie guys that came along on mopeds and they were blocking the car." I hesitated to take a breath and a sip of bourbon.

"And?" Jane asked while setting down her already empty glass.

"They were gonna rape Sarah and kill me."

"They said that?"

"No. But they wouldn't let us leave and they started talking about Sarah doing heroin and having sex with 'em."

"And?"

"Jane, one of them was a nasty-ass white guy with a damaged eye. I thought about you and your father."

"John told you."

"Yes."

"Dammit, Eli. I told you to stay away from that park. He could have killed you."

"But he didn't."

"So what did you do?"

"I had no choice. It wasn't gonna end well. Guy called me a retard and I went off."

"And?"

"We killed 'em."

"Eli! You're not a killer!"

"Guess I am now," I replied and then finished my whiskey.

"Dammit. This makes me so mad I can't stand it. For years, I've dreamed of the day I would look that bastard in the eye and kill him myself. He took my father and, and now he's turned my husband into a killer." She stared for a bit and then asked, "Are you okay with this?"

"Wouldn't matter if I wasn't. We did it. It's over. And now I have to move on."

Jane shook her head and asked, "Did y'all clean up the scene? What'd you do with the bodies?"

"We did clean up, and we took them and their mopeds to a place down by Fort Knox. We put 'em on a boxcar and the last we saw the train was heading off to who knows where."

Jane poured her and me another two fingers. She downed half of hers before I could take a sip and said, "I told you this woman would be trouble. She's either going to get you dead or put in jail."

"I told you she offered excitement."

"Exciting for you, dammit, but not for me sitting around here worrying...." She looked up with fire in her eyes. "You said, *we* killed them. Does that mean you didn't kill all three?"

"I did two. She did one."

"Good. And I guess you get no extra money for this business tonight."

"Correct."

"Let me ask you something, Eli. How do you know that when this job of yours is over, you'll get your money? What if something happens to her? Who pays you then?"

Not wanting to mention Ella, I said, "Guess we need to talk about that."

"You guess? Dammit Eli, you haven't even thought this thing out. I can tell you're in over your head."

"That's not true. I know what I'm doin'."

"Bull! Some pretty girl has you all hypnotized and you're getting careless. Eli, you go through with this and that bitch doesn't pay you, I'll find her and I'll kill her myself."

Cut her off. The whiskey's making her mean.

"Jane. I'm not hypnotized and I'm not stupid. I'll work out the details with Sarah next time we're together."

"Details? With Sarah?" My dearly beloved threw down the rest of her bourbon, looked at the glass and said, "Not bad after all." Then she got that evil grin of hers and said, "Come here."

When I stood up and stepped in front of her, she pulled off my towel and asked, "Any energy left in this thing for me?"

"Guess that depends."

"On what? The details?" I closed my eyes as Jane's warm hands took me. She said, "While I work on this, we both can think about the details."

I stood there enjoying my wife, thinking of Sarah, and wondering, *How does any of this make sense?*

Three rounds of Wild Turkey and one round of Jane left me euphoric to say the least. "Get up," she insisted. "Let's go smoke a cigarette." For a moment, I lay there, eyes closed in a perfect state of paralysis, wondering why something so awesome had to create such a mess. A towel hit me in the face. "I said get your ass up," Jane repeated as she left the room.

Get up asshole. You owe her the company.

When I opened the balcony door, Jane had herself wrapped in a goose down comforter. She handed me a smoke and then lit hers. "Did you take a pack of my cigarettes?"

Seating myself next to her, I said, "Sorry, but it was only a half pack."

"You don't have to be sorry. I don't mind. Just thought I was losing my mind. Knew I didn't smoke a whole pack yesterday."

"I shared them with Sarah."

"She smokes?"

"Apparently."

"Eli, we've talked about your Godly beliefs. Do you still believe he's always watching?"

I lit my cigarette and thought about it for a couple draws. "Yes Dear, I do."

"So you saying everything you've done with this girl is okay in your God's eyes?"

"I hope so."

Jane turned and hit me in the shoulder. "What's that mean?"

"I told you what we did tonight. I pray I won't be condemned for it."

"I don't give a damn about what you did to those hoodie guys. I'm talking about your girl, Sarah. Are you doing anything with her out of line with me and you?"

"I respect our promises to one another."

"You broke them before."

"The Lord knows what I'm goin' through. I'm hopin' he'll judge me on the merits of my efforts to honor the vows I made to you."

Jane stood up and said, "Elijah Allen Haycraft, that's the biggest line of bull I've ever heard!"

"What?"

"Don't what me boy. What the hell? You want to be judged on the merits of your efforts? Is it that much of an effort to be faithful?"

Damn right it is. "You're a smart girl, Jane. I'm a male human being with the same biology as every other animal on this friggin' planet. Damn right it's an effort. Like any other man, I fight my animal instincts every day. But in the end, it's you and my religion that keeps me straight."

That's enough, dumb-ass.

Jane stood there staring at me, wishing she could cry, and finally said, "But you're not sleeping with her?"

Now that's a question I can answer. "No, Honey. I promise you I'm not."

Jane sat back down, took a draw and said, "What about Sarah? Is she a religious person?"

I smashed out my cigarette. "I'd say she has her beliefs."

Chapter 36

Though it wasn't easy, I did make it into work that day. Didn't see John until lunch. He invited me out to the parking lot. We stood behind my truck. He said, "Damn, you look rough."

"Up pretty much all night."

"With your girl, Sarah?"

"It got complicated, but everything turned out okay. Got home late and then had to deal with Jane."

"Bet that was fun."

"I'm assuming you didn't do any more research."

"Correct. Did you ask your girl about the NASA stuff?"

"Yeah. She says the guys we're dealing with were moles in NASA. She believes they're part of a terrorist organization that's already infiltrated the group that supplies rockets for the U.S. Air Force Space Program. It has a lot to do with the global warming, climate change crap we keep hearing about. Apparently these assholes think they can eventually control the weather, as a weapon of sort."

John lit a joint and said, "And these are the same guys that are running for office?"

"Crazy, isn't it?"

John laughed and said, "They're like, super moles."

"Exactly. And here's the kicker. While born in the U.S. they both have Middle Eastern fathers, and both are somehow associated with that guy Amor Saline Al-Riase, who might be selling secrets to the Chinese."

"Wow," John replied. "So you're saying they're also connected to the Doris girl."

"Oh yeah. Think I already told you. Doris lives at the Wellington Estate. John, these people are trying to infiltrate the U.S. Government with their offspring. It seems their ultimate goal is to have blood in the White House."

John took a hit and said, "Ain't that what the Right said about Obama?"

"You got it," I replied.

"Sounds like this Al-Riase guy has big plans for America."

"I'd say."

"Want some of this?" John asked, holding up the joint.

"Better not. Might fall asleep."

John took another hit and said, "Seems to me someone needs to eliminate these guys before they get elected."

I tilted my head, and he knew.

"Oh no. Hell no. Not you?"

My silence said it all.

"You saying that's what this bitch's paying you to do?"

"John, you just said it needs to be done."

"Yeah, but not by you. Let the got-damn CIA do it."

"It's complicated."

"Oh, I'm sure it is!" John blurted. Then he mumbled, "This woman does have you hypnotized."

"Excuse me?" *Same word Jane used.* "What'd you just say?"

John stood silent. He took another hit and held it as long as he could. His eyes were closed and his head pivoted left and right, back and forth, like a hard drive being read. I knew my friend well. Figured he was analyzing. By the time he had exhaled, his face changed from concerned to CONCERNED. "Elijah, you've got to tell me what's going on."

"Not until you come clean with me. I'm not stupid, John. You've been talking to Jane about me and Sarah. What's up with that?"

John motioned his head toward the car and said, "Get in." After we were seated, he said, "You know I've known Jane a lot longer than I've known you. She's like a sister. Woman calls me on the phone, dude, I'm gonna answer."

"She called you?"

"Yes. She asked me if I knew anything about a girl you were seeing. Knew right away who she was talking about."

"And you said what?"

"Told her some woman was paying attention to you."

"Paying attention to me? Why the hell didn't you just tell her I was working for the lady?"

"She already knew." John's eyes got big. "Apparently, *you* told her!"

"I ... I did."

"Ain't no married woman that stupid, Elijah. Especially not Jane. She thinks you're having an affair. And why wouldn't she? You already burnt her ass once."

"But I—"

You need to tell him the truth about that.

John said, "Look. Stop it man. Next to Jane, I'm your best friend. So, don't sit there acting like you ain't dying to put your dick in that girl."

"But I haven't."

"As your friend, I'm gonna take your word on that. But knowing what I know now, I'm afraid you might be in over your head. I wanna help you, man, but you've gotta involve Jane."

"No. I can't. She already knows too much."

John said, "Look at me. Maybe you might think you've got this thing all figured out, but I'm worried maybe you don't. Believe you need a second set of eyes. Someone not infatuated with the girl."

"I'm not infatuated."

"Stop lyin' to yourself, Bro. Listen to me. If Jane sets her mind on something, she figures it out. Every detail. She crosses every T and dots every I. She's the stuff and I know you know it."

"But she's my wife. Why would I wanna put her in harm's way?"

"Then don't. Just let her help you with the details. If you don't she's either gonna worry herself sick or snoop until she figures it out on her own."

Good point. For a moment, I sat staring at John. As usual he seemed uncomfortable.

He said, "Elijah, how come you look at me but never ask about my scar?"

"Hell, I don't know. Guess I figured if you wanted to talk about it, you would."

"But why haven't you ever asked how it happened?"

"I did ask. I asked Jane."

"And what did she say?"

"She said you don't like to talk about it."

"Elijah, Jane did it."

Backing up against the window, I said, "What the? Why? What'd you do to her?"

"I didn't do anything to her. Just pissed her off. And I blame myself because I know how she is."

"What's that supposed to mean?"

"You know how she is. We were drinking beer. Got into an argument about something stupid. Elijah, your girl can't take criticism."

"You don't have to tell me." Each time Jane erupted on me, it had been triggered by criticism.

"She had a bottle opener in her hand when she took a swing. The sharp point got me."

I remembered back and said, "When we first got married, I assumed her anger to be a byproduct of the pressures of med school."

"Are you saying she went off on you?"

Instead of answering, I nodded.

"Did she hurt you?"

I held my hands up, eyes wide open and said, "No scars."

"Don't tell me you like it when she whoops up on your ass."

"She's doesn't really hurt me. I gave her an ultimatum. If I ever feel the necessity to hit her back, we won't be living together."

John shook his head. "I'd say you two crazy ass people deserve one another."

"Probably. So, what else did Jane say about Sarah?"

"Nothing really. Oh yeah, she asked me what the woman looks like?"

"What'd you say?"

John grinned and said, "I told her she was one hot piece of work."

"Jesus."

Chapter 37

During the first weekend in October, Louisville hosts the infamous Saint James Art Fair. Jane and I typically spend a few hours wallowing in the array of artistic expressions. On a seasonably warm Friday evening, we parked four blocks away and walked. I wore jeans and a pull-over. Jane wore one of those long flowery dresses with a low top and no bra. Instead of carrying a purse, she wore a small backpack. Quick as she got out of the car, she lit a cigarette. "Want one?" she asked.

"No."

"Bet if Sarah was here you'd share one with her."

"Never shoulda told you that."

"But you did."

An array of people passed carrying paintings, sculptures and the like. When we were in the heart of things, Jane glanced around at the crowd and said, "Okay Mr. Haycraft, no phones and we're away from the car. Believe we can talk safely now."

From my pocket I removed a new white flip phone and handed it to Jane.

"What's this?" she asked.

"Put it in your pocket. I've still got the one I bought when we went out of town. Now we're good to go. I figure two can play this game. If Sarah and I can have a pair, why can't you and me?"

"Well, aren't you the smart one?"

"Only use these when we can't use our smart phones. Never say my name. Just call me, Sweetie. I'll call you, Honey. Even in text messages, just use Sweetie."

Without stopping, Jane kissed me on the cheek and said, "I love you, Sweetie."

"And keep in mind, when I'm with Sarah, I'll have the battery out of my white phone so she can't see it on her software. As soon as we part, I'll put it back in to see if you left me a message."

"Can I leave mine on?"

"I would think so."

We walked a bit further before Jane said, "So that's it, just the phones?"

Reaching for her hand I changed the subject. "How close were you and John in school?"

Jane stopped walking. "We were good friends. Why do you ask?"

"Talking to him, I'd say you two were a number."

"What the hell, Eli? I know John didn't tell you that! What makes you say such a thing?"

"John says if you call, he's gonna answer."

"And?" she shouted. "What wrong with that?"

Two 20-somethings stood behind Jane, obviously eavesdropping. One raised her eyebrows and tilted her head at me.

"Please lower your voice," I spoke quietly to Jane.

"Don't tell me to lower my voice! You think I slept with John!" she continued.

Don't set her off, dumbass. "Didn't say that."

"Then what are you saying?"

"It's just that I know you two have been talking."

"He told you that?"

I stood there without answering, staring at her eyes.

"John told you we've been talking?" she repeated, quieter than the time before.

She knows you know.

But does she care?

You're getting ready to find out.

"For starters, you need to know that for most of the time my mother spent sick and dying, my father was overseas. John's mother helped take care of Mom. Dad came home long enough to bury her and then he went back. I stayed with John and his mother until Dad came back home. John and I were like brother and sister."

"That's what he said."

"Eli, I called him out of concern."

Thank you. "Concern for what?"

"You know what," she replied.

"You still don't trust me, do you?"

One of the two girls giggled. Jane saw me looking, turned and snarled, "Do you mind?"

Believe they knew better than to say anything. I took my wife by the hand and tugged her into walking. Neither of us spoke as I searched for a spot to sit and smoke. Art enthusiasts mingled elbow to elbow in all directions. We neared the Conrad-Caldwell House Museum, a multi-story stone mansion constructed in the late 1890s. A sidewalk led away from the street to behind the mansion. I had hoped for privacy but got none. Several small groups stood around like social outcasts, smoking and chatting under large trees. I wiped colored leaves away and offered Jane a seat on the small concrete porch. She settled in with her feet on the steps and pulled out her cigarettes. It seemed her anger had begun to subside. When I said, "Let me have one," she grinned. Jane reached out with her lighter. After my first draw, I said, "John says I need to talk to you about what I'm doing, the project, you know."

Still holding her unlit cigarette, Jane asked, "Why would he say such a thing?"

"You know why. He's afraid I might be missing something."

"And I'm afraid he might be right," Jane replied while lighting her smoke. "Fill me in."

I scanned our surroundings and said, "Okay, but first there's something else I need to tell you."

"You look nervous, Eli. Don't you dare stand there and tell me you've been sleeping with Sarah."

"No, but that is kind of what I wanna talk about. All this time you've been accusing me of cheating on you. I told you over and over that I didn't, but you wouldn't believe me. Now I know why."

Jane's face tightened as she asked, "What are you talking about?"

"John told you I did it with Margaret. Didn't he?"

Jane closed her eyes and her head moved slightly back and forth. *What's she thinking?* "Jane, he's the only one who could have told you that."

She opened her eyes and said, "So you saying he lied?"

Bingo. "No dear. I lied. Don't ask me why, but I told him I slept with her. I lied to him to make him think I was something I'm not. It was a big mistake. A stupid guy thing. Jane, I haven't slept with another woman since we got married."

"You lied and made me think all this time that you had cheated on me."

"No. I was drunk, and I lied to make John think I was the shit. Had no idea he would run and tell my wife."

"You never told him any differently?"

"Started to a couple times but didn't. But you can bet your sweet ass I will, now that you verified what I thought. What kind of best friend tells your wife you cheated on her?"

"If you weren't sleeping with that woman, then why were you hanging out with her? She was practically old enough to be your mother?"

For a moment, I couldn't answer.

"What, cat got your tongue?"

"You just said it, Jane. She reminded me of my mother."

"She did?"

"Yes she did. There were times when I needed companionship. Someone to talk to. Someone to sit next to. You were too busy. For me, it wasn't about sex. She was my friend until you ran her off."

"Oh well. She was trying to seduce my husband."

"We were close friends. Just like you and John. Should I run him out of town?"

With Jane, sometimes it's hard to tell if she's about to make up, or about to go off. With nothing more to say, I stood there finishing my cigarette, lady watching and wondering how with all the different versions of females in the world, I wound up with one as unreasonable as my crazy-ass Jane.

"So" she finally spoke, "you swear you never had sex with that woman."

"I do."

Jane leaned back against the building, cigarette in her mouth, pulled her top opened a bit and said, "You're making me hot."

Is this her way of saying I'm sorry? Jane's nipples were suddenly protruding through the material of her dress. While I stood admiring her cleavage, she moved her right leg up a step. Her dress rose to her knee. "What're you doing?" I asked.

She took one more draw, laid her cigarette on the step, and said, "Told you, I'm having an issue." As she spoke, Jane's tongue slid out a little, wetting her lips.

"Stop it," I whispered.

She grinned and said, "I can't," then used her left hand to open her dress enough for me to see she wasn't wearing anything under it. "Guess what Honey?"

I looked around to make sure no one else could see what I was seeing. When I took a deep breath, Jane said, "I'm ... having ... an orgasm."

Your wife is crazy.

Glancing back and forth between bystanders and my wife's contractions, I asked, "Do you realize what you're doing to me?"

"Ohhh baby. Let me see."

"That ain't gonna happen. Not here."

Jane leaned forward to touch me, but I moved out of her reach. She leaned back and said, "I wish I could do for you right here, right now, what you just did for me."

"I didn't do anything."

"Honey, you have no idea." Jane took a draw from her cigarette. As she exhaled, I noticed her staring past me. Turning, I saw what appeared to be a middle aged lesbian couple holding hands. One seemed to be talking to another woman. The other stared our way. "Eli, I believe someone is interested."

"In you, I'd say."

"Should I flash her?"

"Hell no!" I positioned myself between Jane and the woman. "You behave."

I smashed out my cigarette and dropped it into a flower pot. Jane did the same. "Have a seat, Honey." When I sat down next to my flirtatious wife, she said, "You're no fun."

We both watched as the lesbian couple walked off. The looker turned our way and winked. Jane said, "She's cute."

"Are you seriously attracted to that woman?"

"Not really." She placed her hand on my leg. "I'm just trying to tease you."

"Should we go on home and not talk about what we came here to talk about?"

"No. We have to talk."

"Then you have to behave."

Jane removed her hand from my leg, took a deep breath and said, "Fine. Since you're no fun, let's talk about your project."

I stared at her for a moment. *I love my wife.* "Alright, here's the deal. I'm gonna consider you as a consultant. I'll fill you in. When I'm done, you can give me your assessment or advice or whatever."

"Works for me."

"Basically, my girl's a rookie spook. She's the daughter of a rich Dubai businessman and an African American woman from here in Kentucky. Some thirty years ago, while Sarah's mother studied abroad, Amor Saline Al-Riase, a wealthy Emirati businessman, paid her to have his child. He also paid an extreme amount for Sarah's support and her schooling all the way through Oxford."

"Oxford. My, my."

"She was raised here on a farm but spent a portion of her summers overseas with her father speaking his language, learning his Islamic culture, and traveling to places few Americans are allowed to visit. As result, she got recruited by," looking around, I whispered, "the CIA."

"Thought you said she works for Homeland?"

"Turns out that's a cover."

"Seems a stretch," Jane said while rubbing her forehead. "But go ahead."

"During her childhood, Sarah attended a Catholic school, yet got reminded often that she was never to do anything to dishonor her father's religion. The man and woman who owned the farm that Sarah and her mother lived on, taught Sarah Arabic while indoctrinating her with the beliefs of Islam. Long story short, about a year ago, her father informed her that he had arranged her marriage to James Proctor."

Jane's eyes wondered. She appeared to be people watching. I asked, "Are you listening to me?"

"Yes."

"Do you follow me so far?"

"Perfectly. Is Sarah a practicing Muslim?"

"If she is, I haven't seen it."

"She doesn't like, cover up or whatever?"

"No," I replied, "at least not around me."

"Okay. We're to believe that your girl doesn't want to marry the son of a U.S. Senator. She's an American so she doesn't have to do that. Therefore, nothing you've said so far explains why she needs your help."

"Recently, Sarah's mother saw a news broadcast that showed some terrorists being taken into custody. They each had a small shape tattooed on the back of their necks. She recognized the shape. Sarah has one on the same spot on the back of her neck."

Jane stood up and said, "So now we're assuming that your girl Sarah is a terrorist?"

"No. We're assuming her father is. Those who tattooed Sarah were working for him. It happened when she was a child, while her mother wasn't at home. They told her they were removing a tick. Her mother believed their story and figured the removal had left the marking. Sarah said she never thought much of it, considering where it was. But her mother, well, when she saw the newscast, she got concerned. Now they're both convinced there's a connection and that Sarah's father had her tattooed because he has plans for her that involves terrorism."

Looking down at me, Jane said, "You let a spook tell you she didn't know her father is a terrorist?"

"I feel what you're saying, and I am skeptical, but Sarah seems ... convincing."

"Well, yes. I'm sure she does. She's an operative, Eli."

I stood and said, "Hear me out." We began walking back toward the art show. "It was when Sarah started investigating her own father that her mother told her the whole story about him paying her to get pregnant. Sarah always believed that she was the result of a summer fling and that her mother received support from a good father."

"Still seems naïve for someone of her education and occupation. From what you've told me so far, I'd say the government recruited this girl because they already had their eyes on her rich daddy."

"You're probably right," I replied. "But you'd think they would have her overseas watching him. Right now, they've got her working here for Homeland Security. Sarah is convinced that her father, like everyone else, thinks she works for Homeland Security."

Jane frowned and said, "To a terrorist, Homeland Security is a threat."

Good point. "Sarah says she's worried that the Agency will discover her father's ties to terrorism. Then, they'll think she's some kind of double agent and that her mother is in on it. On top of that, she has no intentions of being married to James Proctor, or anyone else her father picks."

"So?"

"So she wants me to help her do away with all three, James, Timothy, and her father."

"Timothy?"

"Timothy Wellington, the guy we just flew out to see in Virginia. He's the son of former Ambassador Marshal Wellington."

"Why all three? Why not just the father?"

"Oh. Well, there's more. In researching, Sarah discovered that James and Timothy are like her. Both were born of foreign fathers under similar circumstances. She actually wants to interrogate them. Among other things, she wants to find out who their biological fathers are."

"She wants to find out? Or the CIA wants to find out?"

"Both. Apparently that's why they approached me in the first place. David Weeper convinced Sarah that I'm the man to help her get them to talk, and he's willing to pay me to do that."

"He's not paying you, Eli. The Agency is."

"True. The Agency is paying me to help Sarah extract information. Sarah's mother is paying me to make sure no one survives."

"In that case," Jane replied, "I'd say Mr. Weeper and the CIA are using all three of you."

"Maybe they are. Hell, I don't know. Regardless, I'd say these two guys and Sarah were conceived for the purpose of infiltrating our U.S. Government. James is running for State Senate. Timothy is running for a seat in Congress."

"And your girl works for the government."

"Exactly," I replied.

"Sounds like this Amor Saline guy wants his grandbabies to have two U.S. born parents."

"Bingo," I replied.

"Okay, you've already met these two guys, James and Timothy. Do you consider them to be as bad as the hoodie guys you and she...," Jane glanced around before saying, "ran into the other night?"

"In a different sense, yes."

"And so, you're willing to do what this woman wants you to do?"

"At this point, I am. What do you think?"

Jane stared into my eyes. "Sounds like you've bought in. Like you've all of a sudden become some kind of a super patriot."

"That's not fair, Jane. You're the one who watches the news twenty-four seven. You're the one who bitches and complains about the assholes running our country. I want the money and the things we can buy with it. I want a house. I want a garage. And providing you do, I want a kid. Honey, the fact that these guys are bad for The United States just makes my job easier."

"Sounds dangerous and, yes, exciting."

For the next 15 minutes, Jane and I strolled through the crowds, admiring artworks. I filled her in on the whole NASA mole, climate change deal, and then finished by saying, "And I guess you can figure out that Sarah thinks her father, James, and Timothy are all part of that effort to steal the weather controlling technology."

"All while they work on getting elected to seats in our Government."

"Exactly," I agreed.

Jane stopped walking, glanced around at display booths, and then asked, "Have you seen enough art?"

"Pretty much," I replied, "Why?"

"I've heard enough. I need a drink, and I want to have sex with my loyal husband."

Chapter 38

The rooster on Jane's phone crowed loudly. She hit the snooze and then pulled her pillow over her head. I heard a muffled, "I don't want to get up."

"Then don't," I replied while heading to the toilet.

"I have to go in. It's my Saturday." As I pissed, Jane spoke louder. "Start the coffee, please!"

Walking to the kitchen, I opened the black flip phone and saw where I'd missed a call from Sarah at 6:12 p.m. I had also missed a text two minutes later that read, **Where are you?**

"Damn." I mumbled to myself. "Should of looked at this last night."

On my return to the bedroom, Jane had repositioned. Her head lay on top of the pillow facing away. One leg and one bare butt cheek were exposed. Stepping next to the bed, I said, "I missed a call and a text from Sarah last night."

"And?" she asked without turning over.

"She wanted to know where I was." I pulled the blanket and sheet over to see the rest of Jane's ass.

"What are you doing?" she asked, still facing away.

"I'm looking at my wife's sweet butt."

"Don't you ever get enough?"

"Isn't that the same thing I asked you last night?"

Jane rolled over and raised her knees as if to tease me more. "You were talking about her while staring at my ass?"

"Is that a problem?"

"Do you talk about me while you stare at her ass?"

"I don't stare at her ass."

"Liar. I know you better than that." She glanced at my half erection and said, "Forget about it. I need coffee, a cigarette, and a few words with you about last night."

Tugging on my sweatpants, I asked, "Last night? What, did I smack your butt too hard?"

"You wish. I'm talking about Sarah. It came to me last night when I was on top of you, but I didn't want to ruin the moment."

While slipping on my shirt, I said, "*You* were thinking about *Sarah* while we did it?"

Jane replied, "You know what I mean, asshole."

My beloved came to the balcony, layered up, carrying the newspaper and a comforter to fight the cool morning air. I had already downed a half cup and was about to light one of her cigarettes. "Were you not going to wait for me?"

Are you kidding? "Yes dear. I was lighting this one for you."

"You're so full of it."

"And that's why you love me," I said. Jane took a seat, covered her legs with the comforter, and reached for the smoke. I lit another one and said, "I'm waiting."

"For what?" she answered while leafing through the morning news.

"Your thoughts about last night."

"Oh. Well, I thought you came a little too fast."

How can a woman be such a bitch so early in the morning? I stared and said nothing.

Jane grinned, struggling to hold back a laugh. "I'm just kidding. You did fine, dear. Men are so insecure."

Men? Isn't that like plural? Why didn't she say my man is so insecure? I took a draw, blew it out and still said nothing.

Jane tuned her phone to streaming country music, turned it up, and said, "Sit this inside the door, please." When I did so and then took a seat, she leaned close. "Okay," she started, just loud enough for me to hear. "There are a lot of things about this project that don't make sense. To begin with, it seems to me that if Sarah is a rookie, whoever recruited her would have eyes and ears on her pretty much all the time. Hell, they might even track her with satellite. Isn't that what they do in the movies?"

"Ah, I believe so."

"Therefore," Jane continued, "at the very least, I question the idea that she wants to do any of this behind their backs. If her father is somehow tied into the people making these rockets, and if the technology is what you say it is, the intelligence agencies would have to be all over it."

"You think?" I whispered.

"Honey, they're watching any person who's within a mile of it. No stones unturned. My guess is they're already watching your girl's little covert operation. Or perhaps they've been orchestrating it from the word go."

"So you think they know about me?"

"Probably. They know she's using someone. And if they know about you, they're having you watched. How well..."

Two girls on the street? Brenda at Bart's Bar and Fish House?

"...she's concealed your identity is something we need to find out. I'd say this whole idea of having you help her keep it on the down low is a setup."

"Setup? Who's being setup?" I asked.

Jane took a sip of her coffee and whispered, "You, dumb ass."

I wanted to go off. To curse and believe Jane simply had a problem with Sarah, or that she might be messing with me. But I knew better. John had it right. My fresh set of eyes was onto something. "Are you done?"

"No." Jane smashed out her cigarette and said, "Doesn't matter if it's the sixth floor of a book depository or the thirty-second floor of a Vegas Hotel, the cover up always involves the death of the shooter. I believe someone is going to great lengths to make this happen. And there's a good reason they picked you. You grew up close to where this wedding is to occur. If no one who lives past that day knows of your connection to these people, it'll look like some idiot from the neighborhood went off on some childhood jealousy act and massacred everyone. It's not just about killing the three you spoke of. If they know Wellington and Proctor were moles, and were set in place by their adopted fathers, that could explain the assassination of Ambassador Wellington. How do we know they don't plan to use this small wedding venue as an opportunity to clean house?"

I didn't know what to say.

"Think about it, Eli. They may suspect that the Senator has been complicit all along. These people might be planning to kill the whole gathering at that wedding."

"Surely you don't think they would kill everyone."

"Honey, somebody shot over five hundred people at Mandalay Bay. Pretty sure fifty-eight died. You think the planners had a vendetta with all five hundred of them? If this goes the way I suspect, they'll be ridding themselves of the Senator, his son, Wellington, Sarah's father, and they'll get you, and...."

"And? And what, or who?"

"And Sarah."

"No!" I said loudly.

Jane put her finger to her lips and then whispered, "If everyone dies except her, it becomes obvious that she's involved. They probably already think she's a double agent. In the movies, they're always knocking off their own that get out of line."

"You think Sarah's a rogue agent?"

"Doesn't matter what I think. These people act on what they think. And they'll do all this while using you as a patsy."

"What a mess."

"And one more thing," Jane said. "Didn't you say there were three hoodie guys?"

"Yes. Why?"

She laid the newspaper on the arm of my chair, and then pointed to a story. The headline read: FOUR BODIES FOUND INSIDE CSX BOXCAR.

That's why she was crying! "I need to call Sarah."

"Not yet. Eli, we need to think this out. We need to decide if and what you're going to tell her. And if you decide to go through with this job, we have to come up with a way to keep you alive and to guarantee the money."

Chapter 39

Ironically, Jane convinced me that the park would be the only safe place to meet with Sarah. Arriving an hour after sunset, I slumped in the cab of my pickup, scanning the moonlit darkness for hoodies and zombies while my mind played with details. If my wife's suspicions were true, at what point would the wedding massacre take place? Who would do it? Would it be the Senator's security team? Or, would they too be killed? I had heard stories of government security people dying mysteriously. Now it all made better sense. Was Sarah aware of everything going on or was she being used, and in either case, how could I avoid becoming collateral damage? The hard part would be picking Sarah's brain without revealing Jane's involvement.

Headlights approached from downhill. As the black Camry pulled in next to me, I removed the battery from the white phone, stuck it in the glove box, and then waited for Sarah to come to me. She slid in and said, "You do know, cops expect killers will return to the scene of the crime."

"Might they also be suspicious of those who change their habits after the crime? Besides, do they even know a crime occurred here?"

"Good point."

"Unless the zombies saw it go down and told the cops, they had no reason to do forensics here."

"You're starting to sound like a detective," Sarah replied. She pulled out her phone, punched a few things, and asked, "Did you quit carrying your iPhone?"

"It's at home. If I have to turn it off when we're together, might as well not carry it."

"But" Sarah said, "you should carry it, turned on, when we're apart."

"What makes you think I don't?"

"You both left your phones at home as a decoy while you went out yesterday."

Becoming a little pissed, I asked, "How do you know that?"

"Jane's car was gone. Both of your phones were at home, turned on."

"When I go out with my wife, we deserve our privacy. What gives you the right to be stalking us? You came to our condo?"

"No, Eli. I used a computer and checked from the satellite."

Between her phone and her computer, the agency has to know what's going on. "Aren't you afraid someone will monitor your computer? Your phone?"

"For this project, I'm not using an agency computer. Trust me, I'm doing all I can to cover our butts. From my phone, they might see me looking at the software, but they'd have to really watch and study to know which numbers I'm looking at."

And they probably do.

As I sat pondering, Sarah said, "Bottom line, you and Jane should both carry your phones."

"Why? Did you ask Jane's permission to monitor her?"

"No, but I like to. For safety's sake."

She doesn't trust us. "Are you saying someone else knows about me, and might be watching my wife?"

"I'm telling you that I don't put anything past the Agency. Eli, it's not my fault that you went snooping into people you didn't need to be snooping into. You have to admit, you got a little OCD on your research."

"Isn't that what you guys do?" I turned on my headlights for a few seconds to check out the road ahead.

Sarah asked, "You nervous?"

"A little, maybe." Turning off the lights, I said, "Let me ask you something. Can we agree there's a chance that on game day, something could go wrong and you could get killed?"

Sarah tilted her head and said, "That's always a possibility."

"Exactly what I was thinking. And in such an event, how do I get my money?"

"You already know you'll get money from my mother. And hopefully some from David."

"Do I know that? I don't count on anything from Weeper. And what if something happens to me? Does Jane get the money from your mother?"

Sarah uncapped the water, took a drink and said, "You've been doing a lot of thinking."

"Just things I figure you've already thought about. You need to ask your mother about the money issue. I'll need some sort of resolution before game day."

"Okay. Speaking of, we need to talk about how this is all going to go down."

"I'm all ears," I replied.

"Would you like to walk?"

"No. I'm good right here."

Sarah's eyes were saying things her mouth was not. She had that same suspicious look as when we first met, before I gained her trust. She said, "You and I will be going down on Friday. I'll deal with the rehearsal and then dinner and drinks. Timothy and the girl will be there."

"Who's officiating the wedding?" I asked.

"One of James's friends. Not a preacher, but he is a marriage minister."

"Is he expendable?"

Sarah seemed to be thinking for a few seconds. "If necessary."

"What time will your father be arriving?"

"He's flying into the country on Friday, but we're not sure what time he'll arrive at the estate. I suspect he'll come in by helicopter sometime before the rehearsal."

"Will there be catering people?"

"Yes," she replied, "but they'll not arrive until Saturday around noon. Guests are scheduled to begin coming in at three."

"And the Senator?"

"I'm thinking Senator Proctor would rather not be at the wedding, period. My guess is he'll stay in Washington Friday night. Fly in on Saturday morning."

I pulled out Jane's cigarettes and asked, "You want one?"

"No thanks. Not now."

After lowering the window, I lit up and continued. "How much security are you anticipating for the wedding?"

Sarah said, "Considering the Senator's leadership position, there should be a company of three."

"What about Wellington? Will he bring his guy?"

"Always does."

"Lots of potential witnesses. You see, Sarah, I'm concerned that there's gonna be all kinds of uncertainties here, like security persons, house help, minister, and catering service. What do we do with these people while I do my work? And what if they get in the way? Do we kill 'em all? Are they all expendable?"

Her eyebrows rose as she answered, "Eli, our plan at this point involves three people. We want to isolate, interrogate, and eliminate those three. That's it. But yes, under the right circumstances, others may become expendable."

"What about your daddy's chopper? Will it stick around?"

"No. It'll be a lease. They depart quickly."

"So when and where are we gonna do this?"

Sarah hesitated. "The barn would be nice. But really, it doesn't matter where if we plan to blow the place up."

"You know if we blow the place up, it's going to involve more than three people."

"Then it is what it is."

Jane is right. This is going to end up being a massacre.

"Tell me," Sarah continued, "how much time do you need to make James and Timothy talk?"

"They don't seem like tough guys. You apprehend 'em. I'll walk in, do my thing and leave."

Sarah said, "Ha, ha. Be serious. These things typically take time. They may come across as pansies, but they may or may not be. So let's don't assume it'll go quickly."

"Okay," I started, "how about we begin with our window of time. We can't do anything until after the local secret service does their sweep on Friday." Sarah's eyes squinted. "I'd prefer to be done long before the Senator's security arrives, whatever time that might be. You should be able to find out. And then, we plan conservatively around that."

Sarah took another sip of water and asked, "How'd you know there would be a sweep on Friday?"

"Research." *She doesn't believe you.* I looked into her eyes and asked, "Do we need a session?"

Her head tilted and she replied, "Why? What about?"

"I sense we're not being honest with one another."

She grinned and said, "Me too. So how *do* we fix this trust situation?"

"I think we could start by going out to see your mother."

"Now?"

"Is she home?"

"Well, yes. I'm sure she is. You surely don't want to go all the way out there tonight?"

"Why not?" I replied. "Tomorrow's Sunday. I don't have to work."

"What about Jane? Isn't she expecting you home?"

"She's working. Besides, she's getting used to me coming in late and then giving her some excuse. She'll be okay."

When Sarah's forehead wrinkled, I got the feeling that she suspected I'd been talking to Jane. "Okay," she answered. "Let's go. We both driving?"

"Yes. I don't wanna leave my truck."

Following Sarah out of the park, I pulled out my white Jane-phone and replaced the battery. When Sarah stopped at a traffic light, I could see a small glow in her car. *Calling Ella?* The light changed before the white phone finished booting. I had to text while driving. **Gonna be a while, Honey.**

On the radio, Brad Paisley sang about Love and War. I monitored mirrors and waited anxiously for a reply from Jane. "Come on, come on, come on," I mumbled. Seconds later it came.

Okay Sweetie. Be careful.

"Perfect." My knees controlled the steering wheel as I deleted the text, removed the battery and stashed the phone. Finally relaxed, I sang along, "...forget about you when you're gone..." I hit the radio's power button, turned to the empty seat next to me and said, "I ain't forgot you, dad. Wish you were sittin' right there with one of those little half-pints of whiskey."

Dust flew from Sarah's tires as I followed her down the dark lane to her mother's farm. The Camry stopped in front of the house while the garaged door opened for me. She wanted my truck out of sight. When I walked out, the door started down. Sarah turned and stepped to the house. The picture window lit up first and then the porch. When the door opened, Ella stood behind the screen in a robe, with a scarf covering her head. Sarah waited for me to catch up. When I stepped up onto the porch, Ella backed off and we entered.

"Lordy girl. Why didn't you let me know you were coming? I coulda made coffee."

"That's okay Momma. Don't think we need coffee at this hour."

"Well, I was just fixing me a drink." Looking my way, she asked, "How about you, boy? You like to join me?"

Why not? "I will, if Sarah has one."

Normally cool, calm, and collected, Sarah appeared nervous, and said, "Might as well."

We followed Ella into the kitchen where a bottle of 100 Proof Bourbon sat next to a short glass on the table. The glass contained a hint of booze and nearly melted ice cubes. While Ella reached into the cabinet for two more glasses, I watched Sarah.

If she wasn't talking to her mother on the phone while driving, who was she talking to?

"Ice?" Ella asked.

"Yes," I replied.

She added cubes to all three glasses and then poured enough bourbon into each to cover the ice. The first sip exploded as I swished it around in my mouth before swallowing. When they both took a seat, I downed the rest of my drink, lowered the glass and said, "Another, please?"

Ella glanced at Sarah and then back at me. She shoved the bottle in my direction and said, "You help yourself, boy."

I did. When I took a seat and a sip, Sarah stared. Ella said, "Man drinks like that he's got something heavy on his mind. What brings you two all the way out here on a Saturday night?"

Sarah answered for me. "Momma, he's worried someone's gonna kill me when all this goes down and he won't get his money."

Anger crossed Ella's already tired face as she slid her chair back away from the table.

I said, "I'm worried she might get killed. That brings up the question about money."

Leaning left with her elbow on the chair's arm, Ella stared as if trying to read me. She took a sip of her drink and said, "Boy, it's your job to make sure nobody hurts my girl."

"Don't recall that conversation."

"It's an understood thing," she replied.

"Well, maybe it was understood by you, but not so much by me. This whole thing's gotten complicated."

Ella frowned. "Is that right? And how so, may I ask?"

"Momma," Sarah interrupted, "Eli and I've been through a lot."

"Is that right? And you're calling him Eli now? Maybe I don't wanna know what you two have been doing."

I shook my head and said, "It's not like that."

Sarah leaned back in her chair. "We've been in some tight spots. Had to do things we can't talk about."

"Really. Well then, is Mr. *Eli* worth the money?"

"Yes. He's good. Very much worth the money."

"I bet he is. Look at you all smilin' and shiny faced."

"He already told you, Momma. It's not like that. So you can quit talking that way."

Ella reached over and ran her fingers through my shabby three inch beard. Though stunned, I sat quietly. She took a deep breath and said, "Bet that feels real good on a belly."

"Stop that!" Sarah snapped. "How much have you had to drink?"

"Don't you be worrying about my drinking. I've got a right to fantasize. Haven't had me a man in years."

Sarah stood and said, "This was a bad idea. We need to go."

"You sit your ass down, girl. I'm just trying to have some fun. I can behave." Leaning back, she said, "Now, you two tell me what it is you need."

Sarah took a seat, threw back her drink and said, "Go ahead, Mr. Jones."

Leaning forward with my elbows on the table, I said, "Ella, I'm thinking your daughter's in over her head."

"Excuse me?" Sarah interrupted. "What the hell are you talking about?"

"Let him speak," Ella demanded.

Looking back at Ella, I continued. "I've decided, either Sarah isn't telling me everything, or she doesn't know everything."

"I don't know everything?"

Ella snapped back again. "Girl, I said let—him—speak."

I finished off my second drink and then said, "There's a ton of stuff going on. I'm beginning to think this wedding is a setup, but not just our setup. Maybe I've been watching too many movies, but it seems to me that there's a good reason someone led Sarah to me. Maybe they think I have the ability to do what she needs done. But I'd say they picked me because I grew up near the Proctor Estate. Ella, I believe while Sarah's planning her little wedding party, the Agency is planning a massacre. And I'm gonna be their fall guy. Now either Sarah knows about it or she's in the wrong line of business. If she does know about it, then she's been bullshitting me, and you."

Sarah reached for the bottle and poured herself another drink. She took a sip and said nothing.

Ella looked at her daughter. "Now let's hear what you have to say."

Sarah's lips puckered out and her nose flared. "I'm interested in what he's saying." Looking my way, she said, "Describe this so-called massacre."

She already knows.

I said, "We've already determined that James Proctor and Timothy Wellington are some kind of political moles. They've been spying on NASA for reasons I told Sarah I wouldn't discuss. But you already know it involves terrorism. And the fact that they're both trying to get elected into government positions pisses you, me, and Sarah off. These guys are puppets of Sarah's father and whoever in the hell he's involved with. My guess, they wanna infiltrate our Government with radical Islam. Bottom line, I'd say these guys need to go."

Ella said, "Wasn't that the idea to begin with? Isn't that why we hired you?"

Sarah said nothing as she sipped more bourbon.

"Yes it is," I continued. "In the beginning, Sarah said David Weeper wanted information. But now I'm thinking someone else wants to do the same thing you want done. They already assassinated Timothy Wellington's father. They're not stupid. They know if we somehow abduct and gather information from these people, none of them are gonna be in shape to participate in a wedding ... and everyone there's gonna know something's up. Ella, they're gonna wait until we gather information, and then they're gonna kill Timothy, James, Sarah's father, the Senator and every single soul present at that damn wedding ... and they'll say I did it, after they kill me."

Ella turned to Sarah. "You know anything about this?"

"Like Eli, I have my suspicions."

"Then why didn't you say something to me?"

"Momma, I don't tell you everything, for your own good. You know that."

"So," I asked, "were you keeping this stuff from *me* for *my* own good?"

Sarah looked at me and said, "David told me that if I could get information from Timothy and James it would help my case against my father. He suggested I hire you to help. That's what I knew from the beginning and that's what I told you from the start. David never mentioned killing anyone."

Reaching for the whiskey, I said, "Yes, but I believe you've underestimated David Weeper. And I promise you, he'd like nothing better than to see me on the wrong end of this. Did he tell you I got in trouble with the law for sneaking up to the Proctor Estate when I was a teenager, and that I just happened to have a gun with me at the time?"

"No. No he did not."

"Well, wouldn't you think that might go a long way toward making me look like the crazy guy who went off at your wedding? Killed everybody?"

Sarah stood and said, "I have to go pee."

As soon as her daughter disappeared, Ella downed her drink and then reached and placed her hand over mine. "Mr. Haycraft, Eli, we've gotten you into more than you expected. More than I expected. Is it too late to put a stop to the whole thing?"

"I think we've gone too far, Ella. No turning back now."

"But if everything you say is true, and they think Sarah has grown close to you, I'm thinking they'll kill her too."

"I didn't want to say that."

Ella squeezed my hand. "Please, no matter what, I need you to keep my daughter alive. Can you promise me you'll do that?"

I placed my other hand on top of hers and said, "As long as she's got my back, I'll have hers."

She asked, "How can I make you comfortable with the money situation?"

"I want the first two hundred thousand up front. The rest after it's over." Ella closed her eyes and sighed heavily. I said, "Eliminating two people has turned into to three for sure and maybe several more in the end."

"That many people?"

"Rest assured, Ella, I'm not gonna kill someone who doesn't deserve to die, unless it comes down to them or me, or them or Sarah. Then they're gonna die."

Ella used her free hand to rub my beard. "I'm sorry I got you into this."

"Don't be. I want the money, and I hate what these people are trying to do to America." I reached up and began caressing Ella's neck the way she was mine. Her eyes rolled back. I asked, "How sick are you?"

She gripped my wrist and looked away while speaking. "Been dealing with this stuff since I was just a little older than Sarah. Thought I had it whooped a couple times. It's back, and this time it's gonna get me."

"How long you got?"

"Months."

"Sucks."

"Yes it does," Ella replied while using her free hand to reach for the bottle. She poured and said, "And I hate putting the burden on Sarah."

"Death is part of life. We all deal with it sooner or later."

"But she's got so much on her plate."

"She can handle it."

Ella stared at me a moment. "I'm going to be paying you four hundred thousand. That's most of what I have. But since I'm gonna die anyway, it doesn't matter. There'll be enough left for Sarah to bury me and then some, and she'll get the farm. So the money's not important to me. I'll give you one hundred thousand up front, another hundred thousand as soon as it's over, and the other two hundred thousand if you keep my baby safe."

"A hundred thousand tonight?"

"Yes. But there's one more stipulation. I need a favor."

"A favor?"

"I already told you, I haven't been with a man in years. Can't even remember the last time anyone besides Sarah touched me. Thought several times about going into town and finding me a man. In the end, I always chickened out. Afraid I'd catch a disease. Now look at me. When this is over, before I go, will you have mercy on a lonesome woman?"

I sat, lost for words and wondering if it was the whiskey talking.

"Will you lay down with me? Hold me? Touch me? Rub me with that beard?"

In a short moment of silence, I learned what it meant to be truly lonesome. My heart broke for Ella. Sarah returned to see me holding hands with her mother. She asked, "What's going on?"

Ella placed her free hand on top of mine. Our eyes met. I nodded my reply. Still staring into my eyes, Ella grinned and said, "Sarah honey, Mr. Haycraft's gonna take real good care of you. I want you to promise me you're gonna do the same for him. You hear me girl?"

Sarah placed one of her hands on her mother's shoulder and the other on top of our hands and said, "I hear you Momma." Then looking at me, she said, "I've got your back. And together, we're going to figure this thing out."

Ella pulled our hands apart and said, "It's real nice out tonight. Would you two join me outside for one more drink?"

Sarah looked at me and said, "I'm good for one more. How about you?"

We sat on a wide, wood slat swing behind the house, me between Sarah and Ella. Large sandstones formed in a circle created a fire pit about ten feet in front of the swing. *A fire would be nice.* Beyond the barn, passing clouds were illuminated by the moon from somewhere behind us. As our legs barely moved the swing backwards and forwards, Ella sipped her drink and then asked, "Elijah, do you believe there is a God?"

"Yes ma'am."

"Any proof?"

"Yes, ma'am."

"He has his own elucidation, mamma."

"Excuse me?" Ella asked.

"His own explanation."

I said, "You might not care for my thoughts."

"That's okay," Ella replied. "I'd like to hear it anyway."

It took a few seconds to figure how to begin. "Well, Ella, I've cut open enough animals to know they have the exact same organs inside as we do. They're all flesh of flesh and bone of bone. Yet something makes us different. Dinosaurs evolved on this planet for billions of years. Didn't none of 'em ever evolve to the point of writin' it down. Man comes along and in a short period of time, look what we've done."

"You saying you believe in evolution?"

"Yes. I'd say for millions of years we evolved and lived by our instincts, just like every other animal on Earth."

"So where does God come in?"

"God is our explanation for what we can't otherwise explain. It's pretty obvious that man is different than any other animal on Earth. A million years from now, ain't no dog, cat, lion or ape gonna use a cell phone, much less create one. We are special. Having been raised in the Church, I choose to believe that at some point in our evolution, God added something to the animal man creating human beings."

"Something?" Ella mumbled.

"Knowledge, Momma."

"In the Bible," I continued, "it says, God looked down on man and was pleased and said let us make man in our image. So, if God is a spirit, and he made man in his image, then I'd say God added a spirit to the animal man, creating human beings. Along with our spirits came the ability to gather, analyze and use information ... which is, as Sarah says, knowledge."

Ella sipped more bourbon and said, "Damn. That's some heavy shit."

"Makes better sense than anything I've been taught," Sarah admitted.

Ella turned to her daughter. "You saying you believe what he just said?"

"All I'm saying is I can believe that a whole lot better than most of what I've been taught."

Ella reached for my hand and then glanced at Sarah's. I took Sarah's hand as her mother began to pray. "Lord, no matter how we got here, we are here. And we're just trying to survive this crazy world you created until we die. Look over my girl and this young man while they do what they need to do. Keep them safe and let them make decisions that are pleasing to you. Amen."

"Amen," I repeated.

Ella looked past me to her daughter. Sarah said, "Amen."

Don't know if it was the bourbon, or what, but both women continued to hold my hands as they leaned their heads onto my shoulders. We swung a slow rhythm while the clouds moved in and out of view. A whippoorwill called its glorious tune over and over in the nearby trees. Somewhere in the distance a bull bellowed its desire for a cow while the horses stood silent in the lot next to the barn. It had become a beautiful night. I wished Jane could be with us.

I left there that night with a bag full of money and a heart full of feelings for Sarah and her mother.

Chapter 40

On Friday morning, October 12th, the day we'd all been waiting for, I rode with Sarah from her mother's place. We were both dressed comfortably in jeans, tee-shirts, light jackets and cross-training shoes. Ella had stuffed us with scrambled eggs, sausage, biscuits and gravy. On our way out into the misty morning, she provided us each with an additional go cup of coffee and then stood at the door waving her goodbyes. It felt like a movie.

Highway miles passed as Sarah and I sipped java while rehashing our plans for the day. It somehow felt like my father and me on our way to hunt whitetail deer. He would plan out every detail. Rarely did things go as planned. All that mattered is that we went home with venison.

At some point, Sarah's voice blended into the road noise as I stared out the window at things I might never see again. *Is this how a soldier feels, sitting in a helicopter, looking out across the landscape en route to a mission? Is it just another job? Kill or be killed?* Halfway across a foggy field of soybeans, I could barely make out several whitetail deer. Beyond that a distant flock of crows seemed special as each bird left tall trees, like jets launching from a carrier. When I lowered the window, Sarah asked, "You hot?"

"No. Just trying to hear the birds. Almost forgot how interesting they are."

Sarah said, "I used to watch the crows every morning."

Turning back to her, I thought, *We're so damn much alike.*

She read my expression and said, "Tomorrow morning, I'll show you my private little spot out behind the barn. We can sit there with our backs against the wood, drinking coffee and smoking a cigarette as we watch the crows fly." When I nodded my approval, she winked.

After that, she tuned the radio to country music and drove without speaking. By the time we passed the sign that read Morganville 5-miles, I had begun to worry about her silence. When the Camry's engine hum lessened on our way down the exit ramp, I asked, "Are you nervous about today?"

Her lips tightened, she nodded and said, "If we were dealing with strangers, it would be easier."

"Like killing an innocent hobo in a train car?"

"So you heard it on the news?"

"I saw it in your face, that night."

"Man was strung out. Had a needle and a gun. I couldn't take the chance. And yes, it bothered me."

"I didn't think the tears were for those three hoodie guys."

"Let me ask you something, Eli. If you were going to watch your father die today would it make you nervous?"

"I did watch my father die."

"Sorry, I shouldn't have gone there. So, are you nervous?"

"Maybe. Not sure. Excited might be a better word. Isn't that what you offered on day one?"

"Yes."

As we made our way through town and headed out the winding two lane road, I stared beyond rock walls at the countryside while considering how many men had fought and died for American freedoms. That day, I too would become a soldier. A patriot ready to eliminate several who were involved in a conspiracy to harm America and what its flag stands for. I would do it for the memory of Jane's father, Captain Bradley Ray Higgins, Special Forces, United States Army.

We pulled in front of the house and parked behind a black SUV. Sarah said, "That's the sweep from Louisville. Let's grab our stuff before they come out."

Charles popped out the double doors and joined us as Sarah closed the trunk, leaving one bag inside. Reaching for her luggage, he asked, "Anything else?"

"No, that's all there is," she answered.

When we entered the front doors, two men in black, one six foot two, the other closer to five eight, both in their fifties, stood as if waiting on us. Sally the cat slid around rubbing against the shorter man's legs. Sarah asked, "How's it going, gentlemen?" Both men nodded. To me, she said, "Jones, this is Special Agent White," pointing at the shorter man, "and Special Agent Black."

Agent White said, "We're wrapping up here. Just waiting to see you and your guy." He looked at me and asked, "How you doing?"

I replied, "I'm fine, sir. Black and White? You people all use generic names?"

Agent Black frowned, looked at Sarah, and commented, "Man's name is Jones, and he asks about generic?"

Good point, dumbass.

Agent White said, "I assume you both are packing?"

Sarah pulled up her jacket to show her belt holster. I unzipped my jacket and pulled it open enough to reveal the 9mm holstered against my lower back.

Agent White got close to stare at my beard and glasses and asked, "That all you have?"

Charles stood watching as I took a step back and said, "That's all I need. Can't say I ever used a gun to kill a man."

He glared back and asked, "You ever killed a man?"

If you would hang out here tonight I might kill you. "Apparently you've never seen my file."

The tall guy said, "Apparently no one's seen your file."

"I have," Sarah spoke up. "Is there a problem?"

Agent White backed away and said, "No, not at all. Ma'am, we've covered every inch of this place, inside and out, including the barn. It's all clear. You feel safe with this guy, we're good to go."

The two suits headed to the door. The short one had already stepped out when Sarah asked, "When exactly should we expect the Senator?"

Agent Black said, "We're told he and his security team will slide in around eight o'clock tomorrow morning. It's up to you two and Wellington's guy to keep things straight until then. We also understand your father will have his own security."

"I figured that," Sarah replied. "Believe we'll all get along just fine."

"Good luck with that," the man stated, "and congratulations on the wedding."

"Thank you," she replied. As the suit disappeared and the door closed, Charles began gathering Sarah's things. She asked, "Where's James?"

"He's gone to the airport to pick up Mr. Wellington and the girl. They should all be back shortly." Charles addressed me. "Bring your bags upstairs. I'll show you to your room."

When we reached the top of the stairs, the old man hesitated at the door of the room Sarah had changed in on our last visit. He pointed to the next door and said, "That one's yours."

My room had two single beds. After dropping my stuff, I checked out the bathroom. "Nice," I commented out loud. "Five Star."

When I turned around, Charles stood three feet from me. "Not quite. We don't have room service here. You want to eat, you make it to the kitchen."

"Sounds good to me," I replied.

"I've already begun preparing a meal for after the wedding rehearsal. I wish your friend Jackson could have made it."

"Trust me Charles, she wanted to come. Who knows, maybe she can free up for your breakfast tomorrow."

The sound of voices came from downstairs. "They're here," Charles mumbled as he turned away. "You need anything, let me know."

I stepped out of the room and to the windows overlooking the pool area. Sunshine sparkled through condensation on the roof system. Four rows of 3 chairs were lined up on either side of the pool and a table sat at the end closest to the barn. *Damn, that is a small wedding.*

Since my last visit, most of the leaves on the trees in the wooded area had either fallen or changed colors. The barn's windows and bay doors were opened. No horses were visible. As I admired the scene, Doris came up the stairs. Stepping next to me she said, "Nice view, isn't it?"

"Sure is."

I kept wondering, *Why did this girl lie about her age?*

Chapter 41

If I said I wasn't anxious, I'd be lying. All the preparation had not mentally prepared me for the game of chess that would play out over the next few hours. Each word spoken seemed like a move on the board. Though I enjoyed speaking with Doris, she came across as nothing more than a pond. Bigger pieces were about. On the first floor I found Charles in his kitchen prepping for the rehearsal dinner.

"Apple pie?" I guessed while sniffing the air.

"Yes it is."

"What's the main course?"

"I'm cooking beef tenderloin."

"Awesome," I replied. "Where is everyone?"

"They're in the barn. Mr. James's mare is not doing well. Found her down this morning. Don't believe she will get back up."

"How old is the horse?"

"Twenty-six."

"That's a long life."

As I spoke, Sarah entered the back door. "Eli ... Jones, can you come to the barn? James needs assistance with his mare."

Charles stared at Sarah's slip of the tongue.

On our way to the barn I said, "Horse is old. Probably needs to be put down."

"How would you know that?"

"Charles filled me in. I believe he paid attention to you calling me Eli."

"Yes, I noticed. My bad. Now listen, when we get out here, keep in mind that James has had this mare since he was a kid."

Would she have me feel sorry for the guy I am to butcher?

In the Proctor barn, beyond areas for feed and grooming there were three European style stalls on each side. They were like executive suites for horses. At the entrance to the third stall on the left, Timothy stood outside looking in. Bo, standing behind him, stepped to meet us.

He and I fist bumped as I eyeballed the partially opened back door to the barn. *Perfect.*

Bo spoke quietly. "That old horse is about done."

Inside, James sat on his heels in a fresh bed of sawdust, holding the mare's huge head in his lap. Seeing me, he said, "She can't get up."

I asked, "Have you called the vet?"

"She can't get here until tomorrow morning. Told me to keep her comfortable until then."

"It's your horse. You need to go ahead and put 'er down."

"How?" James asked.

"Shoot 'er."

"No way," he snapped. "Not going to do that. The vet will give her something."

"Yeah, and she suffers until then."

"I'm not going to shoot Milly."

I entered the stall, squatted and checked the horse's mouth. For the fun of it, I whispered into its ear. Then I laid my ear against its mouth as if she were talking to me. "She's thirsty."

"How do you know that?" Timothy asked.

"She can't reach her water." Rising, I cupped my hand into the water bucket to get water and then offered it to the old horse. Her thick tongue rubbed against my hand. I said, "She's dehydrated. If she gets enough water, she might get up."

I removed the water bucket from the wall hanger to bring it closer to Milly's head. After ten minutes of hand watering, the old horse first raised her head, and then her shoulders. "Get out of her way," I said to James. "She's gonna try to get up and she might fall on you." We all stood back as the mare made several attempts before climbing to her feet.

James said, "Mr. Jones! You really are the horse whisperer." He wrapped his arms around me and said, "I'll never forget this."

Sarah stood just inside the stall door, grinning. Separating from Jimmy, I inspected the mare. Abnormally thin, her boney hips reeked of arthritis. Her teeth were pretty much worn out, and her eyes seemed glazed. After I put the bucket back on the wall, the old horse stood drinking. Turning to James, I said, "You still need to put 'er down. She's in pain and it appears she's been starving herself to death. Believe she'll go back down soon."

I left the stall and headed back toward the house. Sarah caught up and spoke quietly. "You still okay?"

"With what?"

"With what we have to do."

"I'm good," I replied.

Charles came to the door. "Mr. Brown is coming through Morganville now. He'll be here shortly."

"Mr. Brown?" I asked.

"The marriage minister," Sarah replied. "I'll step out front to greet him."

When she started that way, Charles said, "You might want to accompany her. Mr. Brown can be an ass."

Outside, Sarah had taken a seat on the front steps. "Mind if I join you?"

"Please do."

We sat in an odd moment of silence. Cardinals used the fountain in the circle for a birdbath.

I said, "You asked if I'm okay. How about you?"

"Yes," she spoke quietly. "Just want it to be over with."

"Charles says this guy Brown can be a real ass."

"Yes, he can," she replied in a whisper.

As I began to speak again, Sarah rose and said, "Follow me." Nearing the noise of the water fountain, she said, "The doorbell has a camera and a microphone."

"Just like the Wellington place," I replied. "Always someone watching and listening." It was then that I noticed Sarah's hand shaking slightly. *My girl's gonna fall apart.* I needed a way to distract her. A way to take her mind off what was about to happen. "Wish we had time to take a walk in the woods."

"Why? Why would you want to go to the woods?"

"I know you don't wanna be romantically attached when we do our business tonight, but I still can't help but think—"

"Think what?" she quickly asked.

"Well, it's more fantasy than anything else. I mean, while I know you and I should never hook up, I would like to walk into the woods for a session."

"You have something you want to talk about?"

"Nooo. Just hear me out. The subject of the session is unimportant. But when it's over, and you spread your arms, I'd kiss you longer, like that night on the wall."

"Really?"

"Remember, it's just a fantasy, but considering how this could be our last day together, in my mind I wouldn't stop with the kiss. My hands would search you like that first day in the barn, exploring every inch of your body."

"And?"

"I would touch you where I've never touched you. I would kiss you where I believe no man has ever kissed you. I would do everything in my power to assure you that a man can enjoy you for exactly who and what you are. I would tickle you until you lost your breath and then as gently as I could, I would...."

Before I could finish, an older model, baby-blue convertible Mercedes—top up—buzzed down the lane.

"And?" Sarah asked, staring into my eyes, waiting for my words. Tears fell across her full lips. I wanted to kiss her right there but knew I couldn't. I reached and wiped away the tears. She grinned and repeated, "And?"

As the convertible passed on the drive, I said, "To be continued."

Sarah wiped her face, glanced back, and growled, "Damn you, Peter Brown."

Looking toward the car, I asked, "So this is the guy?"

Sarah started toward the house and said, "Like Charles said, he's a real piece of work. With remarkably bad timing."

We neared the porch as Charles came out. I'm thinking, *Dude must monitor that camera.*

The car stopped behind Sarah's Camry. I took a seat on the porch and lit a cigarette. Sarah stood next to me. A man, 5'10" and overweight with hair on the sides of his head only, popped out and immediately started around the car. Charles met him at the bottom step. Handing over his keys the man said, "Park it in the garage, please. Last time I was here, a bird had its way with my windshield. I'll have none of that."

As the man approached, Sarah looked down at me and shook her head. He stopped in front of her and said, "Where's Jimmy?"

"In the barn last time I saw him," she replied.

"Well, I'm going to marry you two, but you must know it's against my better judgment."

"Excuse me?" she asked.

"Girl, you and I both know Jimmy should not be marrying a ... a woman."

I blew cigarette smoke up toward the man's face. He shook his head and asked, "Who the hell are you?"

"I'm the man who's going to kick your fat ass if you continue to speak disrespectfully to this woman."

"Well." he huffed while scurrying through the door and out of sight.

I said, "What a prick."

As Charles drove off in the car, Sarah said, "Man used to be a priest. Now he calls himself a marriage minister."

Are you kidding me? "Is that Father Peter Brown?" I mumbled.

"You knew him?"

"He's a friggin' pedophile. That's why he's not a priest anymore. Used to be at St. Aloysius."

"I think you're right," Sarah replied. "Were you, exposed to him?"

"No, I was raised Baptist, but I know someone he abused."

Sarah said, "James went to that school. That's how come he knows Peter Brown."

As the day went on, I grew tired of listening to James cry over his horse. Doris seemed less than her usual flirty self as she made a special effort to keep her distance from Peter Brown. That fat bastard was in constant surveillance of her as he spent a lot of time whispering with Timothy and James. Bo occupied himself with his phone. not talking, but texting or on social media.

When everyone began migrating towards the pool area for the rehearsal, I moved to the kitchen and spent time with Charles and his steamy stove. He seemed pleased with my interest in his multitasking system of cooking. As James's hairy feline threaded its way between the old man's legs, I commented, "Can't believe you allow a cat in your kitchen."

Charles huffed. "If I had my way, I'd kill it. But then, James would kill me."

When Charles began to set the table, I volunteered to use multiple utensils while stirring multiple pots. Sarah came in and found amusement in the moment. "Charles put you to work?"

I shoved the cat away with my foot and replied, "This isn't work, Sarah. This is art."

From the dining area, Charles—apparently eavesdropping—paused and spoke loudly, "Miss Sarah, your protector has appreciation for what I do."

The exterior door slammed. Seconds later Peter Brown stormed into the kitchen sipping what I counted to be his third glass of red wine. "Where on *earth* is your father?"

Sarah said, "He texted. It's going to be another hour."

"Well, I'm sorry but I cannot wait any longer. I have places to go and things to do. If we don't begin soon, I'll not be able to stay for dinner." Turning toward Charles, he spoke loudly. "How about you, sir? Can you pretend to be Sarah's father so we can get through this arduous moment in time?"

What an asshole!

Stepping out of the kitchen, Sarah said, "That would work. Would you please, Charles? Then when my father gets here, we can explain his duties."

"I need to tend to my stove."

"Jones could do that for you," Sarah replied. She turned to look my way, winked and asked, "Isn't that right?"

I took the hint and said, "Sure. I'd be honored."

Charles looked at Peter and asked, "How long will this rehearsal thing take?"

"I'll have you back in the kitchen where you belong in thirty minutes max."

"Good," Charles replied. "Give me ten minutes to finish my table and I'll be out."

"Very well," Peter Brown sniffled. On his way out, he added, "We'll be waiting."

I stepped out of the kitchen and said, "What an ass."

Charles said, "I warned you."

When Sarah sat down at the head of the table, Charles barked, "That's Mr. James's seat. Don't be touching things."

"Where then will I be?" she asked.

"You shall sit to the right hand of your groom."

"Can you put Jones next to me?"

As she spoke, the white phone in my pocket vibrated. "No!" I said loudly to cover it up. "I'll be close by, but I won't be sitting at the table."

"Then shall I fix a spot for you in the foyer?"

"I probably shouldn't stay in one place. It'll be better if I move about, keeping an eye on things inside and outside."

The old man said, "Come with me."

In the kitchen, the phone vibrated again. *She has to know I can't just pull it out and look.* Charles apparently didn't hear it as he opened pantry doors. Behind them resided an elaborate system for security cameras. There were four monitors. One seemed dedicated to the front door only, while the others cycled among different outside locations. On the bottom shelf a DVR unit flashed.

"Convenient," I commented.

"You can eat here while observing the entire estate. I'm sure Mr. Bo will want to eat at the table."

Bo walked in, "Yes I will."

I said, "No problem. I'll be keeping an eye on things from here in the kitchen. Try to sit where you can see through the foyer."

Charles said, "He can sit next to Sarah."

I said, "That works. And by the way Bo, I'll be tending Charles' kitchen while he participates in the rehearsal. You mind keeping an eye on things out there?"

"Sure," Bo replied as he turned to head that way. "They're ready to get started."

I patted the old man on the shoulder and said, "I have to go pee before you leave."

As I headed that way, Sarah passed and spoke quietly. "I'm going to my car to get the champagne. Join me there, please."

In the bathroom, I pulled out the white phone. The text read: **How are you sweetie? I'm walking.**

I replied: **Be careful, dear. See you soon.**

Sarah waited at the back of her car. When I joined her, she quietly asked, "Having fun yet?"

"So far, so good."

She had the trunk of her car opened. With her back to the camera, she handed me a small bottle and some latex gloves. "Put these in your pocket as I pull out the bag with the champagne."

When she closed the trunk, she whispered. "Let's go to the fountain for a cigarette."

"Sure, but we have to hurry."

After we both lit up, Sarah stood hugging the big bottle and said, "When Charles and I go out for the rehearsal, I need you to put two drops in each champagne glass. No more and no less. Twirl it a couple times and set it down. It'll dry quickly. It's the only drink I know everyone will have. When we do the toast, a minute or so later, it'll be game time. And make sure you use the gloves. Don't want that stuff on your hands."

"Or my fingerprints on the glasses."

"Exactly."

"Is it the same stuff you used on me?"

"Yes."

"Cool. And this'll give us an hour?"

"No. I used more on you. We don't want them out that long. Two drops will keep them out less than thirty minutes, give or take a few. Not everyone's going to wake up at the exact same time."

Sarah took a long draw, dropped her cigarette in the water and started toward the house, mumbling, "Still thinking about that walk in the woods."

Back inside, Charles had already placed an ice bucket on the table for the champagne. Sarah shoved the magnum bottle of California CHANDON Reserve down into the ice as Peter Brown returned. "Come on! Let's go! Oh, champagne! I'll have some, please."

"Not yet you won't," Charles snapped. "That bottle is for the toast at dinner."

"Really. Well, you two come on. We're all ready to get this over with."

As Peter walked out, Sarah said, "Charles, do me a favor and don't open that bottle until we get ready for the toast."

"Gladly, ma'am." Charles went to the kitchen and returned with a 4 foot long, two foot wide, rolling bar. From the back, he began setting up short glasses and a bottle of bourbon. "This'll keep them out of the champagne." The old man poured two fingers into a glass downed it quickly and said, "Follow me, Mr. Jones."

My man's a boozer.

After Charles gave me last second instructions for the kitchen, he and Sarah left for the rehearsal. I watched as they stood in the foyer speaking with Peter Brown. When fat-ass walked away, they were like father and daughter in waiting. A minute later, they left, arm-in-arm to the pool area. I dashed back to the kitchen. After quickly stirring each of the pots, I opened the pantry doors and considered unplugging both the monitors and the DVR. *No. Charles might intend to watch the arrival of Sarah's father.*

Moving instead to the dining area, I put on latex gloves and pulled out the bottle of Sarah's potion. It reminded me of an Iodine bottle. In filling the eyedropper I realized the thin nature of the solution as a couple drops hit the floor. Moving around the table, it didn't take long to treat all the flutes except the one at Sarah's seat. Charles had not provided a flute for Bo. *That sucks.*

While capping the bottle of potion, I turned and noticed the damn cat was licking the floor. "Shit! Shit! Shit!" I wanted to kick James's kitty, but figured it would soon pass out. When I reached for it, the little son-of-a-bitch hissed, scratched at my hand and then backed away. It ripped my glove but fortunately did not draw blood. Soon after that, the cat began moving slowly. Seconds later, it collapsed right there in the floor. *Great. You killed the cat.*

That should make Charles happy.

I scooped the damn thing up and headed for the front. Barely opening the door to avoid the camera, I slipped the cat out and pitched it left toward the edge of the porch. It hit hard and rolled off behind shrubs. *One less obstacle.*

Back in the kitchen, I removed and trashed the gloves, and then stirred pots like a happy cook while thinking about Jane and John.

Chapter 42

Just as I considered sampling some of the old man's food, the backdoor opened and Peter Brown's obnoxious voice roared in. Charles shuffled around the dining room table and into the kitchen with a smirk and concern for his stovetop creations. "Welcome back," I stated as he paused at each pot for a thorough inspection.

"Wellll?" I asked.

"You pass."

"So how'd it go?" As I spoke, Peter waddled in full of himself. "Something smells deeelicious." When he saw me he said, "You missed it, Mr. Jones. I accidently married James and Timothy."

Doris stood in the dining area, far side of the table, earbuds in and staring out the window. James and Timothy entered behind her, arms locked as if they had indeed just become married. They were singing, "Dum-dum-dedum, dum-dum-dedum...." Sarah came in behind them shaking her head. Pausing to speak to Doris, she stared my way. Wondering what was up, I went to her. She led me to the foyer.

Speaking softly, Sarah said, "I wouldn't marry that asshole if he was the last man on earth."

"Can I assume the rehearsal didn't go well?"

"You have no idea. James says he would like Timothy to spend our wedding night with us. Peter said he would be jealous if he didn't get invited, and Bo thinks it's all funny."

"What's about Doris?"

"She's supposed to be my Maid of Honor. When Peter told her where to stand she cried."

"That's odd," I replied.

"I'd say."

"So you weren't involved at all?"

"Just briefly. Peter had me next to James for only about one minute. Told me and ... Doris that he would guide us through the wording tomorrow. As soon as I stepped away, Timothy takes my place. He, Peter and James whisper and laugh and before you know it, Peter is asking them if they take one another to be husband and husband."

When I chuckled a bit, Sarah said, "It's not funny. I've an uneasy feeling about this. I know they're all drinking and perhaps just playing, but if I didn't know better, I'd say that bastard Peter just married James and Timothy."

"That's actually what he said to me. So, where were Bo and Charles during all this?"

"Bo stands up there smiling at me. Charles told them they would all be killed if Amor witnessed their behavior."

Is that right? I thought. "So Amor really is anti-gay?"

"He's a devout Muslim. What do you think?"

"Yet he plans for his daughter to marry a gay guy."

Sarah smirked. "It wouldn't be the first political marriage of convenience."

Bo came in the door from the pool. "Jones! You missed the craziest wedding rehearsal ever. These guys are nuts." He slid past us and then patted Doris on the butt on his way into the kitchen. She turned to his back, gave him the finger and then focused back on the window.

When I shook my head, Sarah asked, "See what I mean?"

The distant pop-pop-pop-pop-pop-pop-pop of a helicopter drew attention. Sarah said "That'll be my father."

I spoke quietly. "Sarah, look at me." She did. "Don't these guys get to you. Your moment will come in few. Everything's ready in here, but I need to know you're okay. Are you?"

"Yes, of course I am."

Bo came back into the dining area as if trying to straighten up and be official. Timothy and James were pouring themselves a bourbon and didn't seem to care.

I said, "By the way, the old man didn't put out a flute for Bo."

Sarah glanced at the table, shook her head and said, "Damn. We'll just have to take him out.... Come on. Let's go meet my father."

We exited through the pool area and stood on the walkway between the pool and the barn. A white chopper came in from the north and began its descent into the yard to the right side of the house from the back. When it touched down the engine immediately slowed and Sarah headed that way. Keeping a distance, I followed and got just close enough to read Airbus H-125. It was a three blade unit that appeared to be high end. The pilot exited first and then lowered a pair of luggage bags to the ground. Two dark skinned men in suits stepped out, followed by one Amor Saline Al-Riase. Inside the chopper, two women remained seated. I could only see them well enough to tell that one had light skin and blonde hair. The other had dark skin and dark hair. They remained seated. Taller than I expected, Amor was an impressive man of Middle Eastern appearance, with a thick, dark, partly greying, well-trimmed beard. He wore a traditional white thobe, long enough to make light contact with the ground, a white silk looking ghutra, and a black braided agal.

Sarah exchanged hugs with her father, and then the two suits followed them toward Bo and me, each carrying a bag. Arriving, Amor gave Bo a hug and then stood staring at me. "We have not met," he spoke over the hum of the idling chopper, in an obvious Arab dialect. "I am Amor Saline Al-Riase. Please, call me Amor."

I said, "As-salāmu 'alaykum, Amor."

Sarah seemed surprised as her father's bushy eyebrows raised, and he replied, "Wa'alaykumu as-salām." Then as if concerned, he asked, "You speak Arabic?"

"No, sir. But I have Muslim friends."

This time he nodded. "You are Mr. Jones?"

"I am."

"You watch after my daughter?"

"I do."

"Someone has threatened her life?"

"Yes."

Turning to his suits, both of Middle Eastern appearance with dark hair and short beards, he said, "These men are here for my protection. Sarah says there will be no need for their services. Do you feel that is the case?"

"Earlier today, government security did a sweep of the entire property. For now, Bo and I have your back. Tomorrow morning there will be an additional detail of three arriving with the Senator. That will be five of us for a small group of guests. I'd say you are in good hands."

Amor nodded in the direction of the chopper while speaking to his men. Only word I recognized was 'American'. He pointed at his phone and referred to it. They both bowed and turned away without a word. When they entered the helicopter, its engine throttled. Bo and I each grabbed a bag and we began our deafened walk to the house. The Airbus lifted and soon disappeared over treetops.

Inside the pool area, Amor found the wedding seating to his liking. He questioned, "Where is Itzel?"

Interesting. He used her real name.

"She's here somewhere," Sarah answered.

"And Maria?"

"No sir. She chose not to come."

Though obviously disappointed, he asked, "And your mother?"

"She is too ill."

His head moved up and down as if to say, "I see."

Charles came into the room mumbling, "Sorry, Mr. Amor, I would have come out but I am busy tending my kitchen."

Amor nearly smiled. As the two exchanged man hugs, Sarah winked at me. I nodded slightly before returning my attention to Charles and Amor.

Amor said, "You have aged my friend."

"We both have," Charles replied with a grin. "I expect you brought your appetite."

"My appetite has missed your fine cuisine."

"This is good. We are about to eat."

"Before the rehearsal?" Amor asked with a frown.

"No, sir. We needed to get the rehearsal completed so Mr. Brown could join us for dinner. I stood in for you."

"Mr. Brown?"

"The marriage minister," Charles replied. "He is inside with Mr. James and Mr. Timothy."

The sound of three men singing flowed out from the dining room. Amor said, "Their voices reek of alcohol consumption."

No one said a word as Charles slid back into the dining room, around the table and into the kitchen. When Amor stepped to the dining room door, stopped and stared, I whispered to Sarah, "What'd he say to his men before they left?"

She whispered back, "Something about the women in the chopper and betting horses. Then he said, 'Enjoy the American entertainment, but be ready at a moment's notice.'"

"Sounds like he doesn't trust us."

"My father trusts no one."

As Amor entered the dining area, Sarah and I followed. Doris had disappeared. James, Timothy and Peter stood near the rolling bar, imbibing. James looked our way and spoke at an elevated volume. "Ah, Amor. Welcome to our world."

Amor replied sternly. "Your world?" Motioning around the room with his hand he said, "Who in this room paid for all this?"

Everyone present suddenly seemed to realize the seriousness of Amor's comments. Timothy spoke in Arabic. "marhabaan (hello)."

Amor replied, "We are in America. Speak as Americans speak." When Timothy nodded, Amor focused on James and asked, "Do you intoxicate at this early hour?"

Doris returned from wherever and simply bowed.

Peter Brown raised his glass and said, "Good evening, your highness."

Amor, hard faced, asked, "Has someone told you that I am a king?"

"Ah ... no."

No longer acknowledging Peter, Amor held his arms open toward Doris, and then Timothy. They approached and Amor hugged them both together. They separated and he said, "Your day will be soon."

Sarah's eyes met mine as if reading my mind. *Another arranged marriage?*

Peter said, "If they had a marriage license, we could make it a double wedding tomorrow."

Marriage license? Where is the license for Sarah and James?

Maybe it's already been used for James and Timothy?

Charles came in with a rolling service cart. "No, we could not," he spoke with authority. "It would require additional guests not already invited." While placing small bowls of sauce at each setting he continued. "Now, please let us all be seated and prepare for dinner. We will start with fattoush and za'atar along with the official toast of California CHANDON Reserve provided by Miss Sarah."

When Peter Brown plopped down in James's seat, Charles said, "Mr. Brown, that seat is reserved for the Groom."

Peter's eyebrows raised in protest.

Sarah said, "*Father* Brown, have you forgotten your vows of humility?"

Red faced with embarrassment, he got up with the whole room staring. Looking at Charles, Peter asked "So where would you have me sit?"

Charles pointed at the seat that would be to James's left, and then assigned others. "Sarah will sit at the right hand of James. Amor, please be seated at the head of the table facing the groom. Timothy will sit at your left, Itzel to your right. Bo, you may sit between Timothy and Sarah."

"And I shall sit here," Charles finished while touching the chair between Doris and Peter Brown's seats.

"Charles?" spoke Amor. "Do we have no place for Mr. Jones?"

"Mr. Jones has opted to eat in the kitchen," Charles replied. He then leaned to Amor's ear and whispered. I'm sure he explained about my surveillance of the grounds with the security system.

"Excellent," commented Amor as Charles began untwisting the wire around the cork on the champagne bottle. Amor turned to me. "But you will join us for the toast?"

I glanced at Sarah. She said, "One glass of bubbly shouldn't be a problem."

"Charles," I asked, "do you have another flute?"

Grinning, the old man said, "Top cabinet across from the oven."

Bo spoke up. "Jones! If you're drinking, I am too."

While sliding his flute to Bo, Charles said, "Bring two, Mr. Jones."

From the kitchen I heard the cork pop. *No one will doubt that bottle.* Before returning, I opened the double doors and searched for the power strip that supplied the DVR and all four monitors. Unable to see behind the units, I traced the DVR's power cord to the power strip it was plugged into. From one end to the other I slid my hand until finding the main switch. Flipping it killed the whole system.

While closing the door, I could hear Charles saying, "What is taking Jones so long?" As his feet shuffled into the kitchen, he spoke, "You could not find—"

Raising the flutes in my left hand I poured drippings over the beef tender with my right. "I felt the meat needed marinating."

"Well, thank you," the old man replied, standing there with the bottle of CHANDON in his hand. "Please, lower the heat while we toast."

On our return, Amor and Bo both gave us a look. Charles said, "Man was marinating my beef tenderloin."

Sarah spoke up, "Charles seems to have found himself a cooking partner."

"Mr. Jones is no stranger to the kitchen," Charles replied as he began pouring champagne. He began with my flute, then his and seemed to purposely move clockwise around the table, assuring Peter Brown's would be the last filled. As he filled Bo's glass, I could almost read Sarah's mind. We both knew Bo would now be drugged and Charles would not.

As he finished his task, Charles turned to Amor. "It would seem fitting for the father of the bride to have the honor of giving the toast?"

Amor replied, "If that is the desire of the bride and groom."

Sarah had that *let's just get this over with look* as she said, "Please."

James nodded and acknowledged, "We would be honored."

Bo, patiently waiting, winked at me. Peter appeared to be using every ounce of discipline to not take an early sip. Amor stood and said, "Very well." He looked around the table making eye contact with each participant before speaking. "It is with pleasure that I have come to America to be with you all. I have waited many years for this great occasion." Raising his glass, he continued. "Please, join me." My eyes were on Sarah's as everyone raised their glasses. Amor finished. "I make this toast to the parents of my many future grandchildren."

Sarah nodded to her father as she tipped James's glass and then took a sip of her bubbly. I tipped Charles and Amor's flutes before tasting the sweet reserve while taking in the room. The sound of more glasses clanging preceded everyone's downing of their demise.

How long?

Doris looked at me and asked, "Would you take a picture of us all?"

"Sure," I said. She handed me her phone. Standing in the corner of the room facing Amor, I had everyone turn my way. When they all held up their drinks, I flashed a pic. "Perfect."

As I showed the photo to James and Sarah, Peter raised his flute, requesting more CHANDON. Charles served him and asked, "Anyone else?"

Bo reached for more, followed by, Sarah. *Really?* I thought. Doris rose to reach for her phone, but as she did, her knees buckled and she fell back into her seat. *That was quick.*

"Itzel?" Amor spoke quickly. "Are you ill?"

When her head fell to the table, the Arab's face became worried. James spoke with a slur, "What is happening?"

Timothy, still seated, also looked weak. Amor braced himself on the table and said, "The drink. It is bad!" Staring up at Sarah's alertness, he said, "shoo sowaiti?" (What have you done?)

Peter had already finished his second drink when he became red faced and shouted, "Dear God, no!"

Bo wavered. Reaching into his jacket for his gun, he said, "Jones, what's going on?"

Amor lowered into his chair as Sarah, already slipping on gloves, busted Bo in the temple. His chair tilted but fell back into place, and his eyes remained closed. Sarah grabbed Bo's 9mm and shoved it into her beltline.

Charles mumbled, "Jones, what have you done?" I turned and hit him square in the face. He fell unconscious across the table disturbing fine china, before sliding onto the floor.

James and Timothy both went out spouting expletives. As they collapsed, I noticed Amor, slumped back in his seat accessing his phone. "Sarah!" I shouted. "He's calling someone!" In one long second, she reached her father and smacked at the phone. It flew out of his hand and onto the table. I grabbed it.

With Amor growing weak, Sarah whispered loudly, "Put it on speaker and mute it!" I did and we could hear voices in Arabic until the call ended.

Still looking at Sarah, Amor mumbled, "'iinahum, siatun (They will come.)" His eyes closed and he was out. Sarah took her father's phone from me, set it on the table and took hers out.

"What're you doing?" I asked.

Motioning toward Peter Brown, she said, "Keep an eye on him while I locate the phone he called."

Perhaps because he was so big, Peter remained the only one awake. His eyes were open, but he seemed paralyzed. I stepped close and asked, "Can you still hear me? He closed and then opened his eyes. I said, "Look at me, you piece of crap. Hope you're saying your prayers, Father Peter Brown. As your life ends, I want you to think of all those kids you abused."

While watching Brown's eyes shut, I pulled out the white phone. When I opened it and began texting, **We are ready, Dear**, Sarah noticed and asked, "What's that? Who are you calling?"

"I'm not calling anyone. I'm texting. You'll see who in a minute," I answered while moving to the door between the dining room and the foyer. "Just don't get excited."

"Excuse me?" As Sarah spoke, our help arrived. Dressed in black, face covered, she entered the dining room. Sarah started to draw.

"Easy!" I said. "She's with us."

Jane pulled off her head covering, shook her hair free, and said, "Hello Sarah. Nice to finally meet you."

Chapter 43

I had felt all along that Sarah suspected my wife knew what we were up to. Nonetheless, she seemed genuinely surprised that I had added Jane to the mission. She huffed, "Eli, what the hell's going on here?"

"She calls you Eli?" Jane mumbled.

I said, "Sarah, I wasn't a hundred percent sure how you would take all this. Figured a bit of experience wouldn't hurt."

"Experience?"

"If you remember, I warned you about my wife on day one."

"Sociopath?"

"Eli," Jane complained, "I'm not that careless."

Sarah and Jane stared wordlessly at one another until I said, "Okay ladies. You two can get acquainted later. Right now we have work to do. Sarah, did you locate the phone?"

Still squinting at Jane, she replied, "Yes."

"And what the hell was that guy saying?"

"Like my father said, they will come. I can tell they're at Churchill Downs, in Louisville. I'll monitor their phone to see how they travel."

Jane acknowledged, "That's an hour and a half drive."

"They'll drive fast," Sarah replied. Staring at me, she said, "I still can't believe you involved your wife."

"Get over it. She's here and she's gonna help. Now, I'm thinking those guys are gonna fly. If they're in Millionaires Row, it may take ten minutes to get to the ground floor and out the gates. Then, from the track to the helicopter would take another fifteen to twenty, assuming it's at Bowman Field."

Sarah took a deep breath and said, "The chopper is an Airbus. At a hundred and thirty knots, they could be here in twenty-five to thirty minutes. Let's figure on an hour from the call. Can we be done that soon?"

"We'll have to be," Jane said while pitching her bag up onto the table with total disregard for the expensive dinnerware. "Start your timer at fifty-three minutes and let's get with it." She removed a hard plastic bio-waste container from the bag, unscrewed the lid, and then unzipped her jacket. Underneath she wore a black shooters vest loaded with hypodermics. "Who goes first?"

"Your buddy here," I replied, pointing down at Charles who stirred slightly, regaining consciousness. "He didn't get any drug, so I knocked him out."

Without hesitation, Jane straddled Charles. Holding her jacket open with her left hand; she pulled out a hypo with her right and then remove the needle tip guard. Before she could inject, Sarah said, "Wait!"

Jane hesitated as Sarah stepped over, reached down and pulled off the old man's head cover, revealing a tattoo similar to the one on her neck. Charles raised his head and slowly opened his eyes. Stepping back, Sarah said, "Sorry old man. Your plan ends today." Turning to Jane, she said, "Do it."

Jane looked down at Charles and said, "Hey there. If it means anything, I will eat some of your southern cooking before this day ends." Without hesitation, she jammed the needle into his neck. His eyes widened for a few seconds, and then he collapsed. Rising to her feet, my beloved dropped the spent needle and its tip into the bio-waste container.

I pointed to Peter and Bo and said, "These two go next."

"What about her?" Jane asked, motioning toward Doris.

"Not now. I have questions for her."

Sarah stared with interest as Jane injected Peter and Bo just as she had Charles and then asked, "That it for now?"

"Yes," I replied. From the bag, I removed a 1/2" diameter, braided, nylon rope, and large, black pull-ties.

Jane capped the bio-waste container and placed it back into the bag. Sarah scanned Bo, Peter and Charles. "Are they—"

"Dead?" Jane finished for her. "Very much so. Hope you didn't want to say goodbye."

Sarah shook her head and squinted. "Now what?"

I said, "Help me out here." Amor and James were slumped into their chairs, heads hanging. Timothy had slid into the floor. Doris, still in her chair, laid face down on the table. "We need to drag them all over here in a row so we can get 'em ready." Sarah and Jane helped me line them up, in their chairs.

As Sarah helped me zip-tie their hands, Jane removed old tethered hoodies from her backpack. She pitched them one at a time onto James, Timothy and Amor. "Only had three," she complained.

Sarah asked, "What's up with that?"

"Jane has a thing for—" *Oops!* As Sarah's glance went to Jane, I said, "These'll help hold 'em up in the chairs."

Sarah and I slipped a hoodie over James's head and pulled it over his arms and the chair back. "Perfect," I thought out loud.

Pulling Doris upright in her chair, Sarah asked, "What about her?"

I removed my own jacket and said, "We can use this for now. I'll get it back when she wakes up."

We repeated the process on Timothy. When we got to Amor, as I pulled down the hoodie, I felt a bulge. "He's gotta gun." Jane and Sarah watched as I reached under and came out with a small .380. "Wonder why he didn't pull this out instead of his phone?"

Sarah said, "He knew he didn't have much time. Needed help more than revenge."

Jane disagreed. "He knew if he pulled out the gun, he'd be dead."

I stuck the gun in my back pocket and then worked with Jane using additional ties to secure the left leg of each of our captured to the nylon rope. As we finished and stood admiring our work, I asked Jane, "Everything ready in the barn?"

"Yep."

"So" I continued, "I guess now we just wait for these four to wake up. Then we'll walk 'em to the barn, get information, bring 'em back here and use a gas leak to blow this place apart."

Sarah, looking at her phone, said, "They're definitely on the move. Heading toward the expressway. I'll know soon if they're going to the airport."

"And if they arrive before these guys wake up?" Jane asked.

"That won't happen," Sarah answered. "They'll all wake up soon."

"Perfect," I replied. "Until then, the food smells good, and I'm starving."

Jane said, "Me too."

Sarah shook her head and asked, "You people can eat in the middle of all this?"

My beloved looked at me. "Sure," we said in unison.

When Jane headed to the kitchen for food, I remained a moment with Sarah. She looked over our handiwork and said, "You guys are good."

Ignoring her comment, I said, "Believe she likes you."

"Why do you say that?"

"Because you're still alive."

"Is that right? Perhaps she knows if I die you only get half the money."

"Didn't tell her that."

"Really," Sarah replied. "Maybe when this is over, we can have a session between the three of us."

Never thought about that. I took a deep breath and said, "Can you babysit this bunch while I check out the gas situation on the stove?"

Sarah backed up against the wall, spread her arms and said, "Sure."

A quiet, "Behave," was all I said while exiting the room.

Jane stood with her butt against the stove, chewing on hot broccoli as I entered. "What was that?" She asked.

"What was what?"

"I was watching, so I ask again, what was that about?"

Now you're in trouble. "She was being silly."

While filling a plate, Jane said, "Looked more than silly to me. You told her to behave." Moving up behind my frustrated wife, I reached around her ribs, pulling her against me. She said, "Stop it, asshole. You'll mess up my needles."

As she sliced off two chunks of tender, I massaged her shoulders and asked, "Having fun yet?"

Turning, she pointed the knife at me and said, "You need to focus, Eli."

Stove, dumb ass. Check the stove.

Jane fixed us both a plate and then backed off while I remained at the stove. She stared out into the dining area as I analyzed. First I turned off the burners to avoid something burning while we finished our job. Secondly, I verified that the burners were electronically ignited. "All I'll have to do is quickly turn the knob past the igniter spot and it's gonna spew gas into the room."

"That's good," Jane replied. Then she asked, "What's the deal with that other girl?"

"That's Doris. I told you about her."

"She's the one with three names and lies about her age?"

"Yep."

Jane said, "If she's under cover, why aren't we killing her?"

"I've been assuming she uses an alias because she's part of the terrorist plot. But John says she draws a disability check and is supported by Amor Saline Al-Riase. I'm thinking he's her father."

"You're talking about the guy with the gun, from Dubai?"

"Yep."

"Thought you said he was Sarah's father?"

"He is."

Jane frowned and said, "You didn't tell me everything. Eli, you should have told me all you know about her."

"Sorry. Didn't think it was important."

"Everything's important. So why don't you want to kill her?"

Staring back towards the dining area, I said, "Something just doesn't make sense. This guy comes right in calling her Itzel. If she is Sarah's half-sister, I just don't wanna kill the girl without knowing why."

"And that's the reason I'm here, to make sure you don't screw up. If she's part of this mess and she's a witness, that's all the reason I need." Staring into my eyes, Jane said, "Look at you. You're a mess."

"I'm okay."

"How about your girl, Sarah? Think she'll be okay?"

"With what?"

"With what we are about to do, dammit. You saying there's more? This girl got feelings for my man?"

"What the hell does that mean?"

"You know what it means."

"She's here to do a job just like us, and that's it." I could almost feel Jane's brain calculating as she stared into the dining room at Sarah. I said, "So far, she seems okay."

"Seems nervous to me."

"We'll see in a few minutes. For now, quit calling her my girl."

Jane turned back to me, grinned and said, "Don't forget. I know you like a book. You care about her, and not just because she's hot."

Sarah appeared at the doorway. "They're starting to move. Who's hot?"

"You baby," Jane replied as she moved past Sarah with the two plates of food.

Sarah looked at me and asked, "What the hell was that about?"

Copying Jane, I said, "You baby." Then in passing, I added, "You said it would be exciting."

You're messing with fire.

Jane and I stood eating beef tenderloin and steamed veggies. Sarah poured another flute of CHANDON.

"You okay?" Jane asked Sarah.

"I'm fine." Then with a smirk, she added "Just a little hot."

OMG. Before Sarah could take a sip, I asked, "You sure that's your glass?"

Jane slid a clean water glass toward Sarah and said, "Better safe than sorry."

As I finished eating, my eyes were on Doris. *She looks so, innocent, sleeping.* "Interesting," I said aloud by mistake.

Sarah, while pouring her drink, glanced my way and asked, "There a problem?"

"No," I answered, crouched down in front of Doris. "Just wondering, would she remember it when she wakes up if someone felt her up?"

"I've got a needle for your ass if *you* do!" Jane barked.

Sarah downed her drink, practically shoved me over and said, "Asshole."

You're instigating a fight, you know.

Before Jane could question Sarah's actions and remark, Timothy distracted her attention as he began to moan. She said, "Round two's about to start."

"Can I just kiss her?" I asked.

Jane turned and said, "You're serious, aren't you?"

I gripped my hands onto the chair back near each of Doris's shoulders and leaned forward to within six inches of her face. Close enough to smell her musk. I could feel Sarah and Jane's scheming attentions. *Bet Sarah's heart is pounding.*

Bet Jane's got her hand on that needle.

In the exhale of a deep breath, I said, "Believe I'd rather wait until she wakes up." As I spoke, Doris's eyes opened. "Whoa!" I spurted, sliding back away from her face.

Sarah huffed, "I'd say she heard everything you said."

Jane added, "Don't think she's in the mood for kissing."

"Welcome back," I spoke softly.

Struggling to speak, Doris asked, "Why?" and then closed her eyes again.

Timothy spoke slowly, "What the hell's going on?"

I rose away from Doris. Jane spoke to Timothy. "We're having a party, sir."

"Who are you?"

"I'm your worst nightmare, hoodie man."

Timothy looked confused as he checked out his surprise attire. James began moving and soon asked similar questions. Amor appeared alert, yet seemed to be purposely choosing not to speak.

Jane addressed them all. "Good evening." Motioning toward Bo, Charles and Peter, she continued. "I say 'good' only because you're not in the same condition as your friends. We have no time to waste, so let me be clear. Your friends are dead. If I wanted you dead, you would be. If you're confused, don't worry, you will soon understand. We will help you up off the chairs and then we are going to take a short walk to the barn. You are attached to one another, but will soon be separated. Please nod that you understand."

Doris spoke, "Sarah, why are you doing this?"

Instead of answering, Sarah moved to the foyer door, opened and held it. Jane stepped in front of Doris, stared down into her eyes and said, "I've been asked to spare you. Please don't make me regret that."

Doris turned to me. I held my finger up to my lips and said, "Quiet," while unzipping the jacket. I helped her to her feet and then put the jacket back on me. Doris braced herself silently against the chair as I assisted James and Timothy, pulling the hoodies up over their heads.

Amor decided differently. He looked down at his hoodie and then up at me. "Kill me now. I know your intentions."

I said, "Maybe you do and maybe you don't. Regardless, I have your gun, and you will go to the barn, alive, one way or another. If needed, I'll knock your ass out and make these other three drag you along. So, please rise and follow."

Amor hesitated but rose with my assistance as I pulled off the hoodie and pitched it on the table. I straightened his head dressings and said, "Want you to look nice for the party."

With all four standing, Jane said, "Any one of us is capable of killing any one of you in an instant. Therefore, please do as we say. Together, we're gonna walk out through the pool, down the hill and into the barn."

"Sarah," I asked, "are they flying or driving?"

"They're moving toward the airport."

Amor said, "They will kill you all!"

Jane looked at him and said, "No. If they come here, we will kill them."

I grabbed my bag. Sarah held the door as Doris led the way following Jane. When Amor was through the door into the pool area, Sarah stepped back to the dining area to place her father's phone on the table. She covered it with a cloth napkin.

Chapter 44

Cool air fell over us when we left the pool enclosure. Everyone moved in an eerie silence as Jane lead the way, mostly backwards, down the short sloped pathway to the barn. Once inside, the evening sun bled through skylights, reflecting off the plastic sheeting that lined the floor and stall facings. Doris began to cry. "Nooooo. Please noooo."

"What the hell?" James spoke loudly in his girlish voice.

Amor said, "They intend to torture us."

Timothy bent over to reach for the zip-tie at his ankle. I kicked him in his side. He grabbed for something to hold onto but found no grip on the plastic. "Don't struggle," I said. "Whether or not you are tortured depends on how much information you give us."

"We'll tell you anything you want to know," James pleaded. "Just let us go."

"You will not!" ordered Amor. "You will remain silent."

By then Sarah had her Glock out, guarding. While cutting a hole in the plastic at a bar in the last stall, Jane said, "Don't worry old man. They will talk."

I used wire snips from my bag to free Doris's hands, then immediately held one of her arms to the bars while Jane used a new zip-tie to loosely secure her wrist. "Please, no," she begged.

As Jane grabbed another zip-tie, I leaned to Doris' ear and whispered, "I have no beef with you." We repeated the process for her other wrist, stretching her arms in much the same manner as I had Sarah's when we first met. I cut her ankle loose from the rope. Moving James and Timothy aside, we began the same process with Amor. He fought us until I punched him in the face. Blood trickled from his nose as we quickly attached him to the stall next to Doris.

It only took a few minutes to secure James and Timothy to the stalls on the opposite side. James now stood stretched, facing Amor while Timothy faced Doris. I said, "Ladies and gentlemen, we have a lot to do and little time to do it. When Sarah first approached me about this night, it wasn't because we were friends. She came to me because someone from my past had told her that I could do what needs to be done and not fall apart later. She told me that if I helped her, I'd be one of the good guys. In a world of opposites, that makes you folks the bad guys. Turns out, Sarah's not really an Agent for Homeland Security. But she does do work for the government in another capacity."

Sarah looked at her watch and said, "We're wasting time."

"This won't take long." Addressing James and Timothy, I pointed toward Sarah's father. "Long story short, Sarah needs information from you guys concerning your association with her father, Mr. Amor Saline Al-Raise. Like each of you, Sarah has that little tattoo on the back of her neck. Its shape is that of the East African nation of Vitora. I'm sure you're all familiar." Turning to Amor, I said, "It's the home of this man's terroristic shenanigans. A place where about twenty women are raped every hour of every day. A place where many of the men consider women to be objects of possession ... where it's okay to order the altering of a child's body to lesson her future sexual pleasure, and then to choose the abusive man she will marry. True Americans do not practice or condone such barbaric behavior."

Jane had been standing idle as if entertained by my speech. Like a coach on the sideline of a championship event, she observed in readiness to intervene if needed. She glanced at Sarah, then back at me while tapping her watch. I opened the bag she'd brought. Removing my silver spoon, I wasted no time sliding off the handle cover, exposing the shiny blade. "Have you guys ever watched someone butcher a fish with one of these?"

Holding the knife near to James's neck, I said, "You start with an incision behind the gills and then down the edge of the backbone. Then you go back and start separating flesh from the ribs."

James literally shook as I turned to Timothy and asked, "Do you know what it makes me when I do this to a fish?"

He remained silent.

Amor mumbled. "It makes you a dead man. Everything you do here will only bring you closer to death."

"I've never been one to worry about death, sir. Not mine and certainly not yours." Turning to the others, I said, "What I do to a fish makes me a fisherman. Some days I fish for bluegill. Some days bass. Today, I have fished for men. You are my catch. Today, I have become Sarah's manerman. Unless you tell her everything she needs to know, I will butcher each of your asses alive." Pointing back at Armor, I said, "This man says you will not talk. We are here to prove him wrong."

As I spoke, a loud thumping noise came from the stall that held James's mare.

Jane looked that way. "What the hell?"

I said, "Sounded like that old horse fell again. You guys watch my fishy friends. I'll be right back."

When I headed toward the stall, James asked, "What are you gonna do?"

"What you didn't have the balls to do."

It broke my heart to see the mare lying there suffering on the floor of the stall. I pulled out Amor's gun, pointed it behind the horse's ear, and said, "Sorry girl. Sorry you had to suffer so long."

As soon as I pulled the trigger, I could hear James crying out, "Milly! Milly!" Other horses blew and stomped at his voice. I quickly pried open the horses' mouth, stretched its tongue and sliced it off with my silver blade.

On my return, James wept. I dropped the tongue on the floor in front of him. "Thought you might want a souvenir."

"How could you?" he shouted.

I replied, "That was much easier than what I am about to do to you if you refuse to cooperate. Sarah has some questions to ask you and your buddy here about your time at NASA. And considering those tattoos on your necks, she'll want to know who your real fathers are and all about your efforts to infiltrate our government."

I turned my attention to Doris. Her head hung, chin resting above her cleavage. "Before we start, I wanna ask a few questions of this pretty lady. Doris? Rosa? Or is it Itzel? Who exactly am I speaking to?"

She didn't acknowledge my request as her head remained low. Jane said, "Let me talk to her."

"Really?" I asked.

Jane moved closer. "Look at me, girlfriend. I don't give a damn about who you are, but I would like to know which of these men is the monster that abused you?"

Slowly, Doris's head rose. Her eyes were bloodshot, dilated, and mean. She growled in a wicked way and then spoke aggressively.

"Who do you think you are? You come here and take over our lives. You don't even know us. You are nothing to me."

Jane stared into the girl's eyes and replied, "Honey, at this moment, I'm everything to you. I'm the person who will decide if you live or die. But first, you need to go away and let me talk to Itzel."

"Why? Why do you wanna talk to her? She's a weak person. She has no control over me, or...."

"Or?" Jane asked. "Or who? Doris? Itzel has no control over you or Doris?"

The girl began squirming, fighting her confinements and groaning. White foam formed at the corners of her mouth. With one hand Jane grabbed her by the hair of her head, forcing her back against the bars. She held the girl until the tremors stopped. The girl's head steadied and she wept as Jane let go. A mild and timid voice spoke. "What use is it now? Why talk about things I choose to forget?"

Jane reached, touching Itzel's tears with her gloved finger. "Your multiple names, are they aliases? Are they fake names used to cover up your identity as part of these men's terrorist group?" When the girl's head shook to say no, Jane insisted. "Then tell me who abused you?"

Itzel's head hung again, moving left and right slowly and then fast. Finally she stopped and when she looked up, her eyes were wild again. "Both of them," she growled like an animal while looking at James and Timothy. "And both of those bastards inside. I'm glad you killed them."

"She's lying!" Timothy shouted.

"Father Brown abused you?" I asked.

"Yes," Itzel replied. "With help from James."

James's eyes squinted. "She's lying to you."

Sarah spoke up. "Did Charles abuse you?"

"He was the first. He helped take away a part of me that I can never get back."

"Damn you!" Sarah cried out to her father. "You did the same thing to her that you did to me?"

"I did nothing to you."

"You had it done."

"It was for your own good," Amor replied.

"That's a lie and you know it! You did it to control me, and you did the same thing to Itzel."

"I live thousands of miles away. How was I to preserve your innocence for your future husband?"

Pointing at James, Sarah shook her head and said, "You saved me for him? He doesn't even want me. You're a stupid old man stuck in the stupid ways of your stupid ancestors and I despise you for what you've done to her and me."

"I have been good to you both."

"You butchered our bodies and now you want to use what's left of us to put your blood in our American government. You're not a true Muslim. You're a terrorist! You've been using these men to steal U.S. technologies and now you want to use me like you used my mother. She despises what you do so much that she's paying this man with your money to help me end your efforts."

Jane stepped between Sarah and her father. "Are you saying this man had the both of you circumcised?"

Sarah nodded her reply.

Jane looked at me. "He really is a hoodie man." Then to Amor she said, "You lousy piece of crap. You have no respect for women. Did you hate the woman who brought you into this world?"

"My mother was obedient."

"Obedient? Mister, you screwed up big time when you came to America. Women in this country fought long and hard to gain equal rights. We'll not allow the likes of you to come here and abuse us."

"Jane," Sarah said, "Let's don't lose focus. What he did to me is unimportant at this moment. We're here because of what he is trying to do to America."

I moved next to my wife, focused on Amor and said, "It's people like you that give Islam a bad name. Good descent Muslims in America came here to get away from the likes you. They came here for a better life where men and women are equal. Where women don't have to cover up and *they* get to choose their spouse."

Amor shook his head and said, "Your democracy is already being destroyed by the women you call equals. They have castrated your perverted male politicians. Men who do drugs and then have sex with young girls and other men while being secretly filmed. They are then forced to make bad political decisions because they are being held hostage by foreign entities and by the old women they call equals."

For a moment, I stood shocked at Amor's comments. *Jane often identifies how politicians cast votes in opposition to the will of the people who elected them.*

Amor grinned and continued. "You think you can do away with me and stop what was started decades ago. I am not the first and certainly will not be the last. American leaders now want to control the weather as part of their efforts to control the world. We will not stop until we control America." Turning to Sarah, he said, "And you, my daughter, should join our efforts."

Jane asked, Sarah, "Are you buying into this?"

"No, I'm not. He's part of everything he describes. My father is an admitted terrorist who destroys people's lives and he wants to destroy the country I swore to protect."

"Thank you," Jane replied. She turned to me and said, "He goes first."

The others watched silently as I cut two 20-foot lengths of rope and created a slip loop at one end of each. Amor pleaded with Sarah, "How can you trade the love of your father for a country of drunken liars? My daughter is not a murderer."

"I killed Alon for what he did to me. You are no better."

When I squatted and reached to raise his thobe, Amor kicked me in the chin. I fell backwards, mouth bleeding. Before I could rise, Jane's gloved hands were wearing him out, first face and then stomach until she knocked the wind out of him. As he struggled to take a breath, she and I knelt and secured his ankles. We quickly looped the other ends of the ropes around bars on either side of Timothy and James, pulled and tied off so Amor's legs were spread, barely touching the ground. He caught his breath, but remained at our mercy. Turning to Sarah, Jane asked, "How much time do we have?"

"They're at the airport. I'd say less than thirty minutes."

Jane took a deep breath. "We need more light."

Sarah found a switch and turned on the overhead lighting.

"Not perfect," Jane said, "but it'll do." Squatting, she poured items from her backpack: latex gloves, a stitch kit, combat gauze and several packages of hemostatic clotting sponges. She spoke to James and Timothy. "We don't have much time. Watch what we're doing. Answer Sarah's questions or we'll do the same to each of you."

Sarah asked, "What exactly are you going to do?"

Jane replied, "I'm about to take something from him the way he took something from you." While slipping on surgical gloves, she said, "I'm thinking maybe we should keep his sorry ass alive. Looking up at Amor, she said, "You will never again feel the inside of a woman. From this day forward, you will squat to pee. You will be a woman. Perhaps Sarah can get you a room at Guantanamo. The boys there can have their way with you until you die."

Jane used scissors to cut open Amor's thobe and then started on his undergarment.

"Sarah! Please! You can't let them do this to me!"

After opening two sponge packs and a pack of gauze, Jane leaned across Amor's legs and kissed me on the lips. "Let's do this." Reaching for Amor's limp penis, she stretched it out and said, "Leave me just enough to stitch."

"Hell no!" I said, "I'm not cuttin' this man's dick off!"

Jane shook her head. "He's a bad man, Eli."

"He's an idiot, caught up in some sick ass religious stuff."

"Bull! He's a punk who wants to treat women like property."

"Yes," I said, "I agree, and I've been wantin' to kill him ever since I found out what he did to Sarah. I'll butcher his ass, but I ain't cuttin' no man's dick off."

"When you found out?" Jane squinted. "How'd you find out?"

"She—"

Sarah interrupted, shouting, "Guys, stop! We don't have time for this."

Jane and I both looked up. Sarah had Bo's pistol pointing at us. Jane huffed, and turned to me. "I oughta cut *your* dick off."

Sarah said, "My father deserves to die, but not like this. I will not mutilate him."

"You don't have to," Jane snarled. "Give me your knife, Eli. I'll do it."

"No," I said. "It's her father. This is not how she wants to do it."

Jane picked up the scissors and reached for Amor's manhood. He begged, "Don't let her do this, Sarah!" He screamed as Jane began cutting.

"Crack! Crack!" Two rounds from the 9mm reverberated through the barn. Horses stomped and kicked the stalls. Jane jumped back and began pacing, shaking her head and holding her ears. Mine rang loudly. James choked on his own vomit.

With each heartbeat, blood shot from the stub of Amor's manhood. He stared down at his mangled penis lying on the plastic in a growing puddle of red. Looking up, his weakened eyes were open, staring at his daughter. A lesser amount of blood seeped from his chest through his garment. He mumbled his last words, "'amut min alkhajali," (I die with shame).

Sarah stood silent, staring at her father as his head fell. When Jane turned that way with madness in her eyes, I stepped over the ropes and stood between them facing Jane. "No, dammit! Give it a minute. She just shot her father."

As Amor's body became limp, Sarah took a step back and said, "Back off, Eli." She pointed the gun at Jane and spoke fast and loud. "Lady, no one invited you to this party. I hired your husband to gain information from these men. You bust in here like you own the place, and I'm okay if you want to help Eli with whatever it takes to do his job. But I told him early on that I would deal with my father. My thoughts on how that would happen never involved you. You had no right. If you weren't Eli's wife, I'd dispatch your ass right here and now."

Jane seemed as startled as me at this enraged side of Sarah. I said, "Jane, remember how pissed you were when I took out the man who killed your father. How you had longed for that moment."

My angry wife took a deep breath and then exhaled. Looking at Sarah, she said, "I came here to make sure my husband *and* my marriage survive this fiasco. If your intentions involve anything less, you'd best pull that trigger now." Turning to James and Timothy who stood in shock, she said, "Eli, you knock them out. I'll take their pants off and we can get this over with."

"No!" James pleaded. "You don't have to do that. We'll tell you everything we know."

Timothy said, "Speak for yourself."

Sarah got close to Timothy, stuck the muzzle of her firearm under his chin, and said, "I've disliked you ever since I figured out your involvement in the assassination of Ambassador Wellington. If you want to walk out of this barn in one piece, you'll tell me everything I need to know. Otherwise, I'll let this woman do to you what she just did to my father."

Sarah began a recording on her phone. It didn't take long for James and Timothy to spill names of those involved in the plot to obtain and sell American space technologies. Some were former NASA associates. As suspected, some were Chinese. When she asked Timothy for the identity of his real father, he mumbled something like, "Victor Pavellavich." It sounded Russian to me.

When she asked the same of James, he said, "My father is Asad Saline Al-Riase."

Sarah seemed surprised. "My father's brother?"

"Yes."

"So why didn't he come for the wedding?"

"He's dead," James replied.

"I didn't know that."

Timothy interrupted saying, "There's lots of things you don't know. There are lots of things we all don't know."

Looking toward her father, Sarah said, "Can you believe he wanted me to marry my cousin?"

Jane leaned to my ear and whispered, "For a religious bunch, they sure are some sickos."

I moved to Sarah, pointed at her phone and lipped, "Stop it." When she paused the recording, I turned to Timothy and asked, "What about her, Itzel? Was she really supposed to marry you?" He nodded. Looking at Amor's lifeless body, I said, "One big happy politically infiltrated family. Senator Proctor was in on all this too, wasn't he?" Both men remained silent. I flashed my knife at James and said, "She's gonna turn that recorder back on and you will tell her about Senator Proctor's involvement or I'll start in on your ass right now."

Timothy shook his head, but James spoke anyway. "I will. I will."

Sarah started recording and asked, "What was Senator Proctor's involvement in the terrorist activity?"

James said, "He knows everything."

"Who knows everything?" Sarah demanded. "I want to hear his name."

"Senator ... George ... Proctor ... knows everything about what's going on."

"With what?" Sarah encouraged.

"With the weather technology and with putting people in politics."

Sarah ended the recording.

I said, "Sure hope your alphabet geeks can stop all this."

"On a good day, that's what counterintelligence does."

Suddenly it seemed we were done. We'd gotten the information needed without laying a hand on either man. *Now what*, I thought.

Jane said, "I need a cigarette."

I glanced at Sarah and asked, "Time?"

"Twelve minutes, give or take."

I said, "Let's have a quick smoke while I figure things out."

Sarah's eyebrows lifted. "Better think quickly."

"OODA," I replied with a wink.

Our captors stared as we stepped to the barn-door-opening and lit our cigarettes. I took a draw and said, "We might not get 'em back inside before they get here."

Sarah glanced at the sky and said, "We should hear the chopper in time to react."

Jane blew smoke at Sarah and said, "I'm still interested in how my husband knew you'd been circumcised."

"My mother spoke to him about it. You need not worry. He hasn't seen my butchered anatomy."

Jane glanced toward Amor and Itzel and then back at Sarah. "It takes balls to shoot your father. I was wrong. That was rightfully your call." After offering a fist bump, she said, "Now, are you going to shoot your little sister?"

Sarah seemed caught off guard and nervous. She took a draw, exhaled slowly and said, "Never had a little sister. Not gonna have my mother much longer." Glancing back at Itzel, she added, "Girl's been a victim all her life."

Jane said, "Then she's a keeper. Eli, you take care of her. Make sure she doesn't get in the way." Noticing Sarah's stare Jane asked. "What's your problem?"

"No problem. Just thinking how much easier my job would be if I had your emotions."

"I don't have emotions."

"Exactly." Sarah looked at me and said, "Okay, what's your plan?"

"Sun's going down. We know they're coming." Staring up the hill, I said, "It's an awesome house. I hate to blow it up."

"It's a house," Jane mumbled.

Looking back at Amor's body, I said, "Believe I have a better idea."

"Oh really?" Sarah smirked. "Explain."

"Don't have time. Let's just get 'em inside ASAP. We can clean this place up later. You'll figure it out as we go."

Jane asked, "And what if we don't like your plan?"

"Then we'll blow the place up with all them in it." I winked and said, "I think you'll like my idea."

Chapter 45

Ten minutes had passed as James and Timothy struggled through the dining room door using their shoulders to carry Amor upright between them. I repositioned the chairs and they gladly returned their dead leader to the head of the table. It took multiple zip-ties to secure him to the chair. Adequate lighting bled in from the kitchen. "Now," I demanded in the process of cutting James, Timothy and Doris loose from the rope, "I want all of you to sit in your original seats until Amor's security arrives. As they seated, Jane tilted her head. "Trust me," I spoke to her and Sarah. "Watch 'em a minute. I'll be right back."

Stepping into the kitchen, I removed Amor's .380 from my back pocket and checked it out. It still had four in the magazine and one in the pipe. I glanced back into the dining room where Sarah stood behind Bo's dead body. Doris sat facing Timothy. Jane, directly behind James, stared my way. When James looked toward Sarah, I showed my wife the gun and motioned her to move out of the way. She understood and stepped over behind Peter Brown's lifeless body.

The sound of a distant helicopter drifted in. Everyone glanced toward the window. Holding the pistol inside my right jacket pocket, I stepped back into the room, stopping right behind Amor. When Sarah said, "They're coming," I drew the gun out, pointed it at Timothy's forehead and pulled the trigger. Blood flew out the back of his head. He collapsed forward as I turned to James. Sarah and Jane covered their ears as Doris doubled over hiding her head. When James tried to rise, I fired two rounds into his chest. Dropping back into the chair, he held a hand over his chest to catch the small amount of blood escaping. His face cringed like a child wanting to cry as I extended my arm and placed one more round into his forehead. His head met the back of the chair and then slowly fell forward until he looked as if he'd fallen asleep. Blood oozed from the front and back of his head. Some dripped on his lap. Some ran down one side of his neck.

Timothy's blood soaked across the tablecloth as I put the gun back into my pocket.

Jane said, "Damn, Eli. This is your plan?"

Sarah shook her head, looked out the window and said, "I can see the chopper's lights."

While straightening Amor's ghutra and agal, I said, "Amor just shot James and Timothy for having a gay wedding."

"Oookay," Jane replied.

Sarah turned. "All I know is they're dead and the enemy is landing. So, how do we plan to do this?"

"I'd prefer we kill whoever comes off that chopper with Bo's gun."

Jane looked at Sarah. "Give it to me. I'll do it."

"No," Sarah replied. "You guys have done enough."

Jane looked at me. We both shrugged our shoulders and said, "Okay."

As Sarah checked the rounds left in Bo's 9mm, Jane began rolling up the rope while moving to the window, monitoring the chopper. "There's two men. One's coming around to the front. The other's coming this way."

"Doris!" I hollered, "Get under the table, now." She stood still as if in shock.

Jane pitched the rope behind the bar. She then grabbed Doris pulling her down, shoved her under the table and demanded, "Keep your ass under there. Stay quiet, and don't move."

Sarah sat down in her original seat and said, "You guys get out of sight. Back me up." She bent over, laying her head on the table. A shadow flashed from the pool area. Motioning that direction, I put my finger to my lips. Jane lowered behind the bar while I slid into the kitchen. Slight creaking came from the front door.

You gonna let him go by?

She needs to take 'em both.

Things grew eerily quiet. It felt like waiting for a deer. Finally, a soft sound came from close by. Frozen behind the security cabinet, I saw first his knee and then more as he moved into the kitchen. He had just reached full view when he began raising his gun. A shot cracked from the dining room and blood flew out the man's back. He returned a reflexive round and then collapsed onto the floor, still moving. A second shot blasted inside the dining room. I leaped toward the man on the floor to kick his gun away. As I did, the sting of another shot pierced my left triceps, and my back began to burn. I couldn't see

Sarah but Jane was having her way with the other shooter. Aiming my 9mm, I watched for an open shot. She flipped the guy to the floor and then disappeared below the table. Another shot rang and things got quiet. No motion. *Oh no! Don't let it be!* I nearly threw up anticipating the loss of both Jane and Sarah.

Looking back, the man on the floor wasn't moving. After a few seconds, I heard Jane's growl and then, "Eli!"

"Thank God," I mumbled. Jane rose from behind the table with her hands on her ears, shaking her head. At the other end of the table, I could make out a man, motionless on the floor. I flipped on the dining room chandelier. Stepping over the man and toward Jane, I found Sarah face down on the floor, moaning but at least still breathing. She had a bullet hole high and a couple inches right of center on the back of her jacket.

"Shit!" I said, while avoiding blood on the floor.

"Eli, there's blood on your jacket. Are you hit?" Jane spoke loudly.

"I'll live."

Jane grabbed a cloth napkin and said, "Hold this on it. Try not to drip."

Looking around, I said, "Too late."

She spoke loudly again. "My ears are numb. I can't tell what you're saying."

"Great!" *One's down and the other can't hear.*
But they're both alive.

Jane continued, "Eli, look at me when you talk. I'll read your lips."

Taking her by the shoulders, I over enunciated. "Be careful. I don't want your footprints in the blood."

She glanced down and then nodded.

Staring at her face I said, "Patch me up later. Take care of her first."

We both squatted on either side of Sarah. I tapped Jane and said, "A least it came all the way through."

"Honey, what you're looking at is the entry wound. She shot guy one. When he fired back, she tried to stand up. Before she could turn, guy two shot her in the back from the pool area. He shot at you as he came through the door. That's when I grabbed him."

Jane put on surgical gloves and handed me a pair. She reached under to unzip Sarah's jacket and began searching. "Good, it's a through and through. Okay girlfriend. We need to turn you over."

As we rolled her onto her back, Sarah let out a yelp. Jane grinned and asked, "How you feeling?" With no reply, Jane looked my way and said, "She didn't go down hard, but I saw her head hit the corner of the table. Could have a concussion." Looking back at Sarah, she continued, "You have a lump on your head, but no broken skin or blood. That's good. Now, I don't want to move your right arm yet, so, we're going to pull the jacket sleeve off of your good side. I need access to the front and back to stop the bleeding."

We managed the sleeve easy enough. Jane wasted no time unbuttoning the blouse and exposing Sarah's bloody chest. She wore no bra. The bullet had exited right above her right breast. Jane ripped open an alcohol pad and handed it to me. "Clean her off."

"Okay." When I began sterilizing the wound, she tensed up.

I said, "Relax. It's just a sensation. Enjoy it." If looks could kill, I would have been dead.

Jane pulled out bandages and opened them while inspecting the outside of the jacket. She said, "Girl, you've gotta souvenir somewhere in that lining." She glanced down as I cleaned blood off Sarah's dark nipple. "What the hell, Eli. Are you that big of a pervert?"

"You said clean her off."

"The bullet didn't come out there! Just hold this blouse and jacket out of my way."

Jane reached under to clean Sarah's back, and in less than two minutes, she had QuickClot gauze and adhesive cloth covering both wounds.

I touched her arm. "That's it?"

"Yes."

"You're fast."

"I do this every day."

Before she could look away, I said, "You don't have to talk so loud. I can hear you."

She looked down at Sarah and said, "It went through your scapular, your shoulder blade, at an angle. And seeing how it didn't go through your jacket, it might have hit a rib also. Bottom line, you're going to need a hospital to clean out the bone fragments. And you will be sore. Now I'm going to cover you up and let you lay here a minute while I tend to Eli." As she began buttoning Sarah's blouse, Jane glanced at me and said, "Show me your wound. Try not to drip."

Sliding away from blood, I knelt while taking off my jacket and shirt. In the process, I checked out the man on the floor with his brains scattered. I asked, "Did you have to shoot him with *your* gun?" She didn't hear me, so I tapped her shoulder. When she looked, I repeated, "Did you have to shoot him with *your* gun?"

"I didn't," Jane answered. "She did." Pointing under the table at Doris, she added, "Girl got the gun Sarah dropped and plugged his ass."

"Good for her," I said while Jane took ahold of my arm. She squeezed and it about sent me through the roof. I took a deep breath and exhaled slowly. *It's just a sensation.*

"Don't believe it hit bone." When she started opening the alcohol pad, I knew I was about to get what I'd just given to Sarah. *Here we go!* On initial contact it felt like a thousand volts of electricity. In my mind, I knew it would only last seconds, therefore, I enjoyed it for every ounce of intensity it offered. Jane saw my deep breath and knew what I was doing. She just shook her head. Sarah stared as Jane applied gauze and wrapped my arm.

Doris lay in a fetal position under the table, whimpering. When I started to reach for her with my good arm, she drew up. Jane said, "Careful. Not sure who she is at the moment."

"Wanna give me the gun?" I asked.

Doris drew up more. Sarah tried to rise. Jane patted her on the hip and said, "Hold on pretty girl. Give that gauze a minute to work. Then we'll get you up." Looking back at me, she said, "Damn Eli. Looks like the bullet went across your back."

I reached to feel for blood.

"You're not bleeding, but I'd say you were about an inch away from being paralyzed." She started placing things back into her bag, and said, "Put your shirt back on and go check out the guy Sarah shot. Make sure he's dead."

"I believe he is."

"Check anyway," she ordered.

I rose, looked around the room and then went to verify the man was deceased. Using my foot, I slid his gun next to his hand avoiding blood on the floor. I had somehow forgotten about the chopper until noise loudened and I could tell it was lifting off.

When I got back to the dining room, Doris stood next to the table, both hands gripping the gun. "Easy," I spoke softly while trying to reach her without stepping in blood. I pried Bo's gun from her hand placed it on the table, and hugged her. "It's all over now."

Jane said, "When you two get done crying, we need to get this one up off the floor."

Pulling away, I said, "Doris, Itzel, whoever you are, can you help Jane while I start fixing things so we can get the hell out of here? That pilot might have seen gun flashes and he's probably already called the cops."

Without speaking, she nodded and then squatted to help Jane with Sarah. I cut all of the zip-ties that were holding Amor, and then leaned him back into the chair.

From the kitchen, I grabbed a garbage bag and returned to start picking up anything we could not leave behind. Things that might hold our DNA. Jane and Doris had gotten Sarah up into a chair. "Does she have a concussion?"

"No," Sarah answered for herself. "I know what's going on."

"Well, that's good," I replied, "cause we need to get the hell out of here. We still have to clean up the barn."

Sarah climbed to her feet, looked around and said, "So what's the deal? We plan on blowing this place up or not?"

"No," I said.

Jane interrupted. "I'm beginning to hear some, but you still need to look at me when you talk."

Facing her, I said, "If we blow this place up and Sarah leaves, it'll make her look complicit for sure. Way I see it, Amor got pissed because it turned out to be a gay wedding. He'd been tricked, so he went off and killed James, Timothy and Peter. Bo shot Amor because he shot Timothy. Amor's security shot Bo and Charles."

Sarah said, "I grabbed Bo's gun and shot one of them. The other one shot me and, and—"

"And I shot him," Doris answered.

"But" I tried to reason, "you would have to stay here."

"Correct," Sarah agreed loudly. "She and I both would need to stay here anyway. That's the only way this all makes sense. No one will question our story with me being shot and both of us admitting to killing someone. You and Jane get the hell out of here. Clean up the barn and go. We'll stay and get our stories together until they come."

Jane asked, "Does what she said make sense, Eli?"

"Yes," I replied while nodding my head. Turning to Sarah, I asked, "When do we see you again?"

Sarah continued talking loudly, "As soon as you guys are gone, I'll call my operator. He'll fly a crew in here right away to make this work. One or two of them will accompany me to the hospital. Turning to her half-sister, Sarah said, "You can go with me. I'll call Mom."

Jane said, "My ears are ringing, but I got most of what you just said. So, after you call your mother, she can pay us. Right?"

Sarah nodded. I wanted to hug her but couldn't. Jane pointed at Bo and Charles, and said, "We need to shoot those two with the security guy's guns."

Sarah and I held up Bo, facing Jane who stood in the doorway. While she held the gun in her right hand she wrapped her left arm over her head and stuck her left index finger into her right ear. Her left bicep covered her left ear. When she pointed the gun at Bo's head, Sarah said, "Wait! Don't shoot him in the head. His blood won't flow and it may be too obvious that it's post mortem."

"Good thinking," Jane said as she adjusted her aim to Bo's chest. After she fired two quick rounds, Sarah and I let go and the body dropped rather naturally to the floor. "Good job," I said with my ears ringing loudly.

Moving to the other side of the table, we lifted Charles. Jane went to the kitchen and retrieved the other man's gun from the floor. This time, Sarah and I covered our ears in the same way Jane had while she shot Charles in the back, hopefully through the heart. We dropped him over the table. I complained, "Not enough blood."

Sarah pulled the old man off the table, allowing him to crumple in the floor. She said, "With all the other blood, locals won't be able to tell whose blood is whose."

"What about, fat ass?" Jane asked, nodding toward Peter.

Doris stood near the window, holding her hands over her ears as we pulled Peter's big head off the table. Each time we let go, he started falling forward again. Jane said, "I'll hold him." She grabbed both of his ears and held him back against the chair. "Just don't miss."

"Hold on," I said. "You can't shoot him with that gun, Sarah." I handed her Amor's .380 and then grabbed one of the hoodies off the table. I tried tying the sleeves around Jane's head to protect her ears.

"No!" she shouted. "Get that off of me."

I understood. Instead, I tied the sleeves around my head and said, "I'll hold him."

Jane squinted at me as she backed off and covered her ears. Sarah stood staring as if trying to figure us out. "Come on," I said, holding Peter's head. "We can't waste time."

Sarah took aim at Peter's chest and pulled the trigger twice, firing only once. I let loose, allowing the big body to slump and then used my foot to push him out of the chair. He fell next to Charles. "Only one round. What do you think?" I asked.

Sarah said, "Good enough."

I pulled the hoodie off my head and tossed it back on the table, next to Jane's bag. "Think all this is gonna satisfy forensics?" I asked.

"Probably not," Sarah answered, "but it's just for the locals. Our guys will run them off pretty quick and then it won't matter. By the time they get here, I'll have my story ready. You guys just keep low until I find out what they know or don't know about you."

"What does that mean? What do you think they know?" I asked. Jane's eyes widened and I knew she could hear our conversation.

"I'd say they know who I'm working with. But considering how this is all going down and the fact that you're still alive and gone, their concern will be to conceal your identity."

Jane looked at me and said, "Still alive? I told you they were planning to kill you. And she knew it."

"No," Sarah pleaded. "I didn't know it and I still don't for sure, but it's a damn good possibility. Especially if this all went down tomorrow as planned. That's why I was good with doing it tonight. It was the best choice to save Eli."

Jane said, "I don't believe you."

"Doesn't matter if you believe me or not. It's the truth. I could have shot both of you in the back by now and left a hero, but I haven't, because—"

"Because you're in love with my husband," Jane snarled as she began stuffing things into her bag. She had been doing a good job of controlling her anger. Months of frustration were about to explode and it wouldn't be pretty. *Lord, take her to a better place.*

Sarah seemed on guard. Her good hand remained near her gun. She took a deep breath, let it out, and said, "Eli, I'm not going to lie. My guys already know who you are. After tonight, I don't believe you have to worry about them. However, it's the locals you may have to worry about. You've been seen in town. I suggest you don't waste time getting rid of the beard, dump those silly glasses, and you might want to cut your hair."

I smiled and said, "Damn. Your mother wanted me to rub her with my whiskers."

Jane huffed, "Excuse me?"

I glanced back and forth between two time-bombs. For the moment, Doris stood listening as if she were enjoying the drama.

Sarah stared cautiously at Jane. "My mother had been drinking when she said that. Guess you could say she has a thing for beards. Just a little fantasy from a lonely woman dying of cancer. I promise you, she didn't mean to be disrespectful."

Jane's face changed. As she began taking deep breaths and letting them out slowly, I knew the routine. Her way of trying to control the crazy. When she began gathering the hoodies, I focused on Sarah. "You okay?" Her expression said no, but she nodded yes. When I looked back to Jane, she had wrapped the sleeves of a hoodie around James's stiff neck. I thought, *No! No!* and then let out a "Pssssst!"

Jane looked at me and said, "Screw you, your beard, and everything else. I just need to go before this gets ugly." She had already begun tying the sleeves.

I reached and touched her arm. When she looked up again, I had my eyes wide open and began lipping, "Don't. Do. That."

Jane stopped and we both looked at Sarah. It was too late. Sarah stared down at the hoodie, up at Jane, and then back at me. While my wife calculated the moment, I waited for Sarah to say something to me. Instead, she spoke to Jane. "Please, don't do that. No one knows you're here. If you leave that tied, they'll connect Eli to the park killings."

Jane turned to me, tilted her head and said, "She knows about the park?"

"Yes I do," Sarah answered. "I just didn't know who the perp was ... until now."

"And now that you do?" Jane asked.

"It's no different than what Eli and I did in the park. So I beg you, let it go." Looking around, she said, "We've done a pretty good job here, but it only works if we keep a low profile. I want my people to forget Eli was here tonight. If you leave that hoodie tied, I promise there'll be an APB out on him before morning."

Jane untied the hoodie and stuffed it into her bag. When I began cleaning firearms, she and Sarah joined me. Doris, still at the window, asked, "Is there anything I can do?"

After glancing at Jane, then me, Sarah replied, "Just keep your eyes and ears on alert. I'm afraid we're going to get company soon."

We placed each gun into the hands of its proper owner long enough to get fingerprints. As we finished, Sarah said, "Eli, I'll probably have to stay overnight at the hospital. Mom will want to come. I'd rather she didn't. Can you convince her to stay home?"

"I'll try," was all I could say.

Moving toward Sarah, Jane picked up two white napkins off the table. "If you're staying here, I need my bandages back. The cops might want to take a look at your injury. They'll know damn well that you didn't have that stuff on hand."

Sarah removed her jacket and began unbuttoning her blouse. When she exposed herself, she and Jane stared at one another's eyes long enough to make me nervous. Jane said, "I don't like many people. I think I like you. My husband cares about you, a lot. I understand." Tears ran down Sarah's cheek. She stood wordless as Jane reached for her neck and pulled her close. Their lips joined and I about died. *What the?* Sarah did not resist. I looked at Doris. She grinned. When the kiss ended, Jane stepped back, still facing Sarah, and said, "I just needed to know." Then she turned and gave me a look.

Don't say a word. I kept quiet. As Jane passed me I glanced at Sarah. She refused to look at me. We both watched and listened when Jane stepped to Doris at the window. Jane asked, "Are you okay with what happened here tonight?"

Doris grinned. "Do I get a kiss?"

Jane said, "No. My husband wanted to kiss you while you were out, but he didn't because I threatened to kill him. Knowing what I know now, I'd say you've had your share of abuse."

"Thank you," Doris said quietly.

"You're welcome." After a couple steps toward the door, Jane hesitated and looked back. "I hope you get help for the DID. Just make sure that in your therapy, you never mention mine or my husband's name. If you do, another personality won't save you from me. Do you understand?"

Doris nodded.

Jane turned to me, said, "Grab the garbage bag. We have to go," and then walked out. When I reached the door to the pool area, she had made it to the outside exit. I looked back at Sarah and asked, "You okay?"

"I'm good."

"Give us a few minutes and then turn the security cameras back on. It's all in the cabinet across from the stove. There's a power strip behind the DVR."

"Roger that," Sarah replied. Before I could leave, she said, "Hey." When I looked back, she was trying to raise her arms. Only the good one made it to horizontal.

Bags in hand I raised both of my arms, nodded, and then turned away. Jane stood at the outside door, wiping the knob and watching me. *Don't like that look.* After holding the door open for me, she wiped the outside knob.

Without speaking, we made our way to the barn. As we snatched plastic sheets, and cut zip-ties from the stalls, I asked, "How's your ears?"

"I can hear. Probably better than you think."

"What's that mean?" I asked.

"It means when this is over, I think I'm done."

"Done with what?"

"With everything. You and me to start with."

I stood there not knowing what to say. Jane ripped another sheet and said, "Don't act stupid. It's been coming. I'm not good for you."

"That's not true. I need you."

"No you don't. You need a different kind of woman. Someone who can cry and be a mommy for you and feel sorry for herself. Someone you can feel sorry for." Motioning toward the house, she said, "You need her. I see how you look at her, and I see how she looks at you."

As Jane began stuffing ropes and plastic from the stalls into a leaf-bag, I dumped a wheelbarrow load of sawdust onto the puddle of Amor's blood. It soaked up nicely. We threw the used, cut zip-ties onto the bloody sawdust and then folded the plastic along with Amor's severed penis and stuffed it and the garbage from the house into another bag. I tried to think of something more to say to Jane, but couldn't. From a distance, the faint sound of a siren bled into the barn. I turned out the lights and said, "We gotta go."

With the bags draped over our shoulders, we scanned the area one last time and then looked like a couple of Santa's sliding out the backdoor of the barn. Over the fence and into the woods we went. Jane walked in silence, following closely behind me on a dark, rarely used path that my friends and I had once used to sneak onto the property as teens. Before long, one siren turned into two. They grew closer and louder and were accompanied by the sound of a helicopter. I hesitated and spoke quietly, "That would be the Feds."

Listening to the chopper, Jane said, "Sure hope those two don't screw it up."

Don't say a word. You'd be smart not to mention Sarah again tonight.

Chapter 46

It only took a few minutes to reach the outer edge of the woods, near Todds Creek. Just inside the tree line, we came upon a dark SUV that I had never seen before. When Jane tapped on the window, the hatch popped and slowly rose. We dumped all our belongings in and pulled out fresh clothes. As Jane removed her blouse, John exited from the driver's seat and joined us.

Are you kidding me?

John said, "Your girl called her mother," while tilting his head toward the back seat. "Said it got crazy but everything worked out."

As I stretched to see the top of Ella's head, Jane removed her sports bra. I said, "Damn. You don't mind showing your tits to John?"

John said, "Ain't nothing I ain't seen be'...."

He stopped short and I just stared at him. Jane slipped on a dress and then spoke while pulling her leggings off. "You two stop it. We have no time for silliness."

When I grabbed my electric razor/trimmer, Jane took a hold of my good arm and said, "Not yet."

Really? What's up with that? "Okay."

"Just get dressed so we can get out of here."

I put on clean jeans, cowboy boots and a flannel shirt before closing the hatch. Jane had already climbed into the front passenger seat. For a few seconds, I stood there listening to the running water, thinking of my younger days.

"Come on Eli!" Jane urged.

I slid in next to Ella, behind Jane. Ella's face looked thinner, eyes sunk back. Still, she looked nice in her long wig. I said, "Hey there. You doin' alright?"

Without speaking, Ella nodded while staring at my face. I noticed Jane looking over her shoulder. She turned to John and said, "Let's go."

As we left the trees, crossed the Todds Creek Bridge and started up the blacktop road, I buttoned my shirt, leaned back and exhaled. It felt good to be seated. Ella finally spoke. "Sarah wanted to know why I came out here tonight."

"What'd you tell her?"

"Told her your wife and this fine black man convinced me that it might not be safe to be alone at the farm, depending on how things went down at the estate."

"That's about the truth of it. Considering the way it ended, I'd say you'll be less likely to be in jeopardy. Sarah's people should be pleased with the results. Hell, she oughta get a bonus."

"She says she's okay, but I don't believe it. What happened? Is she really okay?"

For a moment, I sat contemplating what to say. Ella raised her voice. "Don't ignore me boy. I asked you a question."

I replied, "I'm sure Sarah told you all she could."

"No, she didn't. I asked her if anybody got hurt. She said she didn't have time to talk and would explain later."

"Well, there you go. She'll explain when she can."

"Don't you mess with me boy! I'll not give you a damn penny if you don't tell me what's going on!"

Jane glanced back again as if waiting for my reply. I said, "She got shot."

Before I could explain, Ella began pounding my wounded arm and screaming, "I told you not to let her get hurt!"

I raised my right hand as if to hit her and yelled, "Stop it, dammit!" I could feel blood saturating my clean shirt. "You made me bleed again!" When she paused, staring, I said, "It was chaos. We both got shot. Sarah's gonna be okay. Jane fixed her up. She had to stay behind to wait for the Feds, and she'll need to go to the hospital. Doris is gonna go with her."

"Doris?"

"Doris, Itzel, Sarah's half-crazy, half-sister."

"Half-sister? That's no surprise. If he did it with me, he probably did it with others. No telling how many. Now tell me, where did Sarah get shot?"

"In her shoulder. Jane says she'll be okay."

"She has a sister?"

"That's the way it looks."

"Girl always wanted a sister."

"Well, she's got one now." While speaking, I realized we were not driving toward Morganville. "John, why we goin' this way?"

"Figure the first road they might block off would be the main road through Morganville. Taking a scenic route to I-75."

As we drove on, lightning flashes lit the dark sky ahead. Ella said, "How about you take that shirt off and let me take a look."

While lowering her sun visor and opening the mirror to see Ella's reflection, Jane said, "I'll take care of it when we get home."

Ella came back, "Honey, the way he's bleeding, believe you need to take care of it now."

Jane turned to look at my shirt and said, "Damn Eli."

"Don't damn me. She did it."

Jane said, "John, find a safe place to pull over so I can take care of this."

"There is no safe place. If we stop out here, someone's liable to see us."

In the field to our right, there sat an old wooden barn about a hundred yards off the road. No lights and no house in sight. "Pull off here," Jane said. "Go back to that barn."

Turning right, John killed the SUV's lights and bitched on the way back. "We're making a mistake. What if there's a camera?"

"No power lines," I replied.

We found a spot behind the barn. John backed up and turned the vehicle, facing the way he came in. Jane got out first, tapped on my window and said, "Get out and get that shirt off."

While unbuttoning my shirt, I said, "Give me one of your cigarettes." Jane lit one, took a draw and then stuck it into my mouth. John joined us and fired up a joint.

Ella got out, looked at the flashes in the west and said, "Gonna rain for sure." Then to John, she asked, "Mind if I hit on that?"

John passed the joint and said, "You sure you ain't my mother?"

Ella grinned, took a hit and began observing as my beloved worked like a machine, cleaning and wrapping my wound with gauze. Leaning against the vehicle, she complimented Jane. "You do good work."

"Get lots of practice," Jane replied.

"Doctor?"

"Yes. I'm doing my residency in the emergency room at University."

"Hell, you've seen it all then."

"You have no idea."

"Honey, I grew up in a neighborhood that sends you a lot of your work. Believe I do have an idea."

Jane stared for a moment before saying, "Perhaps you do." As she spoke, the sound of a siren grew out of the otherwise quiet countryside. Accompanying lights flashed in the distance from a speeding police cruiser. We all ducked needlessly while it passed and disappeared as quickly as it came. John offered me a hit. I said, "No thanks. Not here."

He passed it back to Ella, looked at Jane and said, "Your instincts were right as usual. Had we not pulled in, we would have met up with that cop."

Jane reached for my cigarette, took a draw and said, "Don't know about all that. Just glad I could stop his bleeding."

The wind picked up and large raindrops splattered on the SUV. Ella slid into the back seat to avoid getting wet. Jane tossed in her bag, closed the hatch and said, "Let's go!" Strangely, instead of getting in the front passenger seat, she pushed in next to me. Ella moved over to give us room. There I sat between the two of them and it suddenly felt as if we were being chauffeured by John. He didn't mind. With a buzz, he was focused on two things; his Bluetooth music and driving in the rain. Old school R&B brought a grin to Ella's otherwise worried face.

Knowing Jane had an agenda, I decided to say nothing and wait patiently. It didn't take long. A mile or so down the road, she leaned against the door, looked past me and spoke frankly to Ella as though interviewing a patient. "Tell me about your cancer."

Ella hesitated like she might be considering Jane's audacity, but then answered. "Had my first breast cancer diagnosis when I was thirty-five. Doctor did a lumpectomy. Was good for six years, and then it came back. Double mastectomy, reconstruction and lots of prayers. Thought that was it, but now it's back, and this time it's metastatic." Ella stared forward. Jane could not resist her infatuation with tears as she leaned past me to touch the woman's wet cheeks.

"Please," Jane urged, "tell me how it feels to be dying?"

Ella looked at Jane and said, "I get the feeling you've been through this?"

"Lost my mother during my second year of high school."

"What took your mother?" Ella asked.

"Do you intend to answer my question?"

"After you tell me about your mother."

"Promise?"

Ella grinned. "Promise."

She's never told you and she's going to tell her?

Jane looked at me, pressed her lips together tightly, and then turned back to Ella. "My daddy was in the service. Spent too much time overseas. Being alone all the time took its toll on my mother. I held her all I could, but it wasn't enough. Looking back, I know she needed a man. Her loneliness turned her into a drunk. One day she ran a red light and got t-boned. It busted her up enough that she was in lots of pain. She got addicted to oxy. When the doctor cut her off, she became desperate."

"Heroin?" Ella mumbled.

Jane nodded. "I figured it out. She kept meeting up with some hoodie guy. When I started complaining, she said she quit, but I knew better. One night, I followed her to the park where that son-of-a-bitch refused to give her a fix until after she gave him a blow-job. That night, we argued. I told her she was disgusting. Next morning, I found her in the bathtub. Needle in the floor. If my father had been around, he might have been able to help her, but he wasn't."

I sat between the two of them fighting my own tears. After several seconds, Ella said, "You asked how it feels to be dying. It feels lonely. Your momma, she needed a man to comfort her. To hold her close and tell her it's alright."

Jane closed her eyes. I thought for a short second she might be emotional, until she asked, "Is that what you need?"

Ella's lips tightened. She covered her face and said, "Lady, I've been needing me a man for thirty years. Ain't even been *with* a man for near fifteen. Life just hasn't worked out. Now it's about to be over." Anger entered her voice. "And I *still* have no one to hold me at night. My baby Sarah used to, but now she's all grown up and gone away. Like your momma, guess I'm gonna die a lonely woman."

Jane tried her best to be sympathetic. She reached over, took Ella's hand and held it. With her other hand she wiped away my tears. I put my arm around Jane's shoulder. She laid her head on mine. After a half a mile or so, she raised her head and nodded toward Ella. I put my other arm around Sarah's lonely mother. At first she flinched. Slowly, she relaxed and allowed me to pull her to me. I used my hand to lay her head on my shoulder. In the rearview mirror I saw John observing. His squinted eyes seemed to understand.

Moving on down the road, John turned his music up over the sound of the pounding rain. Jane and Ella held hands as I held them both.

Chapter 47

By the time we made the interstate, Jane and Ella seemed to be sleeping. I sat between their warm bodies, contemplating the day's events. Some men go far away to another continent to fight a war, killing men who are likely innocent other than their association to the land or nation where they happened to be born. Jane, John, and I chose to do our fighting on our homeland against men who were in no way innocent. They were evildoers, international thieves with bad intentions for our great nation, the land of the free. If God strikes me dead, I believe everything we did on that crazy day was not just for money.

Miles went by, we left the interstate, and the rain slowed to a mist. As we grew close to the farm, I had nearly dozed off myself when I noticed Ella looking at her phone. "What are you doing? Turn that off."

"Why?" she asked. "What if Sarah calls?"

Raising her head off my shoulder, Jane said, "He's afraid they might track your phone."

I said, "If Sarah needs you, she can call my burner."

John spoke loudly. "Elijah, Jane, everybody duck." We all did right before headlights passed us going in the opposite direction. Jane and I both raised enough to watch a dark vehicle going away. John said, "Looked like a government issue to me. And it came out of Ella's road."

"Check it out," I said. "Brake lights. They're watching to see if we turn in."

Jane said, "Don't turn, John. Keep going straight. Don't even touch your brakes. Ella, turn that damn phone off now!"

We drove another quarter mile before the road curved and the brake lights disappeared. "What do you think?" John asked. "Wanna turn around?"

Jane seemed to read my mind. She said, "Not yet."

After another mile, we reached an intersection. On the left, a gas station had one light inside and another outside over the pumps. A

"CLOSED" sign hung on the glass entry door. Across the street to our right sat the tiny Davis Creek Baptist Church. I said, "John, I need to piss real bad. Pull behind the church. We can wait there a minute before heading back, just in case they're watching."

As we pulled in, Ella asked, "Who are they?"

John answered while circling and parking as near to the building as he could, out of sight. "They're the reason we picked you up tonight."

"They come to kill me?"

"Maybe," I replied. "And maybe Sarah too if she'd left the scene."

Ella said, "Hell, they'd be doing me a favor. I just don't want my Sarah in danger."

Jane said, "No offense, but your daughter put herself in danger when she became an operative. You need to watch those Bourne movies."

"I avoid them just for that reason."

Jane turned to me. "Come on Eli. If you need to pee, go do it. I'm getting out for a smoke."

Everyone piled out. As I stepped toward a tree, Jane positioned herself near the corner of the church building.

Upon my return, John stood talking to Ella. He asked me," How long should we wait?"

"Not sure." Motioning toward Jane, I said, "Apparently she's not convinced." I stepped away to join Jane. She glanced back at my approach. Standing together, we had a view of the gas station, the Church parking lot, and the road from which we came. She seemed nervous. I reached for her cigarette and asked, "You okay?"

"Sorry I never shared my mother's story with you."

"I understand. Breaks my heart."

"I don't understand. You cried for my mother and you never even met her."

"I cried for you, Jane. When something hurts you, it hurts me."

My wife tilted her head, gave me a look, and then ran her hand through my beard. "Remember what you told me about your girlfriend, the one that died of leukemia?"

"Kelly?"

"Yeah. You said you felt bad that you didn't have sex with her."

"Yes, but—"

"I'm betting she was lonely. Do you think it was really about sex, or do you think it was more about wanting someone to hold her and tell her it's alright?"

Trick question. Be careful. "I'd say a little of both. Who knows?"

"That woman back there, she's going to die lonely, like my mother. If I had a beard, I'd hold her."

Whoa. Before I could comment, headlights appeared at a distance. Jane turned to John and Ella and said, "We've got company." In two seconds, three guns came out. John moved to the other end of the Church building. Ella stayed at the vehicle. Jane remained where she was. I thought about it and said, "Jane, they'll recognize me, but not you or John. John! You and Jane get in the vehicle. If you see 'em coming around the building, turn your music up and act like you're making out. Ella, come with me!"

Ella and I moved into the weeds a few yards away. We squatted and waited. "John, Jane," I hollered just loud enough. "We don't wanna kill these guys." Jane put a finger to her lips.

From our position, Ella and I couldn't see the SUV. It apparently stopped in front of the gas station. Headlights shined past the church while a spotlight moved about eventually landing on the Church parking lot. "Maybe they'll move on," Ella whispered.

"Doubt it," I whispered back. "They didn't drive this far not to be thorough." Seconds later the headlights swung right and slowly came toward the back of the church. John didn't wait. He turned up his music. There was just enough light to see that Jane was pulling her dress up over her head. She and John both leaned toward the middle, over the console, and appeared to be making out.

"Damn," Ella whispered again. "Puttin' on a good act."

"No shit," I replied.

As the black SUV came past the end of the building, it stopped. The agent in the passenger seat stared out his opened window. I pulled Ella down to the ground as the spotlight scanned past us on its way to Jane's bare shoulders. She and John both covered their eyes. A loud speaker blared, "Get out of the vehicle!"

No, I thought.

John and Jane remained seated.

"I said get out of the vehicle! Dije que salgas del vehiculo!"

No, no, no. Stay where you are. Make them get out.

Doors opened on the government vehicle. Both suits climbed out. The spotlight remained on. The driver, the shorter of the two, stayed at the vehicle gun up, leaning against the fender. The taller man—gun in one hand flashlight in the other—began slow walking. When he came into the light, I knew they were the same two guys that were at the Estate earlier in the day, Agents Black and White. John had parked close enough to the building that the agent seemed uncomfortable with approaching from that side. Instead he came to Jane's side. With his gun raised, he shined his flashlight in on my wife and best friend. "I can see why she won't get out! Open the door lady."

Jane lowered the window. While squatting to check out John, the man said, "Turn the music down, turn the engine off and then place both hands on the wheel, sir. Lady, you put your hands on the dash." Jane obeyed, giving the agent a good view of her boobs. Looking into the back seat, he asked, "Where's the lady?"

"What lady?" Jane asked.

The agent raised his voice, but remained focused. "Bill, you need to check this out!"

Ella and I remained still as Agent Bill White made his way to the vehicle. Agent Black said, "No one else in the vehicle."

Agent White scanned the area and then shined his light in on Jane. "What's under the dress lady?" Jane apparently had her dress in her lap.

"Me, sir," was all she said.

Agent White said, "Believe we need you to step out of the vehicle, ma'am."

"Are you serious?" John asked.

"Just keep your hands on the wheel, boy," ordered Agent White.

Jane said, "It's okay." She opened the door and then turned and slid out. Her boobs were meant to be attention grabbers as she held the dress over her lady parts. Both men took a step backwards. Her right hand remained under the dress.

I whispered to Ella, "Stay down," and then slowly rose to my feet.

Agent Black said, "Ma'am, what do you have under the dress?"

"Something you don't need to see, sir."

"We need to make sure you don't have a gun under—"

Before he could finish, Jane dropped the dress and quickly raised her 9mm. Standing there in a thong, she pointed the gun at Agent

White's head and said, "Both of you need to drop your guns or I swear I'll blow this man's brains out."

Agent White said, "Calm down lady. We already know who you are."

As the man spoke, John climbed out, pointing his gun. Moving around the front, he said, "Then you already know if you don't drop those guns, both of you are gonna die."

The two men squatted just long enough to put their guns on the ground. John stood guard as Jane slipped on her dress without releasing her gun. Re-aiming, she said, "Now, tell me, who am I?"

Agent Black said, "You're married to that Jones guy with the ugly beard."

Jane said, "Well, since you claim to know who I am, how about you explain who you are and what you're doing out here in the middle of nowhere."

"I think you already know," Agent Black replied.

Jane said, "Refresh me."

"It appears your man went off on a house full of people tonight. Thinks he's some kind of pro."

"Pro?" Jane replied.

Agent White chuckled and said, "Man thought he was all that, but he let his girl get killed."

"No!" Ella shouted.

Jane and John both looked up. The agents reacted by attacking. Agent White knocked John's gun out of his hand and began pounding on him.

Black went after Jane's gun. In what looked like a Marine Corp Martial Arts Move, his left hand grabbed the barrel pushing it up while his right hand grabbed the handle. As he took a step back, I busted him up side of the head. He went to his knees, and I kicked his gun away. Jane went to assist John. She did a leg kick to the small of Agent White's back, then grabbed him and flipped him completely over. Agent Black grabbed my ankle, pulled me off my feet and somehow got a grip on my arm that held my gun. By then, Jane had a knee in Agent White's chest. She began pounding with her right fist. The agent rolled over and popped up, throwing Jane off. By the time the two of them squared off to fist fight, Agent Black and I were rolling in the dirt. John had somehow reached one of the guns on the ground. He fired it in the air.

"Enough!" John shouted. "I'll kill you both if you don't stop, right now!" Everyone seemed to freeze. Jane retrieved her gun. I gathered the other two.

"You guys are making one hell of a mistake," barked the lanky Agent Black, as he climbed to his feet.

John said, "Made plenty mistakes in my life. One more won't be the last."

By then, Ella had joined us. "What about my daughter?"

I pointed my gun at Agent White and said, "You asked me this morning if I'd ever killed anyone. I'm gonna kill you right now if you don't explain what you meant about Sarah being dead."

"I'm just telling you what I heard. They said you went off and killed everybody. Said Agent Smith was one of the shooting victims."

"She got shot, but not by me. One of Al-Riase's men shot her. She was fine when we left."

The agents looked at one another as if not sure. Jane said, "Gentlemen, aren't we basically all on the same side?"

Agent Black began dusting off his suit as he answered. "In this line of business, ma'am, sometimes it's hard to tell whose side you're on."

I said, "Agent Black, right?"

"Yes."

"Mister, we have no desire to kill you or your buddy." I turned to Ella. "Our fear was that you wanted to kill this woman."

Agent White spoke. "We just follow orders."

"Well, your orders are about to change. Real slow like, I want you to pull out your phone, call whoever is at the Proctor Estate, and ask if you can speak to Sarah Smith. Put it on speaker so we all can hear."

The phone rang three times before someone answered. "Special Agent McGinnis."

"Jim. White here."

"Hey Bill. What's up?"

"Not much. Just wondering if I could talk to Sarah Smith?"

"She's not here, Bill."

"So where is she?"

"Damn Bill. You didn't know? She got shot. They just flew her and that little gal up to the UofK Medical Center."

Glances of relief were exchanged as Agent White continued. "So she's not dead?"

"No, no. Kid took a bullet in the shoulder, but she's gonna be fine."

"Then plan-A's a scrap?"

"Haven't heard anyone say that, but I'd say so."

White ignored me when I whispered, "What's plan-A?"

He spoke again. "Jim, is Chief around?"

"Chief Little? Yeah. He's over there with Weeper. Want me to get him?"

"Yes."

Jane gave me a look. "Weeper?"

I asked quietly, "Did he just mention David Weeper?"

Agent White standing there, face swollen from Jane's punches, replied, "You guys know Special Agent Weeper?"

Jane and I both nodded. *Asshole owes me money.*

Through the phone, we could hear a raised voice. "Chief Little! White needs to talk to you."

Jane stood there, not blinking, not letting her guard down. With the SUV door open, Ella leaned against the seat, holding the door frame for support. John stood at attention, not saying a word. Finally the man's voice came across the phone. "Chief Little."

"Chief, White here. Just a bit confused. Not sure what you want us to do with this woman."

"What woman?"

"Sarah Smith's mother."

"What? Hell no! We abandoned that!"

"No one told us."

"Don't tell me you—"

"No Chief, we didn't, but we were about to. We misunderstood. Thought Sarah was dead."

"Well she's not. Scrap Plan-A, we're now operating under Plan-B."

Agent White gave us a thumb up, and then asked, "So what about that Jones character?"

"He's gone. Smith must have told him to get lost. I'd like to shake the man's hand. Our girl couldn't have done all this on her own. We've got a few odds and ends to tie up, but for the most part they did one hell of a job here. And Smith says her man extracted a lot of vital information."

"He's that good?" Agent White replied.

"He's good all right, but his MO worries me. A bit of a sicko, I'd say. I'll show you the pics later."

"Roger that. So what's the status? We going after this guy?"

"No. Not now. I don't believe he's as stupid as you said he was. Could be dangerous, and he's apparently on our side. Man saved a lot of lives, including his own. Plan-A would have been ugly. Looks like nothing but a bunch of bad guys got it here. I'll talk to Smith about Jones later. He's her man. Might be someone she can use again."

"Good. So what's our deal? We done?"

"Yeah. Black there with you?"

"Yes, sir."

"You guys have been at it long enough. Call it a day. We'll stick around here to see what Senator Proctor says to the media. Already overheard his aide saying she bets this tragedy will boost the Senator's approval rating by twenty points."

"Maybe not for long," Agent Black chimed in. "Chances are Smith got the goods on him tonight."

"Perhaps, but guys, that's not something we wanna talk about. Understand?"

"Roger that," Agent Black replied.

"Okay. We'll catch up with you two tomorrow. And by the way, make sure Sarah Smith's mother knows if she breathes a word of this, it could get her and her daughter into big trouble."

Ella nodded.

"We'll tell her chief. No problem." Agent White ended the call and stood staring as if waiting for my approval. When I didn't speak, he said, "Sorry about the stupid thing."

Jane lowered her 9mm. Ella pulled herself up off the seat and asked, "What's Plan-B?"

"Not authorized to say," Agent White replied.

Agent Black said, "I will say this, ma'am. It's like the opposite of Plan-A." Looking around at everyone present, he said, "In other words, you just went from having three protectors present to five."

White reiterated, "Ma'am, I hope you heard and understood what the Chief said about not mentioning today's events. You wouldn't want to jeopardize yours or your daughter's wellbeing. Got it?"

"Got what?"

"You know what."

"I don't know what the hell you're talking about. Do I even know you?"

The agent grinned and said, "Perfect." He then turned his focus to John. "Same goes for you, sir. Not sure how you fit into all this, but like the others, you need to pretend tonight never happened."

John seemed to be thinking. "I get it. And I noticed I went from boy to sir when we got the upper hand."

White stepped toward John who still had his gun up, flat against his chest. "I don't know your name, *Sir*. Perhaps calling you boy was not the best choice in wording. But I can assure you that I did not mean it as derogatory. Not my MO."

John stood at attention and asked, "Government teach you to say that after you insult a black man?"

"Mister, my name is Agent White. I just spoke to you out of respect. I respect every individual I meet regardless of the color of their skin. But let me tell you something. You still haven't told me your name. In my world, if a man holding a gun introduces himself as a black man, he automatically associates himself with every criminal black person that I've had to deal with in over twenty years of service to my country. Hopefully you understand what that means." As he spoke, Agent White reached to shake John's hand. Jane and I were trading glances.

Looking back at Ella, John asked, "You buy what this man just said?"

Ella nodded. "I believe he means what he says. Either way, he's giving you good advice."

John took the agent's hand. "My name is John, and I appreciate your insight. Thinking maybe that's something I needed to hear from a white man."

Agent Black approached John and said, "Nice to meet you, John. Believe you can put that gun away now."

Tensions relaxed. Jane stepped to and spoke privately to John as the two agents headed to their SUV. Agent Black turned back to speak. "Mr. Jones. From what we just heard on the phone, no one from any Agency should be contacting you. As long as Smith's alive, you're her man."

"So to speak," I interrupted.

"That's right. And if someone else approaches, act like you don't have a clue what they're talking about. If they're with us, they'll understand. If they don't understand you've made enemies."

Jane asked, "What about witnesses?"

"Witnesses?" replied Agent Black.

I said, "Believe she's talking about the helicopter pilot and the two girls that were with Amor."

Agent Black said, "Don't need to worry about them. All three are with us."

"Really?" I asked. "Did Sarah know that?"

"Not authorized to say, sir."

Ella said, "Seems shitty to me."

Agent White replied, "Ma'am, it's a shitty line of business."

Agent Black said to Jane, "By the way lady, nice MO with the dress. Sure you're not one of us?"

Jane grinned and said, "That would be hard to say, considering neither one of you are who you say you are."

The man winked and then climbed into the SUV. He closed the door and then spoke out the passenger side window. "With all due respect to you and your husband ma'am, you made an old man's day."

When the SUV started moving, I spoke up, "You guys do me a favor! When you see David Weeper, tell him I look forward to our next meeting."

"Will do," the agent replied as they pulled away.

When they were out of sight, I asked Jane, "What do you mean they aren't who they say they are?"

Jane lit a cigarette and said, "No one on that phone call referred to either of them as an agent."

Chapter 48

Arriving near the farm, Jane, John and I were still a bit leery. John cut the lights and stopped the vehicle just inside the woods, one curve and 200 yards from the house. Ella handed me her key. She asked, "You saying you don't trust those men back there?"

"Hell no," Jane and I said at the same time.

Opening the door, I said, "Jane, I'll text you a smiley face when it's clear."

"Or what, a sad face if it's not?"

I turned to John. "If I text Jane a sad face, you turn this thing around and get the hell out of here. I'll hide and give Sarah a text. Ella, keep your phone turned off. You're the one they were looking for."

It took longer than I expected to clear the property. After texting a smiley face, I sat patiently on the front porch, watching the SUV's slow approach, lights still out. Gravel crunched as John maneuvered to a halt near the mailbox. The three of them looked like tired old soldiers as they moved my way. Jane's attention to Ella struck me as odd. When they reached the porch, though I rose to help, Jane managed Ella up the steps. In passing, John shook his head. "What took you so long?"

"There's a lot here to clear."

We all made our way to the kitchen. Ella complained. "How could you make such a mess in my floor?"

"Sorry. I cleared the garage and then the barn before coming in. I'll clean it up."

"That's okay," Ella replied. "It'll give me something to do tomorrow. Right now, just take them muddy shoes off. You two boys go to the porch. If Jane don't mind helping, we'll make up some sandwiches."

"Sounds good," Jane replied.

John and I moved to the porch. I sat where I could look back at the women. "John," I asked, "you ever seen Jane like this? If I didn't know better I'd say she feels sorry for Ella."

John spoke while relaxing into his chair. "See it anyway you want. Me, I just let Jane be who Jane is."

No wonder she likes him.

Facing the barn, I checked out the distant lightning flashes and said, "Perhaps I need to be more like you, John."

"She didn't marry me, Bro. Believe you're doing alright just being you."

I said, "Thanks."

"Is Ella planning on giving you money tonight?"

Staring into the kitchen, I replied, "I'm assuming so."

"Good. I'd say the quicker the better. She's pretty sick. Saw her stumble earlier."

When they brought the sandwiches and iced tea to the porch, Ella excused herself. "Be right back, y'all go ahead."

"You okay?" Jane asked.

"Gotta take my medicine."

As Ella disappeared, John asked, "Y'all gonna tell me about tonight?"

"No," I answered, "except that it was ugly."

Jane said, "Not your everyday event."

John took a bite of his sandwich and spoke to Jane with his mouth full. "Guy thought you were one of them."

I said, "They both acted like they've never seen a naked woman before."

John took a drink and said, "Elijah, you are one jealous man. Worried about me seeing Jane's boobs."

I waited until I swallowed my food. "Those are my boobs, buddy. Nobody else's."

Jane said, "Excuse me. They're *my* boobs, Mr. Haycraft!"

Ella stepped out onto the porch saying, "At least your boobs ain't killing you." Before anyone could react, she pitched a zipped cloth bag into my lap. "Count it. That's all I have here. Hope you trust Sarah to bring you the rest later."

Before I could speak, Jane said, "We trust her."

One of the phones in my pocket vibrated. "Speaking of the devil." I stood, offering Ella my seat as I answered, "What's up?"

"How's mom?"

"She's fine. Sittin' right here." I switched to speakerphone. "She can hear you. Go ahead."

I set the phone on the table to let them speak as I started counting the money.

"Hey Mom, you okay?"

Ella replied, "Better question is are *you* okay, and why didn't you tell me you got shot?"

"I'm fine. Didn't want to worry you. Problem now is they're saying I need to stay the night for observations on my shoulder, and I have to talk to a psychologist in the morning."

"Damn," I interrupted, "they may never let you out."

"You're not funny." When I didn't reply, Sarah said, "Sorry. I'm worn out."

Ella said, "We all are."

"Good news Mom. I have a sister. Her name is Itzel."

"Half-sister. I've already learned that. I'm happy for you."

"And guess what? She's going to fly home in a couple days. Pretty soon, she and her mother, Maria, are coming to Kentucky to stay at the farm with us. They can be with you when I'm working."

Jane began nodding as if it were a good thing. Ella said, "Okay dear. If that's what you want. I'm sure I'll be needing help."

"Is Jane there?"

"Yes," Jane answered. "I can hear you."

"I hate for Mom to be alone tonight. Can one of you stay with her until I get there?"

Jane said, "I have to do ER tomorrow, but I'm sure Eli won't mind staying."

"You okay with that, Eli?" Sarah asked.

I looked at Ella and then Jane, before answering. "Yes, I'll stay, but I'm probably gonna pass out."

"That's fine. Just don't want her to be alone."

Jane squeezed my leg as I continued counting the money we'd earned under unusual circumstances. My mind drifted. *Was it my infatuation with Sarah? My association with Jane? My desire to be a patriot? Or perhaps just a desire for money?* Regardless of the reason or reasons, never again would I be the same. I had elevated from killing animals to killing men.

"Mom!" Sarah's voice caught my attention. "There's someone coming in. I need to get off this phone. Call if you need me. Love you."

"Love you too." Ella spoke to a dead phone.

Suddenly it seemed all were watching me count. Finishing, I said, "Well Ella, this makes half of what you owe me. Correct?"

"That's right. Providing my girl comes home in one piece."

"She will," I replied. "I'll stay here until she gets home. For tonight, I guess it's just you me and this scraggly old beard."

Ella glanced at me, then Jane. "You trust me here alone with those whiskers?"

Jane looked into Ella's eyes and said, "You really do like that beard."

"Oh, yes I do," Ella replied.

"Well honey, if Eli wants to give you those whiskers, you can have them tonight. Just make sure he shaves before he comes home to me."

That sounds weird.

John and I brought chairs from the kitchen and we all ate together on the porch. Afterwards, John and Jane prepared to leave. My vehicle remained in the garage. Jane had already pushed the money envelope deep into her backpack. John opened the back of the SUV and removed the three bags that contained mine and Jane's clothes, the plastic and other nasty stuff from the barn. He said, "Elijah, I don't want to have this stuff in here if we get pulled over. Can you burn it?"

Looking up, I said, "If it doesn't rain."

Jane and I stood at the passenger side of the SUV, her back to the opened window, saying our goodbyes as John got in and turned on his heavy bass music. I looked at my wife and said, "Trust you guys won't run off with all that money. We'll figure out what to do with it when I get home. And by the way, give John ten thousand before he goes home."

"Really?" Jane asked.

"I told him I would give him five for his research. What he did tonight was beyond that."

Jane glanced at John and then back at me. "I'm sure he'll appreciate it."

I asked, "Are we okay, you and me?"

"Why do you ask?"

"The comments you made at the barn."

Jane stuck her fist into my stomach and twisted as though stabbing me with a knife. "Let's just say I'm doing a lot of thinking, and we have plenty to talk about later."

Wow. "Are you stabbing me?"

"I will if I catch you sleeping with Sarah."

"But you want me to spend the night with her mother. What's up with that?"

"Ella's sick and dying and she's not trying to steal you away from me. Her daughter's in love with my husband and you can't stand there and tell me you don't have some kind of feelings for her. Eli, the reason I went through all this today was to protect you and my marriage."

"And I appreciate your efforts."

Jane growled. "I already told you, I have no desire to live alone, and nobody in the world understands me like you do."

John lowered the volume of his music and said, "Come on guys. I wanna go home."

While opening the SUV's door, Jane continued, "Before you come home tomorrow, you need to make up your mind."

For a moment, I went blank. It was the same ultimatum she'd given me concerning Margaret. I stared, but could not speak. Jane slid into the seat, closed the door and spoke out the window. "You heard what I said."

I stood there with both hands resting on the door and said, "You think John could stay here with Ella tonight? I could go home with you."

Jane placed one of her hands on mine and then focused towards the house. "Eli, I don't want you to look back someday and say, 'I should have been there for Ella,' the way you do about your friend Kelly."

"Kelly was my girlfriend, and—"

"And if she could be here, she'd tell you to be there for Ella. If Mom was here, she'd want me to let you hold and comfort that woman." Jane relaxed into the seat, closed her eyes and said, "Eli, she's suffering. Her time is near. I'm asking you to be there for her tonight."

I didn't really know what to say. Had Jane revealed a part of herself that I'd never seen? *Is she using me to do something she wants to do but can't?*

John looked over. "You ready?"

Jane nodded. As the SUV moved backwards, she spoke out the window. "Keep your white phone on for me. Keep your iPhone covered up. Otherwise your girl's going to be listening."

I'm confused. Women are so messed up.

Jane waved at Ella standing in the doorway. Ella waved back. I watched the bright LED taillights until they disappeared around the curve into the woods. Turning to the house, Ella had disappeared. I pulled out one of Jane's cigarettes and lit up.

You know you're smoking way too much.

After a day like this....

The bags were not too heavy. I carried all three to the back where I sat them against the house. Lightning continued to flash at a distance. While finishing my smoke, I reviewed Jane's comments while wondering if she considered John to be a lonely person.

Besides you, she might be his only friend.

I opened the back porch door, walked in and found Ella sitting at the kitchen table with a bottle of whiskey and two short glasses. I said, "You read my mind."

"Wishful thinking on my part," she replied.

I took a seat. Ella poured two fingers in each glass and shoved one my way. As we savored that first sip, she said, "Been one hell of a day."

"Yes indeed."

I held my glass up for a toast. "To Sarah." We tapped glasses and took a sip.

Ella raised her glass again and said, "To you, your lovely wife, and John." After another sip, she said, "That John seems like a nice fella."

"He is."

"You trust him with your wife?"

I downed my whiskey, exhaled slowly, and said, "Jane lived with John and his mother after her mother died, while her father served overseas. They're like brother and sister. If they were gonna hook up, they'd of done it by now."

Raindrops began to tap on the metal roof over the back porch. Ella said, "Looks like they have to drive home in the rain."

"Ella, can I ask you a personal question?"

She finished off her drink and said, "You can't get no more personal than that woman of yours."

"Do you see your daughter as a lonely person?"

A tear ran down Ella's cheek as she poured herself another drink. After a swig, she said, "It's my fault. I brought her into this world. Thought I was doing the right thing. Older Sarah got, the more that seemed to slip away."

"Appears to me that the people you lived with here were bad people."

"Not necessarily."

"Ella, they were associated with terrorist."

"I'm not sure how much of that they understood."

"But what about what they did to...?"

Ella stared at me. "Sarah told you what they did?"

I nodded.

"Can't believe she told you that."

"She told me in confidence. Please don't tell her I said anything."

Ella finished her drink, popped the glass down and said, "When they did that, I wanted to take Sarah and leave. Hide from Amor and his culture, but the cancer already had a hold on me. Just couldn't walk away."

I said, "What they did to her was insane and unforgivable."

"I agree," Ella replied. "Inhumane. Un-American. Immoral. But believe it or not, I came to realize that Alon and his woman were basically good people. They were caught up in an ancient culture that made them behave in ancient ways. It cost them their lives. Now, because of what they did to my daughter, she may never fully give herself to a man. So yes, my Sarah is lonely."

I thought and then said, "Sarah and I are a lot alike. We were both raised as an only child. So was Jane. Not sure about Sarah, but I can tell you that Jane and I were starving for attention when we met."

"Companionship is a lot about having someone to be there for you, to hold you, to touch you."

I said, "Yes, and I find myself wanting to be there for Sarah. Hopefully, she and I can remain friends."

Ella gripped my arm. "Promise me you won't let my Sarah come between you and Jane."

You mean, if she hasn't already. "I ... I'll keep that in mind. But right now, I want to enjoy my drink with you."

"You enjoy having a drink with an old woman?"

"You're not that old."

"About as old as I'm gonna get. Life slipped by me. I was with one boy before I had Sarah. Only man I've been with in all those years since was Alon."

"Sarah said you and the old man had an unusual relationship."

"Sarah never approved. She knew what *he* helped take from *her*. What she didn't know was what *she* took from *me*. I've been a lonely woman now for a long, long time. This place I live. This beautiful farm. It's been my prison for years."

"You never go anywhere?"

"When Sarah was young, Alon got her into riding those show horses. I tried going to the barn with them. Wasn't a single black person there besides me."

Now I see where Sarah got her attitude. "Are you saying people disrespected you because you're black?"

"Didn't say they necessarily disrespected me, but they didn't pay me much attention. It's about my hair."

"Your hair?"

"Yes, I have, or had bad hair."

"That's hard to believe."

"I'm not lying to you. You might not understand but the hair thing is real. I had everything those other women had. I had money. I had education. I had a good body. But I didn't have good hair. Women there looked at me all funny. Men didn't even bother looking. I tried wearing a scarf and that just seemed to make it worse. Then one day, after I started chemo, I wore the wig the doctor's office had made for me to a horse show. Suddenly, I was turning heads. There were men talking to me that never paid me any mind before. Even the women started talking to me."

"That's crazy."

"Yes, it is. My girl had already been going through similar stuff at school. You know how girls can be. Black girls with good hair or the money to weave got attention. Those with bad hair didn't. As a result there was jealousy and hatred between them."

"Sarah talked a little about that."

"When she saw what I was going through, that's when she cut her hair. Some sort of protest, I'd say."

"So she did have long hair?"

"Oh yes," Ella spoke while rising and stumbling to the refrigerator. "My girl had beautiful hair."

"You sure you're okay?"

Without answering, she pulled off a magnetically held calendar. Underneath it hung a 5"x7" photo. She turned and brought it to me.

"Oh, wow." It was a teenage Sarah with hair to the middle of her back.

"Told you."

"Her hair is beautiful."

Ella took the photo from my hand returned it to the fridge and replaced the calendar. I asked, "Why do you hide it?"

"She doesn't know I have it there. She would take it. Did she tell you she covered up while overseas with her father?"

"She mentioned it." I raised my glass and said "That's messed up, her cutting off all that beautiful hair."

"She did it for me. When I'm gone, she'll probably grow it back."

I hope so. "Tell me, Ella, do you get out and about now? Wearing the wig, I mean?"

"I go to the grocery. To the doctor. That's about it. Guess you could say cancer has a way of turning one into a recluse."

I sat quietly, hating cancer, and trying to imagine Sarah with long hair. Watching me sip my drink, Ella asked, "You ever smoke weed?"

Lightning flashed bright through the windows. "Yep."

"Got some medical marijuana. Wanna try it?"

Thunder clapped. "Can we sit on the back porch and watch the storm?"

She smiled and said, "We sure can."

I grinned and said, "I need to use the restroom first."

"Meet me on the porch."

In the bathroom, I could feel the whiskey buzz while taking a piss. When I washed my hands, my reflection in the mirror said, *Do you have any idea where this is going?*

"No."

On the back porch, Ella sat holding a small pipe. After I took a seat in the rocker next to her, she handed it over and a lighter, and said, "Careful now. This stuff's strong."

I took a hit, held it as long as I could and then coughed it out.

"Told you" she grinned.

After one more toke, I gave it back to her. She hit it twice and then we settled back to enjoy the light show and thunder claps well beyond the barn roof. Sprinkles of rain tapped on the metal roof. About the time I suspected Ella might be dozing off, she took another hit and asked, "You got another one of those cigarettes?"

"Didn't know you smoked."

"Doctors made me quit. Hell, I'm gonna die anyway. Might as well enjoy what little life I've got left."

I pulled out two. Lit one for her and one for me. She took a draw and then exhaled slowly. "Damn that's good. Thank you."

"Thank Jane. They're her cigarettes."

We sat for a minute or so, enjoying our smoke in silence before Ella spoke with a slight slur. "Your wife is an interesting person."

"Yes she is."

"You ever cheat on her?"

"No."

"You know she said I could have them whiskers."

"Yep."

Ella's hand shook as she took another draw and asked, "You gonna give 'em to me?"

I said, "Ella, I believe you to be a God fearing woman."

Her eyes were glassy as she replied, "Yes I am."

I put my cigarette out in an empty bourbon glass and held it out for hers. She took another quick draw and then dropped it in. Sitting on the edge of my chair, I reached to hold her hand and asked, "If I spend time with you tonight, will God condemn us both?"

She swiped her eyes and said, "You can look at it anyway you want. I'm sitting here praying this is God's gift to me."

"God's gift? Or Jane's gift?" I replied.

"Out of respect, I didn't wanna say it that way."

Though thinner than when I first met her, Ella still had an attractive appearance. Her long wig framed a soft loving face. In the dim light, she did not look twenty years my elder. I took her by both hands and helped her to her feet. In an awkward attempt to rub my beard on her face, my nose rubbed against hers. She nearly collapsed. When I wrapped my arms around her to hold her, she reached around my waist and held tight. I could feel each heavy breath she took. "How we doin'?" I asked.

"It feels like I already died and went to Heaven."

As I stood there wondering what to do next, Ella's soft hand gripped my right wrist. She began to hum a classic tune while urging me into a slow dance. The rain became percussion and I hummed along with a woman old enough to be my mother. She rubbed her face against my beard as we slowly rocked back and forth in a small circle.

Several minutes and a lot of rain had passed when Ella began urging my hand down across her bottom.

Jane said hold her.

When I gripped her lightly, Ella began breathing heavily. So much so, it worried me. "You okay" I asked.

"Honey, I'm more okay right now than I've been in forever." She pulled away and said, "I need to freshen up. Give me about ten minutes, and then you come on up."

Not knowing what to say, I just nodded. On her way into the kitchen, Ella stumbled again. I said, "Be careful!" while moving inside and across the kitchen, far enough to watch her feet disappearing up the steps. Moving back to the porch, I nervously lit another cigarette and wondered how far Jane expected this would go.

An ugly noise drew my attention. After putting my cigarette out, I moved into the house. Floor movements above startled me. I heard the first noise again but louder. It sounded sickening. Two steps at a time, I bounced upstairs and into the bathroom. There, I found Ella on her knees, hugging the toilet and vomiting violently. She wore a cotton night shirt that hung to her bare legs. With each heave, the material moved up and down across her bottom. Her wig lay on the floor and her mostly hairless head tapped against the raised seat. "Oh no." It took me back to Kelly on the chairlift. Kneeling down, I rubbed Ella's back softly and said, "I'm here, baby. I'm here."

Finally her heaves began to subside, yet she remained bent over, shoulders rising and falling as she cried. When I felt sure her episode had ended, I said, "Come on. Let's get you up so I can clean you off."

"No. Please no. I'm embarrassed."

"Don't be, Ella. It's not your fault."

When I got her to her feet, she had vomit all down the front of her shirt. I lowered the toilet seat and had her sit. The whole toilet moved a little, loose on the floor, and I knew she'd been through this scenario many times before. With a washcloth, it didn't take long to clean her face and arms. She sat quiet, as if somehow enjoying the attention. When I finished, she took the washcloth from me and attempted to wipe her shirt.

I said, "That's gonna stink. Do you have something else you can sleep in?"

"Across the hall. Check the top drawer next to the door."

"Okay. You sit still. I'll be right back."

When I opened the top drawer, there was no night-shirt, only short sleeved t-shirts. Second drawer had socks. I stepped across the room, opened a closet and fumbled through an array of nice shirts until I found a long silk, cream colored, button-up blouse. "This'll do."

On my return, Ella stood at the sink, taking a swig of mouthwash from a bottle. After gargling and spitting, she looked at herself in the mirror. She rubbed her head. Her face wrinkled and she began crying again. "I'm so sorry. I wanted so badly to be with you."

"You are with me."

"You know what I mean."

Her legs seemed weak as she placed her elbows on the sink. I asked, "You gonna throw up again?"

"No. I'm just upset."

I said, "There were no shirts in the drawers. I found this in your closet."

Ella rose, turned and sort of grinned. "That might have been more appropriate had I not gotten sick."

"It'll do. Just don't want you sleeping in that one. You wanna change here or in the bedroom?"

Without answering, she reached to flip the light switch, turned her back to me and began pulling off her soiled night-shirt. Enough light bled in from across the hall to see that she wore nothing underneath. The whiskey in me wanted what I saw. Common sense said no. She held her arms out and I slipped on the silk shirt. I stood silent as she buttoned up. Turning to face me, she said, "I need to get off my feet."

I helped Ella into her room, and she sat on the edge of the bed with her feet on the floor. Kneeling down, I ran my hands around her hips to hold her and placed my head in her warm lap. For a moment, she seemed content running her fingers through my hair. Then she said, "I need to lie down."

I got up and helped her pull down the comforter. She rolled over onto the bed, in a fetal position, facing the wall. I drug the comforter up to her arms and asked, "Is there anything I can get you?"

Her shoulders began rocking again. She was crying. "It wasn't meant to be. It just wasn't meant to be."

Now what?

I stepped to the door and started to turn out the light. Instead, I looked back at Ella lying there whimpering.

Don't leave her.

I closed my eyes, tilted my head back and prayed, *Lord, what should I do?*

Not sure if it was the whiskey, the pot, or a gift from God, but I heard Kelly's voice as real as the day we sat on that rock in the Red River Gorge. "Hold me, Elijah." It felt so real that I lost my breath. I longed for an opportunity to do that day over, to do more than just hold her hand. To embrace her, the way I should have then.

What are you gonna do?

After a deep breath, I pulled off my boots and then carefully removed my shirt. It relieved me to see no signs of fresh blood on my arm. When I pulled back the comforter, Ella's legs were straight and her blouse had ridden up above her hips. I lied down in my pants and tee-shirt and then scooted against her while sliding my good arm under her neck. I laid my injured arm over her. Seconds later, she gripped both my wrists, pulling them against her breasts. Pain shot through my left arm. I had to move it while my mind went to a better place. Within seconds, I'd reached a comfort zone. While she held my right wrist against her chest, my left hand had wound up on the silk material, low on her belly, still held by her grip. I didn't know what to do. Every few seconds, she shivered. Gently, I pulled her to me and whispered, "It's okay. It's alright. It's ... alright."

I'm not sure how long it took Ella's trembling to subside. I may have dozed off myself, but woke as she rolled over and began rubbing her face against my beard.

Chapter 49

The rooster crowing outside woke me. I'd been standing, steeling my knife in preparation for the first kills of the morning. Instead of hogs, I turned to see the bodies of three hoodie-men, followed by James, Timothy, Charles, Bo, Peter and Amor, hanging upside down, coming my way to have their juggler veins cut. As with any other nightmare, relief came as details faded.

I crawled out of bed and started to cover Ella with the comforter. She looked so peaceful. The night before, she had spoken about being old. In the dim morning light that bled in from the window, she didn't look old. She had called me her "gift." In the end, Ella had become as much a gift to me. I covered her, stepped to the door and looked back. *Lord, if you have to take her, please don't let her suffer.*

Gathering my things, I left the room, took a piss, and spent a few minutes cleaning up the bathroom. I hung Ella's dirty nightshirt on a hook on the back of the door.

On the first floor, I began a search for java. Like Jane, Ella kept hers in the fridge. As the coffee perked, I stared out the back window at a beautiful sunrise. For the first time in a while, I had started my day without the need to plan for Sarah's job. Funny, I missed her already. Standing there I wished for a session—a chance to talk about how she and I felt post operation.

I stepped outside to share my first cup with a cigarette. Jane would be doing the same at home. After a shower, she would head off to work and her daily routine as if nothing unusual had occurred. I would spend my morning considering the outlandish things we had done only a few hours earlier. On day one, Sarah had asked if I would be able to live with myself after the fact. Years ago, my grandfather told me a story about waking up in Vietnam, sharing his coffee with a joint and thinking about the men he had killed the day before. I took a sip of my coffee and thought, *Grandpa, you became a soldier at nineteen, overseas. I became a soldier at thirty in the Bluegrass of Kentucky.* "I need a joint."

The rising sun pushed a cool breeze that rustled leaves. Chickens chased one another near the barn. In the distance a Bob White Quail whistled for his mate. Small feathery cloud formations migrated slowly in from the west.

Saturday somehow felt like Sunday. My mind drifted to those days when Mother took me to the Little Rock Baptist Church for morning service. I would sit next to her listening to Preacher Herman's sermon on good vs. evil, love vs. hate—a faithful man's words of hope for those who just can't figure it out on their own. Did I really figure it out? Or, did my faith evolve by necessity from church services and tent revivals to survival—an ability to live with my thoughts, my desires, my actions, and my crazy-ass wife, without Sunday morning services? That said; it would be nice to sit in a pew next to my mother, watching her pray for the Lord's assistance in dealing with a man whose mind lived in the past.

I spoke softly. "Love you mom." I missed her, and in a way I missed him too. While Mom taught me compassion, Dad made me tough. He made me comfortable with the pains of survival. I am a product of her love and his hate. "I am who I am."

When I went back inside and pulled out my electric razor/trimmer, I noticed my iPhone. I had left it turned off, in the backpack. After booting it, I discovered a recent missed call with a message and a text from 10pm the night before.

The text read: **Unable to reach your white phone. How's it going with the beard thing? LOL**

Yeah right. You're just wondering how far it went.

I put the phone on speaker and listened to Jane's voice message: ***You didn't answer either phone last night. I figure your IPhone was still off. Wondering how things were going. How's your arm? Anyway, I'm leaving for work. Call or text me when you can so I don't worry.***

I texted: **All is good. Shaving. See you this evening.**

I'd just finished shaving when tires crunched in the gravel out front. Opening the door revealed Sarah and Doris getting out of the Camry. Doris had driven. Sarah had her arm in a sling. I stepped out to join them. Sarah came around the front of the car carrying a backpack on her good shoulder. Her eyes looked weak.

No sleep.

Or good drugs for the arm. "Give me your bag. You look tired."

She stopped, gave me the bag and said, "I am."

"I thought they flew you to the hospital. How'd you get your car?"

"The guys brought it to me last night."

"You're home early. Did you already see a psychologist this morning?"

"They told me I could do it tomorrow. I was worried about Mom. Thanks for staying with her."

"No problem. I enjoyed her company." Sarah stared at my comment for a moment and then started towards the house. As she stepped up on the porch, I said, "Try to be quiet. She's still sleeping. I made coffee."

I turned and there stood little sister, staring at my clean shaven face. "Damn," she said, "look at you?" Her voice sounded healthy.

This is a woman who just killed a man yesterday.

"Good morning," I replied. "How are you?"

"My ears are still ringing, but I'm okay. You?"

"I'm good."

We quietly made our way to the kitchen, to the coffee pot, and then to the porch. Doris and Sarah took a seat. I remained standing. Sarah looked up and asked, "How's Elijah Haycraft on the day after?"

"I'm fine."

"Your arm?"

"It's okay," I replied. "Trying not to use it. How about you and your shoulder?"

"I'm tired. My shoulder's a mess, but I'm alright. They gave me good pain meds."

Doris seemed content to drink coffee and let her new sister do the talking.

Sarah continued. "Heard you talked to Agents Black and White last night. What'd they have to say?"

"They knew everything that was supposed to happen. The wedding massacre and all that. They heard you got shot and thought you were dead. They were lookin' for your mother. Apparently to kill her."

"Oh my God."

"Yeah. Ella about died when she heard 'em say you were dead. We got the drop and forced 'em to call their boss on speaker. Some guy named Chief Little."

"Little? And?"

"Guess who he was talking to on site?"

"Who?"

"Special Agent David Weeper. I told you he was playing you all along while setting me up. Next time I see him, it ain't gonna be pretty."

Sarah took a deep breath, let it out slowly, and said, "Sorry about that. Guess it's a good thing you figured him out. We might all be dead."

"Doesn't he owe us money?"

Sarah nodded in agreement, and then asked, "What did Chief Little have to say?"

"He filled Black and White in. Talked about what a good job we all did and told 'em to go to plan B."

"That's a good thing," Sarah replied.

"So" I asked, "you know about plan B?"

"I can figure it out." After a sip of coffee, she said, "Mom's usually up by now. How late did you guys stay up?"

"Longer than I expected. We drank a little. Talked a lot, and then sat out here and smoked some of her medical marijuana. When I came down this morning, she was sleeping like a baby."

Sarah's eyes squinted. "When you came down?" She sat her coffee on the table, rose from the chair and said, "I'm going up to check on Mom."

It became my first opportunity to be alone with Doris since our walk on the Wellington property. As soon as Sarah left the room, she said, "You lied to Doris."

"Excuse me?"

"You told her you don't smoke pot."

"Hold on. Who am I talking to?"

"I'm Itzel."

"Well, you lied to me. Told me you were nineteen."

"Doris is nineteen. I'm not."

"You really are screwed up."

"My life is full of confusion."

I said, "Most of us have that problem. What makes you different?"

She stared a moment and then said, "I've been hurt a lot, and I've known for a while that things weren't right. I deal with gaps in time and all that. Sometimes I can't remember things that happened, and then later I do. It's confusing. Sarah says I should find a good psychiatrist when I move down here."

"For what it's worth, I agree. Hope you remember what Jane said about therapy."

"Sarah reminded me. No offense, but I'd say your woman's as messed up as I am."

I tilted my head. "To tell the truth, Itzel, we all are."

As I spoke, Sarah came back through the kitchen and onto the porch. She stood in front of me and said, "What the hell?"

"Excuse me?"

Her lip curled. "You know what I mean. Mom never wears a silk blouse to bed."

Hope her ass was covered.

"You slept in my mother's bed!"

"Are you jumping to conclusions?"

"Damn right I am. Itzel, I think Mr. Haycraft and I need to take a walk. You mind sitting here for a bit?"

Itzel smiled at me and asked, "Have you been a bad boy?"

"No," I replied as Sarah held the door open.

Itzel raised her voice. "By the way, Doris knew all along that you weren't gay."

I like Doris.

Outside, as we walked, Sarah said, "I need a cigarette."

I pulled out the pack and said, "Last one."

"We can share."

After lighting up, I took a draw and passed it to her. Glancing back at the house, I said, "She's watching."

"Follow me." Sarah led the way to the barn. Inside she passed the cigarette back to me. We finished our smoke in a nervous silence. Me watching her eyes. Her shifting weight from one leg to the other and back.

I asked, "You gotta pee?"

"No." She put out the cigarette and then started. "Remember our first encounter here."

"Yes."

"You handcuffed and tied me to the bars."

"Yes."

"I wish I could do you the same way."

"Why?"

"I want to interrogate you."

Damn. "Okay." I moved against one of the stalls, spread my arms and held the bars. "Go ahead. Interrogate me."

"Why is my mother dressed that way?"

"Perhaps you should ask her that question?"

Wham! Sarah slapped me across my face with her good hand. I gripped the bars and stood my ground.

"I can't believe you slept with my mother?"

I considered, and then said, "Define slept."

Whop! She struck me again. My lack of reaction seemed to infuriate her.

"I can't believe this! I've been putting off sleeping with you out of respect for Jane. And what do you do? You have sex with my mother!" She slapped me again. The sting became a tolerable sensation. Staring at Sarah's eyes, I kept my grip on the bars and waited for more.

"Dammit!" she screamed. "You're enjoying this!"

"I'd say this is hurting you more than it's hurting me. Didn't I tell you it would depend on my perception of *why* you hit me?"

"Damn you Eli. I hit you because you slept with my mother!"

"Your mother misses being held. She says that when you were younger, you were always there to hold her. But now, she's alone. Do you know how long it's been since someone besides you held your mother?"

Sarah began crying.

"Your mother's dying. She's not dead. Remember what you once told me. Everyone deserves passion. Does that not include your mother? She told Jane she would like a man to hold her before she dies."

"But why you? Why would Jane want you to be with my mother?"

"Sarah, you misunderstand Jane. Her father wasn't there when her mother needed him to hold her. She sees her mother in your mother. Jane knows the loneliness of dying, and that's why she asked me to hold your mother. To comfort her. To tell her it's okay and it's alright. I did that."

"But my mother wanted more?"

"... She did."

"And you?"

I placed my finger on Sarah's lips. "What I do with my wife is between her and me. I never talk about it with another person. What I've done with you is between us, and I will never talk about it. Don't you think your mother deserves the same?"

"But did you?"

This time I held my finger to my own lips.

Sarah's face distorted. "Dammit! Dammit!" She still wanted to hit me. I reached and took her by the wrist. Before she could try to raise her bad arm, I bore the pain of pulling her to me with my injured arm. She continued to weep. I laid her head against my chest and held her tight, thinking, *Like mother, like daughter. Sarah is lonely.* While running my hand through her hair, I whispered, "It's okay. It's alright. It's ... alright."

As I held Sarah, my mind pondered the differences between her and Jane. Both strong, hard-headed women, yet Sarah, unlike Jane, had her weaknesses, her insecurities. It gave her a humanness that Jane lacks. Like Kelly. Like Margaret. Like Ella. Like my mother, Sarah has a hole in her heart. She's a lonely person in a world of chaos. She needs someone to hold her.

Sarah's sobbing subsided. She seemed calm as she leaned away to look into my eyes. I released her, took a step back and asked, "Is this session over?"

Sarah pressed her lips together and then spoke softly. "If I ask you a question, will you promise not to lie?"

When I gave her an unsure look, she said, "Our work is over, Eli. There's no need for me to lie to you, or for you to lie to me. Please?"

Don't say it if you don't mean it.

"Okay. I won't lie."

"Yesterday, at the water fountain, the things you said to me. Did you mean them?"

This is not going to be easy. "Can we grab a cup of coffee? Sit in the swing?"

"You don't want to answer my question?"

"Oh, yes I do. Sarah, we both deserve an answer."

She closed her eyes, took a deep breath and nodded. When she opened her eyes, I spread my arms. She said, "Hell no. This session is not over."

Chapter 50

Sarah and I left the barn in silence. On her way through the fence gate, she noticed the three bags against the house. "What's all that?"

While closing the gate, I said, "It's mine and Jane's clothes and all the stuff from the barn last night. Things we need to burn."

"We can burn them while we talk."

Ella stepped out onto the porch as we entered from outside. She carried a cup of coffee and looked nice, wearing jeans, flannel shirt and her wig. She glanced down at Itzel and then up at Sarah's arm, and said, "Oh honey, you had me so worried. How are you?"

"I'm okay. How about you? You look fresh this morning."

"I slept well. Is this your sister?"

"Yes. Momma, this is Itzel. Itzel, this is my mother, Ella."

Itzel stood and said, "Nice to meet you."

"It's good to meet you. Sarah always wanted a sister." Turning to me, Ella touched my face. "You shaved."

"Yep. You heard what Jane said. She wants me clean shaven when I come home."

"Well, you tell her how much I enjoyed those whiskers. And thank you for all you did last night."

"Excuse me," Sarah huffed. "What exactly did he do for you last night?"

Itzel's eyes widened as she gave me a look.

Ella replied, "Oh honey, we had such a good time, until I got sick."

"I bet you did." Sarah had wet eyes. "I came up this morning. I saw how you were dressed. Not sure I approve of what Elijah did for you last night."

Ella shook her head slowly. "No, no Honey. It's not what you think. We drank and we smoked my pot and, and he even danced with me. I had so much fun just talking and having his company. Then I got really sick. Baby, he comforted me while I made a mess of myself. Then he cleaned me up. He took care of me like I was his child. He held me and told me it was all okay until I went to sleep. Please don't think badly of him."

Sarah looked at me with her lips tightened. I stood there not knowing what to say or do. Itzel shook her head and said, "You people are killing me. Did someone say there's pot in this house?"

I went to the restroom and then back to the kitchen. As I poured my coffee, Ella stepped in and held out her cup for a refill. Our eyes met. I said, "Thanks for what you said."

She squinted. "What I said, I said for Sarah. She's acting like a woman in love. Please, you be kind to my daughter's heart."

Moments later, Itzel, Ella and Sarah sat on the swing, covered with a large comforter, watching me tip a small amount of gasoline onto the black plastic bags in the fire pit. I had ripped them open to expose the contents. After balling up a paper towel, I lit and pitched it. Flames flared and the ladies all jumped. Black smoke rose into the clear, cold morning. Ella said, "Come on now, Elijah. Join us."

"You sure that swing's gonna hold us all?"

"Believe we can squeeze you in."

I slid in between Sarah and her mother. As we all settled under the blanket, Itzel lit the joint she'd rolled from Ella's stash. When she took a hit, I asked, "Are we smoking with Doris?"

"No," she replied. "For the first time in forever, it feels good to be me."

But I had been looking forward to smoking with Doris.

It didn't take long for the four of us to kill that joint. While Itzel, Sarah and Ella got to talking about Maria, my mind got caught up on the crows flying overhead. Under the cover, Sarah's hand found mine. I did not resist. Our eyes met and she whispered, "We were supposed to sit behind the barn to watch the crows fly by."

"I squeezed her hand and said, "I'm fine right here."

"But this is not the conversation we planned."

Itzel stopped rattling. Ella turned to me, and I could read her mind. *...you be kind to my daughter's heart.*

Leaning back, I pulled my hand from Sarah's, stretched my arms out across the swings back, stared up at the sky and said, "Don't know about y'all, but right now, all I wanna do is relax here in good company with this awesome morning buzz, while that there black smoke rises the bad stuff we did yesterday up to those birds, and they carry it all away."

Ella leaned back and said, "That's some heavy shit."

Itzel said, "Amen to that."

Sarah seemed to get the hint. When she leaned back, I put my arm around her shoulder, and tugged her close. She finally relaxed and it got so quiet that all I could hear was the creaking of the swing and the caws of those big black birds as they flew my troubles away.

It didn't take long before the plastic's smoke diminished and the burning smell of bloody clothing and raw flesh remained. Sarah complained, "Damn, that stinks."

Itzel giggled and said, "Believe that's our father's dick you smell."

Ella turned. "You didn't?"

I said, "Don't know about you ladies, but I'm starving."

While Ella and Sarah remained on the swing talking, Itzel and I cooked breakfast. I mostly listened as she spoke of her excitement towards moving to the farm with her mother and assisting in Ella's final days. Meeting Sarah while escaping the claws and pains of her past had brought promise for her and her mother's future.

We all pigged out on scrambled eggs, sausage and biscuits. Itzel's excitement continued to dominate the conversation. It seemed each time my eyes met Sarah's, Ella's were watching. The things that needed to be said could not be said at that moment, at that table. Perhaps, Sarah and I could have taken a walk to talk, but it seemed I had not yet found the words.

After eating breakfast and helping to clean off the table, I made myself leave. The ladies walked me to the garage. Every step became painful. I didn't want to leave, yet knew there was so much to do at home. I had to deal with the money. I had to deal with Jane. At some point, I would have to deal with myself and my future considering what I had done, and what I had become.

I backed out of the garage and then stopped. Itzel stood back as mother and daughter came to my open window. After, "You be careful driving home," Ella leaned in the window and said, "I'll have the rest of your money in a week. Please come back and have a drink with me."

Looking up to Sarah, I said, "I'll communicate with Ruth about that."

Ella reached in to touch my face. "Tell Jane I said thank you. Bring her with you when you come back."

"I will."

Looking at Sarah, I said, "Glad we survived."

She nodded with glassy eyes. As I pulled away, she said, "Don't forget, we have unfinished business."

Accelerating down the lane, I looked into the mirror. Ella and Itzel were waving. Sarah watched, but did not wave. *So much left unsaid.* On my drive home, I would have to figure out what to say that evening to Jane.

About a mile before reaching the interstate, a sign read "Unleaded/Diesel". Needing gas, I pulled up to a pump and then went inside for a pack of cigarettes. Back outside, while pumping gas, my eyes were drawn to an entranceway across the road with a sign that read, **Godsey's Pay Lake and Motel**. *Hmm. Never noticed that.*

When traffic allowed, I shot across the road, passed the sign and started back a narrow drive. For a quarter mile, dense woods lined both sides. Like magic, it opened up to a scenic three acre lake and a small, single story motel building, all privately surrounded by tall timber. Fishing rods stood upright in a rack outside the office.

I parked next to another pickup in a graveled area that faced the lake. About a hundred yards away, a couple sat in chairs warming their hands on the small, open fire in front of them. Their fishing rods rested in holders near the water's edge. It made me think of Margaret, which made me think of Jane, which made me think of Sarah. Still buzzing from the pot, I stepped out to smoke a cigarette. Draw after draw, the same thoughts stuck in my head. *What if Sarah dies tomorrow, or the next day, or next week in the line of duty? How will I feel? Will I have regrets?* I pulled out my phone. Two rings later, Sarah answered, "Did you forget something?"

"I found the perfect spot to finish our session."

The sun had just gone down when I got home. Jane's 12-hour shift would soon be ending. I checked the gun safe, the only spot where Jane might have hidden the money. Ella's bag rested between two gun stocks. Counting the money somehow calmed me. Next stop, the shower. On my cell phone, I streamed loud country rock. For thirty minutes, I absorbed hot water, touched up my shave, and thought about my future.

From the moment we met, I began to fall in love with Jane. She filled a void in me. Her attention helped me forget the unforgettable things in my past. Her hands, her beauty, her smartness, her mental and physical strengths seduced me. She made me forget about Kelly.

Margaret came along when loneliness had me in need of a friend. She filled that void but never became a threat to make me fall out of love with Jane. This thing with Sarah felt different. I told myself it wouldn't happen, but it did. She tickled my ego like a new drug, and I slowly became hooked. Sarah had become a threat to my marriage. Her mother's words remained in my head. *Do not let my Sarah come between you and Jane,* and *You be kind to my daughter's heart.* How could I do both?

Even before I married Jane, John warned me that she had issues. Months after we were married, when the proverbial honeymoon had ended, during a heated argument, I found out that I had married my father. Jane possesses an element of my father's rage. Though I will never be able to repair my wife's issues, I understand them, and she understands mine. She knows how to kick my ass and make me like it. She knows exactly when to stop. Jane can see into my mind and tell when the electricity starts and when it has finished. While I love Sarah's tears, there is a part of Jane that cannot be replaced. She is my rock. I have dedicated my life, my love and my loyalty to her. It will never be my choice to walk away from her. My sessions with Sarah must end.

I opened the shower door and like déjà vu, Jane sat on the closed toilet seat. She glanced at my limp state, squinted and spoke over the music. "Should I be worried?"

"Should I?"

Jane stood and said, "Get dressed. I'll be outside."

I blow dried my hair, dressed, and poured two fingers of bourbon. When I stepped out onto the deck, Jane sat bundled up in a hooded coat, with a comforter over her legs. She took a draw off of her cigarette and asked, "Where's your phone?"

"Left it inside, in the bedroom. Where's yours?"

"It's in my purse. You know, I'm never going to feel comfortable again with the whole spying on our phones thing."

"This week, I'll get your number changed. New SIM card and all that. That's the best I can do."

"What about yours?" she asked.

"Might have to do the same for me too."

"Might? What you're saying is that it won't do any good to change numbers if you share yours with Sarah."

"Honey, after what we've been through, I'm not sure we can prevent being spied on if the government chooses to do so. Guess we just have to remain aware of what we're saying around our phones ... from now on."

"That sucks," she replied.

"Yes it does."

"So what's the deal with you and Sarah?"

"I'm never going to leave you."

She smashed out her cigarette and said, "That's not what I asked. Are you going to continue seeing her? I see what she does for you and I'm not sure I can compete. You've become addicted to her."

I thought for a moment and then asked, "Tell me Jane, have you ever done cocaine?" Her expression said yes. "Me too. Did it a few times with guys from the packinghouse. Most awesome buzz I've ever had. From the moment we got it until it was gone, it was all I could think about. That's addiction."

"Sarah is your cocaine?"

"No baby. You are. You're the drug I can't do without. Every moment I spent with Sarah, you were on my mind. You already know I kissed her. I can't lie about that. I could write a damn book on how it happened and why, but that wouldn't change a thing. You were always on my mind. You kept me from going too far."

"But you wanted to."

"That's not a fair statement, Jane. To be honest, I could say that about every hot-ass woman I meet. Maybe someday when I'm old, I won't think that way."

Jane's head moved back and forth. "Then it sounds like the only reason you don't mess around is because you have a commitment. Do you even love me?"

"Jane, you know I love you, but for me, being loyal to a commitment is not about love."

"Why not?"

"Honey, we're human beings. It's our nature to love. We love everything. We love our parents. We love our country. We say we love our dogs, our cats, and our favorite football team. To me, love is a friggin' watered down word that says something excites us. Makes us feel funny inside. Makes us lose our breath. But in the end, it's not love that keeps us faithful and loyal. It's respect. When you respect someone, you don't do things to hurt them."

When Jane picked up her pack of cigarettes, I said, "Give me one, please."

After we were both lit up, she asked, "Did you just make all that respect stuff up, or did you read it somewhere?"

"No. It's not something I read. That's just the way I feel."

"Well, I like it. To be honest, I feel pretty much the same way. It's kind of scary though. You basically admitting that you love Sarah."

"Didn't say that."

"But it's true, isn't it? Be honest. There's something about Sarah that makes you feel funny inside?"

To be honest, yes. "Sarah is beautiful. I find her attractive just like any other pretty lady. But what attracts me to her is her mind. She's a lot like you. Smart and strong. She ain't gonna take shit off of anyone. Neither do you. I like strong women. But Sarah doesn't understand me like you do, and I don't want her to. I'm yours and you are mine. For me, that's the way it's gotta be."

"Oh, my man loves me."

I smiled. "You can bank on that."

"And he respects me."

"Thank you."

Jane stared at my eyes. "Are you going to see her again?"

"I have to go there next week to get the rest of the money. Ella asked me to bring you with me."

Jane rubbed her breasts and said, "We need to go in now."

I downed my whiskey.

* * *

That next morning, Monday, Jane got up early enough to have coffee with me. During our first cup, she surprised me with, "Can we talk privately?" which meant away from our phones.

I replied, "Sure," before taking my phone to the bedroom.

On my return, Jane said, "When you talk to John this morning, ask if he can track down that man, David Weeper."

"Why?"

Jane sipped her coffee and said, "I need a cigarette."

We bundled up, got more coffee and then stepped outside. Our cups steamed like two smoke stacks in the cool morning air. Jane and I both lit up. She took a draw and said, "Remember the hoodie guy in the park? The white one. The one with the damaged eye."

"Yesss. How could I forget?"

"Like you said, I wanted to be the one."

"The one?"

Leaning toward me, she spoke quietly. "I dreamed of the day I would stab that bastard in the back and then look into his eyes and remind him of my father as he bled out."

"I get it. But Honey, we've already discussed that. At the time I figured I was doing you a favor."

"You did." Jane leaned back into her chair and whispered. "Now I want to return the favor."

"What the hell are you talking about?"

She leaned back up to me and said, "I'm going after Weeper."

I nearly choked on my coffee. "Honey, no. We can't kill Weeper!"

"I didn't say anything about you, Eli. Think about all those nights and days I spent worrying about you. Worrying about how I would live without you. When I lost my parents, I died inside and became the loneliest person in the world. Then you came along and saved me. That man used you. He intended for you to die. He tried to take away the one thing that makes my life livable."

With my head shaking, I said, "Jane, he's a government agent. If you kill him, the whole damn world's gonna come down on us."

"He tried to kill you. He may try again." My crazy-ass wife grinned and said, "Guess I'll just have to be careful."

Pain on the outside can be sensational.
Pain on the inside always hurts.
Loneliness lives on the inside.
Elijah Haycraft

Made in the USA
Monee, IL
11 May 2022

96208964R00246